ROCK,

PAPER,

SCISSORS

A NOVEL OF POLITICAL INTRIGUE

STEVE SAMUEL

SIMON & SCHUSTER
NEW YORK LONDON TORONTO SYDNEY SINGAPORE

SIMON & SCHUSTER
ROCKEFELLER CENTER
1230 AVENUE OF THE AMERICAS
NEW YORK, NY 10020

SIMON & SCHUSTER AND COLOPHON ARE REGISTERED TRADEMARKS
OF SIMON & SCHUSTER, INC.
DESIGNED BY KAROLINA HARRIS
MANUFACTURED IN THE UNITED STATES OF AMERICA
1   3   5   7   9   10   8   6   4   2
LIBRARY OF CONGRESS CATALOGING-IN-PUBLICATION DATA
SAMUEL, STEVE.
ROCK, PAPER, SCISSORS : A NOVEL OF POLITICAL INTRIGUE / STEVE SAMUEL.
P.   CM.
1. POLITICAL CORRUPTION—FICTION. 2. WOMEN DETECTIVES—FICTION. 3. SECRET SERV-
ICE—FICTION. 4. CONSPIRACIES—FICTION. I. TITLE.
PS3569.A46675 R6 2000
813'.6—DC21
00-030099
ISBN 0-684-82343-8

ACKNOWLEDGMENTS

I give a thousand heartfelt thanks to my extraordinary wife, Amy Winston, for being the most patient, balanced, and complete person I have ever known. Being married to a would-be writer is no easy task and you have handled this burden with aplomb. Thanks for being so wonderful.

Henry Morrison has been a terrific agent and a sagacious guiding hand throughout this process. His keen eye improved the manuscript exponentially. And his willingness to invest so much of his time to me is much appreciated.

This book would never have gotten off the ground without the help of several people at Simon & Schuster. First and foremost is Betsy Radin Herman. Her initial enthusiasm set the wheels in motion. Sydny Miner carried the ball from there. Her skillful editing transformed a big clunky manuscript into a clean thriller. My thanks also goes out to David Rosenthal for his willingness to take a flier on me.

Several well-known authors have taken the time to read what I have written and then have been gracious enough to say nice things about it, and for that I am grateful. James Patterson was kind enough to read a 500-page unsolicited manuscript many moons ago and to write a letter that served as an inspiration to keep pushing forward. Joseph Finder is a gifted writer who has always assisted me through this labyrinth called the world of publishing.

There were many people who read early versions of this book and provided valuable feedback. Amy Grolnick, Wendy Klein, Dick Miller, Ian Mausner, Jim Donovan, Lynn Testa, and Juliette Cherbuliez were particularly helpful. Dan Winston saved me from my computer on more occasions than I care to count. And fellow writer Jay Nussbaum has been a sounding board and confidant through all of the ups and downs every author endures.

His insights and encouragement helped me realize it wasn't a train at the end of the tunnel.

Last, but not least, I'd like to thank my parents for providing me with the guidance and opportunity to succeed. Mom, I know you're fond of saying that next time around I should choose rich parents. But I think I did pretty damn well this time around, too.

TO AMY AND FRIEDA—

I THANK YOU BOTH FOR ALWAYS BEING THERE.

ROCK,

PAPER,

SCISSORS

PROLOGUE

Reston, Virginia—Late August, 1963

THE unbroken sound of crickets echoed clear across the sunburned field, then drifted into the deep woods where the assassin watched and waited. His target was standing in the elementary school parking lot two hundred yards away, talking to his wide-eyed three-year-old.

"Daddy, that was yummy." Sarah Peterson wiped her sticky fingers on her shorts, streaking the white cotton with chocolate ice cream handprints.

Chip Peterson kneeled to his daughter's eye level and returned the smile.

"I'm glad you liked it, pumpkin." He gently brushed a napkin across his daughter's face.

"Daddy?"

"Yeah?"

"Can I go on the swings?"

Chip glanced at his watch, then stroked Sarah's fine, barley-colored hair. Half the sky was already pitch black.

"I don't think so, sweetie. It's almost nine o'clock. Last night we got out here earlier."

"Pleeeeeeez!"

He sighed, knowing he was wrapped like a piece of reminder string around his little girl's finger. In the week since his return from Moscow he had spoiled his daughter at every opportunity. She had changed so much in the last six months; had barely recognized him when he bounded through the front door of their three-bedroom ranch. For the past seven days Chip had done everything he could to bridge the void his prolonged absence had caused. And from the contented look on his daughter's cherubic face, he knew he had finally earned back Sarah's love.

"All right," he said. "But only a few minutes."

Without waiting for her father to finish his answer, Sarah scurried past the assortment of tired-looking playground equipment. She ignored the rusty monkey bars and the wobbly sliding board and the half-filled sandbox. Instead, she ran directly to the smallest of the four swings.

"Aren't you going to try one of those big-girl swings?"

Sarah shook her head.

"Why not?"

She shrugged.

"I don't suppose you want me to do all the pushing?"

Sarah smiled.

Chip lifted his daughter by her armpits and dropped her into the kiddie swing. She squeezed her legs through the holes in the molded black plastic with some difficulty.

"Mommy buckles me in so I don't fall out."

"You got it, Miss Smartypants." He grabbed the corroded eye hook and clipped it into place.

"Fast or slow?" he asked.

"Fast!"

Chip was in front of her, holding both sides of the swing. He raised the seat above his head, then allowed gravity to propel Sarah backward in one quick rush.

"Higher, Daddy!"

Her Chiclet-toothed smile enveloped him.

Chip savored the moment, and daydreamed of the good times ahead. He and Kim had no mortgage payments to worry about and the '57 Chevy was owned free and clear. They even had stashed a few thousand dollars over at First Federal. That little nest egg was enough to convince them they could afford to have a second child. When to start trying was now the only question. Chip would be in the States for only two more weeks. Once his high-level briefings were over, he'd crisscross the Atlantic one last time. The director of the CIA had already indicated there'd soon be a complete reshuffling of the agents stationed in Eastern Europe. And Chip had received personal assurances that a desk job in Langley would be his if he so desired. Then, he thought, things would be perfect.

"Sweetie, we've got to get home. We'll come back again tomorrow night."

"Two more minutes, Daddy?" She clasped her hands together. "Please!"

As he let out a resigned sigh a light flickered on above him. The bulb buzzed loudly. Within seconds, a swarm of moths and mosquitoes began to circle the sphere as if it was a honey pot.

"Look, Daddy!"

Chip turned toward the football field where his daughter's index finger was trained. From the darkness emerged a man walking a dog. The tall, thin stranger wore a navy windbreaker despite the stifling heat. He was already beneath the closer goal post, strolling calmly toward them.

Chip looked back at Sarah, pushing her swing a few last times.

"I'll bet you don't know what type of dog that is."

"A fireman doggy," she answered proudly.

"Sort of. It's called a Dalmatian. Can you say Dal-ma-tion?"

Sarah shook her head.

Chip smiled.

"Come on, sweetie, let's get going." He grabbed the metal chain that was fastened across her belly. The swing and its squeak both stopped at once. Suddenly the rapid pitter-patter of the dog's paws sounded as if it was upon him. He glanced over his shoulder, prepared for the slobber of a wet tongue.

"Good evening," Chip said with a friendly nod.

The stranger's dark eyes focused on Chip's hands, carefully watching to see if the CIA agent moved for his service revolver.

"Up," he finally said softly.

The Dalmatian rose up on his hind legs, his head nearly as high as Chip's. It was enough to distract the CIA agent for a split second.

The first shot blasted from the pocket of the stranger's nylon windbreaker. It ripped through Chip's aorta, shredding it like hamburger. The second shot splattered Chip's brain stem on the way in, his esophagus on the way out.

The Dalmatian barked angrily, startled by the gunshots. Without hesitating, the gunman aimed his weapon in the dog's direction and calmly squeezed the trigger. The dog yelped once, then fell in a heap beside Chip's crumpled body.

The stranger pointed his weapon at the only remaining witness to his crime. Sarah stared right back at him, devoid of any fear. The gunman's finger tightened briefly on the trigger, then slackened. Killing the girl had not been part of his instructions. He strode away from the scene without looking back.

For a full minute Sarah waited anxiously for her father and the dog to leap to their feet.

"Daddy?" she asked tentatively.

Like a speeding roller coaster rushing at her, panic set in. Her sense of survival took over, even if she couldn't fully comprehend what had just happened.

"Wake up, Daddy!" she pleaded. "Wake up!"

Her tiny fingers worked furiously at the eye hook. She clenched her teeth and grunted, straining the muscles in her forearms until they stung. Her thumb eventually moved the rusted clasp ever so slightly, but not nearly enough to open it.

Tears streamed down her face in jagged streaks while she desperately tried to wiggle from the confines of the swing. She twisted and turned as hard as she could, her toes vainly trying to make contact with the ground. At midnight her throat gave out, raw and scratchy from shrieking. But there was no one that night who would hear her cries, because the closest house was more than half a mile away. She remained suspended in midair, dangling like a marionette.

At ten past twelve she mercifully slumped forward toward her father, sapped of every bit of energy her twenty-eight pounds held. Insects buzzed around her sweat-drenched head, stinging her salty skin without resistance. "Please wake up, Daddy," she mumbled, just as she drifted off to sleep.

At 2 A.M. half the search party arrived at the elementary school. Sarah slept through the initial wave of commotion. Minutes later Kim Peterson grabbed her daughter from the safety of a policeman's arms. The CIA agent's widow held Sarah's mosquito-bitten face tightly against her breast in a futile attempt to shield her child's innocent eyes from the carnage she would never forget.

ONE

THE ROCK

He was devious, because the very certainty of his convictions made him extremely flexible in his choice of means.

HENRY KISSINGER, IN HIS 1954 DOCTORAL DISSERTATION ON
PRINCE KLEMENS VON METTERNICH

1

Greenwich, Connecticut — Sunday, October 25, 1998

GRIZZWALD removed the syringe from his briefcase, carefully measuring a nonlethal dosage. A dead hostage was a complication he didn't need to work around. When the needle was ready he steered his car between the stone pillars of Jessica Baldwin's unguarded Connecticut estate and up her long driveway. Once inside, he knew it would take exactly one minute to reach the third-floor master bedroom. Before encountering his prey, however, he paused to study his surroundings painstakingly. Seventeen years with Special Forces had taught him extreme caution. As always, he would leave nothing to chance.

Sixteen thousand square feet of imposing sticks and bricks stood before him. The century-old Colonial had been featured on the glossy pages of *Town and Country* in 1982, long before its present occupant was old enough to drive. Set on twenty-five lush acres, the mansion's closest neighbor was tucked a thousand yards away behind a thick row of sturdy maples. Grizzwald couldn't see the backyard from the driveway, but he knew the expanse of manicured lawn would provide privacy from Jessica's few neighbors. As for the rent-a-cop in an unmarked Dodge who patrolled this wealthy hamlet, he had passed by six minutes earlier. Although the patrol route was supposed to be varied continuously, for the past five Sundays it had remained constant and predictable. For the next thirty-eight minutes the ex-detective would not be a factor.

Grizzwald had studied his target meticulously; he expected little resistance. From all Grizzwald had observed, Jessica seemed as down-to-earth as one could be for someone who owned custom-built homes on several continents. Her tireless charity work was applauded in Manhattan's elite social circles, yet she was more likely to show up at a grungy watering hole than at any of the stuffy black tie affairs to which she received dozens of invitations. At twenty-six she was unmarried, but engaged to an architect, who, like today, was often out of town. Not a bit of this was of any interest to Grizzwald. All that mattered to him was the $8 billion net worth of Jessica's father, Sam Baldwin. That was an estimate, of course, but he had usually found the CIA's classified files to be accurate.

Grizzwald turned off the engine and stepped out of the car. Within seconds he felt the adrenaline surge that always accompanied this type of operation, the rush giving him a sense of invincibility that could never be duplicated. He savored every last ounce of the sensation, wishing he could bottle it. The capture and the kill had always made him feel alive.

A sudden movement registered and he flinched. He immediately took inventory, sensing he was being watched. Grizzwald scanned in all directions to search for danger and he locked onto the eyes of a squirrel up on a power line. His eyes flitted across the horizon, then moved from window to window of the nine-bedroom house. Nothing appeared unusual. No one else was watching him. Grizzwald smiled. Everything would soon fall into place.

Inside the mansion, Jessica Baldwin thought she heard a car door close. She was standing on the sliding wooden ladder in her second-floor library. Situated in the rear of the house, the thickly carpeted room had a panoramic view of the Long Island Sound.

Jessica glanced at the antique clock on the far wall. It was only 2:30.

"Hold on a second, Dad," she said into the cordless phone. "I think there's someone at the door." She descended the ladder and crossed the hardwood floors of the hallway to a bedroom window that looked toward the front lawn. A shiny black Cadillac sat in the driveway.

"Oh, shit!" she said, and ran down the swirling steps of the vaulted front hallway and opened the door. Warm October air filled the foyer.

"You're early!" she yelled from the top step of the wraparound porch. "The guy who called this morning said you'd be here at three-fifteen!"

The handsome crew-cut driver waved casually and smiled. "Take your time, ma'am." Grizzwald leaned against the front bumper. "Traffic won't be heavy until we hit the Van Wyck."

Having made eight separate dry runs to the secluded street, Grizzwald knew every possible escape route, as well as who could be expected to come and go. The Jamaican maid who unfailingly arrived at 8 A.M. each Sunday morning was always gone by noon. Today had been no exception. Only Jessica's cook and two housekeepers would be inside. The remainder of the domestic contingent invariably had Sunday off. He glanced at his watch. He still had plenty of time, although that would change in a hurry if things got messy. In thirty-four minutes the rent-a-cop would reappear.

To minimize the risk of his being recognized, Grizzwald had always traveled the neighborhood in a different car and wearing a different disguise. Each of those cars, like the Cadillac on which he was leaning, had been procured with a bogus California driver's license and a stolen credit card. Grizzwald had recoded the Visa card with a sophisticated device called an ATM Junior, which he had purchased for $5,800 in cash from the curtained-off back room of an electronics store in Manhattan. Once recoded, the magnetic strip could not alert even the computer wizards who manned Visa's fraud unit that the credit card belonged to someone who had died more than two years earlier.

Grizzwald had been accompanied during that last visit by his partner, Lieutenant McClarty. McClarty was a senior communications specialist with Special Forces who had also spent seventeen years in the marines. They had posed as telephone repairmen on the midnight-to-six shift, placing Day-Glo orange construction cones around the manhole located barely twenty yards from the lip of Jessica Baldwin's property line. Dressed in blue jumpsuits and Vibram-soled workboots, they had silently shimmied down the rusted steel rungs of the narrow manhole. Within five minutes they found the large SNET switchbox and PBX trunking system for Jessica's street. Quickly, McClarty identified the correct wire amid the twisted ganglia of colorful cables and spliced the fiber-optic filament controlling all of Jessica's calls. Once a call diverter and cellular transmitter were added, they were able to eavesdrop on every telephone conversation that took place inside the mansion.

Foiling the security system was slightly more complicated, though it took less time. McClarty used a clever little device known to professional burglars as the Mousetrap. Weighing less than eight ounces, the jumble of insulated wires and sterile silicon chips received its power from an attached six-volt alkaline dry cell battery that could be purchased in any local hardware store. When shunted to the proper cable, the Mousetrap forced the electrical impulses generated by the mansion's security system to enter its circuitry, then its switches closed. Instead of racing along the underground phone lines to the local police station, or to the alarm company that monitored Jessica's estate, the alarm signals remained trapped in a continuous loop until one of the house's eight indoor punch pads could be reset. As an extra precaution, Grizzwald had also disabled the generators that supplied power to the sound cannons on each corner of the house. For the past week, the $200,000 security system had been rendered completely useless.

Grizzwald stood on the driveway and waited, pleased with how events had unfolded thus far. He had intercepted Jessica's call to a Manhattan limousine service, and had considered lying in wait for the sedan to appear just down the road, then ambushing and murdering the driver. But in the interest of simplicity, he decided to call the limo service, cancel Jessica's order, then appear as scheduled. When McClarty called Jessica that morning to confirm her pickup, he knew they had chosen the cleanest option.

Jessica hurried up to the library.

"Dad, I've gotta go. My car's here."

"What time's your flight?"

"Six something. But I haven't finished packing yet."

Sam Baldwin smiled as he glanced at the lone picture on his desk: enclosed in a heavy crystal frame were the two women in his life. "You know you sound like your mother? She starts packing when we're ready to load the car."

She laughed. "Listen, I've gotta run. I'll call you guys in a few days if I can."

"Enjoy Paris, Jessie. And be careful."

"Thanks, Dad."

Jessica sprinted to the master bedroom, the portable phone still in her hand. She looked quickly through the open suitcase spread on top of her king-sized canopied bed, then threw in another dozen pieces of clothing. As she struggled with the zipper, she and a housekeeper poked clothes back into the valise.

"Need help, ladies?" The unexpected sound of a deep voice startled Jessica. She turned to see the driver in her doorway.

"I didn't hear you come in."

"Sorry," he said, employing the boyish, aw-shucks smile that had seduced so many women over the years. "I thought you might need a hand with your bags."

"That would be great. Francine and I *are* having a problem with this thing."

Grizzwald slowly approached them, his clean-shaven face expressionless as he moved closer. Beside the bed was the red panic button. He knew his plan would succeed even if it was pressed. His eyes narrowed like hyphens as they fixed on Jessica. She appeared slightly younger without makeup, although there was no doubt she was the woman whom he had watched through binoculars last Sunday night as she undressed. He leaned across the mattress and grabbed the two flaps of the suitcase that were stretched a hand's length apart. With a forceful jerk he pulled the case closed, the network of veins in his forearms bulging under his skin as thick as telephone cord. Jessica slid the zipper easily around the valise.

"Thanks," she said.

"You going away for a month?"

Jessica smiled. "Just a week."

"You're still on the Air France 6:04 to Paris?"

"Yup."

The driver gripped the handle of the suitcase and lifted the heavy bag to his side. "I'll bring this down for you."

"Do you want Francine to help you?"

"I think I can manage."

"There's that one, too," she said sheepishly, pointing to the matching brown-on-beige garment bag outside her walk-in closet.

Grizzwald grabbed the garment bag by its hook before draping it over his left shoulder. "The next sound you'll probably hear is me falling down all those steps," he said. Between the stuffed suitcase and the length of the garment bag there was barely enough space to maneuver through the doorway.

Jessica laughed. There was something appealing about this guy's self-effacing humor. From his chiseled upper body, and the graceful manner in which he carried himself, it looked as though he could have hauled her baby grand down the spiral staircase without stumbling. What Jessica found most attractive about him, though, was how polite he was.

Grizzwald checked his watch. He still had twenty-seven minutes until the next pass of the security cop.

Jessica slid out of her rumpled T-shirt and went into her bathroom. She brushed her teeth and splashed cold water over her eyes, freshening up for the ten hours of traveling that lay ahead. After she had put on a clean blouse Grizzwald reappeared in her doorway.

"Anything else?"

"No, that's it."

Grizzwald fiddled with the syringe in his pocket. He could neutralize the housekeeper and inject Jessica in almost no time at all. The two others downstairs were the wild cards; if they were within earshot he would have to turn the mansion into a slaughterhouse. Everything had gone smoothly to this point. He decided to stick to his original plan.

"I'll be in the car whenever you're ready," he said with a smile.

"Great. I'll be downstairs in a couple of minutes."

2
Georgetown, Washington, D.C.

S ARAH P ETERSON finished the last drop of her third Bloody Mary, then glared at the painting she had just spent all morning creating. These were supposed to be the precious hours the career Secret Service agent used to bring some semblance of simplicity to her chaotic life. No TV, no radio. Even the thick Sunday *Washington Post* remained rubber-banded on the welcome mat of her two-story brownstone. But the images that had started out as a sketch of sunny memories spent in the south of France had somehow melded into a muddy field under attack by ominous storm clouds. Life had been so simple during those semesters abroad, she thought. Pedaling three miles into town on a rickety Peugeot was all that had cluttered her days. But now she had 372 federal agents reporting to her. And at five feet, six inches, 110 pounds, with round, brown eyes, a pageboy auburn haircut, and an engaging smile, Sarah had little physical resemblance to any of them.

Sarah walked away from the painting and warily took a peek at the laptop that lay open beside her bare feet. The e-mail message from her aunt updating her mother's condition had added an edge to the personality that some of her counterparts already considered too contentious. And ever since a cryptic death threat had arrived two weeks earlier she had had no desire to open her mailbox. She bent down and activated her laptop's sound board.

"You have five new messages," said the synthesized voice of her IBM Thinkpad.

Sarah wiped her hands on a ripped T-shirt Jean-Pierre had left behind when he moved out last year, then sat cross-legged on the scuffed hardwood floor of her spare bedroom. She lifted her cat, Big Guy, onto her lap, which allowed her to see that three of the five messages were intelligence reports that had been sent by reliable contacts in the Middle East. She sent the text of all three of them to the printer in the adjoining bedroom. Sometime in the next few days she'd find the time to read them. Maybe in the tub. At midnight.

The fourth e-mail on Sarah's glowing blue screen had come from Judy Mellonbee, a friend and fellow Secret Service agent who'd recruited Sarah into the neighborhood book club back in '92. "Don't forget that we're meeting at my place on Tuesday night at eight. Hope you can make it this time. We've all missed your usual insightful commentary the last few months. Even your best friend and favorite litigator, Katy Nelson!"

Sarah chuckled. She had locked horns with Katy Nelson during that very first meeting in 1992, when *The Bridges of Madison County* was the topic for discussion. Nelson had gushed on about the best-seller before Sarah summarily dismissed the book as trite and mushy, not to mention that she was troubled by the adulterous relationship on which the love story was predicated. An hour of verbal jousting ensued, with Sarah ably fending off a veritable cross-examination by the aggressive defense lawyer. Once the conversation was steered in another direction, Sarah was certain that she would never be invited back. But to her surprise, she hosted the gathering eight weeks later, and was credited as the catalyst who had infused a measure of enthusiasm into what had become a fairly dull series of discussions. Sarah confirmed that her Palm Pilot would beep a reminder at 7:00 P.M. on Tuesday, then deleted the message from her screen.

Now there was just one message left, and Sarah stared at the last tag line. "Dick Flanagan," she murmured. "Who the *hell* is Dick Flanagan?"

She opened the message.

"Dear Sarah," it began. "Greetings from sunny Florida. It's been a few years since we met to talk about your dad. But I just heard a bit of news that you might find interesting. Call me ASAP. I'm at 407-221-6365. Dick."

Sarah now remembered the last conversation she'd had with her father's former colleague. She had tried to track down every retired CIA agent who had worked with Chip Peterson while he was stationed in Moscow in the early sixties, reaching out to them in an attempt to reconstruct the weeks that preceded her father's death. Sarah's extensive interviews had produced an overwhelming amount of information her mother had never told her. But as she methodically ran every lead to ground, she felt as though she was climbing a sprawling maple tree, trying to touch every single leaf. Each limb led to three new branches, and then three more. After exhausting four months of accumulated comp time, Sarah was left with a thousand open issues to still pursue. And new information trickled in every so often as people remembered things they had forgotten to mention.

Sarah pulled open a filing cabinet in her cramped home office and located the notes of her October 14, 1995, conversation with Flanagan. Her two-hour interview had yielded fifteen handwritten pages, but very little that she didn't already know. With those pages by the phone she dialed the number at the end of Dick Flanagan's e-mail. The phone was answered on the first ring.

"Hello?" It was the voice of an older man.

"Dick Flanagan, please."

"Speaking."

"Hi, Dick, it's Sarah Peterson. I just got your message."

"Boy, that was quick! I just sent it a few minutes ago. Where are you?"

"At my home in Georgetown."

"I hear you're still doing gangbusters over at the Service. Your old man would be proud."

Sarah smiled, and wondered whether she would keep abreast of the D.C. scuttlebutt after she hung up her spikes. Although law enforcement was inextricably intertwined with her DNA, there were so many pleasures she hoped to pursue as soon as she had the time: cooking lessons in Tuscany, helicopter skiing the Alps, a meandering wine-tasting tour down the Rhine, maybe even a shot at breaking three hours in the New York City Marathon. And that was just the beginning. With so much she wanted to see and do, Sarah suspected that once her own retirement rolled around, she would break from the fold and never be heard from again.

"I've got no complaints," Sarah replied. "How about yourself? You still playing golf?"

"Every day. And take it from an old-timer, Sarah, make sure you call it quits while you're young and healthy. There are lots of guys down here who worked until they were seventy, and now they regret it."

"We'll see. Right now I still love what I'm doing and I've got plenty of good years ahead of me before I'd even *consider* retiring."

"How old are you?"

"Thirty-eight."

"Aw, you're still just a pup. Give it another ten years and you'll be ready for green slacks and early-bird dinners."

"God, I hope not," she said with a smile. "That sounds perfectly awful." She swooped up her cat and scratched the top of his head. Big Guy purred softly.

"So you've piqued my curiosity, Dick. What's up?"

"Well, I make no promises that this'll lead anywhere." Flanagan laughed. "Listen to me. I still sound like I'm reporting back to headquarters."

"It's a hard habit to break."

"Tell me about it. My wife gives me a raft of shit whenever I regress. But anyway, here's what I know. There was a lady named Anna Rodzinski who was a translator at the embassy for a very short time in either 1962 or 1963. I can't remember whether she was CIA or State Department, or whether she was even officially on the payroll. She only worked a couple of days a month, if I recall correctly, and only when we were in a pinch. When you and I spoke a few years ago I don't think I mentioned her name."

Sarah quickly skimmed her notes. "That name definitely didn't come up. In fact, I don't think anyone ever mentioned her to me." She put Big Guy on the floor and picked up a pen. "It's spelled R-o-d-z-i-n-s-k-i?"

"It might be s-k-y instead of s-k-i. And if you're going to call her you better do it soon. I heard yesterday that she's over at Bethesda Naval Hospital, dying of lung cancer. Ted Brantley told me she only had a few days left."

Sarah felt a wave of compassion. Her mother had found a lump in her breast just last week; they were now awaiting the results of a biopsy. However, if her family history was any guide, there was a good chance there was going to be a hard fight ahead.

"Thanks for the update, Dick. I'll call her right now and let you know if anything comes of it."

Sarah logged onto her computer and accessed a classified State Department database. Dick Flanagan had been partly correct. Anna Rodzinski had been a part-time employee for the State Department between 1960 and 1964. Born in Manhattan in 1934, and a graduate from NYU in Russian Studies, she had married a career diplomat who had bounced around several Eastern Europe capitals. Although her duties at the U.S. Embassy in Moscow were limited to translating, her security clearance had gotten as high as top secret.

Sarah thumbed through the local white pages, and dialed the hospital.

The phone in Room 1121 rang twice before a young woman answered.

"Hello?"

"May I speak to Anna Rodzinski, please?"

"Who's this?"

"My name's Sarah Peterson. Is she available?"

"Not right now. Can I help you with something? I'm her daughter."

"I'm trying to find out if she knew my father at the U.S. Embassy in Moscow in 1963. His name was Chip Peterson." Sarah waited for an answer, then continued. "I know your mom's very sick, but this is *very* important. My dad was murdered in front of me when I was three years old and I don't think all the people who were involved in his death were ever caught. Your mother might be able to help me."

"Hold on for a second."

Sarah heard muffled conversation.

"Hello?"

Anna Rodzinski's voice was raspy and frail, as if the simple act of breathing was an effort. Sarah could hear the hiss of an oxygen tank in the background.

"Ms. Rodzinski, this is Sarah Peterson. I'm Chip Peterson's daughter. Dick Flanagan told me that you and my dad might have worked together in Russia a long time ago."

There was a long pause before Anna responded. "We did," she said weakly.

"Well, can I ask you a few things? There are a number of unanswered questions about my father's death that I'm trying to resolve."

Anna paused again, this time longer than before. "When you're dying," Anna eventually said softly, "you stare at the ceiling from your hospital bed, thinking about all those things in your life that you regret." She coughed, then said, "One of my biggest regrets is that I never tried finding you. I thought about it several times, but I was afraid."

Sarah's eyes widened. "Why?"

Anna didn't answer.

"Does it have to do with my father's death?"

Anna coughed. "I don't want to discuss this over the phone."

"May I come see you? I can be there in twenty minutes."

Sarah could sense the woman's reluctance and infused her voice with greater urgency.

"Please?"

"OK."

"Thank you, Mrs. Rodzinski. I'll see you soon."

Sarah rushed to her easel and dipped her paintbrush onto the section of her palette that was smudged bright yellow. With one quick brushstroke, a ray of sunlight came shining through the foreboding clouds.

"Much better," she said. She hurried into her bedroom and threw on the first clothes she could pull out of her closet. A comb through her hair and a dab of toothpaste in her mouth and she was ready in three minutes. She grabbed her briefcase and dashed toward her front door. So much for the simplicity of Sunday morning.

3

THE Cadillac was barely a mile from Jessica's estate when Grizzwald stopped the car on a local side street. He had driven down this road sixteen different times and had never seen anyone outdoors. If today was the exception, he could exercise four other options.

"I need to get something out of the trunk," Grizzwald said as he looked at Jessica in his rearview mirror. "I'll just be a second."

Jessica smiled, unconcerned at the slight delay. Then something the driver said registered.

"You're still on the Air France 6:04 to Paris?"

A jolt of fear tore through her. *How the hell did he known what flight I was on? I haven't told anyone!*

Jessica lunged for the door to her right. She was desperate to get out of the car, but Grizzwald was too quick and too strong. He landed on top of her as her fingers touched the door handle. His huge hand smashed up against her face, knocking her two front teeth loose. She tried to scream, but gagged on the spongy rubber ball Grizzwald jammed in her mouth. As Jessica struggled to break free, he slapped a strip of duct tape forcefully from ear to ear. An acrid hospital aroma filled her nostrils and seconds later she felt the sharp point of a needle bury itself deep into the muscles of her left shoulder. The more she struggled, the faster the homemade cocktail of ketamine hydrochloride and Valium raced through her bloodstream.

In her remaining seconds of consciousness all she could think about was the eight-week-old fetus growing inside her womb. Then her world went inky black.

4

SARAH rushed past an unoccupied nurses' station. Clutched in her hand was a bouquet of fresh daisies wrapped in cellophane. Her mother had taught her at an early age to appear with some small gift whenever she visited a hospital patient, and the huge gift shop in the lobby of Bethesda Naval had made the purchase quick and easy.

A small handwritten nameplate facing the hallway confirmed that Anna

Rodzinski was the lone patient in Room 1121. Sarah stood in the doorway for a moment, feeling like an intruder in the death vigil. Several family members were in the room. Mrs. Rodzinski seemed too small for the bed in which she was sleeping. The lines on her face, and the gray in her hair, made her appear much older than her sixty-four years.

Sarah knocked gently. "May I come in?" she asked softly.

"Are you Sarah?" The speaker was a dark-haired, attractive woman in her late thirties.

Sarah nodded.

"Mom's expecting you and wanted me to wake her up as soon as you got here. I'm Marica Rodzinski and that's my husband, Tony."

Sarah stepped into the room. "It's nice to meet you," she said as they shook hands.

"Over there is my brother Frank Rodzinski and his wife, Kathy."

Sarah smiled politely.

"Her lungs sound clogged," Sarah commented. "Has she been aspirated recently?"

"Twenty minutes ago, but at this point the fluid is coming faster than it can be pumped out. Now the doctors don't think she'll make it through the week. She's in pain, too."

"I'm sorry."

Sarah approached the bed, quickly noticing the amount of hardware around it. An IV needle pierced the back of Anna's hand, and had two bags of clear fluid feeding into it. One held saline, the other morphine. Pure oxygen entered the woman's nose through a narrow plastic tube that was taped to her face. A heart and blood pressure monitor beeped methodically beside the bedstand.

"Mom, wake up," Marica said. She touched her mother's leg and gave it a gentle shake.

Anna opened deepset blue eyes.

"Mom, there's someone here to see you."

Anna's gaze drifted in Sarah's direction.

"Ms. Rodzinski?"

A slight smile creased the older woman's face. "You look just like your father," she said softly. "Has anyone ever told you that?"

"Yes, ma'am."

Anna pressed the bed's control box beside her waist until she was sitting upright.

"Come closer." She patted the mattress, inviting Sarah to sit directly beside her.

"That's all right. I can get a chair."

"No." She reached out for Sarah's arm and held it, surprising Sarah with the strength of her grip.

"Mom," Marica said, "we're going to get some fresh air for a few minutes. Can I do anything for you before we go?"

"No, my love. I'll be fine."

"OK. We'll be back soon."

Marica and the three others filed out of the room and closed the door behind them. Sarah set her briefcase on a chair and sat on the bed at Anna's side.

"They seem like good kids," Sarah said.

"They are. I've been very lucky."

"Do you feel well enough to talk?"

"No. I feel miserable, if you want to know the truth. But we may not have another chance to talk."

Anna reached for Sarah's hand and held it.

"Let me ask you something," Anna said maternally.

"Go ahead."

"Do you smoke?"

"No."

"Promise me you'll never start."

"It's one of the few vices I don't have. I tried it once when I was sixteen. Amy Fortenelli and I snuck behind the high school and split a pack of Marlboros. I coughed until I threw up. Then I had to go home because I was so dizzy. Never touched another cigarette again."

"I wish to God that would've happened to me when I was sixteen. I wouldn't have ended up dying this way." She coughed and brought up a wad of dark phlegm that she spat into a tissue.

"You were three when your father was shot?"

"Yes."

"Then you really don't remember him?"

"No. Only from pictures and home movies."

"The last time I saw Chip, he was so excited to be going home to see you and your mother. He was such a proud parent. I guess we all were." Anna swallowed hard and cleared her throat.

"Do you want some water?"

"Please."

Sarah held a cup of ice chips near Anna's chapped lips. The older woman sipped the cold water through a plastic straw.

"Did you know my father well?" Sarah asked.

"Not really. Marica and Frankie were two and three then, so I was very busy with them. And I was only working a few days a month at the time. But whenever I saw Chip we talked about how much we missed being back home. He wanted to be stationed near your family in the worst way."

"That's what my mom's told me."

"Is she still alive?"

Sarah nodded.

"How's she doing?"

"Time will tell. She found a lump and may be about to fight her own battle. Both her parents died of cancer so we're keeping our fingers crossed. We're supposed to get some test results next week."

Anna grimaced again.

"Are you in a lot of pain?" Sarah asked.

"It comes and goes. When it gets real bad I press this little friend." She pointed to a white button that was attached to her morphine drip. "The problem with these damn painkillers is that they knock me out. And with so few hours left, I want to be awake for every one of them."

"I understand," Sarah said. She reached for Anna's cool, brittle hand. Sarah gently stroked her translucent, liver-spotted skin, trying to imagine the pain this woman was enduring just to stay lucid for an extra few hours.

Sarah wasn't sure how long Anna would last. Finally she spoke.

"There's something about my father that you haven't told anyone, isn't there?"

Anna closed her eyes and nodded, tears working their way down her cheeks.

"I hope you don't think I'm a terrible person for not telling you this sooner," Anna said.

Sarah dabbed Anna's face with a tissue, wiping away the tears. "Please don't cry."

"People had freak accidents or disappeared mysteriously. Shirley Ketchums had a sudden heart attack, and she seemed so healthy. I knew at the time it was wrong to keep quiet, but I had two children to raise. Of course, now I've got nothing to lose. What are they going to do, kill me?" She laughed sarcastically and began to cough again.

Sarah studied the dying woman's face. Severe pain and strong medication could warp even the most lucid of thinkers, but Anna's eyes were clear and her voice was steady.

"Just tell me," Sarah said firmly.

Anna breathed the oxygen through her nose and nodded.

"It was on August 10, 1963. I never knew for sure that it had anything to do with your father's murder, but deep in my heart it was something I always suspected. It's why the date has always stuck in my head."

Sarah again held the straw near Anna's dry lips, allowing her to take a sip of ice water.

"It was a Saturday night, maybe ten o'clock. Bernie and I had eaten dinner at a restaurant near our apartment when we decided to go out for a nightcap. We almost went to one of the nightclubs the diplomats and their wives frequented, but we decided to go a little bar called The Vodka House that was just around the corner from the Kremlin."

Sarah leaned closer to Anna.

"Bernie and the manager had a few things to discuss, so I went to the bar and ordered a couple of martinis. I saw your father sitting at a table with a man I'd never seen before. I went over to say hello and the three of us chatted for a few minutes."

Anna suddenly clenched her teeth and closed her eyes.

"Are you OK?" Sarah asked urgently.

"Yes," she replied weakly. She took another deep breath of oxygen. "That was a bad one. The pain comes in waves."

"Some more water?"

"No, but I may need to push that button if the pain doesn't go away."

"I understand. You do whatever you need to do. I can come back later."

Sarah watched Anna gather her composure, and delay the inevitable shot of morphine.

"Your father introduced me to the man he was with. Said his name was Lee Foster, a machine tool importer from St. Louis. I spent less than five minutes with them and didn't see them leave. But I'll never forget Foster's face as long as I live."

"Why?"

"Because three months later I saw it on the front page of *Pravda*. It turned out that his name wasn't Lee Foster. It was Lee Oswald. Lee Harvey Oswald."

The color drained from Sarah's face.

"Are you sure it was him?"

"At first I wasn't, so I didn't say anything to anybody. A few weeks later I translated a classified document that mentioned Oswald had been in Moscow during the summer of sixty-three. Then I found out one of his aliases was Lee Foster."

"Jesus." As Sarah tried to make sense of what she'd just been told, she heard Anna press the button that controlled the morphine. A whirring sound came from the control spigot.

"Witnesses in Dallas and everywhere else started dropping like flies," Anna said, her eyes getting heavy. "Seventy-three people named in the Warren Report ended up dying under very strange circumstances. I'm sorry, Sarah, but I couldn't take that chance. Please tell me you forgive me."

Anna struggled in vain to keep her eyes open so she could look directly at Sarah.

"You're forgiven," Sarah said. She leaned across the bed and kissed the sick woman on the forehead. "You're forgiven," she sobbed into Anna's ear. "Can you hear me?"

Anna grunted something indistinguishable, then drifted off into a deep sleep.

5

Monday

SPECIAL AGENT Sarah Peterson steadied herself and prepared to fire the same caliber weapon that had slain her father so many years ago. The image of the blood-soaked white sheet always flashed through her mind whenever she held a .44. By now she accepted the return of the painful recollection, even if she stubbornly refused to buy into the conclusion reached by the committee that supposedly had spent eight months investigating his death. "*Agent Peterson was killed by a single gunman acting alone.*" Those were the final ten words of the inch-thick confidential report that had never been made public. Sarah knew now the committee had not interviewed every relevant witness before they issued their report. What she didn't yet know was whether skipping over Anna Rodzinski was an intentional omission or simply an oversight. But now more than ever, Sarah was convinced that one day she would learn what really happened that hot August night in 1963.

"Notice how I'm standing!" Sarah said authoritatively, her words resounding throughout the cavernous room. It was time to concentrate on the Browning semiautomatic in her hands.

Thirty-four eager eyes briefly focused on Sarah's scuffed Reeboks, studying every nuance of her body language. Although a few of the stubborn men in the group would never admit it, she was what they all aspired to be.

"Feet? About shoulder length apart," she stated firmly. "Knees? Slightly bent." She froze in place, allowing everyone to observe her straight-backed posture. When the proper stance had been committed to her students' memory, she lowered her weapon and turned to face the Secret Service wannabes who had fanned out along several of the firing range's partitioned stalls.

"Give me three reasons why we fire from this position whenever possible," she said to the twelve men and five women.

"Better balance?" someone to her left responded.

"That's one."

"Better accuracy?"

She nodded. "That's two. One more."

There was silence for a few seconds, then an uncertain answer came from her right. "To compensate for the recoil?"

"Excellent," Sarah answered with a smile. She studied the blond woman who provided the last answer. There was obviously a bright light behind those blue eyes, one that could be kindled if there was a corresponding passion for this line of work. To Sarah, that aspect of her job had always been the most rewarding, and these weeklong classes were the only place where she met eager young women who possessed the rare combination of enthusiasm and God-given talent. More than three dozen female federal agents had Sarah Peterson to thank for the boost to their careers.

"All right, folks," Sarah said to her students. "This is how it all comes together." She loaded a thirteen-shot magazine into her revolver and assumed the position she had just demonstrated. The snout of her weapon pointed at the spot where her target would soon appear.

"Billy, let 'er rip!"

The man inside the bulletproof control room behind her and one flight up dimmed the lights, allowing Sarah to focus on the bowling alley–sized lane she was now facing. Her hands were steady as a surgeon's, her arms extended. Right now she had no idea how fast, or in what pattern, her target would rush at her. That was up to Billy, who was the chief instructor at the range.

Sarah squeezed her trigger the instant the target emerged from its chute.

Most of the rookies in the room didn't realize at first that a black sheet of paper with a white outline was quickly coming toward them. The target zigged and zagged every few feet, blurring the human silhouette on the paper.

A continuous roar poured from Sarah's weapon until its magazine was empty. When the Swiss-cheesed target stopped on its gurney just a few feet from her, only one shot out of thirteen had landed in the sand pit without hitting its mark.

Sarah turned and faced the group. Behind them, in the glass-encased control booth, Sarah noticed a young man in a suit and tie standing with his arms folded beside Billy. His wide eyes displayed that he, too, had been dazzled by her proficiency.

"Sarah, there's someone here to see you." Billy's amplified voice came from the speaker above all their heads. Everyone in the room glanced back at the control room.

"I'll be there in a second," Sarah answered. "In the meantime, set up lane fourteen, please."

"He says it's important."

"I understand," Sarah said with a hint of irritation, "and so's this. Tell him I'll come on up after this round."

Sarah looked at her students. Almost three men to every woman. The ratio hadn't changed much since she had spent her six months at the Secret Service Training Academy.

"Who wants to be our guinea pig?" she asked. Her weapon was offered out in front of her, resting in her palm.

Eight volunteers raised their hands, but not the one Sarah had hoped to see. She locked eyes with the blond woman, almost daring her to refuse. After several awkward seconds the young woman's arm slowly moved towards the soundproof ceiling.

"Good," Sarah said. "I see we have our first volunteer of the week."

The young woman wove her way between her colleagues.

"What's your name?" Sarah asked as she handed her the revolver.

"Williams. Nicole Williams."

"Ever fire a forty-four?" Sarah asked in a whisper.

The reluctant volunteer shook her head.

"Just remember to bend your knees and stay loose. If it's any consolation, the first time I fired a forty-four I missed my first fifty-seven shots."

Sarah backed away. "OK, Ms. Williams," she said, this time loud enough for everyone to hear. "You ready?"

The woman nodded.

Billy saw the gesture and flipped a switch.

The target rushed halfway up the lane before Nicole squeezed off her first shot. It threw her back six inches. She quickly regained her balance and fired five more times. Three pierced the target, two landed harmlessly in the sand pit. The remaining seven bullets never left her clip.

"Not bad," Sarah said, "but you let that first shot kick your ass a little bit, didn't you? Bend those knees! They're your shock absorbers!" She retrieved her revolver and holstered it, then sent her volunteer back to her colleagues with an encouraging pat on the shoulder.

"Let's all take five!" Sarah announced to the group. "Back here at eleven-fifteen!" She hustled up one flight to the control room. When she got there the steel door was wide open.

"Agent Peterson," the suit said, with his hand outstretched, "Brian Hogan. White House staff."

Sarah quickly gave the rosy-cheeked Hogan the once-over. He seemed polite, clean cut, and eager. She glanced at the laminated ID card hanging halfway down his tie. It confirmed he was one of the cookie-cutter interns who spent a year not quite believing they were actually getting paid to work at the White House.

"What can I do for you, Mr. Hogan?" The tone of her voice indicated she wasn't particularly pleased this tadpole had interrupted her training session.

"The President wants to see you."

Sarah eyed him quizzically. "When?"

"Right now. He's leaving for Camp David in less than an hour."

"Did he say *why* he wants to see me?"

"No, ma'am. Mr. Haskins just told me to get you right away."

"Ron Haskins? Chief of Staff Ron Haskins?"

"Yes, ma'am."

Sarah looked at Billy, who made no effort to disguise his interest in the situation.

"You know anything about this?"

Billy shook his head.

"Take over," she said. "Small arms the rest of this morning, then high-powered rifles this afternoon if I'm not back by then."

"No problem." Billy swiveled out from behind the control panel, grabbing his own .44 from his steel lock box.

"Drive 'em hard," Sarah said. "They seem like a solid group." She winked at him, then started toward the rear exit.

"Agent Peterson?" the intern said.

"Yes?"

"My limo's out front."

Sarah shook her head. "I'll take my own car."

A thousand ideas raced through Sarah's mind while her eight-year-old Jeep Wrangler followed the limousine to the White House. She had been in or around the Oval Office several dozen times, and had actually been introduced to the President at the Democratic convention two years earlier. But never before had she actually been summoned to the White House by the man himself. One-on-one. Cool beans, she thought. Very cool beans.

She parked at the East Wing colonnade, self-conscious at stepping inside 1600 Pennsylvania Avenue looking as though she was about to catch a movie with her friends. She hoped the President had been told that time had not allowed her to change into something more appropriate.

Sarah passed by several Secret Service agents as she was escorted through the White House, exchanging a quick hello with each. Almost everyone in this security detail knew exactly who she was.

"He'll be with you in a minute," the President's secretary said once Sarah settled into a seat just outside the Oval Office.

"Thanks."

"He's just finishing up on a call."

"Care to give me a heads-up on what this is about?"

The President's secretary smiled. "I couldn't say."

Sarah smiled too. She had been around enough powerful men and women to know their secretaries often knew more details than the people they worked for. But now was not the time to press this issue. She'd have some answers soon enough. Then the butterflies began their flight around her stomach and for the first time in her life she had cotton mouth. She aimlessly thumbed through a *Time* magazine on the mahogany coffee table, unable to focus on the printed words. She startled at the crisp buzz that came from the intercom that seemed to have more switches than a DC-10.

"I'll bring her right in," the President's secretary said in a low voice.

Sarah rose quickly from her seat, primping her hair before she arrived at the soundproof door.

"Mr. President," the secretary said, "I believe you met Sarah Peterson at the convention in 1996?"

The chief executive sat behind his desk, initialing documents. He dropped his heavy Cross pen, and walked toward Sarah. They met in the center of the large royal blue rug, where the gold bald eagle held thirteen arrows in its left claw.

"I understand they dragged you off the firing range," the President said with an easy smile. "Thanks for making it on such short notice."

Sarah's anxiety eased, which was exactly what the President had intended. Still, she continued to size up the man who held more power in his pinkie than most people held in a lifetime. Sarah had been trained by the best in the business to absorb every nuance of behavior and appearance no matter what the situation, and right now her senses were working overtime. The President was taller than she remembered, and slightly thinner. His gray suit was freshly pressed, his shoes tar black. From his mouth came the hint of a breath mint. More than anything, though, Sarah noticed the manner in which the President was looking at her. The most powerful man in the world was checking her out, plain and simple. By now, of course, she had gotten used to *that* look. It was different with each man, depending on their level of sophistication. Blue-collar guys simply leered. More sophisticated men admired her appearance in a much more subtle fashion. In this setting she felt absolutely unthreatened by the attention. But had they been in a different time and place she probably would have turned her back to him.

Sarah extended her hand to the President while she racked her brains for something witty to say. She vacillated a dozen times in the few seconds before her mouth decided to take a stab at humor.

"Sorry about this, sir," she said, gesturing at her stonewashed Levi's and sweatshirt, "but I didn't think our date was until *tomorrow*."

The President hesitated for a moment, then smiled. His scouting report on Sarah Peterson appeared to be right on target. The chief executive enjoyed working with women who had the courage to display a one-of-the-boys sense of humor in his company without thinking it would be interpreted as a come-on. More importantly, he respected people who could think quickly on their feet. Walking into the Oval Office was intimidating under any circumstances. Being summoned for a meeting with the President without notice was something most couldn't handle with aplomb.

"If you take a seat, we can get right down to business," he suggested affably, guiding her to one of the armchairs that faced his desk. He glanced at the wall clock that had been given to him by the Swiss consulate general. It was almost noon. "I don't have much time and you're probably wondering why the hell you're here."

"I'd be lying, sir, if I told you the thought didn't cross my mind."

The President nodded, but said nothing. For the moment he was concentrating on the single sheet of paper he had pulled from a thick expandable folder with Sarah's name written in block letters on its spine. Below it were a dozen or so similar folders. Sarah found herself straining as inconspicuously as she could to decipher what was written on the three facing her.

Halfway down the stack she saw Chet Moore's file. He was a fellow Secret Service agent stationed in Los Angeles, whom Sarah considered one of the best in the business. She collaborated with him whenever a left coast problem arose.

On the folder below Moore's was Peter Morrison's. Although Sarah didn't know him personally, she knew he was a young ATF agent in New York who was clearly a rising star. Sarah had heard just last week that Morrison was headed for a top spot in the antiterrorism division of the Justice Department.

The bottom folder was Dennis Ralston's. Ralston had spent twenty-some years working for the FBI. One of the highlights of his career had been the breaking open of a major portion of the Pan Am 103 case. Ralston had used an electron microscope to trace minute bits of clothing found among the wreckage back to a store on the tiny Mediterranean island of Malta. As a result of this painstaking effort, the FBI was eventually able to learn the names of the two Libyans who bought the clothing that surrounded the bomb on board the 747. Their indictment *in abstentia* soon followed.

"I see you went to Yale," the President said, a one-page executive summary in his hands.

Sarah quickly turned her focus toward the document the President was skimming. All she could make out were the dark black bullet points running in a column down the left side of the page.

"Yes, sir."

"My daughter tells me it's not really as tough as it's cracked up to be."

"She's right. Getting in was the hard part, sir."

She paused, watching him skim the many highlights of her career. When his eyes moved to the bottom of the page he removed his reading glasses and looked at her.

"You've accomplished quite a bit so far."

Sarah smiled nervously. "I've done the best I could whenever possible, sir."

"Like when you foiled an attempt on the Vice President's life in ninety-four?"

"Well, I was the team leader that day, but Fetterman was the guy who actually spotted the gunman up in the hotel window."

"And the Colombian counterfeiting ring that was dismantled in ninety-seven?"

"I was involved in that operation, Mr. President, but a lady named Diane Howard over at Treasury was the one who really pieced it all together."

"I suppose that story about Reagan your first week on the job was someone else, too?"

Sarah smiled. That *had* been more than just dumb luck. "This may sound funny, sir, but I happened to be looking in the right place at the right time."

The President waved his hand casually, dismissing her modesty. Repeated success, he knew, was rarely accidental.

"Let me ask you something, Sarah. You don't mind if I call you Sarah, do you?"

"Of course not, sir."

"And please don't take offense to my question."

She noticed he was pausing almost imperceptibly now before speaking, measuring each sentence carefully. She recognized this technique as a well-rehearsed trait of every refined politician. It heightened her skepticism; it meant he was calculating the effect of each question.

"Yes, sir."

"Why did you join the Secret Service? The pay is modest, the hours are long, and every day you step into harm's way."

"I'm not quite sure how to answer that, sir. I mean, it's what I've always wanted to do."

"That may be so, but my people tell me you're smart as hell and get along really well with your colleagues. You're also quite attractive. With that combination you could've written your ticket anywhere you wanted to go. Why the Secret Service?"

You're just like the rest of them? If I were a man, you never would have mentioned my looks. Sarah allowed her cooler side to take over. "I guess I thought it'd be interesting and challenging," she eventually replied. "And it's been both."

The President leaned back in his leather chair and steepled his fingers beneath his chin. His narrowing eyes told Sarah he was thinking a hundred miles an hour.

"When people walk into this office, I expect absolute honesty from them. It's a simple rule and one that's not negotiable. You and I have never worked together before today, but I want to be very clear about one thing. When people lay the bullshit on me, or give me half-truths, they're gone. I'd prefer that you not answer, rather than choose not to tell me the whole truth. Is that understood?"

Sarah stiffened. *"You and I have never worked together before today."* What the hell did that mean? she wondered. The President simply stared at her while she considered her answer.

"Ever since I can remember, sir, I've needed to find out what really happened to my father," she said without emotion. "I've never accepted the answers that so-called blue ribbon panel gave my mother."

"And that's why you signed on with the Secret Service in 1981?"

"That was one of the reasons," she answered softly. "The main one. I thought about the FBI and the CIA, but the Service gave me access to almost as much information without having to walk directly in my father's shadow."

Sarah felt hollow. The President had used his position of power to corner her into admitting something she had revealed only to her very close friends. She considered ending the interview, but being sent off to some desolate Third World outpost was not how she wanted to spend the next ten years.

"Your dad was shot in 1963?"

"Yes."

"That's a long time ago, Sarah. Why won't you move on?"

Sarah thought about backing down, about serving up a creampuff response that would make this whole unpleasant discussion go away. But she sensed a plum assignment coming her way and didn't want to ruin her chances. Then she remembered the sickening image of her father lying facedown in a pool of his and the Dalmatian's blood.

"May I answer your question with a question, Mr. President?"

"Sure."

"Your father's what, about seventy-five?"

"He'll be eighty in January."

"And you're fifty-seven?"

"As of last Tuesday."

"That's why," she said fiercely. "You've had almost sixty years to get to know your father and he you. My father and I never had that opportunity."

"And you think someone other than a single gunman is to blame?"

"My dad was spying on the Russians when he was shot twice at close range. His killer was found a few hours later, less than a mile from the crime scene, dead from a drug-induced heart attack. Some secret CIA commission looked at those facts and concluded the killer was acting on his own." She shrugged, then added, "Let's just say I've always had my doubts."

"Fair enough," the President said. "If you want to swing at windmills for the rest of your life, that's your prerogative. Just as long as it doesn't interfere with your performance."

"With all due respect, sir, I don't think I'd be sitting here today if it did."

The President nodded. She *was* as gritty and determined as the confidential report before him said she would be. She had passed her first test. "Why don't we change the subject?"

"That's more than fine with me, sir."

The President leaned back and folded his arms. "Any regrets about joining the Secret Service?"

"I'm not quite sure how to answer that one either, sir."

"Well, you've never gotten any satisfactory answers about your father's death."

"Not yet."

"And from what I've read, you've endured more than your share of obstacles over the years."

"That's an understatement," she said with a smile. "It hasn't been easy, especially those first few years. For a while there it seemed like someone was behind the scenes pulling me back, seeing if I'd throw in the towel."

The President raised one eyebrow. "You believe that?"

Absolutely, she thought, *and from your reaction it sure seems like you know something that I don't know.* "No, sir."

The President quickly scanned his one-pager.

"Two years in Pakistan, then three in Algeria. Those countries aren't exactly friendly toward female professionals."

"Neither was the Academy, sir. I don't know how much detail my file contains," she said, "but most of the practical jokes could've led to a lawsuit and an appearance on *Nightline*." She shrugged and said, "As you probably know, I never made a stink about any of it. That's never been my style."

"Nor mine."

"I simply got even whenever I could." She smiled mischievously. "I'm sure some of those incidents are in my file, too."

The President stood and walked toward one of the picture windows facing the South Lawn. The chopper that would soon ferry him to Camp David had just touched down.

"Let me ask you a personal question, and you *really* don't have to answer this one if you don't want to."

The President smiled when he saw her skeptical expression.

"I mean that, Sarah. This one's a freebie. I won't hold it against you if you think I'm overstepping my bounds."

"Thank you, Mr. President, but I've got very little to hide."

"OK. You're thirty-eight, successful at your job, attractive, and seem to have a good sense of humor. How come there's no Mr. Peterson?"

Sarah chuckled to mask her anger. She had been asked this same question a thousand different times in a hundred ways and had always told the nosy interrogator to mind their own damn business. But this was different. If the President was going to put her in a position of trust, as she suspected, he arguably had a right to know whether there was a dark center inside her glossy exterior.

"I assume this is relevant, sir?"

"To me it is."

"Well, if you ask my mom, she'll tell you that I'm too picky," she said to buy a few extra seconds.

The former prosecutor leaned forward in his high-backed leather chair. "*I'm* asking."

"I've been close a few times," she replied, "but something always made me pull in the reins. I never wanted to back into marriage just because nothing better came along." She paused, thinking about the dozens of men she had had dinner with over the last five years. With almost all of them, she had known within two minutes that she'd rather be curled up on her couch in her sweats watching a movie. But despite these ho-hum dates, Sarah had collected a shoebox filled with letters and notes from men who wanted to spend the rest of their lives with her. Sarah saved every one of these, and read them with her girlfriends whenever they needed a good laugh.

"I suppose one day it'll happen," she added, to give the President what she thought he wanted to hear. "I mean I'd like it to, because I'd like to start a family."

"That's fair enough," the President said. He moved closer to her, pleased that her answer had confirmed what his own investigation of her love life had revealed. "I've got an opportunity for you, Sarah. One that'll move you up to that next level. Are you interested?"

The question startled her, even though the conversation had obviously been moving in this direction. She suddenly felt queasy, remembering the e-mail message she had received two weeks earlier. YOU WILL SOON BE OF-FERED A BUSINESS OPPORTUNITY THAT ON ITS FACE SEEMS IRRESISTIBLE. BUT I AM WARNING YOU, SARAH. DO NOT TAKE IT!!! Sarah had tried every conceivable avenue to trace the source of the e-mail, but her efforts had been futile. The communication had been sent through an anonymous server in Finland who accepted incoming messages from all around the world for redelivery. The server stripped away the sender's header, rerouted the e-mail per the sender's instructions, then assigned it a bogus name. Tens of thousands of vindictive messages had been forwarded in this fashion. And there was nothing the authorities could do to stop it.

Twelve hours later the strange message reappeared, but in a different form. Taped to her front door was a sheet of plain white paper. The message on it was printed in block letters in black ink: CERTAIN PEOPLE SURVIVE BE-CAUSE THEY HEED GOOD ADVICE. THOSE WHO FOLLOW IT LIVE. THOSE WHO IGNORE IT DIE. YOUR FATHER SCORNED GOOD ADVICE AND DIED BECAUSE OF IT. DON'T MAKE THE SAME MISTAKE!

Someone who knew where she lived was obviously trying to intimidate her. This was no longer a harmless Internet threat that could be deleted with the push of a button. This was as close to home as it got. Someone who had recently been standing at her front door was going to hurt her if she accepted this job offer from the President.

"Sarah?" the President asked.

"Yes, sir?"

"I asked if you were interested."

"I'm sorry, sir. I lost my train of thought for a second. Of course I'm interested."

"It goes without saying that this is all strictly confidential."

"I understand."

Sarah moved to the edge of her seat. Round one was over. She had obviously held her own. Round two was about to begin.

"We've recently intercepted a flurry of communications concerning possible assassination plots against Jack Montgomery."

"Phone conversations?"

The President nodded. "And a few faxes."

"Here?"

"No, the Middle East."

"Encrypted?"

"Most of them."

"So someone's trying to take out the Secretary of State." It was a statement, not a question.

The President nodded. "The CIA thinks there may be a Libyan connection, but they haven't made any definitive link yet."

"These are satellite intercepts, I take it, rather than ground devices?"

"You're familiar with the NSA's equipment?"

"Just the basics, really. It's my understanding that the NSA keeps between six and eight satellites in constant orbit."

"Right now there are six."

"And because they can't target any *specific* conversation without a court order, these satellites suck up tens of millions of bits of information every single day. Like huge vacuum cleaners."

"Exactly. Then they sift for key words like 'assassination' or 'explosives.' The NSA's analysts have struck gold a few times using this technique. It's how we thwarted the bombing of the UN building last year."

"Amazing."

"So's the information they've intercepted in the last thirty days. Several groups are apparently determined to kill Secretary Montgomery." The President passed a large National Security Agency interdepartmental folder across his desk, its wax seal broken.

"I assume you've got access to a secure safe?"

"Yes, sir."

"Anyone else use it?"

Sarah shook her head.

The President reached into his top drawer and removed a single index card. On it were six rows of seemingly unrelated letters, numbers, and symbols. The shortest row contained twenty-four characters, the longest thirty-nine. Asterisks, dollars signs, and ampersands dotted the card.

"These are this month's NSA access codes," he said. "This database gives us a hell of a leg up on preventing certain types of terrorism."

Sarah looked confused. She had never been required to enter any special passwords to retrieve data from the NSA's files. "Isn't all of the NSA's information available to the U.S. intelligence community?"

"No. There's certain information the NSA doesn't share with anyone except on a need-to-know basis."

"And I assume these codes unlock that information?"

"Exactly."

Sarah hesitated. "Am I allowed to ask what's in there, sir?"

The President nodded. "The NSA has listened in on every internal communication of every intelligence agency of every country in the world ever since The Cold War started. It's a way to find out what our allies *really* think of our policies. Some of my predecessors thought that this practice was unethical, but I'm convinced it's essential." He leaned forward, as if to emphasize his point. "A single act of terrorism can demoralize an entire country. If the Oklahoma City bombing had been the work of Arabs, it would have ripped the heart out of America. When it comes to preventing terrorism, this president believes there's no such thing as being too aggressive. No one in my administration will *ever* be held accountable for doing what they think is necessary to stop terrorism."

"Don't our allies object, Mr. President?"

"Vigorously," he replied, deadpan. "But they're powerless to stop it. The Israelis try jamming their most secret communications, and so do the Saudis. But most countries don't even know we're eavesdropping." The President smiled. The intelligence network he had quietly spent billions developing was as efficient as any secret mechanism of the government. He gestured toward the index card in Sarah's hand. "Fewer than ten people in the entire world have access to the information in those computer files. I wrestled long and hard over whether to give these codes to you. But given the number of threats against Secretary Montgomery, you'll need help from as many sources as possible."

Sarah nodded, pleased she would soon be able to squirrel around the files few others could access. From the President's remarks it was obvious that skill would be necessary. She looked at the President, waiting for the other shoe to drop.

"I assume you're familiar with the Office of Diplomatic Security?" he asked.

"Yes, sir. I've worked closely with the ODS for years. Most recently when the Israeli prime minister came to the States."

"Good, then it shouldn't take you very long to spool up."

"How so, sir?"

"Effective immediately, you're the number two person at the ODS. You'll report directly to Dick O'Neill. Your only task in the short term will be to protect Secretary Montgomery."

Sarah smiled at the news of her promotion, even though she tried her best not to. But she felt a strange feeling in the pit of her stomach. *Some-*

thing's very wrong with this picture. Someone had known this was coming and had tried to scare her into turning down the job. She held her tongue, waiting to learn more.

"Dick's already preparing an office for you over at the State Department."

The thought of the thirty-two-year veteran who she'd be replacing crossed her mind, tempering her excitement. Stepping on heads had become a necessary evil, but one she didn't always enjoy. Especially when nice guys were left in the dust.

"What about Bob Wakefield?" Sarah asked.

"Wakefield's retiring. He saw the handwriting on the wall and tendered his resignation a few months ago, but he kept it quiet until this search was over. To his credit, he acknowledged he wasn't capable of changing the agency from the top down. And from what I can tell, you are." He stared at her. "Of course, Wakefield's agreed to stay on for as long as you need him so the transition's a smooth one. He'll fill the gaps while you put a system in place that anticipates danger instead of reacts to it. If this works we'll do it with the Secret Service; that will also be your project. Hal wants to retire by the end of next year."

Sarah felt a shiver of excitement and apprehension. Running the Secret Service was climbing into some very rarefied air. "Thank you for the vote of confidence, Mr. President. I'm flattered. I really am."

"You've earned this, Sarah. But don't get complacent. This assignment will be the most difficult one of your life. There are people out there who're itching to strap explosives to their chest and pull the switch if they can just get close enough to Jack Montgomery. There are also people who would love to see you fall on your face."

"I understand that, sir."

The President again leaned forward, his elbows resting on his desk. His serious expression was the same one he wore during the last few minutes of every televised speech from the Oval Office as he stared directly into the camera without blinking. Sarah had been around enough politicians to accept the gesture with a very large grain of salt.

"Jack Montgomery is the most important person in my administration, Sarah. *The* most important. He gets things done behind the scenes. He learned that when he was Kissinger's Chief of Staff in the seventies."

"I understand, sir. May I ask you a question?"

"Of course."

"Do I have the full support of the Secretary? I mean, Wakefield's been with him for years."

The President smiled. "I'll level with you, Sarah. His reaction was much more negative than I anticipated. He didn't think you were ready to take this on." The President waved his hand dismissively. "He finally came around to my line of thinking once he understood how thorough the search was for the right person."

A soft, short buzz came from the President's intercom. He lifted his phone, then listened for a few seconds. "I'll be right there," he said. Behind him Sarah could see the First Lady strolling across the South Lawn toward the awaiting helicopter. The family basset hound was tugging at his leash, eager to scoot up the retractable steps.

"Well, that's it," the President said. He stood, signaling that the meeting was over.

"Thank you, Mr. President," Sarah said as she rose. "I'll do everything I can to protect Secretary Montgomery."

"I'm sure you will." He shook her hand firmly and asked, "Any other questions before you go?"

Yeah, what aren't you telling me? "None right now, sir," she said. "Perhaps after I've had a chance to review this file."

She tucked the NSA file under her arm and left the Oval Office. As much as she wanted to take a few days to think this all through, she knew Jack Montgomery's security team would be awaiting her orders first thing tomorrow morning.

6

IT was cold. Numbingly cold. The dank, stale air brought back vivid memories of her visit to a bat-infested limestone cave when she was just a child. She was frightened then and she was frightened now, though for very different reasons.

Jessica blinked, tentatively at first, then rapidly several times. Although she wasn't quite yet awake she could clearly feel the muscles in her face contract with each successive effort. But no images registered; it was as if she were blind.

With all the energy she could muster she tried to move her legs. Nothing.

Her shoulders budged ever so slightly when she strained to move her arms. Thank God she could move her heavy head. But her hands remained fixed where they were, as if they'd been nailed to the floor. She felt an agonizing sensation in her wrists.

"Hello!" She tried to shout. The word came out slurred and incomprehensible even to her, sounding like a cassette tape being played with a drained battery.

She tried to recall what had happened the last time she was awake. She thought hard, but couldn't remember a thing. It was all a blur. She felt a wave of nausea. It was the same nausea she had felt every morning since she had seen that little pink dot on the home pregnancy test stick. *Oh my God, my baby!*

Jessica tried to compose herself, tried to remember what had happened. There had been a man. She remembered his muscular arms lifting her bags, and the stream of clear fluid that squirted all over her face. Then all of her strength had been sapped from her system. He had held her down like a rag doll.

Jessica lay still, feeling nothing in her belly. Was she supposed to? She didn't know, couldn't remember. She began to panic, swallowing the few drops of saliva that still remained on her parched tongue. When she did, her two front teeth seemed to wiggle.

"Help me! Someone, please help me!" she cried. The words were slightly less garbled, but still incomprehensible. *What was happening?* Then she felt a sharp pain in her arm. The nightmare was starting over.

Jessica closed her eyes, again trying to compose herself. In a few minutes she would wake up in her bed in the Hôtel Marronniers in Paris. She would slough aside the bad dream. The conference on world hunger awaited her and she was ready. She had been excited about this trip for months.

"Don't let me die," she pleaded softly, her words still garbled. "I want to see my baby!"

Before she could speak another word, her world went black once again.

GRIZZWALD hovered over her, still as a deer. The knife in his hand was perfectly steady.

He had watched Jessica thrash for several seconds before she went limp. It would be three hours before she awoke. The second injection made that a certainty.

Grizzwald placed the sharp edge of his knife against her throat. One quick slash would end her life right then and there. He decided to hold off; there was a possibility he would need her alive to collect his ransom. Instead, he flicked a tiny mass of flesh from Jessica's left arm. She didn't even flinch as blood oozed from the circular wound. Grizzwald laughed. He had always wondered whether his homemade anesthetic was as potent as the real stuff. Now he knew.

He bent down close to her ear, touching the soft skin of her neck with his lips.

"You will be mine," he whispered. "All mine."

7
Tuesday

"POSITIONS please, guys!" Sarah ordered. The edge in her voice crackled through the small plastic earpieces of the eleven Office of Diplomatic Security agents whom she had assigned to guard Jack Montgomery.

"All clear!" barked a behemoth of a man who had jumped out of a black Seville.

All of the cars in the Secretary of State's heavily armed motorcade came to a complete halt well inside the underground VIP garage of the Pentagon. The *thump, thump, thump* of the Apache attack helicopter that would now accompany all his convoys could no longer be heard. Neither could the roar of the sixteen D.C. police motorcycles that had leapfrogged in front of one another to block the Secretary's travel route from traffic. Jack Montgomery, the beneficiary of this intricate security machine, continued to work on his laptop. He was nestled comfortably into the tanned Corinthian leather of his armored Town Car, seemingly oblivious to the extraordinary security precautions swirling around him.

Sarah had left the President's office less than twenty-four hours earlier and had hit the ground running. The NSA transcriptions had been fascinating: forty-three telephone conversations translated from Arabic into English.

In all, there seemed to be three separate terrorist groups intent on killing the Secretary of State. All were angry about Montgomery's apparent favoritism toward Israel in what was supposed to be a neutral peace process. One had decided to use a truck bomb filled with ammonium nitrate and fuel oil. It would be detonated by remote control and a Teflon sensor. The second planned to employ a suicide bomber who would tape a large quantity of plastic explosives to his chest, just as the President had warned. The third intended to kill the old-fashioned way: a gunman with access to the Secretary would shoot him from close range. From what Sarah could glean from the intercepted conversations, that assassin had recently entered the United States.

Sarah stepped out of the $700,000 decoy limo in which she was riding, careful to take a moment to look and listen. In view of the various threats, she had insisted that all of the agents who were guarding Secretary Montgomery have their automatic weapons poised and ready. No place, not even a secure area beneath the Pentagon, was considered safe enough not to take these extra precautions. She squinted, allowing her eyes to adjust to the dim fluorescent light that gave the vast subterranean parking lot a hollow, closed-in feeling.

"Let's go!" Sarah ordered.

Jack Montgomery pushed open his back door. The Secretary of State walked briskly toward the building entrance, limping slightly. More than four decades had passed since a sniper's bullet had shattered his kneecap in Korea.

"Rick and Mark in with me!" Sarah directed, no longer speaking into the compact microphone of her collar set. Her crisp, authoritative voice reverberated against the solid walls and concrete support beams. "Everyone else stay here!"

She turned and looked at the man whose job she had just taken. Bob Wakefield appeared much older to her than when she had bumped into him over at the FBI building just a few weeks ago.

"I'll follow you," she told Wakefield.

Each of the men around her was already familiar with her reputation for thwarting domestic terrorism; this, she knew, was the reason she seemed already to have the support and respect of those who would be taking her orders. She could not say the same for Jack Montgomery. His chilly greeting four hours earlier had taken her by surprise. The President had been candid and forewarned her. But Montgomery obviously didn't take kindly to having decisions jammed down his throat.

Sarah and her colleagues hustled forward to catch up to Montgomery. He was already shaking hands with a burly army general who was wearing his dark green dress uniform. Sarah instantly recognized the man with the salt-and-pepper buzz cut and infectious smile as General Buck Perry. General Perry was a farm boy from Georgia who had served in the infantry with Secretary Montgomery during the Korean War. His prairie-stock physique made it look as though his suit coat had lost a size in the wash. As Buck Perry affectionately wrapped his Bunyanesque hand around Montgomery's shoulder, Sarah couldn't help but think what an odd pair the two old friends made. To her, Montgomery was smooth as silk, a refined public figure who had improved with age. Buck Perry was a bulldozer. Of course, Sarah was mindful that as her own looks proved, appearances were often misleading. As Commander of all Special Forces operations worldwide, there was no doubt Buck Perry was every bit as shrewd as his diplomatic counterpart.

Sarah kept pace with the two men, catching clipped phrases of Montgomery's bland mid-Atlantic accent and Perry's vivid Southern drawl. The group followed Wakefield through the deserted corridors, then came to one of the Pentagon's fortified situation rooms. Sarah pushed open the heavy steel door and began to go inside.

"You can wait out in the hallway, ma'am," Perry said sarcastically. He glanced at Wakefield, whose company he had enjoyed for years. "I don't think there are any A-rabs around. I feel pretty safe here." The general smiled at his own flippant comment, as did the two civilians who were standing at the far end of the forty-foot-long mahogany conference table. Both were wearing visitor's badges with their names printed in blue ink; Sarah knew she had seen one of them before.

"That's an interesting choice of words," Sarah said, looking General Perry in the eye. "Because Indira Gandhi used almost the exact same phrase on the morning of October thirty-first, 1984. Thirty seconds later she was shot dead by her own security forces. Sir," she added, smiling blandly.

When no further comment from the general was forthcoming she turned and quickly surveyed the spacious room. On one wall were several large colorful maps pocked with red and blue stickpins. Along another was a row of blinking computer terminals and a battery of secure fax machines and telephones. A web of monster coaxial cables connected the bunker to the outside world. Sarah had seen all of this high-tech gadgetry during her tenure with the Secret Service. However, in light of the highly restricted access area, she was troubled to see the two civilians standing before her. Something was clearly out of kilter, and Sarah couldn't help but wonder whether this meeting had any connection to the assassination plots the NSA satellites had overheard. Although the odds of that were remote, she had learned long ago not to dismiss any possibility.

Sarah desperately tried to remember all she could about the two civilians.

The man to her left was Tom Witherspoon, a brilliant U.S. expatriate who now resided principally in Monaco. As one of the world's foremost arms dealers, he had supplied warring factions in every corner of the globe with genuine and copycat hardware for more than thirty years and was more knowledgeable than almost anyone alive on the topic of sophisticated weaponry. He wore his crisply pressed spread French collar, double-breasted dark blue suit, and conservative foulard tie as comfortably as his own skin. A dab of styling gel kept his fifty-five-mile-an-hour side part in place. He was the one fumigating the room with an oversized Cuban cigar. Although to Sarah's knowledge no current U.S. government official had ever consulted with Witherspoon in a "professional" capacity, rumor had it that envoys from many of the world's capitals had quietly visited his posh Riviera offices over the years.

Next to him stood Ed Gallagher, a handsome, athletic-looking man with sea blue eyes, wavy dark blond hair and matching walrus mustache. Though they had never met, Sarah knew his name from the reams of classified documents she had reviewed during her career. Gallagher had been employed by one of the major oil companies during the 1960s and '70s before making his fortune trading petroleum futures on the Chicago mercantile exchange. He had also consulted extensively for OPEC, which was why several U.S. intelligence agencies had taken an interest in him in the first place. He and Witherspoon had known Jack Montgomery since their days at Harvard.

Sarah observed the two men carefully, not quite sure what to make of their presence. But something about them, and their extensive contacts within the Arab world through their oil and their weapons, made the tiny hairs on the back of her neck stand on edge.

"When it comes to preventing terrorism, this President believes there's no such thing as being too aggressive. No one in my administration will ever be held accountable for doing what they think is necessary to stop terrorism." As the President's words rang through her head she made a decision. Of course she was aware that what she was about to do was deceptive, that it stretched the boundaries of what most civilians considered ethical. But she understood that questionable conduct by protective agencies like the Secret Service and the ODS often kept men like the President and the Secretary of State alive. Those fools who believed otherwise simply didn't understand the way this world worked. Besides, the technique she was about to employ had been executed to perfection several times and no one had ever been the wiser. It was her ability to deftly steer danger of every kind away from her VIPs that had so impressed the President and had certainly triggered her promotion.

Sarah walked to the far end of the room while Witherspoon and Gallagher circled the table to greet Montgomery and Perry. Her thumbs released the spring-loaded brass locks on her briefcase, causing the crisp sound of metal striking metal to reverberate through the room. When she removed the stack of six yellow legal pads she always kept in her briefcase, no one seemed to take notice.

Perhaps I can get you gentlemen some coffee and doughnuts, too? she thought sarcastically.

Sarah knew as well as anyone that men at this level viewed the women around them as glorified secretaries. She found it predictable, yet pathetic, that the putting out of legal pads by the second-in-command at the ODS had not raised any eyebrows. It had been this way throughout Sarah's career, and she had used this antiquated line of thinking to her advantage whenever she could.

Sarah nonchalantly set the legal pads down two feet from the head of the long table, where she surmised Jack Montgomery would be sitting. Concealed within the binder of the bottom notepad were the guts from a Norelco 597 voice-activated Dictaphone, which had been surgically implanted many years earlier by an FBI technician for one of Sarah's prior assignments. The microphone was the size and thickness of a postage stamp and could capture a whisper from as far as twenty feet away.

The taping mechanism itself was just as small, and just as cleverly disguised by the FBI's forensic whiz. The techie had extracted a rectangular swatch of cardboard backing from the writing tablet. After inserting a specially designed microcassette into the hole, he had pasted a thin layer of brown buckram over the cassette. A dash of gray paint made the slight seam undetectable.

Her recording device in place, Sarah and Wakefield headed toward the door.

"We'll be out in the hallway if you need anything," she said to Montgomery with a polite smile.

For the moment Sarah suppressed her urge to warn Montgomery. Within a few hours she would have listened to the tape she had just planted and would know for sure whether her concerns were genuine. If Witherspoon and Gallagher pressured Montgomery into some kind of questionable business arrangement, then she would quietly squash that initiative before it had an opportunity to get legs. If she detected from the conversation that Montgomery was being set up for direct physical danger, then she would take immediate steps to blunt their progress. In the interim, she would maximize her time while she waited for the meeting to conclude.

Sarah sat cross-legged on the marble floor in the hallway with her IBM Thinkpad propped up in her lap. Linking into the main FBI database through a cellular modem, she typed "T-o-m W-i-t-h-e-r-s-p-o-o-n" on her keyboard.

8

JACK MONTGOMERY closed the conference room door behind him, making certain it was sealed. No one outside these soundproof walls would be permitted to hear what he was about to say. Social pleasantries had already been exchanged; now it was time for the Secretary of State to get down to business. Under his instructions, Jessica Baldwin was bound and gagged, her life hanging in the balance. More important to him, her kidnapping had put his own career on the line once again.

The three men who watched Montgomery stride to his seat did so with a certain degree of admiration. They, like most others who came into contact with him, felt his presence, his charisma. There was almost a regal quality about him. Most politicians worked the crowd when they entered a room. Jack Montgomery found the opposite to be more effective; he would let those in the room work their way toward him. A handshake, a few words, even the mere touch of their sleeve. If the kingmaker acknowledged your presence, you could consider yourself a somebody.

"I'm working on a matter that's of vital interest to this country, and therefore of great importance to me." Montgomery settled into his spot at the head of the table. "Right now exactly two people outside this room know of my involvement in this project. I don't expect that to change after this discussion." His focused gaze bore into the eyes of his three old friends. There was no need to issue threats if they violated his demand for secrecy. What each had no way of knowing was that phone records and airline logs had been doctored at the source to implicate all three in Jessica's kidnapping. A simple call from Montgomery and an offender would be in deeper than he ever could have imagined.

"We're at a critical juncture on this project and decisions need to be made immediately," he continued. "Each of you has expertise in an area that I don't. That's why you're here, if you were wondering."

Montgomery reached under the table and pressed a small, red button. A thirty-five-inch flat-screen television materialized where a portion of one of the walls had been. He grabbed an eight-by-ten-inch glossy from his oxblood briefcase and tossed it onto the polished tabletop.

"This woman was abducted Sunday afternoon while on her way to Paris," Montgomery said matter-of-factly. Grizzwald had taken the picture of Jessica six weeks earlier with a Nikon N90S camera from a half mile away. The texture of the image was slightly grainy despite the use of a $10,000 Nikkor 600mm F/4 zoom lens. Jessica was walking along the water's edge of a deserted white sand beach with her two chocolate labs. The large dogs were belly deep in seawater, the one with the blue bandanna around his neck retrieving a piece of driftwood. Doubled around Jessica's left wrist was a burgundy scrunchy; her thick, black hair hung to the middle of her back. She appeared relaxed and at ease with herself, obviously unaware that at Jack Montgomery's direction, Grizzwald had been carefully charting her every move for the past several months.

Montgomery stared impassively at the picture, relieved none of his colleagues appeared the least bit fazed. The Secretary of State also remained unruffled; he had learned long ago to avoid becoming sensitive to the plight of the central players in his plans. He treated his potential victims much the way surgeons approached their patients. Some would live and some would die. Emotional involvement only clouded his ability to execute properly the business at hand.

"And this is her father," Montgomery added. He slid a second color photograph onto the table. It was the head shot of Sam Baldwin, a man who epitomized the upper echelon of corporate America. Starched pinpoint cotton shirt, charcoal Brooks Brothers suit, crisp maroon Windsor knot, tan forehead, and slightly receding hairline. The picture had been torn from an insert to the most recent Baldwin Enterprises annual report. In the top righthand corner of the page was the familiar corporate logo imprinted onto products in almost every home in America. Five concentric circles appeared inside the upper loop of the B in "Baldwin Enterprises," symbolizing the five continents on which the conglomerate did business. "Right now Baldwin doesn't know his daughter's been kidnapped, but that will likely change in the next few hours."

The Secretary of State again locked eyes with each of the men around the table. Of course, it was still too soon to know for sure how far each would go if his plans went awry and he required their active assistance. But from their subtle smiles, Montgomery knew that at this early juncture they would cooperate fully. This effort was going to proceed as smoothly as the plan he devised in 1980. Of the dozen illegal operations Montgomery had engineered since the early sixties, the one concerning the former Shah of Iran had been the cleanest, if not the most brazen. Jack Montgomery had realized within days of the takeover of the U.S. Embassy in Teheran that the hostage crisis would remain at a stalemate until Reza Phalevi, the exiled shah, was removed from the equation. Montgomery thoroughly assessed his options, then positioned himself to meet secretly with the man who every insider in Washington knew would be the next director of the CIA. Together they arranged for the shah's doctors in Egypt to inject the deposed dictator with a virulent strain of cancer cells while he was undergoing a routine prostate exam. Every detail was considered, including the use of a grouping of cells from an individual who had the same blood type as the shah's. The dissident cells were not rejected, and proliferated within weeks of the inoculation directly into the lining of the shah's colon, causing the disease to ravage his body. The shah's expedited death less than two months later paved the way for the hostage crisis to be resolved with all sides saving face. The creative solution rid the United States of the humiliating predicament and catapulted President Reagan into office with a tide of patriotism and fervor not seen since. It had been one of the most gratifying moments of Montgomery's life.

"Why'd you detain her, Jack?" Gallagher asked cautiously.

Inwardly, the Secretary of State beamed. Gallagher's careful selection of the word *detain*, rather than something more combative, was music to his ears. He now knew he could count on Gallagher if he needed his help. "It'll make perfect sense to you in a minute."

Montgomery swiveled for the phone behind his chair. He dialed a number, then spoke a few words to the person on the other end of the line. Almost immediately, Montgomery's relay from the National Security Agency's satellite link-up at Fort Meade connected.

"This is real-time surveillance of a vessel named *The Hercules,*" Montgomery said. Crisp color images appeared on the television screen. Montgomery rotated his chair so he had a better angle at the screen, as did the others. Several diesel-powered forklifts could be seen removing refrigerator-sized crates from inside the dark cargo hold of a huge freighter.

"Right now those crates are being off-loaded from *The Hercules* in Istanbul, Turkey. In a day or two they'll be shuttled south toward the Turkish-Iraqi border. Ultimately, I believe they'll land in a Kurdish-controlled town called Diyarbakir."

Montgomery paused for a moment to allow his colleagues to study the broadcast. Live intercontinental television hook-ups had become commonplace in the early 1970s. But these men knew that selected individuals within the U.S. government could scrutinize whatever target they wished by accessing a sophisticated spy satellite in orbit three hundred miles above the earth's surface. Even from that distance, license plates came into focus as if they were being viewed on a clear day from a third-floor window.

"What's inside the crates?" Witherspoon asked.

Montgomery flashed his smile, knowing Witherspoon was on board. "Bombs, my friend, and that's the very reason *you're* here." He grabbed a stack of black-and-white satellite photos from his briefcase and spread them in front of Tom Witherspoon. A look of understanding washed across the arms dealer's face even before all eight were in place. Although the dark gray shapes looked like nothing more than blobs, to Tom Witherspoon the images were instantly recognizable. He removed a pair of Ben Franklin reading glasses from inside his breast pocket, then lifted one of the photos. He studied it intently for a moment, squinting as he carefully evaluated the weapons that had been photographed three weeks earlier.

"Who owns *The Hercules,* Jack?" Witherspoon asked.

Montgomery ignored the question.

"I assume you recognize those weapons?" the Secretary of State asked.

"Of course."

"Ever sold any?"

"No, but that's only because I can't get my hands on 'em."

"Is that unusual?"

Witherspoon smiled. "Let's put it this way, Jack. Give me an hour to make a few calls and I'll have an Abrams M1A2 tank waiting for you in the parking lot."

Montgomery glanced at General Perry, aware there were few controls in place to prevent the kind of black market transaction the arms dealer had just described. With several trillion dollars' worth of military hardware out there, and the potential for staggering profits staring conscripts square in the face, it was next to impossible to keep some of it from walking off the practice range.

"You don't happen to have an extra one of those bombs lying around that might've fallen off the back of a truck?" Witherspoon asked. "We can probably make a cool million on it, partner. Maybe two."

Montgomery smiled; the most serious of questions were often asked in jest. He scribbled a few notes on one of the pads Sarah had laid before him and said, "Before we head down that road, I want you to tell me from your perspective exactly what the weapons in those crates are and what they can do. I've been briefed extensively about it by my colleagues in the military, but they're not exactly trustworthy when it comes to critiquing the capabilities of their own weapons." He looked over at the general, knowing his old friend was often guilty of this offense.

The arms dealer tapped an inch of burnt tobacco into a heavy glass ashtray, then blew a narrow stream of smoke toward the ceiling.

"The weapon is commonly known as a bunker buster, and the power inside each one is awesome, Jack. They're laser-guided smart bombs that weigh about three tons apiece. They burrow through reinforced concrete and steel like a hot knife through butter. Then they detonate. During the Gulf War, a single one of these suckers took out a bomb shelter inside Baghdad. Blew the fucking thing to smithereens. In just a few seconds half the Iraqi brass evaporated. And what's frightening is that the weapon's been improved nearly one hundred percent since then."

"Are there any shelters in Iraq that could withstand a blast from one of these tomorrow?" Montgomery asked.

"No. In fact, there are only three in the whole world that could even stand a chance. One's in Tel Aviv, one's under the White House, and the third's about a mile beneath your chair."

"What about the Iraqi air defense system?"

The arms dealer shook his head. "The odds would be almost nil that it could stop one of those bombs after it was launched. Their antiaircraft weapons date back to the mid-eighties. Maybe one in a hundred missiles would get knocked out of the sky, but that would be pure luck."

Witherspoon thought for a moment, then asked, "Who's going to kill Saddam Hussein?"

Montgomery pointed to the picture of Sam Baldwin.

"How the hell did he get those weapons?" Witherspoon asked. There was a tinge of jealousy in his voice.

"I'm not sure yet," the Secretary of State replied, "but I intend to find out. There are only a handful of possible sources."

"Why in God's name is Baldwin involved in this?" Gallagher asked.

"Two reasons, as far as I can tell."

"I assume the first is revenge?" Witherspoon asked. "His nephew?"

Montgomery nodded, impressed with the extent of Witherspoon's inside knowledge. "The Kurds did their homework."

On the evening of January 25, 1991, seven Scuds were fired at Israel from the southwest corner of Iraq. All were intercepted by Patriot missiles, but more than five tons of shrapnel from those collisions rained down on a Tel Aviv suburb. One person was killed that night, forty-two injured. The single fatality was Sam Baldwin's nineteen-year-old nephew, who was visiting friends for a few days on his way home from the Far East.

"Publicly, Baldwin refused to comment on the incident and it barely received any coverage," Montgomery said. "He also called in quite a few markers with his contacts in the press to keep the whole affair quiet. He's a guy who hates any kind of negative publicity. Privately, however, I've heard he vowed revenge at any cost. He loved the kid like a son."

All of the eyes in the room widened. Since 1952, Sam Baldwin had parlayed one small machinery factory into a multibillion-dollar empire with diverse manufacturing facilities in eighty-seven countries, none of which directly concerned the munitions business. But given his phenomenal success with everything he touched, there was little doubt that if Sam Baldwin had set his mind on killing the Iraqi dictator, then the assassination was practically a fait accompli.

"And the other reason?" Witherspoon asked.

"Money," Montgomery replied. "Plain and simple, it's a business transaction with billions and billions of dollars at stake. If Baldwin eliminates Hussein, then the Kurds will give him first dibs at the trillion dollars' worth of oil that's sitting untapped beneath the ground in the land they call Kurdistan. It'd be his reward for avenging the slaughter of all those Kurdish civilians Saddam gassed to death in the last ten years."

"So why was Baldwin's daughter kidnapped?" Gallagher asked Montgomery.

"It was a last resort. Apparently nothing else was going to convince Baldwin to stop his attack on Saddam Hussein. Baldwin's willing to upset the balance of world power and he doesn't give a damn about the consequences as long as he pockets a few billion dollars in the process."

The Secretary of State looked at Buck Perry. Two of his most skilled Special Forces soldiers had executed Jessica's abduction.

"If Baldwin kills Hussein," the general said, "then there's gonna be a vacuum of power in the Middle East, the likes of which we've never seen. The internal power struggle in Iraq would cripple their government for years."

"Then I think we should stand back and let 'em kill each other," Gallagher said.

"You know it's not that simple, Ed. Without a strong leader in Iraq, Iranian soldiers would pour across the border like there was a friggin' jail break. Those two countries spent eight years pounding the shit out of each other, and Iran lost more than a million lives. They've wanted revenge since the cease-fire. And if Saddam was dead, Iraq would likely fall within weeks."

"But Iraq's been a threat to the region for years," Gallagher said.

"Of course it has," the general replied. "But if Iran overthrows Iraq, there's absolutely no doubt that our forces would have to get involved, and this time around we'd sustain heavy casualties. Not only do we have a strategic interest in Kuwait and Saudi Arabia, but Bahrain, Qatar, Oman, and the United Arab Emirates would also need our protection because we need their oil."

"That's the main reason we didn't kill Hussein during the Gulf War," the Secretary of State added. "Iraq neutralizes Iran's ambitions for regional superiority. They've been biding their time, waiting for the right opportunity to strike."

"Exactly," added General Perry. "We tracked Saddam's precise location with spy satellites every single minute of the Gulf War and could've landed a missile on his head any time we wanted. But President Bush was smart enough to resist doing what in all likelihood would've gotten him reelected."

"Saddam made certain that we knew he had ordered his entire stockpile of chemical and biological weapons to be fired at Israel and Saudi Arabia in the event he was killed," Montgomery added. "He used a code he knew we had broken a year before the war started when he communicated that message to his artillery commanders. His Scuds may have flown all over the place with conventional weapons attached, but accuracy wouldn't have mattered if it came to chemical agents. Those toxins spread with the winds and remain airborne for months, and a single drop of VX anywhere on your skin causes convulsion and death within five minutes. As you guys know, the gas masks we gave to our soldiers wouldn't have done them one bit of good."

"He's gassed the Kurds and he's gassed the Iranians," the general added. "There's no reason to think he'd hesitate to use those weapons again."

There was silence while each of the men considered the facts that had been laid before them.

"Tom," the Secretary of State asked, "any chance these bunker busters would miss their target?"

Witherspoon pushed his chair away from the long table and walked to the far end of the room. A computerized map of the Middle East took up half the thirty-foot wall. Each of the twelve countries in the region was shaded a different color. Israel was bright yellow. Iraq was a radiant blue, Iran a neon red. The heavily mined four hundred miles between them was brilliant purple. The arms dealer grabbed hold of an electronic pointer and shot a beam of light onto the area representing Iraq. Each time he pressed the Enlarge button, the image of the Y-shaped country grew larger until only a fifteen-foot-wide reproduction of Iraq remained. Every city, every town, every river was labeled. Strategic bombing sites were identified. Key ports. Munitions dumps. The suspected chemical factories were highlighted in red. He fired his pointer on the city of Mosul, then clicked twice. In an instant a huge grid appeared. Streets, parks, even the local post office was labeled.

"The one with the most toys really *does* win," he muttered under his breath as he finished tinkering with the $50-million software. "And thank God for that, because it keeps me in business." He walked back to his chair and said, "From southern Turkey it'd be a chip shot, Jack. The guidance system on those bombs is state-of-the-art. With a couple of satellite photos, Baldwin could land one wherever he wanted."

Montgomery glanced up at the projection screen. Baldwin's weapons were being unloaded, pallet by pallet.

"Suppose our intelligence is correct," Montgomery said, as he stared at Ed Gallagher. "And we're looking at a full-scale war in the Middle East if Hussein is killed. How big a hit will the world's oil markets take?"

"A huge one," Gallagher replied quickly. "Because the guys in the trading pits will panic if there's even a possibility of Iran controlling that much of the world's crude. And if Iran were successful in overthrowing the four countries Buck just mentioned, then Muslim fundamentalists would control somewhere around forty-seven percent of OPEC's output, give or take a point or two."

"What about the price of oil?"

"My guess is that sweet crude would jump to a hundred twenty dollars a barrel. That works out to something like eight dollars a gallon at every gas station in America. You don't need me to tell you that a situation like that would cripple our economy, and destroy a country like Japan that's wholly dependent on Middle Eastern oil."

The Secretary of State closed his eyes and rubbed his forehead, fighting off a migraine. His friends had confirmed the grave consequences if Baldwin succeeded in killing Saddam Hussein: U.S. troop casualties in the thousands, skyrocketing oil prices, biological weapons of mass destruction contaminating the Middle East for years, and the rapid destabilization of the least stable region in the world. Then there was the issue no one had raised, but one that caused Montgomery many sleepless nights: the fallout if Israel, Saudi Arabia, or even Japan caught wind of the upcoming attack on the Iraqi dictator. The Saudis earned more than $100 billion a year from their oil revenues, and several of those billions were spent gathering intelligence to protect their golden goose. Israel's intelligence network was just as effective, even if it spent a fraction of what the Saudis did. Each of these countries would do whatever was necessary to keep oil, the world's lifeblood, flowing through their economic arteries. Trade wars and preemptive military strikes and the seizing of oil fields were very real possibilities. Montgomery was now sure that he had acted properly by kidnapping Jessica Baldwin. Now it was time for him to walk the tightrope.

"Thank you, gentlemen," Montgomery said as he rose from the table. He picked up the phone behind him, dialed a number, then quietly spoke a few words, and the images of *The Hercules* disappeared from the screen.

"Jack, I know this is your bailiwick, not mine," Witherspoon said, "but most of the people I deal with understand that Saddam Hussein maintains the balance of power in the Middle East. He also keeps those religious nuts in check. Even though the status quo isn't the perfect solution, it's the best one available. So if Baldwin's daughter has to die to keep things the way they are, then so be it."

"Trust me, Tom, I couldn't agree with you more. All that talk in the press and in Congress about trying to knock off Saddam Hussein is one big public relations smokescreen. It makes great sound bites, but no one who truly understands foreign policy *really* wants to see him dead."

"Have you discussed this with the President?"

"The President's a goddamn fool, Tom, who's more worried about his place in history than about anything else," Montgomery spat. "He seems to think that his legacy will live on forever if Saddam is assassinated under his watch, and he's made it very clear to me where he stands on this issue. There's no changing his mind."

The Secretary closed his briefcase, eager to lock horns with Sam Baldwin. His colleagues obviously understood that visionaries like Henry Kissinger, William Casey, and Ollie North were sometimes compelled to go against the will of Congress or the President. There was a greater good to be considered, one that operated without the constraints of political or ethical handcuffs. This decisiveness, Jack Montgomery believed, was the ingredient that made great men great. It separated those who made history from those who were swept up by its currents. And Jack Montgomery understood that if *he* didn't act in this instance, no one else would. Few had the power and influence to buck the President or a billionaire like Sam Baldwin, and even fewer had the balls once they had the opportunity.

"Aren't you worried about the FBI?" Gallagher asked.

"They won't be a factor," Montgomery replied definitively. "Baldwin will be told that his daughter will be killed immediately if the FBI learns about this kidnapping. And I've got enough contacts inside the agency to know if they've been notified by anyone."

"Good," said Witherspoon.

"Gentlemen, thank you for your time," Montgomery said as he grabbed his briefcase. "Is there somewhere I can reach you guys if I need your help in the next few days?"

"Ed and I are both staying at the Hay-Adams through Friday," Witherspoon said. "And I'll be happy to lend a hand if you get into a jam."

"Ditto," Gallagher said.

"Excellent. Buck, I'll see you at the White House tonight?"

"Yes, sir."

Montgomery leaned toward General Perry, whispered in his ear for a few moments, and firmly squeezed his hand. Then he walked around the table and shook hands with Gallagher and Witherspoon.

"Gentlemen, have a good day." He walked swiftly toward the conference room door. When it opened he noticed Sarah leaning against the wall, just a few feet away.

Montgomery strode past his security team. "Inman, call the President's secretary and tell her we're on our way!"

"I'll catch up in a second," Sarah said. She took a half step towards the conference room door. Directly in her line of vision were the scattered legal pads at the far end of the table.

Montgomery stopped halfway down the hall to glare at his defiant underling.

"Need I remind you that our President is waiting?" he growled.

Sarah hesitated in the doorway, then rushed to catch up to the Secretary of State and the men around him. When she looked back she saw a smiling General Perry closing the door to the conference room. Tucked under his beefy right arm was one of her yellow legal pads.

9

SAM BALDWIN sat at his desk, a massive flatbed of lightly tinted green glass without drawers. Atop the glass were several sealed folders and Federal Express packages. They contained the third wave of documents he would work on this afternoon. Behind him a wall of windows afforded a panoramic view of Central Park. The trees stretching north for sixty city blocks were splashed with the vibrant colors of autumn, not unlike those of the fake Monet that brightened the waiting area just outside his office. The original, which he bought for $14.8 million at auction at Christie's, hung in the master bathroom of his Trump Tower triplex.

The billionaire took a moment to soak in the spectacular view, distracted by a knock on his office door. He glanced at the video monitor beside his desk and pressed a buzzer.

"Good afternoon, Mr. Baldwin," the handsome young man said.

"Hi, Chuck. Thanks for getting the fire going."

"My pleasure, sir."

Baldwin's office gofer pushed a small wrought iron cart stacked neatly with seasoned and split maple. "Smells wonderful, doesn't it?"

"Sure does." He inhaled deeply to absorb the sweet aroma thrown off by the blazing logs trucked in from his ranch last week.

Baldwin glanced around the spacious room where he spent more of his waking hours than any other. He was pleased with what he saw. After finally conceding to himself and to his wife that he was an incorrigible workaholic, he had set out to give the working quarters a warmth that most chief executives' offices did not possess. The furnishings Francesca Baldwin had selected were both simple and elegant: two couches patterned with a subtle gold-on-ivory pinstripe, a glass coffee table trimmed with pewter and brass, a pair of unobtrusive end tables that served as pedestals for the lavish floral arrangements that were replaced every other day, and several sleek halogen floor lamps. Set off in the corner was a round mahogany conference table where Sam Baldwin held court at most of his meetings. And then, of course, there was the white Italian marble fireplace. The billionaire had spent nearly two million dollars and five years of legal wrangling to obtain the necessary permits to install this rarest of urban amenities in his office up in the stratosphere. According to the New York City Fire Marshal (who lost his job vigorously opposing the plan), it was the only functional fireplace above the twenty-eighth floor in all of Manhattan.

"Thanks, Chuck," Baldwin said once three fresh logs had been nestled onto the crackling fire.

When he was again alone, Baldwin strode over to his walk-in vault. The fifteen-by-fifteen-foot fireproof room was connected to his office by way of a discreet entranceway. Unless you knew the room was there (and few did), you would look right past the slight seam in the oak-paneled wall. He punched in the twelve-digit code that only he and the lawyer who had drafted his will had committed to memory and waved his index finger across a thermal scanner. The scanner quickly matched ten distinct points of his fingerprint and gauged his body temperature to be within normal limits. This prevented a photocopy of the billionaire's fingerprint from being waved across the disk. It also prevented the use of his dead body to gain entry into the safe. Baldwin heard the muffled click of the disengaging locks and the impregnable door slid open easily.

Soft white light flickered alive automatically when his right ankle breached the narrow red beam of the room's electric eye. Cardboard banker's boxes were piled high against the three-inch-thick steel walls, confidential documents no one would be permitted to review until fifty years after his death. On top of one of the boxes was a large manila envelope containing several dozen pictures of Saddam Hussein. Each of the photos had been taken within the last two days by a roving imaging satellite. Although the Iraqi dictator was constantly surrounded by a phalanx of heavyset men who wore mustaches and burgundy berets like his own, those security precautions would be useless against the weapons on board *The Hercules*. Technology, Baldwin thought, was a wonderful tool in the hands of competent people.

In between two neck-high stacks of boxes was a stand-alone fax machine.

The receiving bin contained a single sheet of paper. Baldwin studied it carefully. The message was addressed to no one and bore no signature. There was neither a header nor a footer at the edge of the page to indicate from where it had been sent. It looked like an ordinary invoice, with a list of items and prices set in two neat columns, but Sam Baldwin recognized it as the transmission of his confidant in Istanbul, who had been assigned to guarantee the safe delivery of the powerful weapons the President had helped to secrete on board *The Hercules*.

Baldwin sealed the vault. With more than forty-six thousand employees on his payroll working on developing everything from AIDS vaccinations to faster space shuttle computers, Sam Baldwin delegated almost every matter that crossed his desk. The same was true of the charitable foundations in his name that donated in excess of $100 million a year to worthy causes. However, there were certain projects requiring his individual, undivided attention. Analyzing the document that had come in from northern Turkey fell into that category.

Baldwin opened the 1936 edition of Webster's Universal Dictionary that rested on a walnut lectern beside his desk. Each item on the invoice corresponded to a page and placement of a word within the dictionary. "Two hundred crankshafts @$13.00 per" corresponded to page 200, thirteenth word down. "Twenty-four Phillips head screwdrivers @$4.00 per" referred to page 24, fourth word down, and so on. Although this simple technique was well known to cryptographers, the use of an outdated dictionary made this particular document nearly impossible for others to decipher.

Baldwin was methodically flipping through the yellowed pages of the dictionary when his private line sounded. He reached for the receiver, assuming his caller was either Francesca or Jessica. The list of others who had this number was extremely short: a few very close friends, his principal banker, several other titans of industry, and a prime minister or two, but it had been years since anyone other than Sam Baldwin's wife or daughter had called him on this line. Whenever it rang, he answered it, no matter what else he was doing. Contrary to how the tabloids sometimes portrayed him, he had always believed that business deals could wait, but family affairs couldn't.

"Hi," he said, hoping it was Jessica calling from Paris. He swiveled his black leather chair 180 degrees so he could enjoy the autumn view while he spoke. Raising his feet, he crossed his tasseled calf-skin loafers on the credenza behind him. The polished walnut was lined with family photographs.

"Don't hang up, Mr. Baldwin. You'll want to hear what I have to say." The gravelly voice sounded like it was being produced by an artificial larynx.

"Who is this?" he asked in disgust. "And how the hell did you get this number?"

"Just shut up and listen."

"Is that you, Michael?" he asked, half smiling.

"I said shut up and listen." The caller's tone was serious, the voice still synthesized.

Baldwin instinctively pressed the button beside his phone. The green light indicated the taping system was functioning properly.

"I'm listening," he said, his heart racing.

"We have your daughter. She'll be killed unless you do precisely as you're told."

Baldwin felt his stomach turn, the acid bile stinging his throat. He swallowed hard, trying to push down the fear that was coursing through his body. Now, he thought, was no time to show any sign of weakness.

"If you think this is funny, you're dead wrong."

There was no response.

"What do you want from me?" Baldwin asked without emotion. He spun around and grabbed a pen and a sheet of paper.

The caller waited a few moments before continuing. "I want you to re-think one of the very misguided activities you're involved in."

"Speak English, God damn it, not some stupid code! I have no idea what the fuck you're talking about!"

"If you shout at me again, I'll hang up and Jessica will die."

Baldwin gritted his teeth, but held his temper.

"You're not the Hercules you think you are," the caller said calmly, "and you know what I mean by that. It's time for you to abort this foolish little arms project of yours. If you don't, Jessica will be executed."

"What arms project? I don't know what you're talking about."

"Don't be coy with me!" the caller snapped.

"Leave Jessie out of this. If you've got a problem with something I've done, then take it up with me. But she's got nothing to do with this."

"Oh, she's got everything to do with this, Mr. Baldwin."

"Let me talk to her right now!"

Sam Baldwin used the silence to try to regroup. The pressure against his skull intensified. Tighter. Tighter. Tighter. His ears began to ring from the tension. Still, he maintained the composure that had been so effective through the hundreds of transactions he had consummated.

"Now you listen to me," he said firmly. "You've got exactly one hour to release Jessica. Up until then I'm willing to consider anything you have to say. At the end of one hour I won't negotiate with you under *any* circumstances. And I'll spend a billion dollars to track *you* down. Is that clear?"

"You're being irrational, Mr. Baldwin. But get this through your thick skull. I'm commanding you to keep this conversation, as well as this entire episode, absolutely secret. If you go to the press, the FBI, or any other law enforcement agency, I'll know about it within minutes." He paused for a moment, then decided that Baldwin's forceful reaction justified some piling on. "And that'll mean immediate death for your daughter and your future grandchild."

"What do you mean?"

"I assumed you knew that Jessica was pregnant, but obviously . . ."

Baldwin knew he couldn't maintain control for much longer. "You've now got fifty-nine minutes to commute your own death sentence, mister," he said steadily. "I'll be here waiting for your call."

Baldwin slammed down the receiver. For the moment the monster on the other end of the line had gone away. Now he was left with the demons swirling inside his own head, praying he had done the right thing. If he hadn't, he knew his Jessie would soon be dead.

10

DEEP belowground in a man-made cavern four miles from the Iraqi-Saudi border, a chemical engineer named Hafez al-Aziz began carefully checking the steel canisters that contained Saddam Hussein's deadly potions, making sure they were ready to be used on a moment's notice. Like the fifty other Iraqi engineers who were forced to work at similar sites around the country's periphery, Aziz had received his training at the University of Moscow and understood exactly how these chemicals affected the human body. The ones inside the red vessels contained anthrax. When these spores touched a mucous membrane, black pustules and vomiting preceded a painful death. Inside the blue canisters were VX agents. This nerve gas blocked the body's production of acetylcholinesterase, causing the body to lose muscular control. Convulsions and suffocation always came next. The yellow containers housed botulinum toxin, or botox. These bacterium blocked the body's nerve transmissions, causing instantaneous paralysis. Death followed shortly thereafter.

Perpendicular to the hundreds of metal canisters were tracks that led to an elevator shaft. If the proper signal was received from Baghdad, these canisters were to be wheeled on their pallets to an awaiting truck. That cargo would then be attached to medium-range Scud missiles by an Iraqi artilleryman.

To ensure that none of the engineers intentionally disabled the canisters they were charged with inspecting, these men were rotated every two weeks. If a single canister was found to be tampered with, punishment was swift. In the ten years this program had been in existence, Aziz had been forced to witness the execution of four of his colleagues.

Row by row, Aziz meticulously inspected every fitting. The warning tags were written in German, but the sign of the skull and crossbones was a universal language. These deadly chemicals had been produced by the very same factories that had provided Josef Mengele with supplies for his torture machine during the Holocaust. They were very effective.

It would take Aziz six hours to inspect every last container. When done, he would eat dinner, then lie down on his cot until his clock told him it was morning. Tomorrow he would check every single canister twice. His shift was ending in twenty-four hours, and he knew the consequences if any of these cylinders were found out of order.

11

JACK MONTGOMERY disconnected his secure line, more than a little taken aback by the conversation he'd just had. Sam Baldwin hadn't begged for his daughter's life, as Montgomery expected. He hadn't broken down and agreed to pay any price for Jessica's safe return. Instead, he had put a billion-dollar bounty on the Secretary of State's life. There were always complications, Montgomery knew, but this one had gotten his attention.

The Secretary of State was confident there had been absolutely no risk in personally conveying his message. The half-dollar-sized device that threaded onto his phone made his familiar voice completely unrecognizable not only to Sam Baldwin but to the others who had received similar calls. But that was the least of it. For decades he had taken elaborate precautions to ensure that no one could ever know the substance of any conversation from this telephone, constantly upgrading his equipment as technology advanced. Sophisticated jamming devices were attached to the phone itself, and had been tucked inconspicuously beneath the eaves of the red-brick Georgian revival mansion he and his wife, Betsy, had spent years restoring. When activated, not even the Pentagon's own billion-dollar Mentor Signal Intelligence satellite had the capacity to eavesdrop on his communications. The day he became Secretary of State he had sought and received the strongest of assurances from the chairman of BellSouth that no record of his calls from this phone would be kept. Instead, an exorbitant monthly flat tariff was charged to the line, which permitted unlimited service to any phone, anywhere in the world, and no one could ever reconstruct whom he had called or when those calls had been placed. Publicly, the justification for this extraordinary arrangement was that it permitted him to secretly contact officials in those governments with whom the United States did not even have diplomatic relations. Privately, of course, it was compatible with his radical, and often violent, objectives. With it he could drop the gauntlet in the public square, without ever facing retribution, even from a man with the vast resources of Sam Baldwin.

Although his call to Baldwin had taken a few disturbing turns, once Baldwin had time to consider his limited options, Montgomery felt certain the billionaire would capitulate. That next call was something the Secretary of State looked forward to. He would crush Baldwin like an ant if he had to. He had done it before and would do it again without hesitation.

In the solitude of his library, Montgomery had a hidden wall safe that contained twelve thick files. Whenever he had difficulty sleeping he would remove one in the middle of the night and pore through its pages. He knew, of course, that if the authorities ever got their hands on any of these files his disgrace would be monumental. But that possibility was outweighed by the solace he derived from reliving in vivid detail the particulars of his rewarding operations.

Fear of exposure kept him sharp, kept him ruthless. It seemed like another lifetime since Iran-Contra, the only one of his clandestine activities that had ever seen even an inch of print space. Montgomery had learned volumes from that fiasco, most important how to look effectively for early warning signs that might spell danger. He had also learned to recruit only professionals from now on. The gang Ollie North had assembled was, in retrospect, a bunch of morons. Fortunately for Montgomery, he had had enough foresight to cloak his involvement in that plan from day one. Houdini could not have escaped more adroitly, but Montgomery knew as well as anyone that only cats had nine lives.

Now there was the question of his aggressive new security chief, Sarah Peterson. She had already begun probing in areas that irritated the Secretary's highly sensitive antenna. Whether it was beginner's luck or that she had inherited her father's inquisitiveness, the moment had come to determine whether she posed a genuine threat of exposure. If so, drastic and immediate steps needed to be taken.

Montgomery placed his open laptop on his desk, staring at the glowing screen. In a few minutes he would jettison the information before him into cyberspace. But now it was time to contemplate the possibilities.

"Tripwire" was a sophisticated software program that had been explained to Jack Montgomery two years earlier, only days after he had been appointed Secretary of State. The meeting had been held in the Roosevelt Room in the White House, and had been called for the benefit of arguably the eight most powerful men in the country. The directors of the CIA, FBI, and NSC were present, as were the Chairman of the Joint Chiefs of Staff, the Secretary of Defense, the President's Chief of Staff, and the President himself. No one else except the man who had devised the clever software program was present.

The President had already received his personal briefing inside the privacy of the Oval Office. "Explain to these gentlemen how this system works," he said, and leaned back in his soft leather chair.

The computer genius who worked within a secret division of the National Security Agency was not accustomed to making technical presentations to laymen, so he kept it as simple as he could.

"A program I've named Tripwire has been installed on each of your computers. To my knowledge, no one else in the world has a system like it. This software acts like a silent burglar alarm; it quickly sifts though tens of millions of government files to allow each one of you to know whether someone's tried to gain computer access to one of those files. We do this by bouncing an encrypted signal off an NSA satellite. It's then relayed to your e-mail directories no matter where you are in the world."

It was clear from the expressions of the men in the room that each understood he was being provided with an instrument that had the potential to substantially augment his own individual power.

"Are you talking strictly about classified files?" The question had come from CIA director Henry Keenan, whose penchant for secrecy was renowned even within the closed-lipped intelligence community.

"No, sir, and that's one of the things that's so remarkable about Tripwire. It's been secretly inoculated into every significant government database without the possibility of detection. Access to almost every U.S. government file imaginable will cause the system to activate. Of course, those files will have to be tabbed with a red flag. When triggered, they act like bear traps."

"Meaning what?" barked the Chairman of the Joint Chiefs.

"Meaning this, General. Suppose you've got just one red flag in place, and that's on your own nonclassified military records on file at Fort Dix. Now a ten-year-old kid in Wisconsin who's doing a book report on the army may try to take a peek at that file while he's surfing the Internet, or maybe it's a grad student doing his doctoral thesis on generals of the twentieth century. Or it's a spy like Aldridge Ames, trying to gather as much information on you as possible. Motive doesn't matter. Tripwire simply sends an impulse by wireless remote to the e-mail directories in your respective computers, which informs you that someone has attempted to examine the file you've marked with a red flag."

"How do I know who the intruder is?"

"Tripwire traces the inquiry back through the phone line, or any other connection to the computer. No system that I know of has yet been devised to neutralize its tracking capabilities. And the real beauty of Tripwire is that the person who's invaded your file has no idea that they've just set off an alarm. You're watching them watch you, but they don't know it."

Everyone chuckled before the next question was posed.

"Suppose I don't want this damn thing on my computer." The general grinned as he spoke, aware that everyone around the table knew the possibility of that happening was next to nil. "Is my computer gonna beep like a friggin' alarm clock every time Tripwire sends a message to one of these other guys?" He waved his stubby index finger around the table.

"No, sir. Your installation reacts only to your red flags. Tripwire alerts you by sending you an e-mail. You'll have to check your e-mail directories every so often to see if there are any red flags."

"And my red flags won't set off anyone else's alarms?"

Now everyone around the table smiled, including the President. It was the question the general had really wanted answered in the first place.

"That's correct, General. No one else will know what files you've flagged."

"Will anyone other than yourself have access to the central system that keeps a record of which files have been flagged?" asked the FBI director.

"Well, I could circulate that . . ."

"But you won't," the President said firmly.

"That's correct, Mr. President. No record will be kept. Only each individual will know which files he's flagged."

All eight of the men relaxed. Like the President, each of his top advisers understood that often the most difficult aspect of defeating one's enemies was identifying them in the first place. Whether it was political opponents, nosy journalists, or overzealous prosecutors, that task would now be made much easier for the few the chief executive had chosen to empower. Once an enemy was identified, an appropriate counterattack could be mounted even before the concealed antagonist displayed his fangs.

Within minutes of returning to his State Department office after the hourlong meeting, Jack Montgomery programmed Tripwire to activate whenever access to one of five hundred files was attempted. Included within those files were the names of every person who might have had even an inkling that Montgomery had carried out illegal activities over all those years.

Montgomery noted that in the last few hours Sarah Peterson had made three separate attempts to access a portion of Tom Witherspoon's and Ed Gallagher's top secret FBI file. She had been denied access, of course, but in her efforts to protect him, she had definitely inched way too close to his vulnerable spot.

Just as important, this past Sunday his new chief of security had opened a State Department personnel file that had remained undisturbed for decades. Anna Rodzinski's role at the U.S. Embassy in Moscow had been practically meaningless. In fact, Montgomery had added her name to his Tripwire list almost as an afterthought. But now he was glad that he did, because it allowed him to know that the investigation that had reached nothing but dead ends for so long had suddenly been reignited. Damn, Montgomery thought. He should have eliminated Anna Rodzinski when he took care of the others.

Montgomery lifted the receiver of his secure phone. There was no reason yet to panic, but now Sarah could not be ignored. A little cat and mouse would go a long way toward determining whether Chip Peterson's daughter was smart enough to smell the poison beneath the cheese. With the help of a man known in certain circles simply as Mr. Green, the Secretary would be able to evaluate whether the keg of dynamite on which he was sitting was about to detonate. And if it was, Montgomery would have no hesitation about snipping the fuse before it burned any further.

12

"Nooooo!"

Sam Baldwin's reaction had been completely reflexive, his howl loud enough to penetrate his oak-paneled walls. His loyal secretary rushed toward his office doors, her heart pounding. She had never heard such an agonized sound come from another human being. She hurriedly used her passkey to gain entry to the plush office, expecting to see blood splattered on the bearskin rug. Instead, the billionaire who controlled an entrepreneurial empire spanning 128 countries was sitting perfectly still behind his desk. His skin was ashen and clammy, his eyes wide and staring.

"Mr. Baldwin, are you OK?" June Wilkerson approached his black leather chair to check his pulse. Two of Sam Baldwin's hulking bodyguards followed just behind her, brandishing Heckler & Koch MP5 submachine guns. From their positions in the waiting area it sounded as if someone had somehow breached the tight ring of security encircling Sam Baldwin. Like all of the bodyguards in Baldwin's employ, these two men were ready to step in the way of a bullet for their boss. The family of the man who had done so during a failed kidnap attempt in 1987 had received the proceeds of the $5 million insurance policy the billionaire personally underwrote for all of his armed escorts. The security guards hastily examined the few possible hiding places in the large room. When they were satisfied no intruder had invaded Sam Baldwin's inner sanctum they placed their automatic weapons back in their shoulder harnesses.

"Mr. Baldwin?" June bent over her boss and put her hand on his shoulder, shaking him gently. "Are you all right?" she asked, her voice raised almost to a shout.

Baldwin blinked. "I'm fine," he finally managed, though his pallor and fixed stare made June concerned.

"Mr. Baldwin? Should I call your doctor?"

"No!" Baldwin snapped. He heard the warning of the mechanical voice. *"I'm commanding you to keep this conversation, as well as this entire episode, absolutely secret. If you go to the press, the FBI, or any other law enforcement agency, I'll know about it within minutes. And that'll mean immediate death for your daughter and your future grandchild."*

"I said I'm fine. Now all of you please leave."

"But . . ."

"I said leave! Now!"

The three employees reluctantly retreated to their workstations, though each glanced back in concern. When Baldwin was again alone he pressed the dime-sized black button located beside his video monitor. Six-foot-long titanium rods silently slid into place inside the finely carved walnut doors of Baldwin's office. There were also no passkeys to override this system.

His solitude now assured, Sam Baldwin plunged his head into his trembling hands. His shoulders heaved spasmodically as he vainly attempted to quell his sobs. The more he attempted to gather his composure, the faster the tears streamed down his flushed cheeks.

His surrender to his emotions was absolute, greater than he had experienced when either of his parents had died. He wished only that he could somehow turn back the clock so he could shelter his daughter from the terror that had befallen her.

When Baldwin finally looked up, the huge room was a blur. He swiveled his chair toward the row of windows behind him and grabbed a granite frame from his credenza. The black-and-white picture, with its yellowing sawtooth border, had been taken of Jessica when she was only three days old. She had just been given her first sponge bath and was swaddled in velvety, white cloth. She was crying hysterically despite being in the safety of her father's strong arms.

That moment was the first time in his life that Sam Baldwin had ever felt compelled to actually *protect* someone. This tiny, vulnerable creature had, on her third day of life, looked up at him with desperation in her perfect blue eyes. And Sam Baldwin had melted.

From that day, until Jessica was almost six, whenever Sam Baldwin was not out of town on one of his many business trips, he would check on his daughter during the middle of the night, sometimes three or four times. He would bend down close to her, feel her sweet breath tickle his ear, and caress her forehead and her cheeks. Then he would gently rest his palm on her belly, always mesmerized by the miracle of her peaceful, methodical breathing.

Sam Baldwin set the picture back down on his credenza. God, how he hoped he would be strong enough to practice what he had always so forcefully preached to his daughter. But before summoning the man who would assist him with that decision, he picked up each of the dozen framed photos strewn around his office. In black and white were Jessica's initial tentative steps into her nursery school, as well as her first trip to Disney World. Baldwin couldn't help but smile when he noticed Jessica's missing two front teeth while she sat on Mickey's lap. There was Jessica seated on the horse she had received for her eighth birthday. Dad and daughter had explored every inch of their ten thousand–acre New Hampshire ranch riding bareback. Jessica's adolescence was documented in color. There she was, confidently spiking a volleyball in her high school state championships. The most recent picture was of Jessica and her fiancé, Doug Templeton, on a Kenyan photo safari this past January.

Like most busy executives, he rarely had the time to consider how fortunate he had been until it was about to be snatched from him. Sure, there had been difficult moments. But what parent could say differently? And like most fathers, he wished he had been there more often than work had permitted. However, on balance he knew those three decades were ones he wouldn't have traded with anyone.

Looking at the photographs was a cathartic exercise, transforming his mood from anguish and sorrow into vitriolic fury. His gut-wrenching anger was joined by a craving for retribution he never imagined was possible. Nothing was going to stop him from finding his Jessica. Baldwin activated his intercom.

"June, tell Hank to come in here, please." Baldwin was back behind his desk, completely focused on the task ahead. "Alone."

"Mr. Baldwin?" June asked. "Are you sure you're OK?" It had been thirty minutes since she had returned to her desk. In that time her boss hadn't taken a single phone call, nor had he responded to the buzz of his intercom.

"Thank you for your concern, June. I'm fine. Now please don't ask again."

"Yes, sir."

Hank Savage gently knocked on the doors less than a minute later. He had been pacing like a caged tiger in the cozy sitting area just beyond Baldwin's office door, waiting for the automatic deadbolts he had ordered installed to be deactivated. He heard a gentle click and the doors slid open.

Savage strode into the office, his dark eyes scouring the room for any objective cause for his boss's aberrant behavior. Standing six feet, three inches tall, and weighing just under 210 pounds, his rock-hard frame carried less than 8 percent body fat. His short, sandy brown hair was closely cropped and had a razor-straight part two inches above his left ear. His custom suit coat was tailored to conceal the licensed automatic weapon that was on his left hip. As always, his handsome face and quick smile belied the state-sponsored violence he had committed during his fourteen years in the marines.

Hank Savage had become personally acquainted with Baldwin Enterprises seven years before, just two days after he had earned his silver eagle shoulder insignias. Clothed in full military dress regalia, the newly promoted colonel had impressed Sam Baldwin within minutes of their introduction at a dinner party hosted by a mutual friend. From their initial hourlong discussion it was apparent to Baldwin that Savage was a steel hand tucked inside a velvet glove. He appeared to be a perfect gentleman: Businesslike, polite, and soft-spoken. Yet when Baldwin deftly steered the conversation toward the topic of counterterrorism, it was immediately clear that the soldier was more knowledgeable about the subject than any cog currently employed within the vast Baldwin security machine. In addition, Savage had obviously gained firsthand experience in this specialty, although he was unequivocal in his unwillingness to divulge the specifics of any of his missions.

After three informal get-togethers, which Savage instantly recognized as interviews, Sam Baldwin was even more impressed than before. Savage had displayed a business acumen, as well as ingrained street smarts, that would make him a valuable asset in any organization. Just as important, he had expressed a degree of frustration at the rigid military bureaucracy that stifled any creative initiative. Baldwin wooed Savage away from the marines by offering him more than six times his colonel's salary.

Savage initially signed on with Baldwin Enterprises simply to head up its thirty-member internal security force. Barely a month after his arrival, his appetite for taking on difficult assignments that had nothing to do with security caught the eyes of senior management, including his new CEO. Discreet business projects that were put under his control were completed in record time with impressive results. Deal after deal beat even the most aggressive projections, with costs always coming in below budget. Ventures that had been stalled for years were suddenly free of the insurmountable roadblocks that had paralyzed them in the first place. *Efficient* was the buzzword that appeared in every one of his reviews.

Savage was moved up to the executive suites after two years at Baldwin Enterprises. Ten months later he began accompanying Sam Baldwin on selected business trips. A year after that a seat was reserved for him beside the billionaire on board the corporate 727. Eventually there was no significant transaction that did not pass through Savage's hands. And Sam Baldwin realized that he liked Hank Savage as a person even more than he respected his judgment as an employee.

" I assume it was a phone call?" Savage asked once he had quickly ruled out all other possibilities. He stood across from his boss's desk, his powerful arms folded in front of him.

Sam Baldwin looked up, his bloodshot eyes destroying any pretense of the strong front he had maintained with the caller.

"Yes," he acknowledged softly.

Savage closed his eyelids for a moment, fearing the worst.

"Francesca?"

"No."

"Jessie?"

"Jessie." He waved his head toward one of the wing chairs, inviting his most trusted assistant to sit.

Savage dreaded asking the next question. He kept his voice level. "Is she dead?"

Baldwin shook his head.

"Kidnapped?"

Baldwin nodded. "Someone called a little while ago. He said he'd kill her if I told anyone."

"Did you record the call?"

"Of course."

"How much do they want?"

"Listen for yourself." Baldwin rewound the tape, then played it for Savage. When the synthesized voice finished, the two men stared at one another.

"What are you going to do?"

Baldwin thumbed through the satellite photos of *The Hercules* that had been hand-delivered that afternoon.

"For the next twenty-two minutes I'm willing to listen to what the guy on the phone has to say. After that his hour is up, and I won't negotiate with him no matter what he offers."

"You'll carry out the attack even if they don't let Jessie go?"

Baldwin nodded.

"You're sure that's what you want to do?"

"Suppose I did everything I was told to do. Don't you think they'd kill Jessie anyway, given what we learned in London last year?"

Savage thought back on the four hours he and Sam had spent with a group of British businessmen who had tried to sell kidnap insurance to Baldwin Enterprises. Their presentation had been professional, their statistics staggering. In the seedy but legitimate world of kidnap negotiations, these former members of Scotland Yard were among the profession's elite. They demonstrated with charts and graphs that in countries like Colombia or Mexico or Russia, kidnapping was a thriving enterprise that was nothing more than a transaction involving human flesh. Victims were almost always left unharmed as long as a substantial ransom was paid. In those countries, all but a few kidnappers went unprosecuted because the local police force took their cut of the booty. However, in the United States the situation was different. In America, punishment for violent crimes like kidnapping was both severe and consistent and officers of the law were virtually never on the take. Almost 95 percent of all kidnappers were eventually caught, and their victims were killed almost 80 percent of the time so that potential witnesses at trial were eliminated. This was true even if the ransom demanded was paid. The only bit of good news that Savage could recall from this meeting was the advice of a former Special Forces operative who told them about the Preserve the Porcelain Rule: most sane kidnappers keep their victims alive for as long as possible. "If you're running a china shop," the man had said, "you can't sell broken china."

"I think you're probably right," Savage finally said to his boss. "I think they'll keep Jessie alive for a few days at least."

Baldwin felt nauseous, caught in a whirlpool of despair. Then an idea crossed his mind. If it worked, it would put them in position to save Jessica and keep his plan to kill Saddam Hussein on track.

"Hank, what if we go after Jessie on our own? What are the chances of getting her out alive?" Baldwin had moved to the edge of his seat, stimulated by the possibility.

Hank Savage smiled. The situation reminded him of the most exhilarating mission of his distinguished military career. With twelve men under his command, he had orchestrated and led a rapid reaction force deep inside the Peruvian jungle to secure the release of a U.S. diplomat who had been seized by militant members of the Shining Path. Nearly a day of machete hacking through the thick underbrush eventually led them to ground zero. Because of Savage's meticulous planning and direction, all seven guerrillas were killed, with no casualties on his side.

"With enough lead time to put a rescue team together, and enough cash to throw at the problem, I'd say your odds are fifty-fifty."

Baldwin nodded. "Here's ample lead time: put that team together immediately. Every plane, every vehicle, and every asset of this company will be at your disposal. We've got forty-two men and women working in Internal Security with more than seven hundred years of combined experience in dealing with shit like this. We've also got quick access to every weapon out there if we need to go that route. If you hit any roadblocks, just let me know. I'll take care of them."

"I'd rather not use any of our in-house people for any kind of rescue operation. If something goes wrong, I want to keep Baldwin Enterprises out of it."

"Hank, who you use will be your decision. Just don't fuck it up."

Savage stood and walked toward the row of windows behind the billionaire's desk. Darkness had begun to descend on Manhattan, shrouding the city under a steel gray sky. "Sam, let me play devil's advocate for a minute." He looked down on Central Park, his back turned toward his boss. Though he knew this was not the time for confrontation, healthy debate had always preceded every covert operation in which Hank Savage had participated.

"Go ahead."

"If we can somehow negotiate a way for Jessie to be released, would you do it?"

Baldwin rose from his chair so he could stand at the window beside Savage.

"I don't think I've ever told you this, Hank, but I was in California for a meeting with Paul Getty the week his grandson was kidnapped in Italy," Baldwin said, his gaze fixed on the darkening horizon below. "For months Paul refused to negotiate with the kidnappers; he and I spent hours discussing that decision. He told me that he had fourteen grandchildren, and that if he paid the ransom he'd have fourteen ransom notes on his desk the next day."

"But this is Jessie we're talking about. She—"

"Let me finish," Baldwin interrupted angrily. "A few years later I was in Toronto working on a deal with Seagram's. I took the opportunity to speak with Edgar Bronfman about his son's kidnapping. Even though everything worked out for the best, Bronfman told me in confidence that he always regretted paying the ransom."

"But why? His son was returned alive, and the guy's still got more money than he could spend in fifty lifetimes."

Baldwin shook his head. "It's not about the money, Hank. Don't you get that? Until this moment I guess I never fully understood what Bronfman was going through. But now I do. More than anything in the world I want Jessie back, safe and sound. If I knew for sure that destroying those weapons would do the trick, then I'd do it in a second. But my gut tells me they're going to kill her no matter what we do or what they say. At least this way we'll have a chance if we try to find her."

Savage put his arm around the older man's shoulder. "You realize the odds are increasing that Jessie will die if those missiles keep moving into position?"

"I don't believe that," Baldwin said. "Those weapons and her release are now two completely separate issues. And besides, you know as well as anyone that Jessie's a woman of deep convictions. As much as I love her, and God knows how much, if she were here right now she'd tell me to tell that caller to go fuck himself."

Savage turned toward Baldwin.

"If that's the way you feel, Sam, then the sooner we start, the better."

"I agree. So what do we do now?"

"First, we tell no one about her kidnapping. Hopefully, that'll keep Jessie alive while we try to find her. Second, you'll probably get another call from the guy with the synthesized voice. I'll put a trace on your phone lines. Third, as soon as I leave this office I'll start putting a rescue team in place. They'll be ready to go on a moment's notice." Savage paused, then said, "If none of these pan out, we can always reverse course and give in. Maybe even beat the odds, like Getty and Bronfman."

Baldwin turned and looked Savage directly in the eye. "Hank, you're one of the only people in this damn organization who doesn't yes me to death. So tell me right now, honestly, if I'm making a mistake."

"I wish I had the right answer, Sam. Every situation like this plays out differently. But with your resources, and my contacts, we've got as good a chance as anyone to be successful."

"Maybe there's someone, somewhere, who knows what's happened to Jessie, but is afraid to talk," Baldwin said. "We've got to find that person before they get up the courage to call the FBI."

"I agree."

Baldwin glanced at his desk clock and then at the packet of satellite photos. In fourteen minutes the fate of those bombs would be sealed. "And I want revenge on those fucking bastards who planned this thing!" he hissed.

"Sam, as long as I have anything to say about it you'll get that, too."

13

BOXES were everywhere. They surrounded what had been Bob Wakefield's cleaned-out desk, leaving only a narrow aisle leading to what was now Sarah's doorway. The gremlins had obviously been busy for the last twenty-four hours, although Sarah hadn't seen them pack or move any of her or Wakefield's stuff; it had simply happened. An edict from the President was apparently an effective motivator. Now she had no more view of the deli; instead she had three squeaky-clean windows facing the Washington Monument. Down the hall was Jack Montgomery's spacious office. It had been her third move in five years. Each time the square footage of her office had nearly doubled.

The moving men had done a masterful job of reconstructing how her old desk had been arranged at the Treasury Department. It was almost as if they had taken a snapshot before they lifted a single object. The two pictures of her mother were directly beside her Rolodex. The tiny Eiffel Tower paperweight sat beside her can of pens; she and Jean-Pierre had gotten a good laugh when they bought the cheesy souvenir the last time they were in Paris together. Even the little yellow Post-its that surrounded Sarah's new telephone were in their proper spot. One of those sticky tabs contained the name and phone number of an eligible cardiologist who supposedly was going to knock her socks off. Sarah was skeptical, but she had promised herself that she'd be open-minded when he took her out to dinner next week.

Getting computer access was another story. The guys in the State Department MIS unit promised Sarah her office could be ready within a week. Maybe. Getting rid of Wakefield's IBM 386 took less than ten minutes. The delay would be the upgrades in technology. Digital subscriber lines needed to be installed for the type of system she requisitioned; that would take at least two days. Long stretches of computer cable then needed to be run behind walls and across drop ceilings to customize her request. The President's own office, they told her, had taken four days. If the order hadn't come in from so high, there would've been a six-week wait.

Despite these few glitches, Sarah's first full day protecting Montgomery had been productive. In the four hours since his loaded-for-bear convoy had slingshotted around the Beltway from his meeting at the Pentagon, she had accompanied the energetic Secretary of State inside the White House, the Capitol, and the Indonesian ambassador's private residence on a cul-de-sac in Bethesda. Sarah quickly understood why the President considered Montgomery indispensable. He was clearly one step ahead of everyone with whom she had worked.

Sarah opened her briefcase and set her modem onto her desk. Maybe she'd be able to link into the FBI's database from here. Night had rapidly crept up on the afternoon, and the spotlights that drenched the city's monuments in brilliant white light were ablaze. In homes all around the nation's capital, the minds of most federal workers were a million miles from their cubicles, as happy-hour alcohol soothed away the vagaries of their day-to-day lives, but the gears inside Sarah's head continued to turn. Since leaving the Pentagon she had thought of little else other than Tom Witherspoon and Ed Gallagher and the tape recorder she prayed was still in that conference room. It was time to get some answers.

She bent way down to examine the telephone jack behind her desk. There was no splitter. No dataport. No surge protector, either. This was going to be useless. She decided to pack it in and visit an old friend over at the FBI. He would be able to help her until she was all set up.

"Anyone home?"

It was a male voice. Either Iowa or Kansas, she thought. It bothered her that she hadn't heard his footsteps before his knock.

"Down here," Sarah answered from beneath her desk.

She stood and admired the handsome man in her doorway. He held a can of Coke in each hand. Mid-thirties. Khakis, button-down oxford, black Rockports. More Abercrombie & Fitch than Sears. The lock of careless sandy brown hair that fell over his forehead drew attention to the long, dark eyelashes that framed his brown eyes. She had always been a sucker for long, dark eyelashes. Jean-Pierre had them. So did Kent.

"Andy?" she asked tentatively.

Andy Archer nodded with a smile, his straight teeth just as white as they had been when Sarah last saw them seventeen years earlier.

"Oh . . . my . . . God!" she said. Her eyes were wide with surprise. "I almost didn't recognize you."

"It's been a long time," he said as he approached. "You still look great. You haven't changed a bit."

"Flattery will get you everywhere, Mr. Archer," she said with a smile as they embraced.

"Is that so? Then I guess you *have* changed a little."

Sarah hesitated. She had met Andy when they were seniors at Yale, and had known him only a few weeks when their relationship ended. Their first meeting was at a pub off-campus. She was mixing drinks to put herself through school when Archer and a few buddies bellied up to the bar. To Sarah, he was different from all the dumb jocks who wanted nothing more than to get into her pants. Night after night Archer appeared during her shift, content to talk with her about politics or sports or music while she served other customers. Eventually he asked the question she knew was coming; dinner or a movie when she had a night off? As much as she wanted to, she said, the timing wasn't right. She was dating another guy and didn't believe in seeing more than one person at a time. Archer persisted, sending flowers and chocolate for thirty consecutive days. He wouldn't accept being turned down. When his affections became an issue in Sarah's relationship with her boyfriend, she asked Archer to back off. He reluctantly acquiesced. Two months later they each received their diplomas and went their separate ways, never seeing one another again.

"Are you working here at State?" Sarah asked, changing the subject.

"I've been at State ever since college," he replied, offering her a Coke. "But only in Washington for the last couple of months."

She grabbed the one in his left hand.

"Right after graduation they made me an offer I couldn't refuse. They said they'd send me overseas as a foreign policy analyst for as long as I wanted. It turned into twenty-seven countries in seventeen years."

"Why'd you come back? It sounds fascinating."

"It was a poli-sci major's dream, but I started to miss the stupid things about the States. Like *I Love Lucy* reruns at three A.M. and cramming down a few hot dogs at Camden Yards with the fellas."

Sarah smiled. He seemed to be the same kid at heart, only seventeen years older.

"How'd you know I was here?" she asked.

"There was an announcement posted this morning. Then I saw the nameplate outside your office when I was walking by a few hours ago."

"I noticed that," she said with genuine surprise. "The maintenance crew at the State Department is obviously more efficient than the one at Treasury. It took a month for my desk chair to arrive last time around."

Archer smiled. "I'm *sure* it was a clerical error. We try to be as slow and inefficient as everyone else in the federal government."

"Now, now, Mr. Archer. Let's not be too cynical. Every long journey begins with one small step. If we all do our own little part, maybe we can change a few things around here."

Archer glanced at her sleek laptop.

"Like that?"

Sarah nodded. "For starters. From what I can tell, Wakefield never turned on his computer. The one we tossed weighed about two hundred pounds and was probably made when I was in high school."

"Then I assume there's no DSL in here?"

"No. That's coming in a couple of days."

"Or dataport?"

"Ditto."

"If you want to use the terminal in my office you're more than welcome. I'm about to pack it in for the night."

"Thanks for the offer, but I've got to get going. I've been on the job for all of thirty-six hours and I'm already up to my eyeballs."

"Trust me, I know the feeling." He looked at his Swatch. "Listen, I'm about to catch a quick bite before I head on home myself. Care to join me?"

Sarah paused. She had chased him away once before, and wasn't sure she wanted to do so again.

"If you don't have much time, there's a terrific wiener wagon around the corner," he said. "My man Frankie will load you up with the works. I'll even splurge for a bag of chips and another Coke."

Sarah considered the offer, then decided to decline. Fifteen minutes on the State Department steps with Andy Archer would probably turn into sixty. Maybe even longer if he had his druthers.

"I'll take a rain check if you're handing them out. I've got a ton of work to catch up on tonight." She saw the disappointment in his brown eyes, and said, "How about another day?"

"I'd like that," he said with a smile. "I'll have my voice mail call yours." He shook her hand and held it for an extra second.

"I'll call you tomorrow, Sarah."

"I'm looking forward to it."

SARAH zoomed past the darkened Air and Space Museum, thinking about Andy Archer, but listening to the message Bob Wakefield had left for her at her old office. She was on her way to the FBI building, comforted that Jack Montgomery was incredibly well protected for the remainder of the day at what the Secret Service affectionately called "Eighteen Acres." Sharpshooters were positioned on the White House rooftop, and enormous concrete planters encircled the grounds. No truck or gunman would get within five hundred yards of the State dinner without being physically searched by a team of well-trained federal agents. Wakefield would escort Montgomery home, safe and sound, by midnight.

Once Sarah was inside the FBI building, she went directly to the fourth floor, where the Center for Innovative Development was located. As she expected, Walter Jensen was still toiling away.

"Knock, knock," Sarah said as she entered the room.

Walter Jensen looked up from his spectrometer, pleased to see her. He stepped closer and removed his reading glasses. "You look as beautiful as ever, my dear. I never dreamed I'd want to wrap my arms around one of the big shots over at the ODS." He gave her an avuncular hug, then gently pinched her smooth cheek.

"I guess you heard?"

"Of course. Good news travels fast around here. Everyone's thrilled for you, Sarah. I was going to call you tomorrow."

"Thanks, Walter."

"I spoke to your mom yesterday," he said, the smile quickly disappearing from his face. "She's scared."

"Wouldn't you be?"

"Of course. That's why I assume you're going out to Kansas?"

"Not yet. She told me a few days ago that she wanted me to stay put. She said she'd be fine with her sister's help for now."

"I know she did. But deep in her heart she wants your company. You know that."

"Don't try to lay that guilt thing on me, Walter."

"You're not still mad at her, are you?"

"I was never mad at her," she said defensively. "But she knew my dad's assignments were incredibly dangerous. She could have put her foot down before he got himself killed."

Jensen shook his head. "Your father loved his job. He enjoyed going to work every single day. And your mom was smart enough not to dampen his enthusiasm, even though she wanted him to have a desk job in Washington in the worst way. You think she wanted to be a widow?"

Sarah looked down at her feet.

"Of course not. And the time's long past to put all that baggage behind you. Go see her."

"I wish I could, but if the biopsy comes back positive, then her treatment's supposed to last eight weeks. There's no way Montgomery will let me miss that much time. You didn't hear this from me, but he didn't want me to get the job in the first place."

"Then why don't you fly her out here for a few months? She's got so many friends still living in Washington and the medical care has got to be better than in Kansas."

Sarah closed her eyes while she slowly shook her head. "I don't know, Walter. I've suggested that a dozen times. But she's convinced it'd be too painful for her to come back. She's never really gotten over Dad's death."

"Believe it or not, neither have I." Jensen lovingly stroked her face. "Your dad always asked me to keep an eye out for you if anything happened to him. I'd give up everything I've ever achieved in this business to have Chip back with us."

Sarah understood the enormity of that statement. Walter Jensen was universally recognized by those in federal law enforcement as the forensic scientist nonpareil. The Oklahoma City blast, the World Trade Center bombing, and the Polly Klaas murder were just a few of the significant criminal matters successfully investigated by forensic teams under his direct control. Jensen looked like your average sixty-year-old white male; five feet, nine inches, with brown hair parted on the left side, wire-rimmed glasses. He was neither slender nor overweight, nor did he carry himself with the arrogance that often accompanies creative genius. He enjoyed discussing the Redskins as much as he relished the opportunity to talk about serology. Yet, after his best friend, Chip Peterson, had gotten killed, the forensic wizard redoubled his commitment to solving crime. Eighteen-hour days cooped up in a windowless lab became the rule rather than the exception.

Jensen glanced at the Timex he had worn since the Nixon presidency.

"So what brings the Deputy Director of the Office of Diplomatic Security to my lab at this hour?"

Sarah smiled at the sound of her official title. "I've got a nagging hunch that I need to bring to ground. Thought maybe you could give me a hand if you've got a few minutes."

"For you, my dear, almost anything. Have you run your hunch by Montgomery yet? From what I've heard the guy's got tremendous instincts."

"Actually, Walter, I'm sort of on my own until I've got more facts. As I said before, Montgomery didn't exactly wheel out the welcome wagon for me, and I heard from more than one source that he hates half-baked ideas."

He brought his index finger to his lips. "Mum's the word. So what's up?"

"Two men met with Montgomery this afternoon who are rubbing me the wrong way. I can't put my finger on it, but something's not kosher. One of these guys is a player in the oil markets. The other's a high roller in the arms business. On top of that, word in the intelligence community is that several Arab groups are plotting to kill my new boss. According to the CIA, we're looking at a two- or three-week time frame in which an attempt to get at Montgomery may occur."

"You think there's some kind of connection?"

"I'm not sure yet and that's why I'm here. But don't get me wrong, Walter. The guys who met with Montgomery are spit and polish all the way. Top-shelf brains and the connections to the Middle East to boot. And that's what frightens me."

"I assume you want to take a peek at their FBI files?"

"Yeah, but since I moved offices I've been locked out of your network. Norm over in MIS promises I'll be on the LAN by next week. But I'll believe it when I see it."

"Can you still run basic FOIMS searches from your system at home?"

"Yes, and I did that already."

"What was in their background checks?"

"They came up blank."

"You mean no convictions or arrests?"

"No, Walter. Their files simply didn't exist. The damn things were eighty-sixed. Kaput. Gone."

Jensen made a that-can't-be-so face. "That's not possible."

"That's one of the reasons I'm here."

He stood. "Let's go on down to O'Grady's office. He left for the day a few minutes ago."

"Can't we use yours?"

"I'm in the middle of a computer run on possible suspects in that U.S Air flight that went down last year. It'll probably take another couple of hours."

"Will O'Grady care? I know some FBI types who are pretty sensitive about outsiders touching their stuff."

"Nah. We share terminals all the time."

Jensen led Sarah down the hall. He unlocked the door to his colleague's cluttered office and flipped on the light. Beneath the Mr. Potato Head on a five-shelf bookcase was a yellow Post-it that contained O'Grady's fifteen-digit password. Like every other FBI agent's password, it was required to be changed at least once a week. When the first security screening was complete, Jensen typed in a series of numbers that unscrambled the FBI's classified encryption software. Words instantly replaced the string of unintelligible symbols.

"When you're done, remember to type "ogradyout," no spaces and no apostrophe. You can't log off otherwise. It's a double-check we instituted just last week after a hacker from Australia somehow managed to infiltrate the system. Fortunately, our firewalls kept him from getting very far."

"Will do, Walter. And thanks."

"No problem. By the way, I'll be around for another few hours if you need any help. I've got a report due on the director's desk on Friday that's nowhere close to being done."

Sarah closed O'Grady's door, interested in some extracurricular activity before getting down to business. She was kidding herself if she thought she wasn't looking forward to seeing Andy Archer again, but before accepting a dinner invitation, Sarah decided to take a peek at what he'd been doing for the last two decades. If he passed muster, they would start with the wiener wagon and maybe work their way up to a restaurant with candlelight and a wine cellar. If he didn't, she could tell him she had to wash her hair until he got the hint.

The file she opened to satisfy her curiosity was contained inside the State Department's most confidential personnel database. There she learned that Archer was a senior geopolitical analyst whose area of expertise was the Middle East. He had never been married and had no declared dependents. She already knew he had graduated magna cum laude from Yale. Fluent in Russian, Italian, Farsi, and German, as a GS-17, his salary was in the high nineties. He had also taken up skydiving and rock climbing while abroad, which didn't surprise her. Sarah smiled as she closed his file. If she could ever find the time to set aside an entire evening, dinner was certainly going to be interesting.

Sarah found her way to a list of National Security Agency directories. Armed with the index card the President had given her, she accessed the top secret database he had told her about. As expected, millions of pages existed in the vast library, going back in time to when the OSS was spying on the Nazis in the late thirties. Sarah considered doing a global subject search with either Anna Rodzinski's or her father's name as the keywords, but then decided this was neither the time nor the place to head down that path. Instead, she downloaded onto a disk nearly three hundred pages of information that intelligence agencies from around the world had accumulated within the last day. Perhaps in that haystack was data that would help her learn more about the planned assassinations against Montgomery. She skimmed the information quickly, surprised at the number of cryptic communications between the Mossad and the Saudi Royal Security Force. Although neither intelligence agency was rattling its saber just yet, both Israel and Saudi Arabia expressed concern about the sketchy rumor that sixteen powerful missiles had supposedly been smuggled into the region. Through the hotline that linked Tel Aviv to Riyadh, each country was seeking an assurance from the other that those bombs, if they existed, would not be pointed at their respective capitals.

Sarah doubled back through William O'Grady's access path, steering her cursor to a classified FBI directory; one that only selected government employees could enter. Bill O'Grady was an FBI special agent, whose job description included conducting sensitive background checks on individuals suspected of crimes ranging from fraud to terrorism. As such, he was given virtual carte blanche to examine all of the information the U.S. government had compiled on a person. Sarah had used these same files extensively at the Secret Service.

Sarah typed Buck Perry's name onto the sky blue screen. The system instantly pulled up the general's chronological twenty-eight-page dossier. A slight gap in the sequence in the mid-1960s led Sarah to believe that one or two entries had been expunged. That was something she had never seen before. She deliberately scrolled page by page, absorbing the particulars of General Perry's notable military career. Starting in 1950, the nineteen-year-old infantryman distinguished himself from the rest of the pack, earning the Medal of Honor during the Korean War. He was one of only 131 soldiers to do so. He led numerous successful campaigns in Vietnam. By the time he was forty-two, he was a full colonel. At age forty-seven, he was made a one-star general.

Sarah exited the file, no closer to pacifying the bothersome feeling she had experienced after leaving the meeting at the Pentagon. Buck Perry's confidential file did nothing but reinforce her view that he was a brilliant military strategist who exhibited exemplary loyalty to his country. His only blemish in the eyes of the FBI was an apparent proclivity toward physical violence, although the author of the report noted that this particular tendency was not unusual among high achievers in the military. From what Sarah could glean, there was no direct connection to either Tom Witherspoon or Ed Gallagher.

The next file she decided to search for clues was Jack Montgomery's. She browsed through a host of nonclassified data; the remainder of the information was squirreled away in archives designated for "eyes only" individuals. She was somewhere in the labyrinth, but the tunnel leading to the bull's-eye was blocked, at least temporarily. From what she could view, however, there was nothing concerning a relationship with either Witherspoon or Gallagher. She expected this, and quickly exited her boss's file.

Cross-referencing through a nonclassified IRS file, she obtained the dates of birth and social security numbers for both Tom Witherspoon and Ed Gallagher. She entered that information for Gallagher into the FBI's classified database; in the center of the screen in bold white letters appeared the words FILE DELETED. Sarah cleared the screen and typed in the relevant details for Tom Witherspoon. The same message appeared. The Special Agent rested her chin in the palm of her left hand.

"*Very* interesting," she said. She leaned over to make sure Bill O'Grady's office door was closed.

Sarah typed in a series of commands to determine who had deleted the files and how they could be retrieved. Each attempt was thwarted with the response ACCESS DENIED.

Just as she was about to sign off, a thought occurred to her. This time she asked the computer to reveal the date Ed Gallagher's file information had been expunged from the system. Yesterday's date appeared on the screen.

"You sneaky bastards!" she said. Sarah hurriedly switched screens to retrieve the corresponding information for Tom Witherspoon, confident there would be a match. The computer blinked rapidly, then displayed the identical date.

Sarah logged out of Bill O'Grady's computer and locked his office door behind her, unaware that Tripwire had already sent an e-mail to Jack Montgomery.

14

"ARE you alone?"

"Yes."

"Can you talk?"

Montgomery looked at his door. It was closed. "Yes."

The Secretary of State switched the receiver to his left ear so he could take notes of his discussion with Mr. Green. He was in his private study, already wearing his tuxedo. In an hour he would depart for the State dinner at the White House in honor of the French foreign minister.

"Your new security chief's an awfully thorough lady, Mr. Secretary. Despite running all over town with you today, she stopped at home for an hour or so early this evening to do some research. She looped into a Secret Service database by modem from her home computer. Witherspoon and Gallagher figured prominently in her search."

Montgomery considered pressing his most reliable operative for details as to how he had garnered this information, then opted not to. A quick glance at his laptop and his Tripwire software confirmed Mr. Green's information. Montgomery also knew that a remnant of almost every computer query existed on a silicon chip somewhere within the hard drive. The ability to find it was a proficiency Mr. Green had obviously acquired.

"Did she speak with anyone about this?" Montgomery asked anxiously.

"No. This evening she made exactly three calls. The first was to a lady named Marica Rodzinski. Apparently Anna Rodzinski died early this morning."

"Did she say when the funeral would be?"

"Eight A.M. tomorrow morning."

"Did she say where?"

"Gaithersburg Memorial Gardens."

"And the second call?"

"Some doctor who had left a message on her answering machine. She told him that she wasn't sure if their date next week would still be on."

"Did she say why?"

"No. Only that she was real busy at the office."

"And the last call?"

"Ron Haskins. They discussed a possible truck bombing attack against your motorcade that the CIA believes may take place next month. Haskins mentioned ammonium nitrate and fuel oil. That threat had been passed to one of their operatives in Cairo."

"Did she call the Chief of Staff, or did he call her?"

"She returned Haskins' call."

The Secretary of State thought for several moments. The fact that Sarah was using every tool at her disposal to track down a potential security problem was not surprising. He knew she was a bulldog. That was why he had butted heads with the President with such vigor. Now her curiosity was becoming extremely worrisome.

"Do you need me to do anything else for you?" Mr. Green asked impatiently. "I received another assignment a few minutes ago that'll put me out-of-pocket for a few weeks."

"You're not to accept work from *anyone* until I give you clearance," Montgomery said sternly.

"But it came from the director of the CIA."

"I could not care less who it came from."

The Secretary of State deliberated playing one of his trump cards even though it was unnecessary. A firm rap on the snout always kept dogs in line, but now was not the time to poke his operative with the cattle prod.

"I didn't hear your answer, Mr. Green."

"I said I understand. I'll tell the director that I'm unavailable until further notice."

"Good. And keep a close eye on Peterson. I'm sure I'll have some follow-up work on this one, if you know what I mean. You can be reached at the same pager number?"

"Yes, sir."

Montgomery placed the receiver of his secure phone onto its cradle. There were now decisions to be made as to how closely he wanted to monitor the activities of his chief of security. A few discreet computer queries and an illegal phone tap or two by an extremely skillful devotee was one thing, detailed surveillance was another. Montgomery knew Sarah Peterson hadn't leapfrogged over every man in her business by being oblivious to her surroundings.

As Montgomery pondered how to best walk the fine line between subtle probing and intrusive digging, he noticed the pearl earrings beside his phone, and his blood pressure began to rise. He had told his wife, Betsy, a dozen times that this phone was strictly off limits, even if it saved them a small fortune on her overseas calls. He decided he would give her hell after their evening at the White House. There was no need to argue all through dinner. The Secretary's secure line again rang. He presumed it was Mr. Green calling back with additional information.

"Yes?"

"It's Grizzwald. We need to talk." He sounded every bit as cocky as Buck Perry said he would be.

"Is something wrong?" Montgomery asked anxiously.

"No."

"Then why'd you call here? Contact between us is forbidden unless there's something urgent to discuss."

"There is," the soldier said matter-of-factly. "There's now an additional demand you'll need to inform our wealthy friend in New York about. McClarty and I are unilaterally changing the rules of engagement."

"What in God's name are you babbling about?" Mr. Green's disturbing report, and the pearl earrings, had put him in a foul mood.

"You'll be given a series of detailed wiring instructions that you'll need to follow very carefully. But understand this, Mr. Secretary. Jessica Baldwin won't be released until fifty million dollars is safely deposited into a Swiss numbered account of our selection. As for the source of those funds, that's your concern. We don't care where they come from, but you've got twenty-four hours to arrange for that transfer. And you may want to act more quickly than that. I'm no doctor, but her health seems to be deteriorating rapidly. McClarty thinks it's internal bleeding."

"Have you gone mad?"

Grizzwald didn't respond.

The Secretary of State could feel his anger rising, although he refused to lose his cool. "Surely you're underestimating me," he said impassively.

"As you are me. If I remember correctly, just a few days ago you and the good general made the decision to stake your entire careers on McClarty and me. I think the word you used to describe us was *invincible*."

"That was all of us banding together as a single unit. The sum of the whole being greater than its parts."

The career soldier laughed. "Men in Special Forces don't need help from politicians like you. And though I don't know you personally, I've heard you're smart enough not to do anything foolish over something as intrinsically worthless as money. I mean, there's no principle involved here for us whatsoever, other than cold, hard cash." Grizzwald paused. "Think about it, *Jack*. Fifty million dollars is a few days' work for Sam Baldwin and about what the nose cone costs for one of the general's fancy Stealth bombers. The Pentagon can certainly survive without one of those nose cones. Don't you think?"

"For an intelligent man you're a fool, Grizzwald. Every penny we spend has got to be closely accounted for. You don't just write a check for that kind of money."

"The CIA dropped three hundred million on a building in the middle of Washington, D.C., without anyone knowing about it for years, and the spy satellite program secretly accumulated a few billion in surplus. I think you'll find what we need."

"But . . . "

"And if you don't have our money within twenty-four hours, then we may get greedy. How would you like to come up with a hundred million, Jack?"

Just as the Secretary was about to respond he heard the connection go dead.

"No one double-crosses Jack Montgomery and gets away with it," he said as he softly put down the receiver. He glanced down at the copy of Sarah's security clearance identification. It had been faxed to him along with the remainder of the paperwork before her promotion. "No one," he whispered.

15

SARAH left Bill O'Grady's fourth-floor office, eager to get her hands on the tape she had planted that afternoon. Two FBI agents stopped to try to speak with her as she exited the Hoover Building, but she gave them much shorter shrift than usual. Sarah was popular with those in federal law enforcement, and generally eager to pass along whatever tidbits she could. She had so many different contacts, in so many different places, that her suggestions often helped to get a stalled investigation back on track.

Even though she enjoyed this camaraderie, right now was not the time to get bogged down in other people's problems. She had much on her mind, not the least of which was the legal pad Buck Perry had been clutching. She needed to know as soon as possible whether it was the one she had positioned at the bottom of the stack. If not, she desperately wanted to learn what had been discussed at the meeting.

Sarah stopped her Jeep at the security gate of one of the Pentagon's sixteen outdoor parking lots. A no-nonsense marine took down her license plate number and mumbled something into his walkie-talkie, then directed her to park in a restricted area just a few yards from the east wing entrance, where she registered at the front desk.

Sarah wound her way through the nearly deserted hallways of the Pentagon, a laminated UNESCORTED VISITOR badge pinned to her lapel. She eventually found the office of the supervisor in charge of the building's nighttime maintenance. A white-on-brown plastic nameplate was at eye level, just outside the door. Sarah knocked, then stepped inside.

"Ms. Mansfield?" she asked the fortyish woman with blond hair and dark eye shadow. Her gray steel desk looked like a 1940s icebox turned on its side and was stacked high with papers. The various piles obscured the open quart carton of chop suey that gave the small office its pungent odor.

Dottie Mansfield looked up when she heard Sarah's voice. "What can I do for you this evening?" she asked. She had a slight southern accent.

Sarah entered the office. "I'm on Secretary Montgomery's staff and I need just a couple of minutes of your time."

"All right. What's up?"

"The Secretary was in a meeting here this afternoon, down in SR-Three, and he left some important papers in there by mistake. I need you to open that conference room for me for just a second so I can get them."

Mansfield eyed Sarah warily. Very few people knew about the secret conference rooms buried deep below grade. In fact, all of the public literature disseminated by the military indicated that the Pentagon contained only five floors, which supposedly included the mezzanine and the basement levels. They were described as storage areas. The guides who led the public tours answered all questions concerning the "situation rooms" by saying that it was architecturally impossible to dig down that deep because of the building's proximity to the Potomac River, and droned on about silt levels and water tables.

"I don't know if this makes any difference," Sarah said, "but General Perry was in on the meeting."

The tiniest flash of fear came across Mansfield's face. The mention of Buck Perry's name had its desired effect. Sarah knew that no one inside this building messed with the general and got away with it.

"Can I see your ID?"

"Sure."

Mansfield studied Sarah's credentials, tilting her State Department card so that the hologram flickered back and forth. Then she said, "Come on! I'll run you down there right quick," as if they were suddenly the best of friends.

The two women hurriedly cruised through the corridors, nodding at the few servicemen they passed.

"I'll say one thing about this job," Mansfield said with a smile, "it certainly has its perks." She motioned to the two marines down the hall. "Good-lookin' men everywhere."

"I can see that."

"You married?"

"Nope."

"Then this is your kinda place."

Sarah's mood turned somber as they rode down the small elevator leading to the basement. She was about to learn whether her well-intentioned plan had failed. If so, there was no doubt things were going to get ugly for her in a hurry and from every direction.

"There you go," Dottie said as she unlocked the conference door. "I know it's a mess. General Higgins hosted a dinner meeting in here a few hours ago and I haven't had a chance to send someone in to clean things up. Quite frankly, I didn't expect anyone down here until tomorrow morning."

Sarah took a step inside the darkened room. She patted her hand blindly against the wall, fishing for the lights. When she felt the three dimming switches against her fingertips she turned them on one at a time. Light spilled into every corner of the room.

"I'll just be a second," she said apprehensively.

Sarah surveyed the filthy fine bone china that was spread the length of the table. The smell of garlic and picked-apart roasted chicken made Sarah's stomach turn. In the center of the table was a heavy glass ashtray piled with crushed cigar and cigarette butts. The thirty high-backed leather chairs had each been pushed back haphazardly a few feet away from the long mahogany table.

Sarah walked to the end of the table, where Secretary Montgomery and his colleagues had congregated during their meeting that afternoon. A single legal pad was in the spot where Buck Perry had been sitting. It had writing on the top page, and several sheets of paper had obviously been torn from it.

Sarah grabbed the pad and slid it into her briefcase without even so much as a glance. She quickly searched underneath all of the chairs and the table just to be certain another hadn't fallen, but there were no others in sight.

"Thanks," she said to Dottie when they were back in the elevator. She did her best to smile.

"You find what you were looking for?"

"I think so," she replied, although she sounded as unconvinced as she felt. "But if not, can you give me a list of the people who attended General Higgins' meeting? One of them may have accidentally picked up what I'm looking for."

"Sure thing. Let me know if you need that list."

Sarah returned to her Jeep and drove to the far end of the huge parking lot. Then she turned off the engine. With the Pentagon behind her she was able make out a sliver of the Potomac through the row of trees on the river's edge. Beyond that, in the distance, was the white marble obelisk of the Washington Monument. And somewhere in that city were Tom Witherspoon and Ed Gallagher. What they were up to, and who they were with, she was not yet sure.

"Please, God," she said. She closed her eyes and reached for her briefcase on the passenger seat.

TWO

THE PAPER

The chess board is the world, the pieces are the phenomena of the universe, the rules of the game are what we call the laws of Nature. The player on the other side is hidden from us. We know that his play is always fair, just, and patient. But also we know, to our cost, that he never overlooks a mistake, or makes the smallest allowance for ignorance.

THOMAS HENRY HUXLEY

16

SECRETARY MONTGOMERY made himself comfortable behind the President's desk while he absorbed the latest reconnaissance images of *The Hercules*. The photos had been hand-delivered to him by a reliable NSA courier ten minutes earlier, just after a string quartet from the Marine Band had played a minuet to announce the entrance of the French foreign minister and his wife. Montgomery had politely excused himself from the dais, informing the President there were urgent matters that required his attention.

The Secretary of State was now alone in the Oval Office. Outside the door an army corporal stood at attention, rigid as a mannequin, with the razor-sharp bayonet of his M-16 held at eye level. His white gloves were crossed over the polished barrel of his rifle.

"Ask General Perry to join me at once," Montgomery barked into the intercom that was beside a framed picture of the First Lady. "He's attending the State dinner." As a lark, he flipped through the President's huge circular Rolodex. He nodded when he saw what he suspected he'd see. There were Sam Baldwin's various phone numbers typed onto an index card.

"Yes, sir," one of the President's Secret Service agents responded.

Jack Montgomery took a few moments to look around while he waited for his colleague to arrive. The Oval Office had always held a mystique that even Jack Montgomery had a difficult time wrapping his arms around. Although it was somewhat illogical, simply being inside this room rejuvenated him, almost gave him a sense of invincibility. The presidency was just a hurdle away. He could taste it, almost touch it with his fingertips. Two years until the President's reelection, then four more as the Secretary of State. Eight years in the world spotlight would put him in as good a position as anyone to capture the brass ring. That presumed, of course, that no foreign policy disasters occurred under his watch. If millions were killed from an anthrax or VX attack, then everyone in the administration would no doubt be washed up for good. That was all the more reason why Baldwin needed to be stopped, and quickly. Aside from all those lives, Montgomery's lofty personal ambitions were at stake.

General Perry entered the room and sat in the same armchair the President had offered to Sarah the day before. He didn't remain there long.

"Let's get some air," Montgomery said.

Together Montgomery and Perry rose, careful not to utter anything that might be the least bit incriminating. In 1970, Richard Nixon had placed hidden microphones in every corner of the Oval Office, a move that eventually cost him the presidency. Although there was no indication the present commander-in-chief had done the same, there was no sense in taking any chances.

"Baldwin's weapons are moving south through Turkey by railcar," Montgomery said softly. They were strolling casually along the west wing portico, the columned walkway that led into the Rose Garden. The night air was brisk and their breath made white plumes in front of them. "He's continuing with his plans to attack Hussein even though he knows about his daughter."

"Perhaps we should cut off her ear and send it to him," the general suggested angrily.

"That's fine with me, but those bombs are the least of our problems right now. Several things have occurred in the last few hours. I think we have a situation that needs to be . . ." He paused for a minute, searching for just the right word, " . . . ameliorated."

The general's blue eyes widened. "Tell me," he said. For an instant, he thought back on the last time he had felt this much concern. General Perry was one of the men who had carried out a portion of the Secretary's most vicious dirty work over the years, including the removal of the developer of the Tripwire software. In Buck Perry's mind, if there was any risk whatsoever that Tripwire's architect might one day use his knowledge as leverage against Jack Montgomery, that risk had to be eliminated. The computer whiz's body was never found.

Montgomery removed a folded sheet of paper from the silk-lined breast pocket of his tuxedo.

"For starters, this evening someone attempted to gain access to each of our Level Two FBI files. The time registered on my e-mail was approximately thirty minutes ago, or just after ten o'clock this evening. Tripwire traced the connection back to an office on the fourth floor of the Hoover Building."

"Whose office?"

"Someone named William O'Grady. He's a forensics agent who apparently works incredibly long hours from what I've been able to determine thus far."

"You're sure he's the one who tripped the alarm?"

"No, but who else could have? I tried calling his office a few minutes ago and no one answered. But I'll know for sure soon enough. I've already requested a copy of the surveillance videotape from the fourth-floor hallway near O'Grady's office. It'll take my inside source at least forty-eight hours to get that on the sly."

"That's way too much time, Jack."

"I agree, and that's why I want you to handle this situation as you see fit. You've got my blessing to correct the problem."

"Done. So what else is wrong?"

"I received a rather disturbing phone call from your man Grizzwald this evening. He and McClarty have decided to extort fifty million dollars from Sam Baldwin before they'll release his daughter."

"Jesus F. Christ." Buck Perry spat out a splinter of his toothpick.

"You think he's bluffing?" Montgomery asked.

"No. Grizzwald's the coldest, meanest, toughest, smartest son of a bitch who's ever worked for me. Guy's a friggin' barracuda."

"Let me lean on him for a day and I'm sure he'll back off. In the end this'll be Sam Baldwin's problem, not ours."

"I'm not so sure of that, Jack. We may want to take out Grizzwald and McClarty, as well as their hostage. The few people in the military who know they're gone think they're on a high-risk training mission in Southeast Asia. If they don't return, no one'll be the least bit surprised."

"Let's just take it one day at a time."

"That's fine, but we've got to be ready to untangle ourselves from this mess if we have to. I'll be ready to let the fucker fly, as we say in Special Ops." He paused. "Any more bad news while you're at it?"

Montgomery's expression became even more serious. "Unfortunately, Buck, there is. Sarah Peterson triggered Tripwire from her computer on two separate occasions today. The first occurred while we were meeting with Ed and Tom at the Pentagon this afternoon. The second was a few hours later from her home. It may all just be a coincidence, but . . ."

A look of concern crossed Buck Perry's face. "Why in God's name would she be focusing on us?"

"I'm not sure yet, Buck, but I've got my best covert guy on it. He told me preliminarily that Peterson conducted a slew of separate FBI searches throughout the day, most of which had nothing to do with to our activities. Of course, those didn't activate Tripwire."

General Perry shook his head slowly. "Jack, I don't like the smell of this one little bit."

"Neither do I. But we've got to be careful about how we handle her. She's a sly fox with incredible instincts. If we get too close, she'll figure it out."

"Then why the hell'd you let her join your staff in the first place?"

"Look, Buck, you know the President insisted on her transfer and that my opinion meant nothing. So let's not dwell on something we can't change."

General Perry looked up at the cloudless sky and sighed, watching his breath dissipate into the cool air. "Suppose she knows about us?"

"Then she'll be treated just like everyone else who's ever learned too much."

"Even though she's your chief of security?"

"That'll have no bearing on my decision."

A look of relief came over the general's face. "Good. Just make sure you let me know as soon as I need to move on her."

"You'll be the first to know."

The two old friends shook hands firmly as they made their way toward the White House. Buck Perry stopped in his tracks and stared through the bulletproof glass that distorted his view of the illuminated Oval Office.

"Life's funny, isn't it, Jack? You remember hugging the dirt in that foxhole in Korea? Two skinny teenagers shittin' in our pants while guys died all around us."

"Like it was yesterday."

"Who'd have ever thought that we'd be standing here outside the President's office, just the two of us?"

"Me," Montgomery answered dispassionately. "I've thought about it every day for more than twenty years. And now that it's real, no one's going to take it from us. And I mean no one."

"Amen, Jack. I'll make damn sure of it."

"So will I."

17

" I think she's moving."

Jessica thought she had only closed her eyes for a few minutes. She tried to cry out, but was still not sure whether what she was experiencing was actual or imagined until Grizzwald squatted beside her and whispered into her left ear.

"I'm taking the tape off your mouth," he said. "If you scream you'll be very sorry. Do you understand?" She could feel his warm breath on the side of her neck.

Jessica nodded furiously.

"Good. As long as you cooperate we won't hurt you. But we're prepared to kill you if you make things even the least bit difficult for us. Do you understand *that?*"

The petrified hostage again gestured with her head.

"Good."

Grizzwald pushed aside Jessica's nest of matted black hair and ripped the tape from her face.

"Ouch!" she cried before she took in gulps of fresh air. As oxygen filled her lungs, the scent that filled her nostrils triggered a familiar response. What was it?

"How about the blindfold?" Lieutenant McClarty asked.

Jessica instinctively whipped her head to her right, trying to locate the source of the sound. Something intangible about this voice told Jessica that the man who was standing beside her was less of a threat than the man who had removed her gag.

"Please take it off," she said in a plaintive whisper, directing her plea to McClarty. "Please."

Grizzwald nodded to his colleague. "Take it off." They both knew what their plan for Jessica was once they'd been paid. Identification wasn't going to be an issue.

McClarty bent down and caressed Jessica's soft cheeks. It had been months since his rough hands had touched such supple flesh. The unexpected contact sent a surge of fear through Jessica's body. She stiffened, though she tried to conceal her reaction.

When her blindfold had been removed, Jessica hastily scanned the sparsely furnished space around her. The small room was dark, illuminated only by the steady flame inside a gas lantern just a few feet behind McClarty.

Jessica noticed that the wide floorboards on which she was sprawled were chocolate brown knotty pine and badly stained, giving her the impression from their width and condition that the structure they were in must have been more than a hundred years old. A small Shaker table and four distressed chairs were just beyond the lantern, and a sturdy maple armoire missing one of its solid wooden doors was pushed up against the doorway to her left. To her right was a second door. It was closed. The two windows across the room had tattered shades drawn past their sills. Although there seemed to be ample space between the shades and the peeling eggshell-colored paint on the wall, no light came through. It was obviously nighttime, Jessica thought, although she still wasn't sure which night. She had lost the concepts of time and space while she was unconscious, and those aptitudes were slow to return.

Jessica next turned her attention to the man whom she recognized as her kidnapper. Kneeling beside her, Grizzwald appeared unaffected by the temperature, which seemed as cold as a meat locker to Jessica. He wore olive green fatigues and a tight white T-shirt. From what Jessica could see, there was not an ounce of flab anywhere on his body. His arms were thickly muscled and his shoulders were as broad as a swimmer's. But what struck Jessica more than anything was that despite his size, all of the component parts were in proportion. As she scrutinized the man who had seemed so helpful inside her Connecticut bedroom, Jessica guessed he was in his late twenties. He had actually just turned forty.

"Where am I? Why am I here?" she asked in a low voice.

Grizzwald ignored the questions. "Don't speak unless you're spoken to. If you do, you'll be punished. Do you understand?"

Jessica nodded.

"We know all about your liberal politics and your rich daddy and your plans to save the world, and frankly don't want to hear any of that shit."

"But why me? I've done nothing to you."

The crack of skin meeting skin sounded like a fly swatter slamming down on a wooden table. The slap snapped Jessica's head violently to the right. She swallowed her cry of pain. When she tried to protect herself against another blow she finally realized her hands were tied securely to the feet of a rust-pocked radiator.

"Apparently you *didn't* understand what I just said, so let me make myself clear. Failure to obey my rules will result in immediate and severe punishment. Now do you understand?"

"Yes," she whimpered. Grizzwald's handprint was clear on her cheek. "I'm sorry."

"You'll be released only after all of our demands have been met. We've already been in contact with those who hold the key to your freedom and they understand what they must do to secure your safe release." Grizzwald paused. "In the meantime, don't do anything stupid because I'll kill you in a heartbeat if I have to."

Grizzwald removed a handgun that had been tucked into his waistband near the small of his back. He twirled the .45-caliber Colt on his index finger like a Western gunslinger and unloaded all but a single bullet from its chamber. Then he pressed the snout of the weapon against Jessica's forehead. She closed her eyes.

"This chamber holds six rounds. If I so much as have an inkling that you're trying to escape, we'll play a little game of chance. The first time you do something wrong, I'll squeeze the trigger three times. That'll be a fifty-fifty chance of what my ballistics friends call a very controlled energy release. Any additional violation of my rules will result in six squeezes to this trigger. You don't need me to do the math for you on that one, do you?"

"No."

For the first time since the blindfold had been removed, Jessica looked Grizzwald in the eye. His features were difficult to distinguish. She strained to focus, but realized her vision was slightly blurred. Was it from the residue of drugs in her system? She wasn't sure.

"May I speak?" she asked apprehensively.

Grizzwald nodded, his arms folded across his chest. "Go ahead."

"I'm two months pregnant," she said as she began to weep.

"We know that. In fact, we know quite a lot about you."

"So I'll do whatever you ask as long as you don't hurt my baby."

Grizzwald sneered. "Lady, you'll do what we ask or it'll cost you your life."

She began to cry. "May I please ask another question?"

"Yes."

"Will you untie my hands? I'm freezing and my wrists are killing me."

"Get her a blanket," Grizzwald ordered McClarty. He reached across her body and sliced through the bonds with a quick flick of his Swiss Army knife.

Jessica felt a terrible cramping in her belly. Was she going to miscarry? She took deep breaths and forced herself to remain calm. Perhaps these were just hunger pangs. God only knew how long it had been since she had eaten.

"May I please have something to eat?" She rubbed her wrists.

"And bring in some food," Grizzwald said just loudly enough so McClarty could hear in the adjoining room.

The other man returned a moment later with two gray army blankets in one hand and some bread and cheese in the other. "It ain't much," he said as he bent down to give it to her, "but it's either this or K-rations."

Jessica sat up slowly. She wrapped one of the woolen blankets around her like a cape and spread the other over her long legs. She bit down on the hard bread, determined to eat for the sake of her baby. She winced when her loose teeth tried to break through the crust and she used her incisors to tear off a piece.

Grizzwald and McClarty had left the room, but Jessica heard the soft murmur of their deep voices in what looked to be an adjacent bedroom. She surveyed her surroundings, trying to evaluate whether she could escape if given the opportunity. Of course, right now she knew that would be premature; she had no idea where she was or how high a jump it would be from one of the two windows. Besides, she was way too weak at that instant to make it very far. But as she gingerly rubbed the swollen side of her face, and thought of the baby growing inside her, her sense of survival was telling her to run the instant she could. If she didn't, she knew it would just be a matter of time before McClarty would touch the remainder of her body the way he had stroked her face. Either that, or Grizzwald would find a reason to play his little game of Russian roulette.

18

SAM BALDWIN remained huddled in his office with Hank Savage throughout the night, waiting for his private line to ring. At 10:00 P.M., Savage had put out a few very discreet feelers to some of their more shadowy contacts, probing to see if anyone had any information on who might have kidnapped Jessica. If so, prearranged code words could be freely exchanged over the telephone. For now, however, the amount of useful information they received was negligible.

If either an informant or the man with the synthesized voice called again, then the call would be traced. Assurances had been given to Victor,

Sam Baldwin's trusted contact at the phone company, that he would once again be paid a princely sum in small bills for his discreet cooperation. Nothing more needed to be said. Baldwin had used Victor's services twice before. Each case had been a failed extortion attempt against the CEO of Baldwin Enterprises and had been handled by Savage without the involvement of any law enforcement agency. It was tidier that way. No publicity. No need to waste time in court. And much more final.

The wait was interminable. Baldwin and Savage listened to the tape of the synthesized voice dozens of times, trying to pluck out any nuance that might give them additional clues. They cataloged a group of potential suspects, but the list was pure conjecture. Opening the phone book and choosing a name at random would have been just as accurate. No matter how badly each wanted to press forward, they both understood they needed more information before they could react.

Each man became more tense as the seconds slowly ticked, their emotions oscillating between frustration and fury. Even more than his boss, Savage could barely wait to get his powerful hands on the coward who was torturing his friend and employer. Savage had been infatuated with Jessica since their first meeting at the Baldwin Enterprises Christmas party at the Rainbow Room six years earlier. Despite the strong attraction, he had never acted on his affections, deciding that a failed romance might jeopardize his standing with her father.

The billionaire spent much of the time again staring at his photographs of Jessica. Time and again he turned to Savage for comfort, always receiving the assurance from the war-hardened ex-marine that he would also be taking this same tack if he were faced with a similar dilemma.

It was just past 1:00 A.M. when Baldwin's private line rang. Both he and Savage lunged toward the glass desk.

"Hello?"

Baldwin spoke calmly. Savage stood silently beside him, listening in on the speaker.

"Burning the midnight oil?" Montgomery's mechanically altered voice asked smugly.

"Let me speak to Jessie," Baldwin demanded.

"I'm disappointed in you," Montgomery said. "My people tell me those weapons are still on their way toward the Iraqi border."

"As am I. Your hour expired at four fifty-two last evening. You and I now have nothing to discuss."

"Maybe so. But as punishment for your insubordination, there's now an additional demand. It's going to cost you fifty million dollars if you want to see your daughter again alive. You'll receive wiring instructions at a later date."

"Let me tell you something, mister. Last evening I exercised one hundred thousand options of Baldwin Enterprises stock at a value of just over ten million dollars. That's public information that I'm sure you can verify as soon as I hang up on you. What only *you* will know is that those proceeds will be the first installment of the funds I intend to expend to put your head on a platter."

"That fifty million dollars is nonnegotiable, Mr. Baldwin. And before you go to bed tonight, I want you to think about all those people who will die along with Jessica and her baby if you've miscalculated about those weapons. Their blood will be on your hands."

Montgomery disconnected the line before the billionaire could beat him to the punch.

Baldwin pressed the contact button on his phone.

"Are you there, Victor?"

"Yes."

"Were you able to trace it?"

"No, sir, you weren't on long enough. But there was something very strange about that signal. I'll need some time to analyze it."

"You do that. And you make sure you come up with the right answer, is that understood? It'll be worth your while if you do."

"Yes, sir. As soon as I know anything I'll let you and Mr. Savage know."

19

"PLEASE be the one!" Sarah implored.

Her Jeep was parked on Pentagon property, but was as far away from the main entrance as possible. Only a sea of white-painted parallel lines surrounded her in this section of the parking lot. There would be no one around to hear her cries of either dismay or joy.

Until that Tuesday night in the middle of October, the satisfaction of simply moving quickly up the Secret Service ladder had been enough of a professional reward for Sarah Peterson. As a child being raised by her mother in northern Kansas, she had dreamed of following in the footsteps of the father she had never really known. Other little girls in the small town of Kimeo talked of becoming nurses and teachers, while Sarah told everyone who would listen that one day she would be on a first-name basis with the President, just as her slain father had been. Of course, that type of talk was summarily dismissed as schoolgirl fantasy. However, when Sarah graduated with top honors from Yale, the *Kimeo Ledger* announced that she was forgoing a free ride to her choice of graduate schools to begin her law-enforcement training at the Secret Service Academy.

Every advancement since then had been a struggle, but her career had gone exactly as she had diagrammed. She had been able to work side by side with some of the most powerful people in Washington, and become privy to information that might one day help explain her father's murder. The combination of her performance and personality made the many obstacles she faced as a woman in this male-dominated field eventually surmountable. Even though she could have made ten times her salary had she chosen Wall Street instead of Pennsylvania Avenue, she had no regrets—at least up until the day she planted a hidden tape recorder in a stack of notepads in the basement of the Pentagon. Although that technique had worked a dozen times before because so many men had underestimated her by pegging her as nothing more than a secretary, Sarah now had an awful feeling that the brio and willingness to take risks that had carried her this far had finally caught up with her. If the pad in her hand wasn't the correct one, then she knew Montgomery would soon be wise to what she had done. No matter what the President had told her in private about aggressively fighting terrorism, he would never be able to save her hide on this one. Her very public flogging wouldn't be far behind.

She carefully angled the top edge of the notepad towards her, then gradually opened her eyes.

"Thank you, God!" she exclaimed as she slumped with relief in her bucket seat. She hurriedly peeled the tissue-thin coating that held the microcassette in place as if she were a kid opening presents on Christmas morning. Once it was exposed she dumped it into the palm of her hand.

Sarah removed a custom-designed tape player from her briefcase. She rewound the tape, put on her earphones, then pressed the Play button. Jack Montgomery's no-nonsense voice was the first thing she heard.

"I'm working on a matter that's of vital interest to this country, and therefore of great importance to me."

Sarah lowered the volume and listened carefully as Jack Montgomery impressed the need for total secrecy on his colleagues. Then he delivered a cold and sterile recitation of how the daughter of someone named Baldwin had been kidnapped and might soon be killed. The fact that this woman's life hinged on the assassination of Saddam Hussein was even more shocking.

She listened in astonishment, scribbling a stream of keywords onto the top sheet of the legal pad: *Hercules, Baldwin, Paris, Saddam Hussein, Witherspoon, Gallagher, the Hay-Adams.*

Sarah was numb when the tape ended. Although the recording had provided her with a wealth of intriguing information, it had also left her with several important questions to be answered. Filling in those gaps without attracting attention wouldn't be easy, she knew. Jack Montgomery was a power broker who had performed favors for people on both sides of the political aisle. Every one of those people yearned for the opportunity to pay him back. The many enemies he had collected throughout the years were in hiding for now, waiting for him to falter. They were wise enough not to take on a powerhouse who was at the top of his game. At a minimum, openly criticizing Montgomery could derail a career. If you were foolish enough to draw his wrath, it was political suicide. Sarah suspected that if she stepped on the wrong land mine, Montgomery would know in an instant that danger was about to drift his way. For the first time in her life she suddenly felt alone, with nowhere to turn and no one to trust.

She listened carefully to the recording a second time, trying to pick up any nuance of the discussion she might have missed; but even another go-round left her wondering whether the Baldwin woman was already in the hands of Buck Perry's two efficient killing machines and how much time she had before the deadly chemical weapons Montgomery had described would be released into the atmosphere.

Sarah's thoughts turned to Andy Archer. He had studied every facet of the Middle East for the last twenty years and probably knew more about Saddam Hussein than almost anyone on the planet. She would pick his brain to find out whether Saddam's death really would bring about the doomsday scenario Jack Montgomery had indicated. If so, many lives were in jeopardy, not just one kidnap victim's. The burning oil wells of Kuwait would be child's play compared with this disaster. Sarah felt the flames licking at her feet as the ramifications of her next step began to set in. The pressure was now on for her to do the right thing. But what was the right thing?

Sarah heard the sound of knuckles meeting glass. She flinched, then saw a uniformed security guard standing beside her Jeep. He was speaking into a black walkie-talkie as he peered into her driver's-side window. Although Sarah wasn't sure, she thought he was the same man she had seen talking with Buck Perry in this parking lot just last week.

20

TWENTY minutes after Jack Montgomery had dialed the penthouse to the Baldwin Building, the billionaire's private line again rang. Baldwin and Savage started, hoping the man who had just demanded $50 million would once more be initiating communication. Any clue, no matter how insignificant, had the potential to be the one that would lead them to Jessica.

"Yes?" Baldwin asked eagerly.

Savage activated the built-in recording device on his boss's phone even though he knew all calls on this line were being recorded digitally by Victor at the phone company. The belt and suspenders approach was one of the reasons Savage had risen so quickly at Baldwin Enterprises.

"Sam? Is that you?" Doug Templeton, Jessica's fiancé, asked. "I didn't think I'd be able to reach you this late. Francesca said you were working on something important, but I never thought you'd still be there."

"Unfortunately, I am." Baldwin tried to keep the disappointment out of his voice. Both he and Savage deflated when they heard Templeton's familiar New York accent. "A deal came up suddenly that we couldn't pass on. If everything goes according to schedule, it'll close next week."

"Sam, I'm worried about Jessie. I haven't heard from her since she left on Sunday, and that's not like her at all. We always speak a couple of times a day even when one of us is out of the country. I tried calling her at her hotel a few minutes ago. But they told me she never checked in."

Baldwin looked at Savage, who was standing across the desk shaking his head vigorously.

"Don't worry about her, Doug. I spoke to her this afternoon and she said everything was fine. She may have switched hotels at the last minute. She also mentioned that she was having trouble reaching *you*. You're in South Carolina?"

"Yeah, with a cell phone that's apparently a piece of shit. What's the name of the hotel where she's staying?"

"You know, I didn't even ask. If she calls again, I'll get her number for you. In the meantime, stop worrying. Jessie's a big girl. You'll probably hear from her after she's done running around Paris with some young stud."

Doug laughed. "That's what I was afraid of." Templeton paused. When there was no response from his future father-in-law he said, "Listen, I'll let you get back to work. You sound tied up."

"Just trying to get the hell out of here so I can get a few hours of sleep. Have a good night, or what's left of it."

"You too."

Once he was off the phone Baldwin turned to Savage and asked, "How long do you think we can keep this from him?"

"Not long."

"A day? Maybe two?"

"At most."

"He's going to complicate things," Baldwin said.

"I know."

"If he doesn't speak with her soon, I think he'll panic and call the police either here or in Paris."

"Wouldn't you?"

Baldwin nodded.

"We may run out of time trying to find Jessie if Doug does something stupid without realizing it," Savage said.

Baldwin slumped in his chair and covered his face.

"Why don't you go back to your apartment and get a few hours of shuteye?" Savage suggested. "I can stay here and hold down the fort."

Baldwin shook his head. "No. I don't want to have to face Francesca. This news will destroy her."

"You're going to keep her in the dark?"

"At least for now. If she finds out, I know she'll go to the FBI."

21

"EVERYTHING OK, here ma'am?" the Pentagon security guard asked Sarah through her unopened window.

She rolled down the window. Now that she took a second look at him, Sarah was convinced he was the man who had been chatting with Buck Perry last week beside the general's green Bonneville while a tow truck jumped the dead battery.

"Yes, I'm fine," Sarah answered firmly.

She glanced in all directions. No one else appeared to be nearby. She noticed the flashing yellow turret light on the roof of the guard's Chevy Blazer, then accepted the encounter at face value. The guard was apparently with the crew who regularly patrolled the Pentagon's seventy acres of parking area.

"I was just about to leave," Sarah said with a smile, "but thanks for asking." She shifted her Jeep into first gear. Seconds later her car was roaring alongside the Potomac, the illuminated monuments in the distance on the other side of the river. The Blazer's whirling yellow light quickly disappeared from her rearview mirror.

Sarah drove to her Georgetown brownstone and scanned her surroundings to see if anyone had followed her, then parked in front of Mr. DelVecchio's home two doors down. At age seventy-five, Alberto DelVecchio was still extremely robust and helped Sarah till her vegetable garden every spring. When she was out of town during the summer, DelVecchio would tend the patch as if it was his own, picking ripe cucumbers and tomatoes before the squirrels had a chance to poach her harvest.

As Sarah searched the length of her darkened street, she tried to formulate a checklist as to what she should do next. Her feelings of uncertainty brought back memories of her first nighttime parachute jump when she cross-trained at the Marine Corps Air-Ground Combat Center in Twenty-nine Palms, California; she would soon be leaping from safety into the black abyss. If the chute opened, everything would be fine. If it didn't, there would be a long free fall before she slammed into the ground.

Sarah's initial reaction was to contact the FBI and let them sort through the fallout the conversation from the Pentagon would no doubt cause. She dismissed that knee-jerk reflex almost immediately for three reasons: First, the tape itself did not prove that anyone had actually been abducted or that any crime had indeed been committed. Without tangible proof or confirmation to present to the authorities, Montgomery's statements were virtually meaningless. Sarah feared that if the plan had been aborted for one of a thousand different reasons, then she would be the one who ultimately had egg on her face. Facts could be twisted, claims of tape-doctoring would be levied against her, and all everyone would remember was that the number two person at the ODS had bugged her own boss's private meeting.

Second, Montgomery had boasted he would know in an instant if anyone had gone to the FBI and that Baldwin's daughter would be killed immediately if that occurred. That meant he no doubt had insiders at the bureau. Sarah was extremely concerned that without additional information, she would cause someone's death before she had an opportunity to expose the plot safely and completely.

Third, Washington was Jack Montgomery's town. He had worked in and around the nation's capital for the better part of forty years. Sarah knew that in order for Montgomery to successfully complete a scheme of this magnitude, he must have had assistance from someone well up the ladder inside either the FBI, the CIA, or possibly both. He had said as much during the meeting. That meant she could not trust anyone with this waiting-to-explode scandal until she had all of the facts.

Sarah felt the pressure of this burden of information slowly building inside her. Because the ever-present shadow of Watergate hung like a storm cloud over Washington, the implications for the entire country were enormous. While trying her best to protect the Secretary of State, she had unwittingly become a lightning rod. Was she also being used as a pawn by the President?

As Sarah weighed her options she noticed a large bundle of green cellophane pushed up against her front door. She hurried up her steps to get a better look, surprised to see a dozen long-stem red roses in a glass vase. "Dear Sarah," the small card wedged between two petals said, "Fate sometimes has a way of intervening in life's plans. I'm looking forward to seeing you again. —AA P.S. Call me in the morning at home if you'd like to get together tomorrow night. I'll be out of the office all day." His home phone number was written on the bottom of the card.

Sarah placed the flowers just inside her vestibule and rushed back to her car, her spirits rising. She wanted to do nothing more right now than to unwind over a bottle of Jack Daniel's with Andy Archer. It would be fun. Spontaneous. Frivolous. Even though it was past midnight, she knew Archer would hop out of bed to meet her for a drink. But Sarah resisted the urge. There would be plenty of time to be impulsive once this current crisis was over. But she did dial Andy's number. He answered on the first ring.

"Thanks for the flowers," she said softly. "You made a rotten day much better."

"Ditto. So why're *you* up so late? You're supposed to be easing into the new job."

"Just trying to dig out. I've got too much on my plate and not enough time to do it."

"Me, too. My eyes are crossed from staring at this damn computer."

Sarah again considered inviting him over, but knew now was not the time.

"This may sound like I'm blowing you off," she said, "but I won't be able to make it for dinner tomorrow night. Something's come up."

"I understand."

She could hear the disappointment in his voice.

"Maybe next week?" she suggested.

"Sounds good. We can talk after the weekend."

"Now that I feel incredibly guilty," she said, "do you mind if I bounce a work question off you?"

"Not at all. I'll start the meter right now."

"What's your hourly rate?"

"Don't ask. You can't afford me."

Sarah laughed. "You're an expert on the Middle East, right, with a concentration on Iraqi-Iranian relations?"

"Well, that was an easy one. Yes."

"That's not the question, Andy."

"Oh," he said, feigning surprise.

"Suppose Saddam Hussein had a heart attack and died tomorrow? How would that affect the stability of the region?"

"Why do you ask? I get briefed by the CIA all the time and they've never said anything about a heart condition."

"Just a rumor I heard from a reliable source in Baghdad," she lied. "And if it's true, it'll certainly have implications for Montgomery's security. He's supposed to be in Cairo next month."

"Well, there are two schools of thought on the sudden removal of Saddam Hussein. The first is that Iraq would quickly choose someone to take his place, and that democracy would eventually take hold. This theory has people dancing in the streets of Baghdad, delirious that *their* Hitler is finally dead."

"You think that's likely?"

"No. I'm in the other camp, the one that's sure there'd be a bloodbath within the Iraqi government while every general with any clout tried to assume power. If that happens, then the region would destabilize and all-out war with Iran would break out."

"Give me your odds."

"I'd say eighty-twenty in favor of destabilization."

"Is that why we haven't been more aggressive in trying to depose him?"

"Yeah, and why we didn't topple him when he jerked around the UN weapons inspectors. Think about the number of times he's given us a reason to go in there and mow him down."

"It seems like every six months."

"That's just about right. And it's been that way for the last eight years. But he knows we won't do it unless he really crosses the line and attacks either Israel or Saudi Arabia. I'm also convinced he's a schizophrenic who'll probably shoot his load of chemical weapons one day."

"Suppose he does. Are those weapons really as deadly as everyone says they are?"

"Absolutely. One nine-millionth of one gram of anthrax is fatal one hundred percent of the time. That's an amount the size of a single grain of salt crushed into a thousand pieces. If Saddam fired the biological agent botox instead of anthrax, then much less than that will do the trick. It's two thousand times more deadly; the most lethal substance known to man. And he's supposedly got several tons of the stuff stored in underground caverns."

"Can any of this be neutralized once it's released?"

"As a practical matter, no. Once it's expelled into the atmosphere, it has the potential to kill every single person on the planet. It also makes whatever earth it lands on completely uninhabitable for a couple of hundred years."

"Then how come no one's killed Saddam and taken out his stockpiles?"

"Because he keeps all those fundamentalists in the region honest, especially the Iranians. Everyone's also even more afraid of what'll happen if he's gone. It's the old story of the devil you know being better than the one you don't. Saddam's son is supposed to be much crazier than he."

"You weren't this smart at Yale," she said mischievously.

"You never gave me the chance to show you."

Sarah laughed. "Good night, Andy," she said. "I'll call you in a few days to work something out."

"You know where to find me."

"And thanks again for the roses. They're beautiful."

"My pleasure."

Sarah started her car and sped to the FBI building. Walter Jensen had said he'd be working late and she hoped he was still there. She had a feeling that Montgomery would never have told Witherspoon or Gallagher about the kidnapping unless he had some very incriminating information about them to ensure their cooperation. And as she rode the elevator to Jensen's office, Sarah had a hunch where she could find that information just in case she needed a bartering chip to fend off her new rivals.

Walter Jensen was typing feverishly at his computer.

"Come on in," he said to Sarah with an inviting smile.

She complied and set her briefcase beside his hard drive.

"You OK?" he asked. "You look tired."

"I am. I also can't believe you're still here."

Jensen shrugged. "What can I say?"

"I take it you didn't have time to find those backup disks on Witherspoon and Gallagher?"

"Not yet, but I found an index that should really help. How soon do you need 'em?"

"Yesterday."

"How about tomorrow morning?"

"That's fine. In the meantime, I need another favor."

"You know, you look just like my daughter right before she asks to borrow my car keys."

Sarah tried to suppress a smile. "Come on, Walter, don't give me a hard time on this one."

"Jeez, I didn't realize I was touching a nerve." He raised his hands in mock self-defense. "So what do you need?"

"Another few minutes on O'Grady's computer since you seem to be tied up on yours."

"No problem."

"Using his encryption codes."

Jensen slowly shook his head. He knew Sarah was experienced enough to appreciate the position she was putting him in. "I'll take you over to O'-Grady's office. If he shows up we can always go elsewhere."

"You think he might come in *now*?"

"Maybe. The guy almost never sleeps. I actually tried calling him fifteen minutes ago to discuss this damn report. When no one answered I figured he might be on his way back to the building."

"Jesus," Sarah said. "And I thought *I* worked long hours."

They walked the silent corridor to O'Grady's office, where Jensen entered a succession of lengthy passwords and was offered a host of file options.

"I assume you can find what you need from here?"

"I think I can manage."

"I'll be down the hall if you get stuck."

"Thanks, Walter. I owe you one."

When Sarah was alone she tapped directly into the FBI's most closely guarded files, the existence of which the bureau had denied for decades. Although she and Jensen had attained equal levels of security clearance, the State Department's computers could not access this database, which was stored inside the FBI's Cray supercomputers. This battery of $500 million hardware was located in a steel-reinforced concrete vault in the basement of the Hoover Building, and was guarded twenty-four hours a day, 365 days a year, by five marines. Their shoot-to-kill orders ensured that no one would be able to access or remove the hardware that housed nearly a century of the nation's dirty laundry.

Sarah took a few minutes to familiarize herself with the various directories, then found herself at the porthole of knowledge only the most trusted of individuals inside the government were entitled to enter. The file she accessed was the bureau's entire research bank on every person who, in the estimation of the hundreds of collecting agents who had contributed research over the decades, posed a potential threat to the democracy.

All told there were more than ten million entries that had made it onto what J. Edgar Hoover and his confidants had arrogantly called "the Bible." This most secret of the FBI's databases dated back to July 27, 1908, one day after the FBI was officially created by an act of Congress. It included tens of thousands of entries no longer than a single paragraph. It also included listings on individuals like Lee Harvey Oswald and James Earl Ray that took up billions of bytes on the hard drive.

Sarah typed "Thomas L. Witherspoon" into the system. Six listings appeared. She skimmed through the various dates of birth, addresses, and occupations, quickly identifying the correct Witherspoon. Then she opened the twelve-page report.

Many of the twenty-seven separate entries concerning Witherspoon con-

tained information that had no business appearing even in a highly classified FBI file. Medical history, IRS returns, and even the names and last
known addresses of several of Witherspoon's alleged mistresses. These details were interesting to Sarah, but did not provide the type of fodder Montgomery would have needed to ensure his old friend's silence about the
kidnapping. Then Sarah saw it: in 1983, Witherspoon's primary holding
company sold more than $300 million worth of Silkworm missiles to Israel.
Although no further explanation of this garden-variety black market arms
transaction was contained in this file, Sarah immediately understood why it
was there. The Silkworms were a significant portion of the hardware that
had been shuttled through various shell countries as part of the Iran-contra
deal. That information had been widely reported in the press and would not
raise any eyebrows. But the connection no one had ever made was that in
1983, Jack Montgomery had been the U.S. Deputy Ambassador to Israel,
stationed in Tel Aviv. At the time, two shadowy arms dealers were executed
gangland style, their severed testicles jammed inside their mouths before
they had been shot. Had Witherspoon been involved in these hits? And had
Montgomery profited from the illegal exchange of weapons? Sarah didn't
know, but her gut told her she had just found a very big stick to swing at her
boss if the need arose.

Sarah rubbed her hands, sure that a thorough examination of Ed Gallagher's file would reveal something just as incriminating, but it was late
and she was exhausted. Sarah decided to go home and try to sleep until sunrise. Then she'd be ready to try in earnest to find out where Jack Montgomery and Buck Perry were holding a young woman named Baldwin
hostage.

22

JACK MONTGOMERY was transported in his armored Town
Car back to his sprawling Virginia home just after 2 A.M. Dinner at the
White House had stretched out longer than he would have liked, but these
State affairs always did. With all that pomp and circumstance, there was no
wonder the federal deficit continued to swell. As did the waistlines of most
of the attendees.

Montgomery changed out of his tux into his terry-cloth robe and wandered downstairs to his study to take one last look at his computer before he retired for the night. He checked his e-mail directory; Tripwire had sent another message less than thirty minutes earlier. Although that, in and of itself, was cause for concern, the source of the signal was even more perplexing: it had originated from Bill O'Grady's office on the fourth floor of the FBI building. Montgomery, however, knew that was impossible. Buck Perry had personally assured him over a snifter of Grand Marnier that the curious FBI agent was dead from a single shot from the general's own .357 Magnum.

23 *Wednesday*

BUCK PERRY returned to his corner office at the Pentagon, stuffed to the gills from a three-hour power breakfast in the executive dining room at the Congressional Country Club. Over scrambled eggs, crispy bacon, and hash browns doused in gravy, he had cajoled a group of moderate Republicans into reconsidering their compromise plan to scrub the development of the RAH-66 Comanche attack helicopter. Perry had argued that the $4 billion project was necessary to keep America's rapid reaction forces one step ahead of the next generation of terrorists. Of course, he mentioned nothing about his secret slush account that siphoned a percentage of the funds at his disposal to an offshore Bahamian bank. With another infusion, the general's well-disguised account would bloat like a stuffed pig.

"Any messages?" he asked his secretary as he jabbed a toothpick between his teeth.

The young woman removed her earphones and stopped transcribing the general's dictation. "Just these." She handed General Perry two pink slips of paper. "It's been a quiet morning."

Perry glanced at the first and then at his watch. "Montgomery called two hours ago?"

"Yes, sir."

Perry nodded, then looked at the second message. "Who the hell's Dottie Mansfield?"

"I think she's the maintenance supervisor who sent around that memo about smoking in the building. I heard her crews keep finding cigarette butts in the garbage cans."

Although the Pentagon had gone smoke free, Perry was way too busy to make the trek outside every time he needed a cigar. In his mind, those rules were for clerks, not him. "Why the hell's she calling me?"

"I have no idea, General. But she said it might be important. Something about one of the situation rooms downstairs."

Perry crumpled the message and fired the pink wad into the garbage can. "If she calls back before I get around to calling her, ask her what the hell she wants."

"Yes, sir."

The woman put her headphones back on, then continued transcribing the general's memo to the Chairman of the Joint Chiefs of Staff on the necessity of proposed upgrades for the Bradley A3 tank. If agreed to by General Higgins, more than $8 billion in funds previously earmarked for other military projects would be diverted to Buck Perry's use. Then the general would find a way to direct a portion of that cash to Tom Witherspoon and Ed Gallagher as a reward for their continuing cooperation in the kidnapping of Jessica Baldwin.

24

JACK MONTGOMERY stood alone in his private study, beside the row of built-in bookshelves extending from floor to ceiling. He was scheduled to meet with the Russian foreign minister in less than half an hour to discuss recent troop deployments in Chechnya; but the designs of the heavy-handed Soviet hard-liners were the furthest thing from his mind. When the most recent Tripwire communication was coupled with Grizzwald's brazen insubordination, as well as the persistent probing of certain FOIMS files by his chief of security, the Secretary knew the time had come to consider pulling the cord on this jinxed operation. He picked up his secure phone to discuss the deteriorating situation with General Perry.

"Buck, it's me," Montgomery said somberly. "We've got another problem. A big one."

"I just got your message a couple of minutes ago and was about to call

you back. What the hell's wrong now?" The general had collaborated with
Jack Montgomery on a host of similar matters, but had never before heard
such distress in his old friend's voice.

"I got a second Tripwire message from O'Grady's office very late last
night."

"That's impossible, Jack! You know that!"

"Tell that to my computer."

"You're sure it's not just a technical error? Unless someone else is using
his computer."

"Look, Buck, I don't have an answer for you right now. The only thing I
do know is that someone entered 'Thomas L. Witherspoon' as a computer
search of a top secret FBI file at one thirty-four A.M. We'll know who it was
as soon as I get that damn tape from my source at the FBI. But that'll take
some time."

"Oh, Christ."

Montgomery said nothing.

General Perry scratched the bristles of his crew cut while he thought.
"Jack, as far as I can see, we've got exactly one good option at this point, and
that's to bail the hell out of this fucking mess while we still can. My CO in
Special Ops training always told us that if you've gotta swallow a turd, then
for God's sake don't nibble around the edges."

"What about Sarah Peterson?"

"We'll get the hell rid of her if she knows too much. As long as she hasn't
gone to the FBI yet, I don't give a rat's ass who she is. As for McClarty and
Grizzwald, I say we eliminate them and their hostage, too."

"You think all that's feasible under the circumstances?"

Perry ground his teeth. There was no doubt both of their careers were
now on the line. He, more than anyone, was aware how remarkable
McClarty and Grizzwald were. They had been painstakingly culled from
thousands of recruits for the ultraselective Delta Force, then meticulously
trained in every aspect of covert intelligence. They were walking encyclo-
pedias when it came to paramilitary strategy and execution and had experienced some of the most challenging real-world battle situations. The
proposition of trying to defeat them was daunting.

"I think so," the general finally said, "only because I think I know where
they are."

"How?" Montgomery asked anxiously. "Where?"

"Before I gave Grizzwald the green light for this operation I tapped his
phone. I know where they're hiding."

"So?"

"So I've got Special Forces guys at my disposal just a couple of hours away. These boys are chomping at the bit for a challenge like this. Those treasonous bastards will never know what the fuck hit 'em."

"Can we still keep this secret?"

"Shit, yeah. My men will only be told that these three targets must be eliminated and disposed of where they'll never be found. It's amazing what they will do in the name of national security. One time they tossed a guy from Pakistan into a wood chipper, then they scattered what was left a few miles out in the Atlantic. If you think finding the fuselage of TWA Flight 800 was difficult, finding Jessica Baldwin will be damn near impossible."

Jack Montgomery knew he had to take the decisive action Buck Perry was suggesting. Unlike every prior covert operation he had orchestrated, too many breaks had cut the wrong way too quickly. Montgomery knew that with no bodies, and no prompt report to the FBI, it would be almost impossible for any investigative agency to pick up their scent. Buck Perry had successfully handled challenges like this for the last thirty-two years and now was no time to change gears. Dance with the girl who got you there, the general had always been fond of saying. And those who followed his orders knew that the girls who had gotten him this far were named Smith & Wesson, or Browning or Beretta.

"Do it," Montgomery finally said. "I'll be at your office in a little while so we can monitor the situation together. We'll also decide what to do with Sarah Peterson. She may make it stickier for us."

"Don't worry about her, Jack. I'll handle Peterson myself if there are any complications."

25

SARAH watched from afar, a thousand frost-laced tombstones separating her parked Jeep from the slowly moving funeral procession. Thirty minutes earlier Anna Rodzinski's coffin had been laid to rest behind the black iron gates of Gaithersburg Memorial Gardens. Some of the marble headstones near her grave site had little American flags stuck in the cold dirt nearby, some a smattering of wilting flowers. Others looked like they hadn't been visited in years.

Several times during the brief ceremony Sarah considered joining the semicircle of bundled mourners who had gathered around Anna's flag-draped coffin, but she decided to pay her respects after everyone was gone. Even though the Rodzinski family had graciously welcomed Sarah into their mother's hospital room, and had informed her of the funeral arrangements, Sarah ultimately thought it would be best to observe the burial from the seclusion of her car, rather than to interrupt the service with the presence of an outsider.

Sarah waited for the twelve-car procession to drive west on Clopper Road toward Seneca Creek State Park before she stepped out of her Jeep. She watched two gravediggers get right to work as soon as the procession exited the cemetery. They were already shoveling dirt into the six-foot hole when Sarah walked towards it, wreath in hand.

"Do you mind if I have a few minutes to myself?" she asked one of the men.

"No problem, ma'am. We'll be back in a few minutes."

The two men hopped into their Ford pickup and parked thirty yards farther down the road. Another cup of hot coffee on a cold morning would be just fine with them. Once she was alone she bent down on one knee to place the ring of flowers alongside the ones the Rodzinski family had left behind.

"Anna, I don't know if you were awake when I told you this in your hospital room," Sarah said in a low voice, "but if you can hear me now, I want you to know that I'm not angry at you. If I was in your shoes, I probably would've done the same thing to protect my family."

Sarah looked around, feeling slightly foolish. She wasn't even quite sure that she believed in God, or in heaven, or in the afterlife. But she had felt compelled to speak to Anna Rodzinski. Maybe it had to do with the guilt she felt for not being with her mother. Maybe she just genuinely liked the woman whom she had only met that one time. But Sarah knew for sure that Anna Rodzinski's death had opened a door that had been closed for so long.

"For what it's worth," Sarah added, "My mom said that my dad would've done everything in the world to protect his family. She forgives you, too."

Sarah stood and closed her eyes for a moment. In that instant, all that was swirling around her seemed so calm.

"Rest in peace, Anna Rodzinski," she said softly. "And thank you."

• • •

FIVE hundred yards away from where Sarah's head was bowed, a black Ford Explorer with tinted windows was parked outside the grounds of the cemetery. In it was a man with high-powered field binoculars and a small notepad. He recorded his observations in meticulous detail and snapped a roll of pictures using a Konica telephoto lens.

26

BUCK PERRY hastily assembled four members of one of his elite tactical squads and briefed them about their assignment. Their main training area was near Kingston, New York, about a hundred miles north of Manhattan. Like most Delta Force members, these soldiers were constantly on the go, always drilling in different "theaters" so that no situation would be unrehearsed once they were confronted with it.

The squad was directed to slip into the sleepy town of Monterey in the Berkshire mountains, where Perry believed Grizzwald and McClarty were hiding. If the timeline played out on schedule, the surgical strike would take less than three hours. Six hours after that they'd be on a C-130 to Saudi Arabia for a three-month training mission. And no one would ever have a clue that Grizzwald or McClarty or Jessica Baldwin had ever set foot in western Massachusetts. No one, perhaps, other than Sarah Peterson; but General Perry would see to it that she would soon be dead, too.

The four young men were dressed in business suits when they piled into the black Ford Taurus. Exactly three miles from their destination they would don beige, green, and black fatigues. The black nylon bags each lugged were loaded with eighty pounds of guns, ammunition, and eaves-dropping devices. To General Perry, the most important tool each carried was the eight-ounce perforated silencer that corkscrewed onto the nose of each of their automatic weapons.

In the brief call to his men, General Perry divulged just enough disinfor-mation to further motivate his soldiers. According to the general, the two men and one woman who had secluded themselves in an abandoned farm-house were detestable terrorists who had committed a string of atrocities against U.S. interests, from train derailments in the Midwest to bombing at-tempts at JFK. These bloodthirsty radicals were a menace to the public. Additional innocent American lives would be lost unless they were eliminated without a trace.

Within ten minutes, the four soldiers were winding their way up Route 9, along the eastern bank of the Hudson River. The trip was similar to another mission they had secretly executed under General Perry's orders in 1994, when three Lebanese terrorists vanished from Geneva, Switzerland. Word of that mission never became public, and the Continental Airlines 767 that had been the terrorists' target landed at Newark Airport without disruption. It had been a glorious day for General Perry and the Delta Force, even if the need for absolute secrecy demanded that no one would ever congratulate them for their heroic work.

It took less than an hour for the covert squad to drive their way through the hills of Columbia County. They cut east on Route 23, toward the Massachusetts border, and traffic picked up considerably until they drove through the small town of Great Barrington.

Once they were in Monterey they had turned left onto Blue Hill Road. After two miles the pavement had turned to gravel. A mile after that it was dirt. Overgrown trees from Beartown State Forest stretched as far as the eye could see. No house could be seen from the deserted road on which they were now parked, but an unkempt narrow clearing in the trees indicated something was back there. Captain Phillips, the team's thirty-four-year-old commander, and his three colleagues pushed their car into a dense thicket of wild rose bushes, and maneuvered it so that it faced the road in case a rapid escape was necessary. All four of the soldiers had put on sheer, black leather gloves, and smeared their faces with charcoal.

"Johnson and Abbott, go have a look," Captain Phillips whispered to his two crew-cut subordinates. He and Lieutenant Spangler remained crouched in the tangled bramble, making sure no one had come up from behind.

The two corporals hunched down low as they wove their way between the trees toward what appeared to be an abandoned house. They walked even more slowly, aware that in this rural setting, the gentle breeze carried the noise of cracking twigs for hundreds of yards.

When Corporal Johnson reached the ragged clearing surrounding the shabby farmhouse, he signaled Abbott to remain in the woods. Johnson crept belly to earth until he was adjacent to the one side of the stone structure that had no windows. A wisp of smoke trickled from the top of the stone chimney, confirming the smell they had noticed from the road. Now there was no doubt someone was inside.

Johnson tiptoed around the rear of the one-story structure and squatted beneath a single-hung window. He slowly unzipped his nylon bag and removed a sensitive eavesdropping device that was used with a pair of lightweight headphones. He put the foam rubber over his ears, pressed the Teflon sensor against the peeling paint of the window frame, then activated the machine. Johnson cocked his head sideways, listening as intently as a doctor using his stethoscope. He nodded to Corporal Abbott, who had circled around the clearing to cover his buddy's flank.

Johnson hurried away from the house, mindful not to make any noise. When he reached Abbott's position he pointed to the hand-forged weathervane that was bolted to the peak of the slanted shingled roof. Both nodded when they recognized the wrought iron fox chasing the rabbit. It was the very one General Perry had meticulously described a few hours earlier.

"There are voices coming from the back bedroom, sir," Corporal Johnson whispered to his commanding officer once he and Abbott had returned to the hidden Taurus. "Those bastards are inside."

"Are there three?"

"Impossible to tell, sir, but it sounded like at least one male and one female."

Captain Phillips nodded. "Good. It's show time. Let's make this short and sweet with no mistakes. Let's get in and out with only *our* weapons being discharged, is that clear? We've got an anxious general in Washington waiting for my call."

The four soldiers slowly approached the house. Two stayed on each side of the dirt pathway that led from the main road to the old structure. With their silencer-equipped assault rifles pointed forward, they made it to the clearing without arousing suspicion.

Captain Phillips surveyed the situation, motioning for his men to fan out around both sides of the house. Thirty yards separated the stone structure from the circle of trees around it, and the team leader wanted his charges to remain fixed in the woods until all were prepared to advance at once. When Corporal Johnson was finally in position, the captain removed his black glove so that each soldier could spot the white flesh of his right palm. He counted down by lowering each finger.

First five, then four, then three, then two, then just one. Show time.

27

SARAH sat at her desk and savored her first cup of hot Starbucks, mentally preparing herself for the struggle she knew lay ahead. The time had come to learn as much as she could about the woman who had gotten kidnapped. After that she would do her best to determine where that woman was being held before she bowed out and let the FBI move in quickly.

Jack Montgomery and Buck Perry were formidable men who had each steamrolled over countless adversaries as part of their alleged commitment to public service. Soon the world would see them the way Sarah now did: no longer pillars of success, but as deadly thugs. They might be caricatures of the towering public figures they had once been, but Sarah knew they were dangerous, particularly because they had so much to lose. *What the hell am I about to get myself into?* she wondered, but she knew she had no choice but to follow her instincts.

Sarah logged onto her computer, using the built-in modem of her Micron TransPort Xke to interface with the server in her old office. After entering a series of appropriate access codes, the first nonclassified file she tapped into was the Department of State Missing Persons Index. The MPI, as it was known, was a list of every U.S. citizen who had traveled abroad and had been reported as missing. The lengthy register was updated whenever a person was either added or subtracted from the list, but at a minimum it was revised three times daily. It generally swelled during the peak summer travel months when concerned parents had no idea of the whereabouts of their backpacking offspring. Nine times out of ten the missing person would surface with only a bruised ego, embarrassed their parents had caused a fuss because they hadn't phoned or written as often as they had promised.

Sarah typed in BALDWIN. The database gave Sarah one matching entry to her inquiry at the same moment the encrypted Tripwire alarm bounced off an orbiting NSA satellite and sped into Jack Montgomery's laptop. Sarah's initial enthusiasm at immediately identifying someone on the MPI with that surname was dampened as soon as she opened the file. As it turned out, one Leon Baldwin had gone trekking in Nepal in September 1989 and had never been seen or heard from again. After two months without familial contact, the State Department conducted a thorough investigation and concluded that Leon Baldwin had been killed while attempting to scale Mt. Everest. His bereaved family continued to cling to the notion that their thirty-year-old son had been seized by Muslim fanatics for political reasons, although the asterisk beside Leon Baldwin's name indicated to Sarah that the State Department considered the matter closed.

Sarah carefully reviewed the early-morning cables that had been received from Paris even though she knew her next attempt was going to be futile. These cables contained information that would eventually be added to the MPI, but which had not yet been manually entered into the system. Eight reports had come in from the French capital, none of which concerned a Baldwin. No one with that surname, other than the unfortunate Leon, was known by the State Department to be missing.

Undeterred, Sarah logged into the FBI's own missing persons files. Because one of the State Department's main responsibilities was to secure the borders of the United States from unauthorized ingress and egress, it worked closely with federal, state, and local law enforcement agencies to keep track of individuals who were unaccounted for. Although most of the people who appeared on this list were young children whose faces would eventually find their way onto the back of a milk carton, all reported adult disappearances were included as well. Of the twenty-five people named Baldwin on the list, none had been reported missing within the last year.

Sarah stared blankly at her computer screen, her chin resting in the palms of her hands. It was inconceivable to her that some law enforcement authority somewhere in the world had not yet been informed of Ms. Baldwin's kidnapping, if in fact a kidnapping had taken place. She began pacing the blond hardwood floor of her second-story makeshift office in frustration. Each time she approached the room's threshold she would turn on her heels with military precision and head back toward her desk. Instead of focusing on her blank computer terminal, she would steal a glance past her desk and through the three-sided bay window looking out on a dormant cherry blossom tree. In early April the tree would burgeon into shades of brilliant pink, but right now the branches, like her thoughts, were barren.

For fifteen minutes she traced, then retraced her steps. Then an idea popped into her mind. She quickly straddled her swivel desk chair and glided smoothly up to her computer.

ALL FLIGHTS, she typed, U.S. TO PARIS.

The computer blinked a few times before spitting out a list of eleven airlines and 104 flights. She typed in the dates of the last three days, which caused the list to narrow marginally. Only two of the eleven airlines offering service between the United States and Paris did not do so every day.

PASSENGER QUERY, she typed and entered.

PASSENGER NAME? was the response.

SURNAME—BALDWIN, FIRST NAME—UNKNOWN.

In less than a second the computer sorted out the three matching names from the thirty-two thousand passengers who had been scheduled to fly from the continental United States to Paris within the last three days:

1. Jessica Baldwin, Air France Flight #007, JFK—Orly;
2. Roger Baldwin, TWA Flight #376, O'Hare—DeGaulle; and
3. Melissa Baldwin, United Airlines Flight #046, JFK—Orly.

Sarah allowed herself a slight smile. She scrawled the two women's names, ignoring Roger Baldwin for the moment. As she stared at the sheet of paper on which she had scribbled a few notes from Montgomery's meeting at the Pentagon, she circled the word *Hercules* over and over again. The wet ink from her fine-tipped Flair soaked through the single page, leaving green dots on her blotter.

"Of course!" Sarah said, now focusing on the name of the ship. But before examining that directory another avenue needed to be opened. She hurriedly thumbed through her Rolodex, stopping when she arrived at Henri LeClaire's index card, and punched in a number on her phone.

"Air France, Henri speaking. How may I help you?"

"Henri, it's Sarah Peterson. I need a favor," she said without any prelude.

"But of course, madame," replied LeClaire.

"And I hate to be a pain in the ass, Henri, but promise me you'll put everything else aside and act quickly. The clock's ticking on this one."

Sarah explained what she needed. But as she turned her focus to the vessel named *The Hercules*, she had no idea how truthful Tripwire and Jack Montgomery had made her last statement to Henri LeClaire.

28

BUCK PERRY pored over the top secret Delta Force files he had compiled on McClarty while Jack Montgomery examined those on Grizzwald. They were alone in the general's Pentagon corner office, trying to determine whether, in the clarity of hindsight, there had been any advance warning that their two henchmen would double-cross them to the tune of $50 million. So far there was nothing. Every report indicated that both soldiers were extremely loyal, and had obeyed authority on every prior occasion.

In retrospect, Montgomery understood that he had presented the opportunity of a lifetime to two proficient grunts who had never earned more than $57,000 in any year. The Secretary of State had virtually given them an invitation to stroll into Fort Knox and wheel out a truckload of gold bullion. If nothing else, Montgomery thought he had learned a valuable lesson for his next operation.

The two power brokers quietly studied the documents before them, awaiting word from the general's tactical squad, when there was a tentative knock at the locked door. Both men ignored it. To them, there was nothing more pressing than what they were doing. The second knock was louder and was accompanied by a woman's muffled utterance.

"General Perry?"

The voice was unfamiliar, but the accent sounded like it could have come from one of the general's old Georgian neighbors. If not for the southern inflection, he would have continued with what he was doing.

"May I help you?" he asked loudly, still at his desk.

"I need to talk to you, General. It's important."

Perry pushed his chair away from his desk with an it's-going-to-be-one-of-those-days thrust. He spread the early morning edition of *The Washington Post* across his desk to obscure the files.

"What is it?" he asked gruffly when he opened the door.

"Sorry to disturb you, General." Her rounded shoulders shrugged, her soft expression turned to one of embarrassment.

"Do I know you, ma'am?"

"Dottie Mansfield. I'm one of the building's maintenance supervisors. We've met a few times at staff meetings, but I'm not sure you'd remember me."

Buck shrugged. He attended so many meetings that they all blended into one another.

"I called you earlier and left a message with your secretary."

Suddenly it dawned on Perry that he had crumpled the pink slip with her name on it into a little ball. He removed the cigar from his mouth and held it way down behind his thigh.

"Sorry about the stogie, but I just don't have the time to step outside every time I wanna smoke. And I don't need someone bustin' my balls about it either. So if you're here to give me a hard time, then you can just turn your pretty little self around and take it up with General Higgins."

Miss Mansfield looked completely befuddled.

"General, I have no idea what the heck you're talking about. If you want to smoke in your office with your door closed, that's your own business."

"That isn't why you called this morning?"

"No, sir."

Buck shrugged. "Well, make it snappy, 'cause I've got someone in here with me."

Dottie peeked through the crack in the door, immediately recognizing Jack Montgomery. The cabinet member's distinctive white hair made him easy to identify even from behind.

"Actually," she said, "this is about someone on the Secretary's staff."

Buck Perry opened the door wider, inviting the perky blond inside. She accepted the gesture and walked toward one of the wing chairs facing the general's desk. Instead of sitting, she leaned her right hand against the curved upholstered top of the chair. Perry followed her in and took up a position just a few feet from her. Montgomery remained seated, although Dottie's statement had aroused his curiosity.

"Maybe I'm being paranoid," she said, "but something very strange happened late last night that I wanted you to know about. I would've gone to my supervisor, but he's out of town until next week."

The two men stared at her. Dottie Mansfield transferred her weight uncomfortably from one leg to another. From her awkward body language, it was apparent she now wished she had minded her own business.

"You know what," she said as she took a baby step toward the exit, "why don't we just forget I even came in here?"

"Don't be silly," the general said. He dropped his large arm like a boom, blocking her path.

Dottie fidgeted for a moment, shifting her eyes between the two men. There was no doubt she had captured their undivided attention.

"Well, a young lady from the Secretary's staff came by my office last night to tell me that she'd left some very important papers in one of the situation rooms down on Level J. She said something about a meeting between you and the Secretary. After I checked her security clearance I took her downstairs. And sure enough she said she found what she was looking for."

"So?"

"Well, the strange thing was that she picked up a plain old legal pad that didn't have *any* writing on it. I mean, there was *nothing* on there at all. The whole thing seemed fishy to me, so I asked one of the security guards to keep an eye out for her when she left the building. He watched her get into her car and park at the far end of the lot. When he approached her window she had some sort of tape recorder on her lap."

"What was her name?"

"Sarah Peterson."

A jolt of rage shot through Buck Perry's nervous system. It was the same primal impulse he had felt when he had learned of Bill O'Grady's apparent computer snooping. But with Dottie Mansfield eyeballing both of them for any reaction, Perry and Montgomery remained outwardly unfazed.

"I'm sure there's a simple explanation," the general said calmly. "And we'll take care of it."

Dottie Mansfield smiled pleasantly as she began her retreat towards the door. "Well, that's it. Like I said, maybe it's nothing. Have a good day, gentlemen."

Buck watched the maintenance supervisor walk through the set of glass doors that separated his secretary's desk from the corridor. Dottie looked back and waved. The general smiled politely, returning the gesture. Once he was back behind his desk he looked at Montgomery.

"Unbelievable."

"Actually, Buck, it's quite believable. Like father like daughter." He quickly opened his laptop and accessed his e-mail. There, on the top line, was a Tripwire message that had been delivered only four minutes earlier. Suddenly it all made sense to him. The second message from O'Grady's office, Sarah's absence from the State dinner at the White House, and her repeated FOIMS searches of Witherspoon and Gallagher's FBI files.

"She was just searching the State Department Missing Persons Index," Montgomery said while he shook his head. "Last name: Baldwin, First name: Unknown."

"Jesus fucking Christ, Jack. How come you didn't have someone tailing her after what she was up to yesterday? She should never have gotten this far."

"Don't second-guess me on this one, Buck," Montgomery snapped. "I made a decision based on what I knew at the time. Obviously, now a more aggressive approach is required."

"I presume you'd like me to handle this immediately?"

Montgomery nodded.

"You have her home phone number?"

Montgomery snapped open his briefcase and leafed through his address book.

"Yes." He placed the page with Sarah's phone number on Buck's desk.

"Set up a meeting at my house," the general directed. "I'll overpower her before she knows what hit her."

Sarah's phone rang twice before her answering machine picked up. Montgomery glanced at his watch as he listened to the recording. Convinced she was within earshot of her machine and was screening her calls, he said: "Peterson, this is Secretary Montgomery. I'm in General Perry's office over at the Pentagon and need to discuss an upcoming assignment. So call me at once so we can arrange a convenient time to meet. Thank you."

"Does she carry a beeper?" General Perry asked.

"Yes. I'll try that in a few minutes if we don't hear from her. If she doesn't respond to either call, then I'll try something that's a little more persuasive."

The general nodded, then unlocked the center drawer of his desk. He removed his 9 mm SIG-Sauers and inserted a thirteen-shot, staggered-column clip into the handle.

"Nosy bitch," he said as he locked the revolver inside his briefcase.

29

SARAH was anxious for her package from Henri LeClaire to arrive and she used the time to do some additional electronic tinkering. LeClaire had assured her that the items she had requested were going to be personally delivered by his most reliable Air France ticket agent on the next available flight between JFK and National Airport. She would have her parcel in the next couple of hours as long as traffic wasn't too heavy on the Beltway.

Sarah heard the answering machine click on in her living room, but ignored it. The beeper attached to her belt vibrated five minutes later. She ignored that, too, because she didn't recognize the phone number on the tiny display screen. Using her modem to link her home terminal into the State

Department LAN, Sarah dialed into the files the State Department shared with the U.S. Coast Guard. Because each agency was charged, at least in part, with the prevention of illegal entry of both unwanted persons and contraband, a joint database had been authorized by Jack Montgomery shortly after he became Secretary of State.

QUERY: ALL VESSELS, she typed.

COUNTRY OF ORIGIN?

UNKNOWN.

VESSEL NAME?

She glanced down at her notes of the conversation that had taken place at the Pentagon.

HERCULES OR THE HERCULES.

26 MATCHES FOUND.

"Shit," Sarah said in disgust.

DISPLAY LIST, she commanded.

Her light blue screen instantly became a blur of white letters.

She opened each of the files one by one, carefully skimming the profile of each vessel. The data she examined was a compilation of register information similar to that used by each state's motor vehicles department. She quickly eliminated many of the vessels from consideration because they were relatively small leisure crafts docked in private boat clubs around the United States. After an hour of probing, she concluded that only three were seaworthy international freighters with the ability to transport the types of heavy weapons Tom Witherspoon had described.

Sarah immediately dismissed the Hong Kong–based *Hercules* as a possibility. The records Sarah retrieved indicated the vessel had never been further west than Singapore. As for the other two, Sarah decided either could have been the correct ship. Both were over two hundred feet long and contained substantial cargo holds below their main deck. The Greek-registered freighter sailed extensively in the Mediterranean and the Adriatic, but also made its way around the Indian Ocean. The same was true of the Liberian-based ship, though its captain seemed to prefer hauling merchandise in the North Sea.

Sarah reached into the coin-filled Mason jar she and her mom had once used to hold raspberry preserves. As she did so, she realized that she needed to call her mother to try to persuade her to come east. Walter Jensen had supposedly lined up a top-notch oncologist at Johns Hopkins who was interested in taking over her care. She hadn't yet had time to speak with him either.

"Heads Greece, tails Liberia," she said. She cocked her thumb and flipped a quarter in the air. It landed in her left palm. She slapped it down onto the back of her right hand.

"Greece it is," Sarah declared when she saw the left-sided profile of George Washington.

She spent the next hour reviewing the files on the twenty-year-old boat whose home port was in Athens. Every captain, every major shareholder, and every corporation that had ever owned even a minority stake in the vessel was examined. There was nothing that suggested a connection to the mystery at hand. She cursed in frustration at the valuable time she had wasted.

Sarah repeated the tedious exercise for the Liberian-based vessel. It was currently piloted by an Irishman named Captain Seamus Dunn. After thirty minutes of tunneling she smiled in triumph. The file indicated that this *Hercules* was owned by World Sailing Inc., a Liberian subsidiary of Universal Delivery Services. UDS, a Bermuda shell corporation, was an affiliate of Global Cargo Corp. In turn, GCC, another shell corporation, was a wholly owned subsidiary of the megacorporation Baldwin Enterprises; its majority shareholder being one Sam Baldwin. Although Sarah was certain *The Hercules* was a pimple on the back of the Baldwin Enterprises corporate juggernaut, it had given her a handhold in what she now knew was the most important investigation of her career. She diagrammed the various companies by joining little green lines with arrows, eventually circling the billionaire's name at the top of the pyramid.

"It's almost noon, Sam Baldwin," she said as she looked at her Seiko desk clock. "Do you know where your daughter is?"

30

"SHE'S definitely home," Montgomery said to General Perry. "How do you know? She didn't call you back or answer our page."

The Secretary of State angled his laptop so the general could see the screen for himself.

"Six minutes ago she queried a coast guard vessel file. Her key words this time were 'Hercules or the Hercules.' She's getting closer by the minute."

"We can't allow her to keep going, Jack. She'll ruin us."

"I agree. But I've got a plan that will finish her off."

31

CAPTAIN PHILLIPS and his men moved silently from the safety of the woods to the jagged stone walls of the farmhouse. Their rapid advance demonstrated a precision made possible only through endless drill after drill. Outside, no car had passed their position for more than an hour. It was perfectly quiet for a mile on all sides of the old house, except for the muffled sound of voices inside. As long as all went according to plan, the three traitors inside would die before they knew what was happening.

Noiselessly, Captain Phillips slid sideways with his back against the house until he reached the front door, while Corporal Johnson checked the back. Each had a teammate squatting beside them with a silencer-equipped assault rifle aimed at the door. A gentle squeeze of either trigger would riddle anything that moved with more than thirty rounds per second.

The back door opened first; Johnson and Abbott tiptoed inside. The front door opened an instant later, and Captain Phillips and his escort entered. They converged in a small center hallway that led into a slightly larger living room. The common area contained two rickety wooden chairs and a pathetic excuse for a table. A few feet away, dying embers smoldered in the fireplace, but the sweet smell of marijuana overpowered the scent of burning wood.

The commanding officer quickly surveyed the interior. The one-story gingerbread structure appeared to contain a tiny kitchen and two other small rooms. He surmised from the layout both were probably bedrooms. The dark floors were solid stone, which made him pleased: there were no creaky floorboards to signal their attack.

With a flick of his index finger, Captain Phillips directed Johnson and Abbott to stand just beyond the back bedroom. Once they were in place, he and his partner positioned themselves outside the closed door of the first bedroom.

The three men nodded to their commanding officer.

Captain Phillips once again counted down with his fingers, this time from three.

BOOM!

The flimsy wooden doors flew off their hinges as the four commandos stormed into each room, their lethal Beretta PM 125 submachine guns leading the way.

"Hold your fire!" Captain Phillips shouted as soon as he saw what was inside the first bedroom. The barrel of his assault rifle was leveled just inches away from the two people in the room.

"Corporal?" Phillips yelled. "Anyone there?"

"All clear!" came the reply. "No one in here!"

Captain Phillips kept his weapon fixed on his two targets.

"Where are they?" he demanded loudly. A forceful push of his silencer against one of their temples emphasized his intent.

The young Japanese couple raised their hands in submission, but said nothing. A soot-stained crack pipe and several empty vials lay at their feet. Their unfocused eyes were wide with a mix of terror and confusion.

Captain Phillips's partner searched under the cot.

"Nothing under here, Captain."

"Cover me," Phillips said as he bent down. He quickly lifted their dusty sleeping bag off the floor. There was nothing underneath. He noticed the two backpacks leaning against the far wall. On both was the plain red dot of the Japanese flag and several Grateful Dead buttons.

"Fuck!" Phillips said. "Do you speak English?" he asked the man in the bed. His gun was relaxed toward the floor.

"Little," said the young man. He appeared to be about eighteen.

"What are you doing here?"

The reed-thin woman with the straight black hair reached to her left and grabbed a large map of Massachusetts. She traced the length of the Appalachian Trail with her index finger. The trail cut through the woods less than a quarter mile from this abandoned farmhouse.

"We outside for a month," she said. "We just want one day inside. We very sorry."

Captain Phillips looked at his three colleagues. All had assembled in the same room, though Corporal Johnson kept his weapon focused on the door. "Let's get out of here," he ordered.

"What do we do with them?" Corporal Abbott asked.

"Nothing," the team leader said. "With the drugs they're carrying, they're not telling anyone about this."

The four men disappeared. The failed mission had bought Sarah more time to find the billionaire's daughter; but it also bought more time for Jack Montgomery to find her.

32

THE rumble in Sarah's stomach made her realize just how quickly the afternoon had crept by. She had immersed herself in the FBI's extensive file on Sam Baldwin. She was generally familiar with some of his many accomplishments, but was astonished that a person could be worth $8 billion, and have his hand in so many worthy endeavors, and still remain essentially anonymous. As for the FBI file itself, Sarah found its contents both fascinating and astounding: fascinating that if Jessica had been kidnapped as planned, Jack Montgomery had chosen to take on such an imposing adversary, an individual who had accumulated so prodigious a fortune from such impoverished roots; and astounding that FBI agents had actually been paid with taxpayers' funds to delve so deeply into Sam Baldwin's personal life in order to harvest this material. That old power monger, J. Edgar, was smiling in his grave, Sarah thought.

She glanced at the clock when she finished reviewing the file and realized she had completely lost track of time. It had been nearly two hours since she had called Bob Wakefield on his cell phone to tell him she would be out for the remainder of the day, and maybe longer. Now Henri LeClaire's courier was late and no one had called with an explanation. She flipped on the radio to catch the latest transit and traffic report, then grabbed the box of sourdough pretzels she always kept in her bottom drawer. They would hold her over for a while. Before she disturbed LeClaire, who had already gone out of his way to accommodate her spontaneous request, Sarah wanted to know if traffic had snarled LeClaire's courier.

The lead story concerned two Israeli F-16s. The supersonic fighters had breached Saudi Arabian airspace just after 7 P.M. Israeli time. In a hastily arranged press conference, Tel Aviv was claiming the incident to be an unfortunate mistake, that faulty radar had caused the jets to stray five hundred miles toward Riyadh. An Israeli general with a chestful of medals used a series of maps to explain that at the speed of Mach 2, it had only taken a few minutes for his warplanes to drift that far off course. Then he acknowledged receiving the Saudis' official protest, but downplayed King Fahd's warning that next time his F-16s would be shot down.

"Let him try," the general said with a confident smile as he bid adieu to the assembled journalists. What he did not say was that within the last twenty-four hours, Israeli production of gas masks had quietly been cranked up to Gulf War levels. Soon every Israeli citizen would have one.

Sarah took a moment to consider the story, convinced no mistake had been made. Given what she had read in the top secret NSA database, she was certain the Israelis were sending the Arab world a very strong message. The Israelis, she knew, understood more than anyone in the region that a few strategically delivered chemical warheads could alter the tenuous balance of power in a heartbeat. With tensions running so high, the bombing of *any* population center would be the spark that lit the powder keg. If hostilities boiled over, Israeli fighter jets could scramble to any point in the Middle East in less than twenty minutes, and with a payload of nuclear weapons always at the ready, the Jewish state was obviously announcing to its neighbors that they were prepared to turn whatever country was harboring the bombs on board *The Hercules* into a huge parking lot if those missiles led to an attack that affected the sovereignty of Israeli soil.

The next news story affected her like a bucket of ice poured down her back. It concerned the mysterious disappearance of FBI Special Agent William O'Grady. His government-issue Ford had been found at the bottom of a shallow creek near his suburban Maryland home, although there was no sign of the thirty-four-year-old man. Police divers were busy dredging through the muck looking for answers. More details would follow as soon as they became available.

The connection clicked. O'Grady's computer had no doubt played a part in his demise. Then she saw her own reflection framed in the seventeen-inch illuminated computer screen on her desk, and a chill shot up her spine.

Sarah hurriedly began to log off, but was interrupted by a sharp knock on her front door. The sudden noise made her flinch. Escape through the back door or see who was out front?

Sarah put on her navy blazer and unharnessed her service revolver from her shoulder strap. She had never backed down from a good fight when there was valuable information at stake. She moved toward the hallway steps with her Smith & Wesson .357 Magnum cocked and ready.

33

WITHIN minutes of making his call to Sarah's brownstone, Jack Montgomery knew he had blundered. It was Forensics 101: the tape would be the first piece of evidence the men wearing surgical gloves would stuff into their Hefty bags when they went looking for suspects in her homicide. The Secretary had carelessly created another footprint that now needed to be erased and when Tripwire showed Sarah had accessed the FBI file on Sam Baldwin, his sense of urgency accelerated.

Montgomery quickly made two phone calls. The first was to a man who had devised a method to secretly infiltrate the computer systems of the four major U.S. credit card companies; he could determine the precise whereabouts of a target, so long as that target had recently made a purchase with plastic. Montgomery directed this operative to monitor all of Sarah Peterson's credit card uses until further notice.

Montgomery's second call was to Mr. Green, who in anticipation of receiving the Secretary's call had already assembled the Kahles Helios ZF69 optical sight that attached to his Mauser SG66 sniper rifle.

The Secretary of State issued a simple four-word directive that had no possibility of being misconstrued: "Eliminate Sarah Peterson immediately." Articulating few details other than the utmost secrecy of this task, he ordered the tape inside Sarah's answering machine to be hand-delivered to him, so he could dispose of it as he saw fit.

34

MR. GREEN knelt on the backseat of a stolen black Ford Explorer, as still as a deer listening for danger. Each of the windows was deeply opaque, tinted ostensibly to mute the sun's glare. A collapsible cardboard shield was expanded across the front windshield.

Montgomery's operative was waiting for Sarah to emerge from her residence, carefully evaluating everyone who walked by. Although the darkened glass made the car a virtual one-way mirror, he still needed to know if anyone appeared to take notice of the Explorer. No one seemed to.

Mr. Green had arrived at Sarah's brownstone within six minutes of hanging up with the Secretary of State. The Explorer sat directly across the street from her front door, less than fifty paces by foot, but the assassin had no intention of stepping onto Thirtieth Street where he might be remembered by a passerby. His job for Jack Montgomery would be carried out from the safety of this vehicle, just as it had been done a half dozen times before.

The back window was open just enough to allow the inch-wide snout to poke out when it was time. It would take less than two seconds to spot his target in the telescopic lens, another three to fire. The 9 mm slug would leave his weapon with nothing more than a gentle swoosh. Then he would be gone before anyone was aware that a shot had been fired on this quiet Georgetown street.

35

SARAH pulled aside one of the drapes that framed the bay window of her home office. From here she could see the bottom few brick steps leading to her front door, though the top three, as well as the platform with the bristly welcome mat, were blocked from this angle. As for the street itself, nothing looked peculiar: Mr. DelVecchio's schnauzer two doors down was barking as usual, a white BMW was backing into a prized parking spot just in front of her building, and a taxi had pulled up beside a fire hydrant thirty yards away. By all accounts it was a normal Wednesday afternoon in Georgetown.

She began to cautiously descend the old wooden steps that led to her front door. The sheer white curtains covering the glass allowed her to see that Ernie the dry cleaning guy had squeezed two weeks' worth of clean blouses on wire hangers onto her front door knob. But the curtain obscured her view of who was there. Sarah hesitated, checking the handheld Dictaphone in her coat pocket to make sure it was on. A similar tape had been discovered at the scene of a homicide in February 1996, when a Jersey City woman had been composed enough during her rape and murder to activate a small recording device in her pocket. She had even prompted her assailant to say his name immediately before he completed his crime. The murderer had been arrested within days.

When Sarah was four steps from her front door the silhouette of a woman with a package in her hands began to materialize. Cautiously, Sarah moved forward. When she was at the bottom landing she moved the curtain aside a few inches, her Magnum out of its harness. The young blond woman appeared no older than twenty. She was wearing a tailored navy blue uniform and a starched white shirt. On her lapel was a pair of gold aviator's wings. Sarah turned the knob and stood in the open doorway.

"I'm so sorry I'm late," the Air France employee said apologetically. "The fog at Kennedy this morning was terrible. We sat on the runway for over an hour."

"No problem. I'm just glad you're here."

ACROSS the street, Mr. Green's heart accelerated when the woman in the blue airline uniform ascended Sarah's steps. In a moment he would have a clear shot at his target, and he found that terribly exciting. It always was. He raised his perfectly weighted rifle to shoulder level, then slid the very tip of the barrel through the small crack at the top of the car's window.

Mr. Green focused on the center of the doorway and sighted through his scope. When Sarah's door opened, she was in the center of his crosshairs.

36

"HELLO!" Jessica cried out.

The door to the adjoining room was ajar just a crack, although she couldn't see from her prone position whether Grizzwald or McClarty was beyond it. If so, neither had made any noise in what she estimated had been the past thirty minutes. Jessica remained confined to this one spot, told she would be severely punished if she strayed even a few feet from it.

"Yes?" Grizzwald answered from the doorway.

"The pain is getting worse. I need you to call a doctor."

"That's impossible."

"Please! I'm afraid my baby's dying!"

Jessica had occupied most of her time in captivity by either trying to sleep or counting the striations in the wooden planks of the ceiling. She fought to keep calm, but each time one of her abductors simply entered her room, fear and apprehension battled for space inside her brain. So far, fear had won every time. The memory of Grizzwald manhandling her in the car was one she couldn't purge from her mind. Jessica was sure that the vicious slap that had loosened her teeth was just the beginning of what was in store for her. No one had ever hit her as hard.

When the cramping started, Jessica's worst fears multiplied. She tried to convince herself that the pain in her belly was nerves. But in her heart she knew that wasn't the case.

"You can see a doctor when you get out of here," Grizzwald said coldly. "But if your kid dies before then, it won't be my fault. The people on your end are dragging their feet."

Jessica restrained herself from protesting. Another smack across the face would only worsen the situation.

"May I use the bathroom, please?" she asked. "Maybe that'll help."

Grizzwald loosened her restraints and Jessica stood. She took a tentative first step before she became lightheaded and had to reach for Grizzwald's right arm to steady herself. As her fingers curled around his huge bicep she felt as though she had grabbed hold of a brick.

Grizzwald supported her through the door and to the winding staircase just down the hallway.

"I'm OK," she said as she gripped the worn handrail.

She slowly climbed the steps, followed by her captor. When she was halfway up the stairs she looked to her right, enabling her to peer through a cracked, web-covered window. There, about a hundred feet beyond the filthy glass, was the craggy neck of an old fieldstone lighthouse. In the distance she could hear the faint sound of sea gulls honking. Down below she could make out the spray of seawater crashing against a black stone jetty.

When Jessica reached the landing at the top of the stairs, she glanced back down through the hallway window, praying her mind had not played tricks on her. The odd configuration of the lighthouse's foundation was unique and had been among the many places of interest her father had pointed out to her when they sailed on his forty-foot yawl in this part of the Long Island Sound when she was a teenager. But now that she knew where she was, she had no idea how she would extricate herself from this remote location.

"Move!" Grizzwald spat and pushed her forward toward the dank and smelly bathroom.

37

SARAH reached for the shoe box–sized package that was wrapped in brown paper.

"Thank Henri for me, will you?"

"Of course." The young woman paused. "Is that it?"

"That's it."

"There's nothing you want me to bring back to Henri for you?"

"Just my thanks."

"OK. Au revoir."

"Au revoir."

Sarah lifted her load of dry cleaning and watched the young woman scoot down her steps.

MR. GREEN remained steady, staring at the spot on Sarah Peterson's blouse that covered her sternum. His powerful Kahles Helios telescopic lens magnified the image thirtyfold. A simple squeeze of his index finger and Sarah would be dead before she hit the ground.

But unfortunately the young blonde would see too much; she would also have to die.

Mr. Green's finger began to tighten on the trigger when something held him back. Then it registered; it was the taxicab three cars away, the driver waiting for Henri LeClaire's courier to return to the car. Three victims would invite too much publicity. If the taxi had a two-way radio, the police would be on their way within seconds.

Mr. Green lowered his rifle. There was no need for things to get messy. Besides, he was in no hurry. He knew eventually he'd have a clear shot at Sarah Peterson, with no one else around and no one watching.

38

SARAH ran upstairs as the Air France employee entered her awaiting taxi. She had intended to leave her brownstone in the next few hours to do some on-site digging, but the news report concerning O'Grady condensed that timeline considerably. She tossed two days' worth of clothes into an overnight bag, then picked up the phone. One last call before she headed out the front door.

"Good afternoon, Baldwin Enterprises. How may I direct your call?"

"Sam Baldwin, please."

"Thank you. I'll connect you to his secretary."

A moment later the phone rang once. "Mr. Baldwin's office?"

"Is he there, please?"

"I'm afraid he's unavailable. Who's calling?"

Sarah put down the phone without leaving a message. As much as she wanted to force the issue immediately, she knew it would simply be a matter of time before one of the world's wealthiest men would drop whatever he was doing to talk with her.

39

HANK SAVAGE entered Sam Baldwin's den quietly, doing his best not to startle his boss: the man's nerves were already frayed like the torn end of a nylon cord. He had convinced Baldwin to return briefly to his Trump Tower apartment, which was just across the street from the Baldwin Building.

Baldwin had spoken with his wife, complaining of a rail-splitter of a migraine. That gave him an excuse to retire to the sanctuary of the downstairs den of the sprawling triplex. As much as he longed to commiserate with the woman with whom he had spent the last twenty-nine years, and to hold her tightly, he hadn't yet mustered the courage to tell her about Jessica, nor how he had decided to handle the problem.

"Sam," Savage said softly as he entered the dimly lit room. He was still wearing his suit and tie, still looking like he had just stepped out of a Sunday *Times* Armani ad in spite of thirty hours without sleep.

Sam Baldwin was slumped into an oversized leather club chair that he had brought back from les Puces, the huge flea market at St. Oeun, just outside Paris. It pained him to remember that he had asked Jessica to scout for a matching chair during her visit.

Sam pointed the remote control at the projection screen television, flipping between news broadcasts. With the caller's warning about secrecy still ringing in his head, he was praying that no aggressive journalist had somehow caught wind of what would surely be the blockbuster news story of the year.

"Come on in and close the door," Baldwin told Savage.

"Anything going on here?"

Baldwin raised himself in the chair, careful not to spill the tumbler of Stoli he was holding down near his hip.

"Doug called again. He's ready to call either the FBI or the State Department."

"Did you tell him he shouldn't?"

"Yeah. I told him not to worry, and that I'd heard from Jessie this morning. But I think we should send the Cessna down for him right now, before he gets suspicious and goes to the authorities. We need to break this to him in person."

Savage nodded. "I'll speak with Billy and send him down to South Carolina immediately. They should be back here by midnight."

"Did you call Istanbul yet?" Baldwin asked.

"Yes. I took a room over at the Plaza to make sure my outgoing calls couldn't be monitored. I spoke to Hobson at our facility in Ankara and instructed him to travel to Uskudar tonight to personally give our message to Patel. He was specifically told not to use the phone, since we've got to assume they may be listening to Patel's line."

"And?"

"And Patel was instructed to continue delivery of the shipment even if he was told by phone to do otherwise. He also was given a series of passwords that'll enable us to reverse that course if we have to. Sam, I know how you feel about those weapons, but we need to be flexible."

"We'll see. In the meantime, I want them assembled and ready to be fired."

Savage took a step closer and lowered his voice. "I've lined up several top-flight men if we need to use force at any time. I've also arranged to have a private jet at our disposal in case they need to be flown to a remote location."

"Excellent."

"Anything else?"

"No."

"All right. I'll see you back at the office whenever you're ready. But take your time. You look like you could use the rest."

40

WITH LeClaire's package cradled under one arm, and her compact valise in the other, Sarah hurried down the steps. As she reached for the doorknob she stopped dead in her tracks. Something wasn't quite right: *The black Explorer parked across the street.* Its front windshield was covered with a sun guard even though it was an overcast October day. Sarah peeked through one of the door's sheer curtains. The Explorer was still there. But one of the passenger windows was opened just a crack. *Danger.*

Sarah rushed upstairs and headed toward the rear of her brownstone. She bolted down the back steps two at a time. When she reached the bottom landing she carefully scanned the area surrounding her small vegetable garden. Nothing appeared unusual. There was no sign of an intruder. She yanked the back door open and ran through her neighbor's yard, then doubled back around the corner and jumped into her car.

Her heart pounded as her Jeep sped toward the Hoover Building. She constantly checked her rearview mirror for any sign of the Explorer, or for any other car that was suspicious. No one was following her. She took a deep breath and grabbed her car phone out of the cluttered glove compartment. It was time to contact Sam Baldwin.

41

HANK SAVAGE turned toward the door just as Francesca's voice came over the intercom from the kitchen, one flight up in the ten-thousand-square-foot penthouse.

"Honey, could you pick up line three, please? One of Jessie's old friends wants to talk to you."

Baldwin pressed the intercom button. "Could you get her number, dear? I'm here with Hank and can't really talk to anyone right now."

"Please, Sam. She's quite insistent. She said something about trying to get together with Jessie in Paris."

Baldwin quickly pressed the blinking white light. "Hello?"

"Hi, Mr. Baldwin, it's Holly Whitmore. Remember me? I went to high school with Jessie."

Baldwin snapped his fingers, stopping Savage in his tracks. There were only forty-two kids in Jessica's high school graduating class and the name Holly Whitmore did not even come close to ringing a bell. He pointed to the phone on the end table beside the couch. Savage delicately lifted the receiver.

"Sure, Holly," Baldwin said affably. "How are your folks?"

"They're fine. How about you and Mrs. Baldwin?"

"We're both doing just great, thanks." He paused, then asked, "So what's this about trying to get together with Jessie?"

"Well, I'm heading off to Paris tomorrow and Jessie and I talked about getting together for dinner. We've tried to meet in New York a couple of times, but it never seems to work out. I think we're each going to be free on Saturday night, but stupid me lost the name of the hotel where she's staying."

Savage looked quizzically at his employer. "Bullshit," Savage whispered as his hand covered the receiver.

"I hate to tell you, Holly, but I'm not really sure myself. Why don't you tell me where you'll be, and if I hear from her I'll give her your number. I'll probably speak with her in the next few days."

"Sure thing. They're trying to squeeze me in at the Intercontinental. If there's no room, then I'm not really sure where I'll be."

"Well, I hope you two connect."

"Thanks a lot, Mr. Baldwin. I hope we do, too."

Baldwin and Savage placed their phones down simultaneously.

"I think we just got our first break," Savage said excitedly as he rushed toward the door. "Let me see if Victor was able to trace the call."

HANK SAVAGE returned to the penthouse apartment, slightly winded from his mad dash to a phone booth on the corner. He was greeted by an anxious Baldwin.

"Well?" he said.

The two men knew this was their first real break.

"Holly Whitmore called from a cell phone that's registered to a private residence in Georgetown."

"What's 'Holly's' real name?"

Savage handed a small piece of scratch paper to his boss. "It's an unpublished listing, but of course Victor's got access to that information."

Baldwin's eyes widened with anticipation. Suddenly, finding Sarah Peterson was the second most important task in the world.

"Hank, I want you to go to Washington now and find this woman. Use one of the corporate jets. Once you find her I want you to squeeze every bit of information out of her, at gunpoint if you have to. If you think she was involved in Jessie's kidnapping, or that she'll go to the FBI when you release her, then you're to handle the situation as you see fit. Am I being clear?"

"Perfectly," Savage said. "And it'll be my pleasure," he added without a trace of a smile.

42

A s soon as Savage had left, Baldwin slowly climbed the spiral staircase that led to the middle floor of the triplex. He dreaded what he was about to do. Not only would his terrible news drive a stake through his wife's heart, but it also had the potential to imperil his daughter's life: Francesca wouldn't hesitate to follow her own course of action if she disagreed with the tack he was taking. Despite this, Sam knew he had to deliver the bad news to his soul mate. He had sworn that at the altar twenty-nine years ago, and had already kept this secret from her longer than his conscience would allow.

Francesca stood at the stove, her left hand covered by an asbestos mitt. Her right stirred a cauldron of her delicious homemade tomato sauce with a wooden spoon. A tortoiseshell barrette clipped back the wings of her shoulder-length brown hair, allowing Sam to see her face. His wife's smooth skin and bright green eyes still made men's heads turn, and the easy manner in which both she and Jessica carried themselves made it apparent that the apple hadn't fallen far from the tree.

Francesca smiled when she saw Sam in the doorway. Tied around her waist was a red and white checkered apron. Printed in large black letters were the words MY HUSBAND MAKES THE MONEY, BUT I'M THE BOSS! How true, he thought, as he lovingly stared at her.

"Hi, babe," Francesca said as she lowered the gas flame on one of the stove's eight burners. "Are you feeling any better?" She approached him and put her arm around his shoulder.

"No. My head's still pounding."

"Did you take something?"

Sam nodded.

"Should I call Dr. Reece?"

"No," he answered somberly. "I want you to sit down." He steered her toward their huge living room, stopping in front of the black Italian leather sectional. "I've got something very important to tell you."

"Is everything all right?" she asked, beginning to look alarmed.

"No. We've got a big problem."

Francesca reached for her husband's hand. "What's wrong?"

Sam bowed his head. "Jessie's been kidnapped. And she's two months pregnant."

"Oh no!" Francesca screamed as she crumpled into her husband's arms. "Oh God no!" She began to cry.

"How did this happen?" she asked with her face buried in Sam's chest. "Who's got my Jessie?"

"It's going to be OK," he said as he gently rubbed her back. "It's going to be OK."

For several minutes she wept in his arms. Eventually she pulled back from his comforting grip and blew her nose. Her eyes were puffy and bloodshot. Sam brushed aside the hair that was pasted in streaks against her face.

"Do the police have any idea who did this?" she asked between sobs, trying to regain composure.

"The police don't know she's been kidnapped."

An expression of incredulity replaced the one of anguish.

"What do you mean they don't know?"

"I haven't told anyone yet except Hank. Her kidnappers said they'd kill her if I went to the police. They said they'd kill her immediately if I even told you."

"When did this happen, Sam?"

"I got a call on Monday."

Francesca took a step back. "Monday?" she shouted. "This happened two days ago and you're telling me today? What the hell were you waiting for?"

Sam moved towards her. "I was trying to protect you, Fran. I thought I could make it go away before I told you it had happened."

"She's my daughter, for Christ's sake! How the hell could you keep this from me?"

Sam grabbed her hand. "Listen, Fran. Don't let them do this to us. Don't let them break us apart. We're on the same team and we need each other more than ever! So let's not fight about this. Please!"

Francesca nodded.

"I should've told you sooner. I'm so sorry, sweetie."

He wrapped his arms around her, weeping as he rested his head on the back of her neck. "What do they want from us?" Francesca asked.

"It's complicated. But they want fifty million dollars."

"Why is that complicated? And why don't we just give it to them?"

Sam closed his eyes, trying to decide the best way to explain. Francesca had no knowledge of the bombs on board *The Hercules*.

"It's complicated because of something very secret, and very important, that I'm planning to do."

Francesca pulled back again. "And what would that be?" she asked warily.

"I'm planning on killing Saddam Hussein."

Francesca put her hands over her swollen eyes and shook her head slowly.

"The President made some very special weapons available to me to make this happen, but I can't go into all this right now. He doesn't know about Jessie and he can't be told. In fact, no one can be told."

"I don't believe this!" she yelled. "I don't believe this!"

"Listen, Fran, it may not be as bad as you think. We got our first solid lead a few minutes ago. That woman who called a few minutes ago might be able to help us find Jessie."

"No, Sam! You know who's going to help us find Jessie? The FBI, that's who."

"You can't do that, Fran! They told me they'd kill her if anyone finds out, that they'd know if we went to the FBI."

Sam sat on the soft leather couch, pulling his wife onto it beside him. "Please, please, please let me and Hank try to get her back," he said as he put his hand on her knee. "I'm begging you to keep everyone else out of this for now. Have I ever failed you, Fran? Ever?"

Francesca shook her head no.

"And wouldn't you trust Hank with your own life?"

She nodded.

"We're putting together a plan, Fran, but it's going to take some time. You have to let us try."

"I don't know."

"Don't you think I'd call the President or the FBI if I thought that would work? Don't you think I'd do *anything* to get Jessie back?"

"Can't you just pay the ransom?"

"No. There's a lot more to this that I can't explain right now. I've got to get back to my office to meet with Hank. If you want to come with me you can."

Francesca shook her head. "No, not now. Maybe in a little while. But right now I want to be alone."

Sam stroked his wife's face gently with the palm of his hand. "I love you, Fran. I promise we'll get Jessie back." He kissed her cheek, then stood. "Please trust me."

Francesca nodded weakly. Her brain was spinning a million miles an hour, but through the confusion she began to chart a path to get her daughter back alive. And that path was very different from the one her husband was traveling.

43

HANK SAVAGE placed a call to Washington eight minutes after Sam Baldwin had ordered him to hunt, interrogate, and possibly kill Sarah Peterson; that was how long it took the ex-marine to sprint from the entrance of Trump Towers, across Fifth Avenue, and to the suite on the eighteenth floor in the Plaza for which Baldwin Enterprises was paying $625 a night simply to use the phone.

The man Savage chose to call was Tom Logan, a highly decorated former marine who had also become a trusted employee of Baldwin Enterprises. For payroll purposes Logan was officially listed as a military procurement consultant. In point of fact Logan spent most of his time lobbying Congressmen whose districts were directly affected by the company's fortunes. Like the few others whom Hank Savage had recruited to Baldwin Enterprises, Logan was bright, loyal, and persistent. And discreet.

Logan was at his Capitol Hill desk when he received the urgent request from his old friend. It took him less than fifteen minutes to drive to the Georgetown address Savage had provided.

Once he arrived at Thirtieth Street, he parked his car beside a yellow fire hydrant forty yards from the front steps of Sarah's two-story brownstone. Even if there had been a parking spot that afforded him a better view of her front door, Logan would have bypassed it. His assignment was to shadow any relatively young woman who exited the building. He was, however, to avoid at all costs the possibility of detection or suspicion either from the target herself or from her neighbors. Although Savage could not provide a physical description, from the sound of her voice Savage estimated she was in her early to mid-thirties. Additional details, and perhaps a photo, would soon be available. And with the virtually unlimited resources of Baldwin Enterprises at his disposal to buy information, it was just a question of time before Hank Savage would know everything there was to know about Sarah Peterson.

44

I T had been more than eight years since the Air France heroin scandal rocked Paris straight up to the Palais de Justice, eight years since Special Agent Sarah Peterson found herself at the core of a national crisis. At the time she had been posted at the U.S. Embassy at 2 Avenue Gabriel, specifically assigned there at the behest of the President to devise a system to thwart a rash of terrorist attacks on American interests throughout Europe. The spree of random violence had left hundreds either dead or wounded in its wake.

As part of her campaign, Sarah utilized informants from around the world. Early one morning, she received a tip through a backdoor channel unrelated to her assignment: France's preeminent forger, Jean Luc Billoux, had been recruited for a new initiative by the French underworld. Instead of altering American passports, as Billoux had done for years, he was forging diplomatic identification. With these falsified documents, drug runners were able to pose as diplomatic couriers on Air France and avoid inspection of their baggage.

Sarah had quietly passed the information onto her close friend, Henri LeClaire, who was working as a security agent for Air France at the time. After a secret three-month investigation by French Internal Affairs, the magnitude of the smuggling operation was exposed, as were the six-figure government payoffs that allowed the open spigot of narcotics to flow directly into the heart of France. Scores of simultaneous midnight arrests soon followed and only days later, LeClaire catapulted from his prior position to an appointment as station manager at JFK International, a plum spot coveted by every Air France employee. In gratitude, LeClaire made it clear that if he could ever come close to returning the favor for Sarah, he would do so without question.

● ● ●

SARAH had proceeded directly from the front entrance of the Hoover Building to an emergency stairwell on ground level. At this point she wanted to be seen by as few people as possible, aware that Jack Montgomery had confidants in every one of the bureau's departments. Although whoever was in the black Explorer probably didn't realize yet that she had slipped out the back door, she had no way of knowing whether others were looking for her.

Sarah entered one of the dimly lit screening rooms where FBI forensic technicians analyzed surveillance videotapes. The locked room was only large enough to accommodate four chairs, and one row of would-be standees behind each seat. Directly in front of the chairs was a slanted control panel containing hundreds of black dials and knobs. The images on the two thirty-five-inch Sony televisions just above the instrument panel could be altered in several thousand ways when someone with Walter Jensen's proficiency tinkered with these switches. Facial hair could be affixed or removed, eye color or nose shape could be modified, or an image aged. The cutting-edge instrumentation could also be used to enhance grainy bank robbery footage so that an all points bulletin could be accompanied by an intelligible photograph. When used in conjunction with the FBI's vast photo library, as Sarah intended to do, the machinery could also compare a suspect's image with the millions of mug shots in the agency's database.

She removed a videotape cassette from LeClaire's package and popped it into the VCR, then dialed Walter Jensen's number. He answered on the tenth ring.

"I need your help one more time," she said.

"Where are you?"

"Two floors down in the screening room."

"I'll be right there."

A minute later the forensic scientist was sitting in the chair beside hers. "What are you watching?"

"Footage from an Air France gate at JFK."

"Why?"

"I'm trying to find somebody."

"Who?"

"You'll see in a second."

Jensen focused in on the screen. In the lower righthand corner of the two television monitors was Sunday's date, which was obviously the day the footage had been taken. In the lower lefthand corner was a digital clock synchronized to New York local time to a thousandth of a second. In the upper righthand corner, in tiny white letters, AIR FRANCE GATE 18D—JFK.

The color video image had obviously been taken with a camera positioned a few feet above eye level. The lens pointed downward from behind the ticket counter, capturing the back of an Air France ticket agent and, more important, an anterior view of every passenger who was checking in.

"When Pan Am 103 went down over Lockerbie," Sarah explained, "the initial theory was that a Lebanese student had been duped into carrying the bomb on board the plane. Air France bought over a thousand video cameras, which they installed at nearly every one of their permanent international gates. Even though it turned out the bomb on 103 was put in the cargo hold by someone with tarmac access, the airlines discovered that these gate cameras had an enormous deterrent effect on criminal activity. Smuggling, for one, decreased dramatically, so the program was expanded."

"I know all about it," Jensen said. "The INS uses those cameras all the time to stop illegal immigration."

"Exactly." She removed a computer printout from the shoe box and spread it on the small slab of Formica in front of her.

"And what's that?"

"When each passenger arrives at the gate, the exact time they checked in is recorded on Air France's gate computer. The time in the computer is synchronized with the time set in each video camera so that anyone viewing the video tape knows exactly who they're watching check in."

"So who're you looking for?"

"A woman named Jessica Baldwin."

"What does she look like?"

"I don't know, but the FBI's mug shot is apparently fairly recent."

"Mug shot?"

"Yup. And that's how I need your help. You work this thing a hell of a lot better than I ever could. I always have trouble pulling up photos from the system."

"You're sure we've got her picture?"

"I know there's one on record. Her FOIMS file said she's been arrested several times. Last one was two years ago out at Luke Air Force Range in Arizona. She and a few hundred others chained themselves to the front gate."

"You have her Social?"

"Right here."

Jensen slid towards the computer to type in Jessica Baldwin's social security number. Using his match, he entered several commands, and Jessica's latest intake photo immediately filled the screen on their left.

Sarah stared at the image of a beautiful dark-haired, green-eyed woman.

Jensen fast-forwarded the tape, slowing it down to real time each time a passenger who even remotely resembled Jessica checked in. After thirty minutes of stopping and starting the footage, the last passenger boarded Air France Flight #007.

"She didn't get on that flight," Jensen said as he rewound the tape.

"No."

"So where is she?"

"I don't know that yet, but I intend to find out. I also plan on finding out what happened to your friend Bill O'Grady."

"You think there's a connection?"

"Right now that's my guess. I also think that Witherspoon and Gallagher are somehow mixed up in this pot, too."

"Holy smokes! If that's the case, then I'll do everything I can to get the backup files on those two guys by the time you get back. Ralph down in Archives called to say the pouch from outside storage should be here any minute."

"Great. I'll be back soon to look them over."

45

TOM LOGAN sat at the wheel of his blue Grand Am on Thirtieth Street. He had been waiting impatiently for thirty minutes outside Sarah's brownstone before he decided to make a move. From the sound of Hank Savage's voice, Sarah Peterson obviously needed to be found, and found quickly. Savage did not excite easily, Logan knew, and when he did it was always for a good reason.

He strolled through the narrow alley between Sarah's building and her neighbor's and noticed two metal trash cans secured to a handrail by way of a steel link bicycle lock. Logan picked up one of the badly dented silver lids. Inside the container was a thirteen-gallon Glad bag filled with trash, a sure sign someone had been home since the last pickup. But from what he could see through the windows, no one was inside the brownstone.

Logan returned to his car and reached for the ringing cell phone on his passenger seat.

"Hello?"

"Where the hell have you been?" Hank Savage asked curtly.

"I stepped out for a second to look around."

"Any sign of her?"

"None. Her apartment's dark and I don't think there's anyone inside. You sure you've got the right address?"

"I just double-checked. There's no doubt the woman we're looking for made a call from a phone that's registered to that apartment."

"Do you know the make and model of her car yet?"

"My guy at Motor Vehicles says she drives an eight-year-old red Jeep Wrangler, with D.C. tag number A-S-W 1021."

"Excellent. I'll look around to see if it's parked nearby. I've also got a few buddies in the D.C. police force if you want me to have them search for her car."

"No!" Savage answered emphatically. "Not yet. Right now I don't want the cops involved."

Logan looked through his rearview mirror and saw a police car slowing down at the adjacent stop sign on N Street. The black-and-white passed through the intersection, apparently without taking notice of his illegally parked car.

"Let's try something," Savage said. "I'll call Peterson's number right now. If she's home, a light should go on."

"Good idea."

Savage dialed Sarah's number and heard her answering machine pick up on the fourth ring.

"No luck," Logan reported when Savage called him back.

"Sit tight, Tom. I'm on my way. Our jet's all fueled and I should be there in an hour or two. If she comes home between now and then leave a voice mail message for me at the Plaza Hotel in Manhattan, Room 1834. But do *not* call Mr. Baldwin's home or office under any circumstances, or even mine for that matter. We're operating under the assumption that someone may be listening to all of our phones."

"Will do, Hank. I'm on the corner of Thirtieth and N Street in a blue

Grand Am. When you get here that's where you'll find me, unless she's come and gone and I'm following her."

46   S A R A H was parked beneath a sprawling curbside maple on Twenty-ninth and P, just two blocks from her Georgetown brownstone. Her brief conversation with Sam Baldwin a few hours earlier had left her perplexed, wondering whether the billionaire had any inkling that his daughter might soon be killed. As much as she wanted to call Baldwin and identify herself, she knew that would result in Jessica's death. Sarah was sure her boss had taken the elementary step of listening in on Sam Baldwin's home phone. For Christ's sake, even *she* had done the same without a court order. Sarah had been coached early on in her career by William Casey himself that violation of the Fourth Amendment was really no big deal, one that would frequently be overlooked by sister law enforcement authorities. "Just don't get caught too often," the former director of the CIA had said with a wry smile. That being the case, Sarah's upcoming plan would go a long way in allowing her to gauge how far Jack Montgomery was prepared to go to protect his dirty little secret. And if her hunch was correct, he was prepared to go all the way.

Sarah kept the driver's side door to the Jeep unlocked, her keys still in the ignition. Every second would count if this plan didn't work. She walked to a nearby pay phone with her jacket collar turned up and dialed 9-1-1.

"D. C. nine-one-one. What's the nature of your emergency?"

Sarah heard the beep on the other end of the line. This call, as she had expected, was being recorded.

"There's a prowler on Thirtieth Street in Georgetown!" she said urgently. "Between N and O! I think he's got a gun! I saw him get into a big, black car with tinted windows! Maybe an Explorer or a Jeep or something like that! Please hurry, I think he's still in there!"

"I'll send the police there right away, ma'am. Did you see what this man looked like?"

Another beep. Static and a police squawk box in the background. "No! I didn't really get a good look at him! Please hurry!"

"What's your name, ma'am?"

"I don't want to say. I'm afraid he'll come after me!"

"Try to stay calm, ma'am. The police will be there very soon."

Another beep, and the sound of plastic keys being clicked on a computer keyboard. Sarah had heard enough. She calmly placed the phone back onto its cradle. In a few minutes she would have her answer.

She turned the corner slowly, stepping onto the familiar street where she had lived for the past seven years. She had stood in this spot five hundred times, maybe a thousand, but this instant something felt different. Something was out of place. It was this intangible aptitude, she knew, that made her almost peerless in her business. It was not so much acute vision, but rather what the brain did with the information; "court sense" sports psychologists called it. It was the ability to take a snapshot of a situation and realize before anyone else that one of the thousands of bits of information the eyes had captured did not belong. The feeling came over her like a tidal wave, transporting her back in time.

March 30, 1981

The carnage she had witnessed that afternoon had been at once the most horrific and fortuitous event up to that point in her life. It was her first week on the job, twelve days after she had loaded up her Volkswagen Beetle after graduating third in her class from Yale. As part of her training, Sarah had been invited by the Secret Service to tag along for the day. She was standing across the street from the Washington Hilton when she made the off-the-cuff remark that instantly put her career onto the fast track. Ronald Reagan's chief of security was standing beside her, casually pointing out logistics and sight lines. It was then that Sarah commented if *she* were making the security decisions, the herd of photographers and pedestrians on the far sidewalk would be pushed back another fifty yards. The composition of the crowd was making her jittery. The President's security chief scoffed at the suggestion, dismissing it as the overactive imagination of a woman who was barely two weeks out of college and didn't know any better. Sarah persisted, repeating the remark to the FBI agent beside her. Seconds later Sarah saw the man with the squared-off eyeglasses raise up from his crouch behind a crowd of onlookers. Her warning scream to the Secret Service agents who were surrounding the President was drowned out by that first awful shot ripping through the forehead of James Brady. Chaos ensued for several minutes, but word of Sarah's insights filtered all the way to the Oval Office over the next few days, ensuring that her ascent was under way. And from the experience she had learned a single critical lesson: that her God-given instincts and intuition were superior to anybody else's, even better than those know-it-all career security men who had twenty years under their belts.

SARAH refocused her attention on the present when she heard the sound of fast-approaching cars. A red turret light was whirling, but there was no siren. It was the classic convergence when the report of a prowler had been received. Sarah smiled. Her hard-earned tax dollars were being put to good use.

The police car accelerated past her, then came to an abrupt halt across the street from her brownstone. A second cruiser came down Thirtieth Street. This one had gone the wrong direction down the one-way street. Now the Explorer's escape would be blocked unless the driver opted for the sidewalk.

Sarah remained on the corner, her eyes fixed on the scene. A powerful beam of light cut through the tinted windows of the Explorer. Now the cops, and Sarah, could see the silhouette of a man sitting in the backseat.

"Open that door very slowly!" Sarah heard one of the policemen say into his megaphone. "And keep your hands on top of your head!"

A small crowd gathered behind her. A similar one formed on the other side of 30th Street. Sarah recognized many of the faces; they were friends and neighbors who frequented the same local restaurants and watering holes that she did. Sarah watched a third cruiser appear. Then a fourth. Now the police were blocking off pedestrian traffic, forcing oglers to move back from the scene. The report of a gunman had obviously caught their attention.

Sarah saw the back door of the Explorer open slowly, but she was too far away to see very much. Four pistols were trained on the man inside. Mr. Green kneeled on the street as instructed, then spread-eagle on the pavement. As a pair of handcuffs was slapped around his wrists, Sarah decided to get a closer look.

She flashed her identification to a young cop and headed toward the Explorer. A second cop tried to block her path, but she waved him away with her badge. Sarah saw the Mauser with the telescopic lens on the backseat. Then she locked eyes with the gunman and gasped. It was Andy Archer.

47

JACK MONTGOMERY was alone in the den of his Virginia home, leaning on one of the polished walnut sides of his nine-foot Brunswick billiard table. Behind him, on the smooth, emerald green felt, were two hand-crafted cue sticks and several solid colored balls. They were what remained of an evening of eight-ball and bourbon the Secretary had spent with the Chief Justice last week. It was Montgomery who suggested to President Reagan in 1985 that the vacancy on the high court be filled by an old Harvard buddy. And it was Montgomery who schmoozed with several key senators to insure a 99–1 confirmation vote. Only the liberal Democrat from Massachusetts had opposed the nomination. Since then, the Secretary of State and the Chief Justice had gotten together regularly to decompress over a few cocktails; but those enjoyable hours were now the furthest things from Montgomery's mind.

The Secretary of State's right hand clutched the remote control while his eyes fixed on the thirty-five-inch Sony Trinitron exactly twelve feet away. He fast-forwarded the videotape he'd just received until it corresponded to within half an hour of the time the second Tripwire message had been triggered from Bill O'Grady's computer. Then he watched it at double speed, freezing each time someone else passed through the metal detectors that framed the front lobby of the Hoover Building. Ten minutes later Montgomery confirmed that Sarah Peterson had entered the building.

Montgomery ejected the tape from his VCR, placed it back in its sleeve, and inserted a second tape. This one showed Sarah walking down the hallway of the fourth floor, entering Bill O'Grady's office, and staying for about half an hour. Montgomery now had no doubt he had taken the correct precautions by assigning someone to muzzle his chief of security.

As he rewound the tape, Montgomery's phone rang. He listened carefully while an operative reported that Sarah Peterson had not purchased anything with her credit cards within the last seventy-two hours, but she had guaranteed a late arrival at the Four Seasons Hotel in Manhattan just a few minutes ago. The American Express Gold Card she had used bore the name Holly Whitmore. That had complicated the search, the operative said, until they checked billing addresses rather than names. As it turned out, Ms. Whitmore's invoices were mailed each month to Sarah's Georgetown brownstone.

48

MOHAMMED EL-FATAH stood in the darkness beside the railroad spur, wishing his wife and five children were still alive. They would have been proud of what he was doing to avenge their deaths. In the nine months since one of Saddam Hussein's cluster bombs had leveled their tin-roofed shanty, El-Fatah had become a different man. No longer was he a humble shepherd with six mouths to feed. Now he was a revolutionary, a warrior, who believed he was destined to topple one of the most ruthless tyrants of the millennium. Allah had obviously taken his loved ones for a reason.

El-Fatah had been up in the mountains tending his goats on that fateful day. The attack helicopters had swooped in without warning. Before the dust had fully cleared, his grief-stricken face was flashed on millions of television screens by CNN. Forty-eight hours later he was on a plane destined for Washington. It was the first time he had ever been more than ten kilometers from Tikrit, the Kurdish village in northern Iraq where he had been born in 1960 and where his family had perished.

There was a secret meeting with men who claimed to have connections to the President of the United States; a blur of interpreters and Secret Service agents and limousines and a maze of underground hallways. The session lasted less than an hour. Before a new day arrived, El-Fatah was back on Iraqi soil, buoyed by promises of revenge.

For months he anxiously awaited word from Washington. He dreamed of fire falling from the sky, and the ground burning ferociously out of control as it had during the final days of the Gulf War. El-Fatah, like every Iraqi citizen, had never been told the truth about the torched Kuwaiti oil wells, but he had seen plumes of black smoke drifting for hundreds of miles, and he had smelled the caustic fumes of burning raw crude. The Iraqi propaganda machine had blamed the inferno on President Bush, deceiving its people into believing that America intended to turn the region into nothing more than ash. Now El-Fatah hoped the United States would concentrate its awesome firepower on the despised dictator in Baghdad. In El-Fatah's mind, even a takeover by the savage Iranians would be a change for the better. If Saddam unleashed his chemical weapons, as he had always vowed he would, that was fine, too. A quick death would be better than the hollow life he was living without his family.

As the weeks passed, El-Fatah grudgingly gave up hope that any progress had been made during his short meeting in the Pentagon. Eventually he began to believe the whole episode had been a cruel delusion. Despair and depression, El-Fatah knew, could break even the strongest of men. He himself had imagined spiders crawling all over his body within days of his stint in solitary confinement at the hands of the corrupt Iraqi regime during most of 1996.

Then one day an emissary arrived. Speaking perfect Kurdish, he told El-Fatah that a wealthy supporter had finally been located. Weapons would be shipped in a few months that could destroy Saddam Hussein and those around him. Powerful bombs would move by train to the Turkish town of Diyarbakir, which was controlled by Kurds. El-Fatah was told to familiarize himself with that part of Turkey and then meet the shipment when it arrived. He would help select a remote location from which the weapons could be fired.

The former goat farmer counted the days, barely able to contain his excitement. After what seemed like an eternity, the middle of the night of October 29 finally arrived. El-Fatah had remained belly to the ground for hours, his ear pressed against the cold steel track. In the stillness of the night he would be able to feel the vibration of the moving train long before he could hear it coming toward the deserted rail spur.

As the train approached, thick soot chugged from its smokestack, blending into the blackness of the night sky. The conductor navigated the rusted tracks at a walker's pace. He had no idea what was contained inside the two rail cars behind the engine, nor did he care to find out. What he *did* know was that he was being paid ten times the normal conductor's rate, and that he had been warned at gunpoint to tell no one about this midnight excursion.

The train came to a halt with a low squeak of the steel wheels. The doors to both rail cars opened as El-Fatah approached. Six men dressed in black jumped from the containers, automatic weapons in their hands. When they realized that only Mohammed El-Fatah was there, they greeted him in English. Behind them, in sealed crates that were falsely marked as refrigerator parts, were the weapons that had been on board *The Hercules*. And just as El-Fatah had hoped, those weapons had the ability to set the sky on fire.

49

SARAH cautiously returned to the crime lab on the fourth floor of the Hoover Building, more mindful than ever that Jack Montgomery might have drafted others to flush her out. She avoided making eye contact with two agents who were chatting near the elevator bank. Her goal was to get in and out of the building as fast as possible, and to exchange information with Walter Jensen before she took her next step.

"How'd it go?" Jensen asked casually, masking his relief that Sarah had returned to the FBI building safely. "Did you learn anything interesting?"

"You bet."

"What?"

"I think I know what happened to O'Grady."

Jensen's eyes widened. "Really?"

"I think so, but I've still got a few questions to answer before I'll be sure."

Jensen resisted his desire to cross-examine her, aware that Sarah would give him more details when she was good and ready. But the backup files on Witherspoon and Gallagher he'd managed to procure made him very wary about her further involvement in this investigation. He put his arm around her, his grim expression making no secret of how he felt.

"I admit I don't know most of the details," he said paternally, "but I think it's time we called in reinforcements to help you out. Everyone agrees that you're one of the top five agents in the business, Sarah, so I'd say this no matter who was in this situation. Even if it was Clem Barker, and he's the best investigator the FBI's seen for the last fifty years. But I get the feeling you're getting in over your head."

Sarah shrugged.

"I can talk to Director Cody, right now," Jensen persisted, "and have him assign the Bureau's best agents to this matter. I'll call him at home if you want me to."

"Thanks for the offer, Walter, but I'll pass. I'll be fine."

"Please let me help you."

Sarah pulled away from Jensen's benevolent grip. "No," she said firmly, "not yet."

"You know you're being as stubborn as your father? He always wanted to handle things all by himself. That's probably what got him killed."

Sarah shot an angry glance at Jensen.

"I'm sorry," he said. "I shouldn't have said that."

"Listen to me, Walter. The people who murdered Bill O'Grady will kill both of us if they find out about this. I'm talking about guys who're wired straight to the top of the FBI. Maybe higher."

Jensen reached for the padded stool behind him and sat down. In thirty-three years at the FBI he had never once had a second thought about confiding in one of his colleagues.

"Believe me, when the time's ripe to hand this mess over to someone else, nothing will make me happier. I've got a knot in my stomach the size of a cantaloupe and I'm looking over my shoulder every two seconds. For God's sake, Walter, my mom may have to start cancer treatment and I haven't had the time to line up the right medical care here so she can just get on a damn plane and not worry about logistics. But right now I've got to see this through for just a little while longer. There's so much at stake here and so many people depending on me, even though they don't know it."

Sarah opened her briefcase and removed a sheet of paper and an envelope. She hastily scribbled on both sides of the paper, folded it, and sealed it inside the envelope.

"I'm leaving for New York City right now. If you don't hear from me within twenty-four hours, then I want you to give this to Evelyn Dunbar over at *The Washington Post*. She's the one journalist I trust with this information. She'll know what to do when she gets the letter."

"I'll tell you honestly that I'm tempted to open it."

"I know you are. But I know you'd never do that unless I said you could. Trust me, for your sake, it's better that you don't know."

Jensen tucked the envelope inside the breast pocket of his sports jacket. "Be careful, Sarah Peterson. There are lots of people in this world who care about you."

"Please don't worry about me. I've been taking care of myself for a long time."

They hugged tightly.

"These may change your opinion about going at this alone." Jensen lifted a small stack of papers from his desk and handed it to her. "They're copies made from a backup disk."

"Did you look through them?" she asked.

"Quickly."

"What do they say?"

"They say there's a damn good reason why their files were sanitized. The FBI knew that Witherspoon's been involved in some pretty nasty shit for a long time. He's as dirty as they get."

Sarah hurriedly stuffed the papers into her briefcase. "I take it you didn't find those missing pages from General Perry's file?"

"Not yet, but there are hundreds of boxes of microfiche in the basement that may contain them. From what I can tell, the reels from the mid-sixties are there. I'll start looking through them as soon as you leave."

Sarah walked to the door and opened it. "Thanks, Walter. I'll check in with you soon. In the meantime, make sure you don't use your computer to find any of this stuff, OK? That's the reason they went after O'Grady."

"Sure thing," Jensen replied appeasingly, even though he knew that he'd have to log onto one of the department's PCs if he was going to do his usual thorough job.

50

"H O W long ago did this happen?" Hank Savage asked incredulously. He was inside Tom Logan's car, trying to evaluate the series of events Sarah's call to 9-1-1 had set into motion. The black Explorer had already been towed and pedestrian traffic along Thirtieth Street had returned to normal.

Logan turned on the interior light and checked his watch. "It's been an hour and a half."

"And you're sure Sarah Peterson hasn't gone in or out of that brownstone?"

"Of course I'm sure. I've been watching that damn door for hours."

Logan's car was now parked legally just down the street from Sarah's front door. When the woman in the silver Lexus had pulled out from this spot he had executed a three-point turn just as quickly as he could.

"I'm going to try to get inside her apartment right now," Savage said. "Even though she's not there, I'm sure I'll learn plenty. And every second obviously counts, because someone else is trying to shut her down. So here's what we'll do. Stroll into that alley over there and throw out something that's in your pockets. When you're near that side door I'll dial her telephone number one more time and let it ring twice. Get as close to that door as possible so we know it's her phone that's ringing. You got it?"

"Yup."

"Go ahead."

Logan hopped out of the car and closed the driver's door just enough so the dome light went off. Savage waited for Logan to approach the narrow alleyway before he picked up his flip phone. He watched Logan remove a Hershey's wrapper from his pants pocket and search for a place to dispose of it. Savage dialed Sarah's number just as his scout was about to lift up the lid of the trash can. Logan leaned close to the side door that led to the kitchen of the brownstone. After two rings Logan casually walked back to the Grand Am.

"That's definitely the right house," Logan said once he was again behind the wheel. "It rang twice, then stopped."

"Good. I'm going inside."

"I'll go with you." He swiveled to his left, reaching for the door handle.

"No. Stay here in case there's trouble."

Savage handed him the cell phone, along with the strip of paper that had Sarah's phone number on it. "Dial this number and let it ring twice, then hang up if you need to warn me about something. Then meet me on the corner of Thirty-first and N."

Savage walked up the brick steps of the brownstone. He rang the bell several times, his black leather gloves pulled tightly against his fingertips. While he waited, he casually looked back at the cars lining both sides of Thirtieth Street. The outline of his colleague's head was barely visible through the front windshield of the Grand Am.

Savage tried the bell twice more before he removed the switchblade from his suit pocket. He looked through the curtained glass to determine if anyone was home, then began jimmying the lock to the front door. The slender blade fit easily into the seam between the door and its sash. In less than thirty seconds his gentle push opened the old door. He lingered in the downstairs foyer for the count of ten, relocked the door, then slowly proceeded up the flight of creaky wooden stairs. He took great pains to transfer the bulk of his weight to both wooden banisters, clutching them tightly like parallel bars until he reached the top landing. Once he was there he pressed his ear against the door. He entered the apartment only after hearing no noise.

The front hallway was unlit, as was the remainder of the second floor. A glimmer of light entered through the bay window that faced Thirtieth Street. Savage removed a pencil-sized Maglite from his pants pocket, testing it low to the ground before going any further. He had encased the clear face of the flashlight almost completely in black electrician's tape so that only a pinpoint of light could shine through as he made his way around the apartment. Shoes and socks were strewn about the hardwood floors of the hallway, making it seem as though Sarah had left her home in a hurry. The beam from his flashlight caught the wide eyes of a cat hiding underneath the living room couch.

Savage turned left toward the rear of the brownstone where he suspected Sarah Peterson usually slept. He passed her answering machine and flipped its plastic lid. There were eighteen messages indicated on the digital counter. He pocketed the microcassette, more concerned with obtaining the potential information on it than revealing someone had taken it.

The unmade queen-sized bed took up much of the master bedroom. On a small mahogany nightstand beside it were several *People* magazines. Across from the bed was a shoulder-high walnut dresser that had been placed just beneath an antique oval mirror. A gold necklace and two women's rings were on top of the dresser, as was a teak Oriental jewelry box that had been Sarah's grandmother's. Several pieces of mail were also scattered among the jewelry. Savage glanced at a BellSouth bill to confirm he was in the correct home. He studied the eight-by-ten-inch black-and-white photograph that he assumed was of Sarah's parents. It was framed inside a square block of Lucite. The handsome couple was standing in front of the White House, both looking full of life. From the crew cut and beehive hairdo, Savage surmised the picture must have been taken in the early sixties. A more recent picture of Sarah's mother was beside it.

Savage opened the top drawer, not really looking for anything specific, but he knew that most people who had something to hide often attempted to conceal their valuables by putting them in with their underwear. He removed a dozen pair of high-cut Calvin Kleins, along with a black lace thong. Then he noticed a large white envelope tucked way in the back of the drawer. He peeked inside and saw a batch of color Polaroids.

"Nice," he purred as he ran his eyes up and down Sarah's nearly perfect naked body. Eight of the twelve pictures were of Jean-Pierre, in happier times before Sarah had caught him in bed with another woman. Savage slipped two compromising pictures of Sarah into his pocket and returned the balance to their hiding spot.

Savage rummaged through the walk-in bedroom closet, surprised at the number of pairs of shoes that were inside. He quickly took note of the remainder of her stylish wardrobe before heading to the front of the apartment where Sarah's office was located. Once there, he pushed aside the lace curtains that adorned the bay window. Then he drew the three blinds. When the last one had been pulled the room fell into complete darkness. Now a curious neighbor would be unable to observe even a fiber-thin shaft of light slowly making its way around the darkened room.

The beam of Savage's flashlight ran along Sarah's two fax machines, her shredder, a pair of computers, and the clutter of paperwork on her desk. He looked behind her high-end Hewlett Packard, quickly spotting the small metal plate on which "Property of the U.S. Treasury Department" was imprinted. Then he focused on the spines of the assorted books that were neatly stacked in the bookcase on the far left wall. Of the hundred or so volumes filling the four shelves, more than half had something to do with antiterrorism or another related law enforcement topic. Savage had no idea what to make of it, but he was eager to spend more of Sam Baldwin's money to have a second background check run on the mystery woman as soon as he returned to Manhattan. The first, which had been hurriedly run moments after Victor at the phone company had provided a name and address, had mysteriously come back completely blank.

The rigged legal pad beside Sarah's computer was the next item to capture Savage's attention. He desperately searched the drawers for the tiny cassette that had obviously been plucked from this space, but it was nowhere to be found.

The single sheet of yellow paper beside the legal pad jumped out at him. A series of peculiar green dots were scattered about the page, although there was nothing written on that particular sheet of paper. Savage shined his flashlight onto the perforated page. At first he saw nothing; but when he rotated his left wrist in a tight spiral, the shaft of white light caught the yellow page at just the right angle. Savage's eyes widened when he saw the imprint of the word *Hercules* circled a few dozen times. Beside it was the name *Baldwin*. He inspected the page more closely, quickly identifying several other recognizable names, and many that were not at all familiar.

Savage frantically rifled through the desk drawers for additional information, randomly stuffing an address book, several loose pieces of paper, and a stack of documents from the fax machine into a black nylon knapsack. When he realized he'd been in the apartment for nearly thirty minutes, he decided not to press his luck any further. He started for the front door with his cache of Sarah's booty securely in his possession. Then the phone rang twice and stopped. It was Tom Logan's signal. Savage froze in his tracks and took out his gun.

51

ON a clear morning Sam and Francesca Baldwin could look up from their pillows in their master bedroom and see for a hundred miles in all directions. New Jersey to the left, the Atlantic Ocean way out there to the right, and a million buildings in between. Guests who were allowed up to the top floor of their Trump Tower triplex marveled at the sight, staring from what seemed like the center of the universe. And with the push of a button beside their king-sized sleigh bed, concealed fifth-century shoji screens blocked out the windows and sealed off the room from the rest of the world. Total privacy, eighty floors above street level.

Francesca sat alone in her bedroom, staring vacantly northeast toward her daughter's home in Connecticut. Virtually all of the tears her eyes could produce had already fallen onto the parquet floor. It had been two hours since Sam had kissed her good-bye, and twenty minutes since he had last checked in to make sure she was OK. In that time she had opened up the Manhattan white pages and jotted down six phone numbers. They included the deputy director of the FBI, the mayor of New York City, the police commissioner, and several reputable private investigative agencies. The kidnap and ransom specialists, such as Kroll-O'Gara Company and Control Risks Group Ltd., were shady, yet legitimate businesses, that employed former spies and special operatives to negotiate the release of wealthy clients at astronomical hourly rates. They also provided security services to try to prevent the type of situation the Baldwins found themselves in. When you were worth several billion dollars, you were regularly solicited by these folks.

What Francesca was going to do with these phone numbers she wasn't yet sure. But she felt as though she had to do *something*. The joy of her life, her reason for living, was in the throes of hell, and Francesca had a difficult time believing that she'd be able to sit on her hands throughout this ordeal without taking some steps on her own to secure her daughter's release. Watching from the sidelines had never been Francesca Baldwin's style. She often chose to get her hands dirty, injecting herself into tasks that others of her social and economic status found distasteful. She knew that this quality was no doubt one of the reasons why her husband had hesitated telling her about the kidnapping in the first place.

Francesca tried to decide what she could possibly do to get her daughter back alive. Throughout twenty-nine years of marriage she had never gone against the wishes of her husband, nor had she ever felt the slightest desire to do so. They agreed on almost every issue and were about as compatible as two strong-willed people could be. Not only did she trust her husband implicitly, but she had no doubt he was trying as hard as he could to bring about the result they both longed for. But that knowledge alone was not enough to satisfy Francesca.

She slowly walked to the sitting area that faced Central Park and sank into an oversized armchair. A call to any of the first three numbers she had copied would no doubt send teams of law enforcement agents scrambling. She knew the kidnap of Jessica Baldwin would be given the highest of priorities and a hundred agents, maybe more, would be assigned until the case was solved. But even if secrecy was promised, it would only be a matter of hours before the name of her daughter would be leaked to the press, and Jessie's life would be over, if her kidnappers were to be believed.

Francesca picked up the cordless phone, then put it down, still unsure what to do. The mayor and the police commissioner were both indebted to her after she had written a check for $18 million to cover the cost of 35,000 new bulletproof vests for every member of the New York City police force. Francesca had graciously refused a dinner in her honor and had insisted that her donation be kept anonymous. Upon their insistence she did accept a small wooden plaque with a gold inscription as a token of the city's gratitude, although it was now buried in the bottom of a box in one of the apartment's dozens of closets.

The deputy director of the FBI was another story. He was a hard-nosed former prosecutor who did everything strictly by the book. When a disgruntled former Baldwin Enterprises employee made claims of money laundering against the conglomerate in 1996, a formal investigation had been opened. Although the six-month probe cleared the company of any wrongdoing, the slash-and-burn method in which the inquiry was conducted left Francesca with the knowledge that she would probably not receive any preferential treatment by the man in charge at Federal Plaza.

Then Francesca remembered Sam had said the President had apparently played a role in getting them into this jam in the first place. If that was so, then he was probably the person who had the best chance of getting them out of it. If he couldn't, Francesca would consider blowing the whistle on him. She would have no qualms about bringing him down, along with everyone else who had played a part in her daughter's murder. But that was a decision she hoped she would never need to make.

She rifled through her large address book, eventually finding the telephone number of the President's secretary. Francesca had coordinated several charity events to raise millions for the Special Olympics, which was one of the First Family's pet projects. Although this phone number was not a direct link into the Oval Office, it would at least get her past the switchboard that ordinary folks had to contend with when they called 1600 Pennsylvania Avenue.

Francesca picked up the phone, then put it down; her head felt like it was going to explode. If her husband caught wind of what she was about to do, he would have a stroke, but her gut was telling her that this was the correct thing to do for her daughter and her unborn grandchild.

Finally, she lifted the receiver and punched in the number. If the President didn't return the call, she felt sure he would regret he had ever met Francesca Baldwin.

52

HEARTY mums of brilliant gold encircled the marble columns that lined the five-star hotel's front entrance. High above the semicircular cobblestone driveway, on flagpoles protruding from the facade of the third floor, were the flags of the United States, Israel, France, and Japan. The colorful banners whipped noisily as gusts of wind disturbed the midnight air. The hotel's entrance, a study in polished walnut and glass, was surrounded by a slab of carved pink sandstone that arched perfectly above the doorway. When Secretary Montgomery emerged from his limousine, he felt the warmth from the heat lamps that radiated down on the few who could afford a night's stay at the Hay-Adams Hotel.

"Good evening, Mr. Secretary!" the uniformed doorman announced obsequiously. He pulled open the door of the armor-plated Town Car before it even came to a full stop.

Montgomery bolted forward and grunted. His battered oversized briefcase swung in his left hand while he quickly made his way toward the hotel entrance. Once inside, he hurried through the richly decorated lobby. From the seventeenth-century Medici tapestry and the fine English antiques, to the gilt moldings and blue and white porcelain ceilings, it was all museum quality. There were purple velvet chairs and bouquets of bursting flowers atop every mahogany coffee table. Montgomery ignored it all. He was a frequent visitor to the hotel, which was a magnet for important meetings that determined the fate of millions of people around the world. Located just a block from the White House, the Hay-Adams had been the epicenter for those in power since the 1920s.

The Secretary paid virtually no attention to the pleasantries extended by the hotel's accommodating staff and hurriedly made his way down the carpeted steps to the left of the lobby. With his security staff specifically directed to remain behind, Montgomery alone entered the John Hay Lounge, where he suspected he would find Tom Witherspoon and Ed Gallagher. The richly paneled tea room doubled as an informal bar.

Montgomery stood in the doorway, observing his two friends sitting on a couch just across the way from a blazing red-brick walk-in fireplace. They were casually perusing *The New York Times* by the warmth of the hearth, while being treated to the soothing music that flowed from the polished Steinway in the corner of the room. The tuxedoed pianist had already played for hours, and would continue on until his last two listeners retired to their rooms for the evening.

" D o you care for a cocktail, Mr. Secretary?"

The question startled Montgomery, even though it had been asked in a hushed tone worthy of the clubby room.

"I'm so sorry, Mr. Secretary," the waiter said deferentially. "I didn't mean to alarm you."

"I'll take a Stoli straight up."

"Yes, sir."

"Make it a double."

"Of course, sir."

The waiter vanished just as quickly as he had appeared.

Montgomery walked beside the curved arm of the couch on which Witherspoon and Gallagher were sitting. No one else occupied the soft leather armchairs spread around the cozy room. The congenial surroundings would have brought back fine memories under different circumstances, reminding him of his time spent socializing in the reading room at the Harvard Club in New York City.

"Hiya, Jack," Witherspoon said amiably after he had glanced up from his newspaper. "Can I buy you a nightcap?"

"We need to talk," Montgomery said, his pale blue eyes cold.

Ed Gallagher folded his paper and looked at Montgomery.

"Pull up a chair," Witherspoon suggested. "Rusty'll be here in a minute to line you up with a drink."

The waiter appeared with a six-ounce tumbler of clear liquid before Witherspoon could press the call button. He held out his silver tray and Montgomery grabbed hold of the pale green glass.

"Put it on my tab," Witherspoon said.

"Another round for you gentlemen?"

"No," Montgomery said curtly.

The waiter left the room without comment.

"What's wrong, Jack?" Gallagher asked.

Montgomery swallowed the chilled vodka in one rapid gulp. "Let's go upstairs."

"I don't like the sound of this," Gallagher said.

Montgomery scanned the room. Once he was certain the piano player was too far away to hear the exchange, he said, "You shouldn't. We've got some very big problems."

Witherspoon extracted himself from the deep depression in the over-stuffed couch. "Let's go up to my suite. There's plenty of room."

The three men walked in silence to the elevator, stepping inside the pan-eled enclosure when it arrived. A young blond-haired couple entered the el-evator at the lobby level, speaking German. It was apparent from the tones in their voices, as well as their conspicuous glances, that they recognized the Secretary of State. Montgomery stared at the carpeted floor, pretending not to notice. The elevator doors opened to the eighth-floor hallway.

"I'm down this way," Witherspoon said.

He guided his party past the antique end tables laden with fresh flowers to Room 804. Witherspoon tossed his houndstooth sports jacket onto the floral-patterned couch. The two-bedroom suite was equipped with a Jacuzzi and a black marble wet bar.

"Something to drink before we get started?"

Montgomery nodded, as did Gallagher.

He grabbed a bottle of Absolut from the fully stocked rack and poured three drinks.

"Ice?"

Both men nodded again and Witherspoon dropped two cubes into each glass.

"So what's the problem, Jack?" Witherspoon asked. The arms dealer stood beside a pair of French doors that opened onto a small balcony with an unobstructed view of the darkened Lafayette Park. Beyond that was the floodlit front facade of the White House. Witherspoon released the clasp on the lefthand door to let in some cool, fresh air.

"I heard from Buck's two men this morning. They're demanding fifty million dollars before they'll release Baldwin's daughter."

"That's outrageous," Witherspoon said.

"They'll never get away with something like that," Gallagher added.

Montgomery shut his eyes for a moment. His two old friends apparently did not fully appreciate the degree of leverage Grizzwald and McClarty possessed.

"You're wrong," he said soberly. "It's not outrageous and in all likelihood they will get away with it. Those bastards are holding Jessica Baldwin somewhere on this big planet, smug that it's damn near impossible for us to root them out."

Witherspoon and Gallagher exchanged worried glances.

"Us?" Gallagher asked cautiously.

"Yes, us," Montgomery replied. "You both agreed to help if anything went wrong. Now I'm taking you up on your offer."

"Hold on, Jack," Witherspoon said with his hands out in front of him. "We volunteered to lend a hand. But it sounds like you're taking our offer way too far."

The Secretary quickly calculated his options. There were two possible approaches: one was the carrot, the other the stick. "As of now we're all in this together," Montgomery said calmly. "Coconspirators are defined very broadly under the federal statutes."

The men recoiled. Witherspoon and Gallagher had always known that Montgomery was a cold-blooded bastard; but forty years of friendship should have meant something to Jack Montgomery. Witherspoon considered a threat of his own, then thought better of it. There was no doubt the cabinet member possessed information that could send both he and Gallagher off to jail until they were very old men.

"Why don't you get Buck's commandos to take them out? He's always bragging about his Special Forces."

"That's a good idea, Tom. Unfortunately, we tried that a couple of hours ago and frightened some Japanese tourists instead."

"Jesus," Witherspoon said.

All three men stood silently, trying not to provoke one another any further. Gallagher turned to stare at the White House while Witherspoon continued to glare at Jack Montgomery.

"How quickly could you each raise twenty-five million if you had to?"

"You're joking," Witherspoon said. Then he added angrily, "There's no fucking way the two of us are gonna get stuck with this tab."

Montgomery decided to soften his position. Perhaps the carrot would work more effectively than had the stick. "When all is said and done, Tom, you're going to make quite a pretty penny on this transaction."

"And how do you figure that?"

"The President told me yesterday that he's leaning toward giving Buck the go-ahead on a new weapons system that'll require more than ten billion in outside bids. I'll bend the President's ear and push him over the edge in that direction. Once it's official, you'll each be given a packet of information that'll guarantee the success of your bids. You'll recoup your share of that fifty million three times over."

Witherspoon smiled, as did Gallagher. This sounded better. Nothing wrong with an interest-free loan to a friend in trouble.

"How come you didn't say that in the first place?" Witherspoon asked, pouring himself another drink.

"Even if I had a gun to my head it'd take two days, maybe three," Gallagher said.

"Ditto," Witherspoon said. "Twenty-five million in cash won't be easy to pull together on such short notice. I don't have that kind of liquidity."

"I understand," Montgomery said. "But time is of the essence. I'll tighten the screws on Sam Baldwin while you guys see what you can do. We still may come out exactly where we want if we play our cards perfectly from here on out."

Montgomery snapped his briefcase shut and stood. "Now if you'll excuse me, gentlemen, I need to call to our newest business partner."

"Baldwin?" Witherspoon asked.

The Secretary of State nodded.

53

WITH his gun drawn, Hank Savage peeked out the bay window facing Thirtieth Street. Savage's search inside Sarah Peterson's brownstone had netted dividends that would be useful as soon as all of it could be digested. Now it was time to quickly assess the situation before deciding how to react. Tom Logan wouldn't have pushed the panic button without a good reason.

At first Savage saw nothing that warranted cause for alarm. Then he noticed the uniformed policeman lumbering down Sarah's front steps.

The solitary officer walked three-quarters of the way down Thirtieth Street before he leaned toward the driver's window of his police cruiser. Savage watched carefully as the young black cop spoke with his partner and he decided to cut and run, rather than to stick around and try to dodge the two cops who were now walking back toward the brownstone. He ran to the rear of Sarah's home and down the back steps three at a time. As long as Tom Logan was at the appointed spot within the next twenty seconds, Savage judged he would be able to escape from the premises without a compromising encounter.

54

AFTER two years in office, there were several aspects of the President's day that had become extremely predictable. At 6 A.M. he would breakfast on whole wheat toast and black coffee while voraciously reading that morning's New York Times, Washington Post, Wall Street Journal, and The Times of London. If another periodical contained an article that one of his aides believed would be of interest, it was photocopied and highlighted for his consumption. Between 8 A.M. and noon, the President would huddle with individual members of his cabinet or his close advisers. Full-blown cabinet meetings were reserved for Monday mornings, then added as crises warranted.

Afternoons generally consisted of high-visibility outings that had the potential for favorable coverage on the evening news. These ranged from meetings with foreign dignitaries to visits to school, hospitals, and housing projects. If the President was going to engage in some form of activity to help the oppressed, then the media was always invited so that he and the First Lady could be photographed pushing their public service agenda.

Evenings were ordinarily spent at one fund-raiser or another where controversial policy positions could be carted out in front of friendly audiences. Catchy sound bites were always woven into these speeches in the hope they would be carried on the eleven o'clock news.

Between this frenetic schedule were blocks of an hour or so in which the President would do nothing more than return phone calls. These usually occurred right after lunch and just before dinner, as well as late at night if a particular emergency required his attention. In all, the President received an average of eight hundred phone calls every single day. Each one of these calls was logged onto an electronic messaging system by exact date, time, caller name, and message, if any. The days of little pink WHILE YOU WERE OUT slips being handed to the President had gone by the wayside during the Reagan administration. And with the advent of more sophisticated software, the tracking of every electronic impulse that entered the White House had developed into an exact science.

As for the routing of these messages, more than half were culled by aides and never reached the President. Most of these consisted of calls from citizens with one gripe or another who felt they had the right to get on the horn with the commander in chief simply because they had voted for him. These calls were returned either by a low-level staffer or by a form letter that thanked John or Jane Q. Public for their concern.

The President took an active role in deciding which of the remaining four hundred or so calls he would return personally. So much of his professional success had been attributed to his uncanny ability to garner support from diverse political factions. Every day dozens of congressmen, mayors, businessmen, and religious leaders called, and a return phone call from the President himself made the party on the other end of the line feel as though they were the most important person in the whole world.

On the evening when Hank Savage was snooping around inside Sarah's brownstone, the President was at Camp David. His small dinner party for the Chinese prime minister and his wife lasted until 10:30. After devouring a wedge of hot apple pie, the President excused himself from the table, telling his two guests through a translator that he needed to attend to a few matters before retiring for the night. In his rustic office, he skimmed the printout of phone messages that had come into the White House since he had last checked the list at 6:30. In all there were forty-two new messages for the President to consider. He took the list, red pen in hand. The first twelve received an S next to them. This indicated to his secretary that a staffer should respond. The President circled the next two entries. This meant that he would handle these calls himself. Then he ran down the list, quickly scribbling S in the margin beside almost every entry. When he got to the thirty-eighth call he thought for several minutes. Received at 6:44 P.M., it was from a woman who had identified herself as Francesca Baldwin. The notation attached to the message indicated that Ms. Baldwin believed her call was extremely important and that she had to speak with the President himself, rather than to one of his assistants.

The President marked an S in the margin beside Francesca's message, then went on to consider the last four calls on the list. When he was done he went back to call number thirty-eight. Although he wasn't sure why Francesca Baldwin would be calling him, he had his suspicions. He knew the First Lady and Francesca had worked together on several occasions, but he was sure that those successful charity functions would not have spurred Francesca to dial up the Oval Office. On the other hand, the bunker busters the President had secretly made available to Sam Baldwin two months earlier were another story. If Francesca had caught wind of her husband's involvement in the assassination of Saddam Hussein, there was no doubt in the President's mind that she might attempt to step in and object. The transfer of those powerful weapons, as well as their link to the White House, had been arranged under such extraordinary secret precaution because of the ramifications of their use. The President had gotten the strongest of assurances from Sam Baldwin that only those with an absolute need to know would be told anything about weapons being transported on board *The Hercules,* and of course, utterly no one was supposed to be told about the connection between *The Hercules* and the Oval Office. To further deflect the possibility of suspicion, the President and Sam Baldwin had agreed that there would be no communication between them once the transfer of weapons had occurred.

The President scratched out the S beside Francesca Baldwin's name. In its place he circled the entire entry. He would call Francesca personally as soon as he could squeeze in a few free minutes.

55 *Thursday*

SARAH stood on the sidewalk outside of the towering black glass Baldwin Building, her eyes cast skyward toward the monolith's top floor. Located in midtown, it had taken her only six minutes to stroll here from the Pierre Hotel, which had not been her original destination to spend the night. But she had taken only two steps inside the room she had reserved at the Four Seasons Hotel before a feeling of urgency had come over her.

My American Express card!

The scene outside of her brownstone had temporarily clouded her thinking. The sense of betrayal Andy Archer had caused ran deep through her marrow. But now was no time to lament. If he was as tenacious and resourceful as he had always been, then he'd be back in her face before she had time to blink. So would Jack Montgomery. By booking a room with her credit card, even in the name of Holly Whitmore, Sarah realized she had left a big, fat footprint they could easily find. She walked to Sixtieth and Fifth and checked in at the Pierre under an assumed name, paying cash up front for a two-night stay.

It was the morning rush, with hundreds of aggressive New Yorkers jockeying for sidewalk space. A few steps to Sarah's right were the five revolving doors at the foot of Sam Baldwin's gigantic world headquarters. Each spun like a gyroscope as suit-clad workers scrambled to make it to their desks on time.

Sarah was dressed in an elegantly tailored blue suit and she observed the scene for a few minutes before she spotted her opportunity. She approached a twenty-year-old black kid who was trying in vain to lock his bicycle to one of the thousands of DON'T HONK YOUR HORN! street signs. The messenger had a well-worn knapsack strapped to his back and a brown envelope tucked under his arm.

"You on the clock right now?" Sarah asked.

"Yeah, but what's it to you?" The messenger was struggling to get the thick silver chain around both of his tires and he answered without barely looking up.

"You with Speedy Deliveries?"

He turned his head and scowled. "Shit no! The company's A-One."

"I've got an envelope I need delivered upstairs right now."

The kid shook his helmeted head. "You gotta call it in. It don't work this way."

"Listen, I'm late for an appointment in SoHo. And you're going inside anyway, aren't you?"

"Yeah, but . . ."

Sarah displayed the concealed folded bill that had been cuffed in her palm. "Fifty bucks for two minutes of work. That's not a bad return on your investment if you ask me."

The messenger had given up trying to get the lock around both tires and the metal post. When the frame and back wheel were fastened he grabbed hold of the front wheel. "There ain't no drugs in there?"

Sarah raised a small white envelope to allow the sun's rays to shine through it. Inside was a single slip of paper.

The messenger studied Sarah carefully, using every ounce of his street sense to decide if this was a setup.

"Don't tell my boss," he said, snatching the envelope and the crisp green bill in one motion.

"I won't say anything if you won't," Sarah answered with a smile. "It's going to the top floor, to Sam Baldwin. And if anyone asks, you don't remember what I look like."

"Ditto," he replied as the fifty got buried into his pants pocket.

Inside the lobby he rolled the fat front tire along the smooth black marble. "Yo, hold that!" he yelled, his black high-top kicking the elevator door back open. The people inside pushed backward, making way for the kid with the baggy pants who was holding a single wheel.

The messenger made his two scheduled deliveries, then pressed the button for the top floor. The elevator opened, the heavy glass doors with the Baldwin Enterprises logo stenciled at eye level straight ahead. Beyond them were three women whom he correctly assumed were secretaries. They were sitting behind neatly ordered desks, busily tapping away at their computers. The messenger approached the entrance, then gave the double doors a push. Nothing happened. He looked to his left and then to his right for the buzzer.

"May I help you?" A female voice came over the intercom. She was staring over the frame of her reading glasses, still at her desk some twenty feet away.

"I got a letter for Sam Baldwin."

"Do we need to sign for it?"

"Nope."

"Then push it through the mail slot, please."

The secretary waited for the messenger to disappear behind the closed elevator before she sauntered toward the locked glass doors. She began to break the seal then glanced at the print on the front of the envelope:

PERSONAL AND CONFIDENTIAL—TO BE OPENED BY MY FATHER ONLY!

TO: SAM BALDWIN

FROM: JESSICA BALDWIN

The secretary hesitated, her long, cranberry red fingernail already a quarter of the way across the top. Ordinarily she would open and date-stamp everything Sam Baldwin received.

"Mr. Baldwin," she said timidly after she barely cracked open his door. "I know you didn't want to be disturbed, but this letter just arrived for you." She tentatively walked it to the round conference table where Baldwin, Hank Savage, and Doug Templeton, Jessica's fiancé, were scrutinizing a pile of documents. Handing the envelope to her boss, she left the room as quickly as she could.

"What's that?" Savage asked. He had safely exited the back door of Sarah's brownstone, leading the two policemen at the front door to believe no one had been inside. Then he had hurried back to New York to evaluate and share his information with Sam Baldwin. In his hand was one of the nude photographs of Sarah that he had taken from her home.

When Baldwin saw how the note was addressed he ripped it open. His lips moved rapidly as he silently read.

"Is it really from her?" Templeton asked excitedly.

"No," Sam Baldwin said. He handed the neatly written page to his future son-in-law.

"Read it out loud," Savage said eagerly.

"'Dear Mr. Baldwin,'" Templeton began. "'Please forgive me if your daughter's name on this envelope gave you false hope that this letter would be from her. But I thought it was the only way to get it routed to you both quickly and confidentially.'" Templeton unconsciously nodded. "'I need to talk with you immediately about a matter that I'm certain is of utmost importance to you. However, I have reason to believe that the use of your phone lines would put my identity, as well as Jessica's life, in jeopardy, and I'm not prepared to do either of those at the present time. Accordingly, if you'd like to hear what I have to say, proceed to the southwest corner of Fifty-fifth and Fifth. Directly outside the Peninsula Hotel is a bank of three public phones. The one in the middle will ring at precisely 8:55 A.M. this morning. I will let it ring ten times. If you don't answer it by the tenth ring

I'll presume you have your own methods of finding your daughter. Sincerely, Holly Whitmore.'"

"Fantastic!" Savage exclaimed.

Baldwin briskly walked across his spacious office, positioning himself beside the blue tinted window facing Fifth Avenue.

"Can you see those phones from way up here?" Savage asked.

"Yeah, but it looks like there's a lady on the one in the middle."

"Is it her?" Savage asked impatiently, referring to the picture of Sarah he had lifted from her armoire.

"I can't tell. We're up too high."

"What time is it?" Templeton asked anxiously.

"Holy Christ, it's eight minutes to nine! We've only got three minutes!"

Baldwin yanked his suit coat off his chair. "Shit! We'll never make it!"

Both Savage and Templeton rushed behind Sam Baldwin as he bolted toward his office door.

"Doug, you stay here just in case she calls!" Baldwin yelled over his shoulder. He was already past his startled secretaries.

Savage quickly caught up to his boss and entered the billionaire's small private elevator. His dark brown eyes were narrowed and his jaw set with concentration. In the span of two minutes he had changed from sympathizer to soldier. He made certain the holster strap of the handgun concealed under his tapered suit coat was unhooked. Although it would only save Savage a second or two if he needed to use it to coax Sarah to come with them, he had learned in situations like this every that second counts.

"*Come on . . .*" Baldwin shouted impatiently. He pounded his hand against one of the richly paneled walls. "What's taking this fucking thing so long to get down?" He looked at his watch. It was six minutes to nine.

The elevator doors finally opened and both men darted toward the bright sunlight. Savage knocked a middle-aged woman backward, and Baldwin followed his block. They zigzagged around the sea of sidewalk traffic until they reached the northwest corner of Fifty-fifth and Fifth. Across the street were the three public phones Sarah had identified in her note. The phones on each end were occupied, the middle one now free. Baldwin started across Fifty-fifth Street, unaware that a taxi to his left was flying through the intersection.

"Watch it!" Savage screamed. He extended his arm quickly, catching just enough of his boss's shoulder with his fingertips to slow him down. The cabbie leaned on his horn and roared past them both without lifting his heavy foot from the accelerator. The driver gesticulated wildly at the men through the back window as his yellow cab zoomed west on Fifty-fifth Street.

Baldwin frantically wove his way between the bumpers of two cars caught in traffic, undeterred by the close call. Although Sarah's deadline had passed, Baldwin did not know by how much. When he heard the middle phone ringing, he leaped over the curb and onto the sidewalk, lunging for the receiver. He forcefully knocked aside the hand of a man in a gray business suit who was about to use the phone.

"Hello?" Baldwin said desperately.

"What the fuck is wrong with you, mister?"

Savage menacingly stepped between the two men, a good six inches and fifty pounds larger than the would-be caller. The man in the suit shook his head and walked away, muttering under his breath about the number of rude assholes in New York.

"Who's this?" Sarah asked.

"It's Sam Baldwin. I got your note."

"I was about to hang up."

"Please don't."

"I wasn't sure you wanted to talk to me."

"I do, very badly. Who are you?"

"I can't tell you that right now, or maybe ever. But I think I've stumbled onto something very important concerning your daughter. But before I go to the FBI I need you to answer a few basic questions."

"Wait a second," Baldwin interrupted, "I can barely hear you." He pressed his index finger tightly against the opening of his right ear. Just behind him was a homeless man with a scraggly, food-encrusted black beard who was pontificating loudly to anyone who would listen. *"Repent before it's too late!"* he bellowed. *"The end of the world is near! Jesus is the answer!"*

Pedestrians cut a wide swath for the unsteady figure as he turned right at the corner and headed south on Fifth Avenue.

"You still there?" Baldwin asked.

"I'm here."

"I want you listen to me very carefully. Under no circumstances are you to go to the FBI. Is that understood?"

"I have to go, Mr. Baldwin. I'll call you again at your office in a few hours. You'll know it's me because I'll say it's your cousin Amy. When you hear that message, go back to the pay phone and I'll call you there."

"But how can I get in touch with you before then?"

As Baldwin waited for Sarah's response he heard the voice of the homeless man getting louder and louder on the other end of the receiver. His eyes widened when he realized how terribly close Sarah must have been. He cupped his palm over the phone.

"She's on a pay phone just around the corner!" he barked at Savage. "If you find that idiot who's yelling about Jesus, you'll find her!"

56

HENRY MCCLARTY had devoted decades of his life to understanding every aspect of high-technology communications. Part Marconi and part Edison, by sixth grade he was capable of soldering together a few rudimentary components of Radio Shack equipment to create his own walkie-talkie. By the time he had graduated from high school he had invented a device that enabled him to route long-distance telephone calls through local switching stations so even transatlantic calls cost him only pennies. When this creative aptitude was coupled with the intensive training he received from the U.S. Army, a talent was born that often served to protect the lives of his fellow Special Forces members. McClarty routinely slipped deep behind hostile lines to bollix his adversary's communications network, paralyzing the enemy from calling in backup troops after they had been hit with a surprise attack. The rout in Basra on February, 24, 1991, was a classic example of his impact, when he parachuted during the dead of night into the town of Al-Amarah, located in Iraq along the Tigris River. The one-two punch of his jamming equipment, and that on board a nearby AWACS jet, crippled the Iraqi leadership's ability to communicate with its troops. Minutes later, at 0400 hours local time, the ground war in Operation Desert Storm commenced in the southwest portion of Iraq. As a direct result of McClarty's expertise, the military leaders in Baghdad learned that fighting was under way only because it was reported on CNN. By then, any chance that the Iraqis could stem the tide had been irreparably lost.

ON the morning when Sarah made contact with Sam Baldwin from a street pay phone in New York City, McClarty traveled to the train station closest to where Jessica Baldwin was being held. There he called Jack Montgomery from a pay phone exactly like the one used by Sarah Peterson. He looked as though he were going to a Land's End catalog shoot, and blended effortlessly into the group of commuters who were milling about the station's platform. No one would remember seeing him that morning, which was precisely his intent.

The small train station had only two banks of telephones, and McClarty had chosen the deserted one adjacent to the outdoor parking lot. He set a playing card–sized black box with a tiny punch pad on the front face onto the sloping stainless steel ledge just beneath the coin return slot; it would trick the phone company's computers into thinking sufficient change had been inserted to place the long-distance call from Minneapolis.

"Mr. Secretary," he said matter-of-factly, making no attempt to disguise his voice.

"Grizzwald?" Jack Montgomery asked anxiously.

"No, it's McClarty. I assume you're ready to wire the money?"

"Not yet, but . . ."

"You've got thirty-six hours. At midnight tomorrow we'll kill her. Maybe before then if Grizzwald gets his way. He's getting very antsy. I know I don't have to tell you that he actually enjoys killing, and even more so the moment just before the kill."

"Listen to me, McClarty. I've read your file again very carefully and I've got no doubt that this foolish extortion scheme is all Grizzwald's idea. If you agree to cooperate, I can end this silly little charade before anyone gets hurt. I promise your slate will be wiped clean, that you'll be reinstated to full military rank, and that no record of any of this will exist in any government file."

"Are you finished?"

"Do yourself a favor and give it some thought. I know you think Grizzwald's worth following, but he's not. There's no question about his military skills, but he's a bad seed who's taken you down a stray path. And even if you don't agree with that assessment, then think about your folks in Chicago. You wouldn't want your elderly parents to fall victim to an unfortunate accident, would you? From the pictures I've got here on my desk, their old house on Maplewood Road looks like such a fire hazard."

Jack Montgomery pressed the Caller ID button as he awaited a response to his threat. Ten digits instantly appeared in the small window beside his volume button. He reached for a pen and quickly jotted down the phone number.

"Area code 612-823-2710," McClarty said blandly once he saw the yellow warning light on his small black box. "You want me to be in Virginia, Jack? Maybe the house next door to yours? Then it'd be really easy to find us. Hold on and let me reprogram this thing." McClarty pressed a few buttons and the numbers on Jack Montgomery's gray Caller ID screen flashed to one that had a 703 area code. "C'mon, Jack," McClarty added, "don't insult my intelligence. My nephew can do better than that. Maybe when we're done speaking you'll press star sixty-nine and *this* phone'll ring." He laughed.

Montgomery scratched out the numbers he had written, embarrassed he had been caught attempting something so facile.

"I'll think about your proposal," McClarty said. "But get this straight. If my parents are *ever* harmed, in *any* fashion, you'll be the one looking over your shoulder. Remember, the security around you exists only as long as you're Secretary of State. After that? Well, you know. And that lovely wife of yours looks like such a nice lady. That pretty blond hair and those pearls that match. She'd look terrible with half her face gone."

Montgomery said nothing.

"In the meantime," McClarty added, "you've got less than thirty-six hours before the game ends and we disappear forever."

"I understand."

"And tell General Perry not to bother wasting his time looking for us in that old farmhouse in Massachusetts. Maybe he thinks I didn't know he was listening in on my conversation with Grizzwald last week. But that's grade school stuff, Jack."

With a tug of a little green wire, the useless numbers on Jack Montgomery's screen vanished. Out of curiosity the Secretary pressed *69. It rang three times before a woman answered.

"Good afternoon, the White House. How may I help you?"

Montgomery smiled and hung up the phone. *Touché*, he thought. *Touché.*

57

IT took only an instant for Sarah to realize that Sam Baldwin was stalling for time. Not only did his inflection change dramatically, but the cadence of his speech was noticeably choppy. Sarah's instincts screamed at her to move quickly, and she did. She dropped the phone and left the spiral metal wire dangling at the corner of Fifty-third and Fifth, just two blocks from the Peninsula Hotel.

By the time Hank Savage reached the abandoned phone, Sarah had blended into the tide of pedestrian traffic along Fifth Avenue. Savage's eyes darted in every direction, hopelessly scouring the bobbing heads for her.

On their way back to the Baldwin Building, both Hank Savage and Sam Baldwin examined every face that crossed their path, even though they knew it was an exercise in futility. Sarah was very close and only time would tell whether she had blundered by remaining in the area.

Within minutes of his return to his penthouse office, Baldwin received another call on his private line. He put the call on his speaker.

"I need to know right now whether you're in a position to wire the fifty million, Mr. Baldwin," Montgomery said. Even through the synthetic distortion the caller's intensity was apparent. "If not, then tell me now so we can kill her mercifully."

"If you kill my Jessica," Baldwin said, "then you might as well kill yourself, too. Because I'll devote every waking minute to making sure that your death is a painful one."

"If you're so concerned about your daughter's safety, then why are those weapons still moving into position? Where the hell are your priorities?"

"I already told you that topic was no longer open for discussion."

A ringing silence enveloped both sides of the call as Montgomery considered his next move. "Suppose I can work out a way for Jessica to be released within the next thirty-six hours?"

Baldwin snapped his head in Savage's direction. *The caller had blinked first*, the billionaire's sparkling eyes said. "If that happens within twenty-four hours, not thirty-six, then I'd be willing to talk."

"I'm not making any promises, Mr. Baldwin. I want to be very clear about that. And you better be prepared to wire fifty million dollars upon my next phone call. Because if you're not, then whatever happens to Jessica is your responsibility, not mine."

The three men exchanged glances when they heard the click.

"You're really willing to negotiate?" Savage asked.

"Only so I can flush him out and kill him," Baldwin replied coldly. "Now I know he can be broken."

Savage quickly circled around the desk, punched in a phone number, and put the phone on speaker. It rang once before Victor picked up. "Anything this time?"

"Nope. My screen showed the call coming in, but I couldn't pick up the signal. It's just like I explained to Mr. Baldwin a few hours ago. Whoever's making these calls either has an incredibly advanced jamming system, or he's somehow scrambling his impulses into a central computer so they can't be traced. I hooked the call into our most restricted nine-one-one software, but even that wouldn't give me a street address or phone number."

"Victor, this is Sam. Suppose this isn't someone with a ton of technical know-how or a multimillion-dollar phone system. Does anyone have the clout to set up an arrangement with the phone company to prevent their calls from being traced?"

"Jeez, I've been working here almost twenty years and I've only heard of it a few times. But if I had to guess, there are probably a thousand people tops who could swing something like that."

"Like who?"

"Well, all of the top guys in the CIA, the FBI, and the NSC for starters. I know for sure they've got unbelievably secure phones. Then you've got a handful of generals and admirals who could probably push hard enough to justify an expenditure like this. Of course, the President and his cabinet do anything they want. And then there are a small group of corporate officials who're working on extremely sensitive government matters. They might be able to wangle something like this on a temporary basis." Victor paused, then said, "I'm sure there are others that I'm missing, like diplomats at the UN, but that should put you in the ballpark."

"All right, Victor," Savage said. "Make sure you stay on top of this."

"Will do."

Baldwin hit the release button. "I've got a theory," he said as he stood facing the row of windows behind his desk. "I think whoever's the mastermind behind Jessie's kidnapping is beginning to panic. I think he's lost control of the situation."

"What the hell makes you say that?" Templeton asked.

"A few things. First of all, from what Victor just told us, it's clear this guy's not your average thug. He's obviously someone important in either the government or the business world. Now that makes sense, because he knew about *The Hercules* and his initial ultimatum was obviously politically motivated. Then, out of nowhere, comes a huge ransom demand. That's totally illogical if the motive for Jessie's kidnapping was purely political. Why wouldn't he have asked for the cash up front if there was a profit in it for him? He's got to know that pulling that amount of money together would take some time, no matter who was involved."

Savage nodded.

"And there's something else," Baldwin added as he rolled up the cuffs of his white sleeves. "Hank, how many background checks have you run on Sarah Peterson?"

"Two."

"And what've they shown?"

"Absolutely nothing, except that she's a federal employee, grade level GS-fifteen. But her job description is missing from the reports we've been able to tap into. That's the first time my government payroll guy has ever struck out on anything like this."

"You think you'll have something on her soon?"

"I hope so. I'm calling in an old marker with a contact at the Secret Service."

"Well, let's think this through," Baldwin said, still fixed on his hypothesis. "If we assume a high-ranking official ordered Jessie's abduction, then we've got to believe he wouldn't have actually carried it out himself, right?"

"Definitely," Templeton said.

"So now you've got some freelancer doing the dirty work for someone who's in a position of power, and who's got everything to lose if his name surfaces, right?"

Both men nodded.

"And then out of the blue comes a ransom demand from a guy who says he might let Jessie go within the next thirty-six hours, even though I've told him in no uncertain terms that I won't pay him a penny."

Savage's dark eyes widened as he began to understand what Sam Baldwin had obviously already concluded. "So some big shot hired a mercenary to kidnap Jessie," Savage said, looking at Baldwin.

"Bingo."

"And now the kidnapper or kidnappers are hiding somewhere waiting for instructions, and figure out that if they turn the tables on the person who hired them, they'll get the biggest payday of their lives. The mastermind obviously can't go to the police or the FBI, but he can pass the demand on to you."

"That's how I see it," Baldwin said. "And since *I* won't pay him anything, *he'll* somehow scrape together fifty million."

"It's all very clean," Savage said with a slow nod. "But how does Sarah Peterson fit into the picture?"

"That I don't know that yet," Baldwin admitted. "And that's why we need to get our hands on her as soon as possible. She either tells us what she knows or she doesn't tell anyone at all."

"Let's stop screwing around," Templeton said. "I agree with Francesca. I say it's time for us to go to the FBI with what we've got right now."

"Absolutely not!" Baldwin replied emphatically. "If I were in the kidnapper's shoes, and the rules of the game suddenly changed, then I'd kill her and scramble for cover." His expression showed that he knew just how desperate a situation they were still in.

"As her fiancé, I say it's time we go to the authorities."

"And as her father, I won't allow it." Baldwin leaned forward and stared at Doug Templeton.

"Then exactly what the fuck do you want to do?"

Baldwin lifted the sheet of paper that contained Sarah's cryptic notes after she had listened to the microcassette.

"I'll send Hank to the Hay-Adams right now," Baldwin said. He turned to Savage and asked, "There's someone named Witherspoon staying there?"

"Yes. I called this morning and confirmed it."

"And what about this other guy, Ed Gallagher?"

"Same thing, but he wasn't in his room when I called."

Baldwin nodded his approval of Savage's information. "It's time for us to send a message." The blue veins near his temples throbbed as he clenched his teeth in anger. "And we're going to exact as much information as possible while doing so." He paused, then said, "If you don't have the stomach for something like this, Doug, then leave the room so you don't hear any of this. But promise me you'll give me this one shot at rescuing Jessie. If this doesn't work, then I'll drive you myself to FBI headquarters."

Savage looked at Templeton and nodded. Although the ex-marine showed no outward sign of excitement, deep inside he was turning handsprings. With Sam Baldwin's explicit go-ahead to pay a visit to the Hay-Adams, it was clear the quiet storm would finally have an opportunity to roar.

Templeton remained mute in his seat for a moment, then returned the nod. "Go for it," he said softly to Hank. "Go for it now."

58

ANDY ARCHER drove through the Lincoln Tunnel, seething at how he had been humiliated over the last eighteen hours; all those rubberneckers watching him being led like a dog into a squad car, then a freezing jail cell that reeked of urine. But more than anything, the image of Sarah Peterson's face was what he would remember most. First she had gasped in surprise. Then she had smiled while the police had tightened the handcuffs around his wrists and pushed him into the squad car. With her smug grin she had punctuated the moment and flipped him the bird without so much as lifting a finger.

Fortunately for Archer, someone had obviously expended some very significant political capital to spring him so quickly and so unequivocally. The police captain who gave him back his belongings (including the fully loaded Mauser) even apologized for the apparent mix-up. It was certainly helpful to have friends in high places.

Now Archer's assignment was personal. Sarah Peterson had spit in his eye. She had gotten a head start and was already in Manhattan. He knew that. She had already reserved a place to sleep while she was there. He knew that, too. And when she returned to her hotel room, Archer would pay her back for making him look like such a fool in the eyes of the man who he felt sure would one day be President.

59

SARAH drove her Jeep across the New York–Connecticut border and entered the quaint town of Old Greenwich, focused on harvesting more facts concerning the whereabouts of Jessica Baldwin. After that was accomplished, she'd take Walter Jensen up on his offer by turning this investigation over to a team that had the resources to more effectively complete the end game. As long as she didn't spin her wheels, she hoped all this would be achieved before Saddam Hussein was killed, and the gears of his chemical arsenal were set in motion. But she had little doubt that the pile of sand at the top of the hourglass was getting smaller by the minute.

"Oh shit!" she exclaimed as the thought of Walter Jensen jogged her memory.

She pulled her car in front of a tiny antique store and rifled through her attaché case in search of her address book. It was stuffed inside the sunsplashed pages of a Club Med brochure that she'd been meaning to look at for weeks. The vacation she and two girlfriends had taken to Cancún six months ago now seemed like a different decade. Sarah sighed, then dialed the forensics lab.

"Walter! I'm glad you're there."

"Sarah? Where are you?"

"In Connecticut, just a couple of miles from Jessica Baldwin's house. But before I went over there I wanted to make sure you didn't do anything with the envelope."

"I've still got it."

"Thank goodness."

"Any luck finding Jessica Baldwin yet?"

"Not really, but I may have something by the end of the day."

"That's great. Maybe you'll give old Clem Barker a run for his money after all."

Sarah smiled as she glanced at her watch, knowing she had received the ultimate compliment from Jensen. "If you don't hear from me in twelve hours, or by midnight tonight, then give the envelope to that reporter at *The Washington Post*, just like we discussed."

"Will do."

"How about that microfiche on General Perry? Did you find that yet?"

"No, but I think I've narrowed it down to four or five boxes. They all seem to be from 1963."

"When in sixty-three?"

"It's hard to tell, but it looks like late summer or early fall."

Sarah remembered her conversation with Anna Rodzinski. "I'll call you again in a couple of hours. Just remember what I told you about going online to do any research."

Jensen's heart skipped a beat, although he said nothing. He *had* heeded her warning about not accessing any of the FBI's classified files to conduct his research, but he had used his computer to examine the list of documents that were indexed at the Library of Congress. That was OK, he thought, wasn't it?

SARAH ended her conversation with Walter Jensen and began the short drive east toward Jessica Baldwin's home. The further out of town she went, the more impressive the scenery became. The winding roads were tree lined, surrounded on both sides by finely manicured lawns. The houses in the affluent community were an eclectic blend of styles, ranging from traditional Tudors with tan and dark brown moldings to cubist Frank Lloyd Wrights that appeared to be suspended in air by glass and steel. Some were barely visible above their tall front hedges, some totally obscured by stone walls that were too high to scale. Others were several hundred yards from the public roadway, set way back behind wrought iron front gates.

"I guess I'm not in Kansas anymore," Sarah said to herself. She wove her way through a series of hurdle-sized white picket fences that were positioned like slalom gates exactly ten yards apart. Sarah had never seen a private road with this type of speed barrier. The forced crawl allowed her to admire the magnificent homes on each side of this secluded lane. In all, she guessed there were twenty or so houses from the point where the road had curved to Jessica Baldwin's home.

Sarah parked her Jeep in the driveway of the last house on the dead-end street, in the exact same spot where Grizzwald had parked his rented Cadillac sedan a few days earlier. Through the thick bushes and trees she could see a sliver of the Long Island Sound beyond Jessica's huge backyard. Sarah walked up the multicolored slate pathway to the wraparound porch. With her hands cupped like blinders she pressed her forehead against one of the narrow strips of glass that were on both sides of the front door. Aside from the life-sized bronze Rodin statue at the foot of a carpeted spiral staircase, there was nothing about the cavernous front vestibule that caught her attention. She rang the bell, relatively certain there would be no answer. Then she waited more than a minute after the second ring for someone to respond. When no one did, she walked back down the four front steps, glancing back when she thought she heard a noise. That's when she noticed the brass mail plate affixed to the front door at knee level. She looked around, then leaped up the stairs two at a time.

Sarah knelt down on the bristly welcome mat and noticed the raised words U.S. MAIL on the tarnished brass. She lifted the thin rectangular metal plate. It opened on to an elliptical hole that looked directly into the sea of white Italian marble that was Jessica's front foyer. Sarah bent forward and peered intently through the slot. There was a pile of letters strewn on the shiny floor; most appeared to be bills of one sort or another. But one caused Sarah to do a double-take. Underneath the same L.L. Bean Winter Sport catalog from which she had ordered a pair of blue corduroys last week was an unmistakable piece of mail. Unmistakable, at least, to someone like

Sarah, who had spent thousands and thousands of hours studying every nuance of the security business. To the average person, however, the rectangular box would have appeared to be simply a set of replacement checks sent from a bank.

Sarah pushed her right hand through the oval mail slot. When all five fingers made it inside easily she forced her forearm forward to try to grab the package. When that failed, she removed her arm from the narrow hole, took off her jacket, and gave it another try. This time her arm went in slightly further, just beyond her wrist, before the metal began constricting her flesh. Sarah gritted her teeth and pushed her arm forward with a quick thrust.

"Ouch!" she screamed. An exposed corner of jagged metal had ripped the skin away from the underside of her forearm. She looked over her shoulders, making certain her involuntary reaction to the pain had not alerted one of the neighbors.

At first the wound appeared to Sarah to be only an abrasion; then the raw skin began to bead with tiny droplets of blood. With part of her arm still inside Jessica's foyer, Sarah opened and closed her index and middle fingers as if they were the blades on a pair of scissors. She realized after several tries that her desperate attempts to snare the package were going to be useless. She twisted her waist so she could peer into the slot to determine how far away her effort had left her, gauging the distance between her fingertips and the small box still to be more than six inches. Closer than that, on one of the envelopes, was a small pool of her blood.

Sarah gingerly began to pull her arm out of the hole. Then she realized the skin on her swollen arm was caught on the sharp edge that had caused her laceration. She slowly pulled back a couple of times, knowing a full retreat would excoriate the area between her elbow and hand. When that failed to extricate her arm, she rotated her wrist a quarter of an inch, setting fresh skin on the spot with the barbed metal. She closed her eyes tightly, took in a gulp of air, and prepared herself for the inevitable.

"Agh!" she blurted as she yanked her arm out of the slot. The force of the clean pullout sent her toppling backward towards the porch steps. She braced herself with her uninjured arm, keeping her from falling backward down the stairs.

She regained her balance and surveyed the extent of the wound. The steady bleeding had stopped. She crudely cleansed the wound with a handful of saliva and put her jacket back on, determined to see if there was another way to get her hands on the package.

A stroll around the grounds did little to convince Sarah that she was going to be successful during this visit. Although a rock through one of the ground-floor windows would have permitted her to gain entry, Sarah was certain an alarm would have sounded before the glass fully shattered. She wandered to the backyard, where the putting green lawn met a row of jagged rocks on the curved shoreline of the Long Island Sound. There she strayed to the edge of the narrow white dock where Jessica's modest speedboat was moored in place. Sarah looked out at the choppy water, squinting to see some of the dozen or so boats bobbing in the distance. She stared back at the large house after she had admired the panoramic view and that's when she noticed, up on the third floor, that one of the three bay windows that flooded Jessica's master bedroom with sunlight was partially open.

60

THE soldier with the high-powered field binoculars crouched down behind the weather-beaten storage bin filled with life preservers. Although the probability that the woman wearing the navy blue blazer could see him from this distance was extremely remote, his instructions to remain undetected had been unequivocal. General Perry himself had delivered the stern warning that immediate demotion would follow in the event there was a deviation from his precise instructions.

"General, it's Krystoviac," he reported as soon as Sarah had walked back around the front of Jessica's house. The reception on his cellular phone crackled because of the trawler's distance from the nearest receiving station. "You said you wanted to be informed immediately if anything unusual occurred here?"

"What's happened?" Perry asked anxiously. Even though the general knew Grizzwald and McClarty would probably not be foolish enough to return to Jessica's home, during his years in the military Perry had witnessed men do some remarkably stupid things. Perhaps Jessica had told her captors where her safety deposit box key was located, or where stacks of unmarked bills were secreted in a wall safe. There were also valuable works of art that could be taken from the premises. In any case, the general had taken every precaution. If nothing materialized, then the negligible inconvenience of tying up two Special Forces men was worth the effort. Besides, after the fiasco in western Massachusetts he was determined to cover all of the bases.

"A young woman was just traipsing around the backyard sticking her nose in every goddamn window," Krystoviac said. "I couldn't really see her face because we're almost a mile out, but it sure as hell looked like that pretty young thing who was guarding the Vice President a few years ago. She started to climb up this friggin' support beam that leads to one of the upstairs bedrooms, but she had a devil of a time getting up that damn thing. After ten minutes she went back around the front of the house. That's when we lost sight of her."

"Did she drive away?"

"I don't know, sir. She might have gained entry from the front. Do you want us to approach the house and detain her if she's still there?"

"No! Just maintain your positions and report back to me if she returns."

"Aye, aye, General."

"By the way, Captain, that couldn't have been the lady you're thinking of because she was with me here in Washington just a few minutes ago."

"Like I said, sir, I'm pretty far away."

"Keep up the fine work, Captain. And don't hesitate to call me at once if you see anyone else around that house. If anything urgent comes up and you can't reach me, then leave a message for Secretary Montgomery. He'll know how to find me."

"Aye, aye, sir."

Without missing a beat, Buck Perry dialed the Hay-Adams, instructing the hotel operator to put him through to Tom Witherspoon immediately. When told that both of Witherspoon's lines were busy, the general insisted the operator interrupt one of Witherspoon's calls.

"Tom, it's Buck. I can't get into all of the details right now, but I've got to know what's happening with the money."

"Don't tell me something else's wrong," Witherspoon groused. He was seated on a Louis XIV padded armchair, his papers spread on the leather-topped Victorian rosewood writing desk in front of him. A chambermaid had opened the lace curtains, allowing the brilliant sunshine to spill into the room.

"Nothing's wrong," Perry responded. "But before I get us out of this situation once and for all I need to know the cash will be available, and fast."

Witherspoon felt the butterflies turning in his stomach. In all the years he had known Buck Perry, he had never heard the soldier who seemed to have antifreeze in his veins sound so anxious.

"I had two of my bankers on the line when you jumped in," Witherspoon replied. "It'll take a thousand calls to get this accomplished without faxing paperwork all over the place. But it should be ready by day's end."

"Do it discreetly, and don't leave that room until it's a done deal. We need to pay those two bastards as soon as possible so we can put this fiasco behind us. Things are starting to unravel."

"Then let me get back to my calls, God damn it. I just hung up on a guy who's trying his best to help me scrape together ten million dollars."

"Is Gallagher having any trouble getting his half?"

"Look, Buck, I have no idea. The only thing I know is that you just forced me off the line with a Senior VP at Credit Suisse. God knows if I'll be able to get him back on the phone."

"Then go ahead and make your calls. I'll be out of pocket for a little while, but you can leave a message on my voice mail here at the Pentagon if you run into any snags. I'm the only one who's got the password to my line."

General Perry hastily shoved a folded map of Connecticut into his brief-case. It had been years, maybe decades, since he had felt so pumped up. When his nine-inch hunting knife was secured beside his loaded revolver, he closed and locked the briefcase. Now that he knew where Sarah Peterson was, he didn't want amateurs like Andy Archer doing his work for him.

61

LAGUARDIA Airport was relatively deserted at midday, a brief lull before the throng of hectic commuters rushed around the airport to catch overbooked flights to every sector of the country. The Marine Air Terminal, set almost a mile west of the main gates, appeared to Hank Savage as though it had been evacuated. Despite the sparse crowd, he had concealed his crew cut with a blond hairpiece and a tape-on mustache. A prosthetic paunch and blue contact lenses further added to his disguise. Even if the inevitable FBI inquiry this trip would cause somehow wound its way to this spot, it would lead to a description of a man who did not exist. Of course, the fact that he was flying a commercial airline, instead of one of the Baldwin corporate jets, practically ensured that any investigation would never get that far. Filing a flight plan with the FAA in order to save a few minutes was a risk he decided wasn't worth taking.

Savage paid cash at the gate for his ticket with well-worn twenties, and curb-checked his compact valise so the gun inside would avoid X-ray detection. With a Delta Shuttle flight leaving for Washington, D.C., every hour on the half hour, Savage had his choice of seats for the forty-five-minute jaunt to the nation's capital. He selected one by a window, halfway down the narrow aisle of the Boeing 737. Passengers were sprinkled both in front of him and in the back of the aircraft, and he knew neither flight attendant would have time to take notice of the heavy-set businessman who kept his face buried inside his *Wall Street Journal.*

He walked the quarter mile to the United terminal upon his arrival at National Airport, where he waited eighteen minutes for the passengers on board United's flight from Seattle to retrieve their luggage before he blended in with the crowd flowing out of United's baggage claim area. Once he was seated in the back of a smoke-filled taxi, he directed the Nigerian driver to drop him off at the corner of Sixteenth Street and Pennsylvania Avenue. Because the White House was barely fifty paces away, Savage knew his request was one the cabbie received many times every day.

The short walk from the wrought iron fence surrounding the North Lawn to the Hay-Adams Hotel was uneventful, except for his jog around the group of Asian tourists who were snapping pictures at everything that didn't move. The ex-marine had found himself in the line of fire between the tourists and the art deco facade of St. John's Church, which was directly across the street from his intended destination. He quickly crossed Sixteenth Street, rubbing his gloved hand across the bridge of his nose just in case one of the Japanese tourists had activated his camcorder. Although his disguise cloaked his actual features, Savage knew the FBI had a stable of men like Walter Jensen who could analyze a videotape down to a pixel if given sufficient time and initiative; and he was well aware he was about to provide them with the latter.

In his expensive Italian suit and floral silk tie, Savage mingled easily among the affluent crowd after entering the hotel. Half smiling at the few who made eye contact with him, Savage found his way to the men's room adjacent to the Eagle Bar & Grill.

"Good afternoon, sir," said the tuxedoed washroom attendant when Savage walked in. He was busily rearranging the accessories on one side of the black marble sink, making certain the cotton hand towels were perfectly symmetrical with the box of Kleenex. On the other side of the basin was a row of erotically shaped bottles filled with amber-colored colognes.

Savage entered the oversized stall and locked the door behind him. He dropped his trousers and boxers to his ankles, then peered through the narrow space between the stall door and the metal partition before opening his small valise. The attendant was mindlessly wiping down his workstation with a wet rag.

Savage propped his small suitcase on his bare thighs and assembled his deadly Luger to the soothing sound of Tchaikovsky's *Dance of the Swans* as it wafted out of the built-in Bose ceiling speakers. He had broken down the weapon into its component parts before setting off for Washington, spreading the various pieces among the ill-fitting articles of clothing he had purchased with cash for this trip. As part of his training with the marines he had been required to learn how to take apart, then reconstruct, no fewer than a dozen different weapons while blindfolded. At one point in his military career he had been able to accomplish the feat in less than sixty seconds while wearing a pair of Gore-Tex mittens. In the luxurious men's room in the Hay-Adams Hotel, his sheer calfskin gloves presented no problem.

Before flushing, Savage slapped at the roll of toilet paper two or three times. He ripped the perforated sheets, and added a few conspicuous crumples for effect, certain his time squatting over a marble seat had appeared authentic. He exited the stall, primped his artificial hair, then left the bathroom with his Luger tucked into his front waistband.

"Good afternoon," he said with a slight nod to the elderly couple who followed him into the elevator after they had enjoyed a fine meal at the Eagle Bar & Grille. "What floor?"

"Four, please," replied a man with a thick German accent.

Savage pressed the button for the fourth floor, then the one for the sixth. He would have gotten out on a floor other than the one where he knew Tom Witherspoon occupied a suite even had no one else joined him in the elevator.

"Guten abend," Savage said to the couple as they left for their room.

Both smiled, but neither returned the pleasantry.

Savage exited on the sixth floor and quickly made his way across the carpeted hallway to one of the two emergency stairwells. The walls were painted in 1970 East Bloc government gray, the black concrete steps just as bland. Rising up from the basement to split the winding rectangular staircase was a six-inch standpipe that hissed like a steam engine on a freighter. The black numbers that had been stenciled onto each reentry door were bordered with a razor-thin outline of violet paint.

Savage climbed up two flights and pulled open the heavy fire door to the eighth floor. The thick woolen carpet muffled his footsteps. He walked noiselessly down the hall and took a moment to press his ear against the doorframe outside Suite 804. As he listened to one side of Tom Witherspoon's telephone conversation, he glanced in both directions to determine if anyone else was in sight. The sturdy mahogany door muffled Witherspoon's voice to something less than a whisper. Savage smiled. He was pleased to know the old yellow walls were as solid as he had suspected. When he was certain the coast was clear, he rang the bell outside the door. The beige calfskin gloves were assurance there would be no prints for the FBI to dust.

"Yes?" Witherspoon yelled.

Savage stood there patiently, deciding not to respond. Instead, he pressed the illuminated button again. A moment later the pinhole of light shining through the peephole disappeared for an instant before the door swung open.

"Yeah?" Witherspoon asked impatiently.

Savage looked past the arms dealer's shoulder, taking notice that the phone on the antique desk was off its hook.

"Good afternoon, Mr. Witherspoon, I'm Chuck Dobbins, the assistant concierge. I need to check your thermostat for a second or two. We just received a complaint from the guest in Room 704 that your HVAC unit might be leaking. We wanted to examine it before calling maintenance."

"Whatever," Witherspoon replied as he strode back to his chair. He picked up his conversation where it had been left off, though he lowered his tone a few decibels. Savage strained to catch this side of the exchange while he tinkered with the heating and air-conditioning controls. The arms dealer was switching back and forth between French and English, obviously talking numbers and bank accounts.

"I'm going to take a look at the unit if you don't mind," Savage said to Witherspoon obsequiously. He was doing his best to appear as though serving the hotel's wealthy guests was his only purpose in life. Witherspoon talked on without responding, unaware that Savage had walked across the room behind him. When his phone line went dead, Witherspoon appeared confused.

"Hello?" he said.

"Hello?" This time he spoke louder. "Bernard, are you still there?" He took the phone away from his ear and stared quizzically at the receiver. "For Christ's sake, what the hell's wrong with this thing?" He switched lines, but could not get a dial tone.

Savage was still bent down near the base of the heating unit, the compact pair of wire cutters placed back in his pocket. He looked up innocently, trying to sound as helpful as he could. "Something wrong?"

"You know anything about phones? This goddamn thing just went dead."

"Let me have a look."

Savage stood behind the seated Witherspoon, holding the cradle of the receiver in his gloved hand. He feigned an attempt at diagnosing the problem while he peered over Witherspoon's shoulder. It took less than five seconds for him to skim Witherspoon's handwritten notes to confirm what he had strongly suspected; that the man seated just inches away had been involved in Jessica's abduction, and that he would be able to exact a measure of revenge.

Savage unbuttoned his jacket, giving him free access to the smooth black handle of his Luger. Witherspoon also possessed a concealed weapon, but it was in his suitcase in the adjoining room.

62

ANDY ARCHER paced the length of the sixteenth floor of the Four Seasons several times, not yet certain what to do. The USA Today remained undisturbed just outside of Sarah's room, but the calls he had made from the hotel lobby had gone unanswered. Likewise, his knock on the door had received no response. Perplexed, he flagged down a chambermaid who spoke little English and persuaded her that he had locked himself out. Moments later he was inside the room where Sarah had only spent a few minutes before leaving the hotel without checking out.

He looked around carefully. No toothbrush, no clothes, no suitcase. Only a small piece of hotel stationery with a handwritten note taped to the bathroom mirror: "AA—Maybe next time. Maybe not." Somehow Sarah had slipped through the net and spit in his eye once again.

Archer decided he would track down every taxi driver who frequently parked in front of the Four Seasons during the middle of the night, waiting for a fare. Like the cabbies who positioned themselves at airports, there were regulars who were fixtures at every one of Manhattan's deluxe hotels. He would discreetly speak with the overnight bellhops and garage attendants to see if anyone knew where Sarah had gone. He would also check the phone records for this room to see if arrangements for another hotel stay had been made, even though she was still registered as Holly Whitmore in this hotel. Someone surely would be able to tell him something, especially if they were quietly offered a small fortune. But until he got his hands on Sarah Peterson, he knew Jack Montgomery was going to be furious.

63

WALTER JENSEN wearily grabbed the roll of microfiche and placed it onto the black plastic spindle. He spun the gray handle slowly, allowing his bloodshot eyes to quickly skim the reports other FBI agents had written more than three decades earlier. He was wedged in a tiny carrel beside an alarmed emergency exit in the basement of the Hoover Building. His hands were filthy, having spent the last four hours threading the thin film under a square of glass, past a projection tube and back around onto an empty reel. He had lost count after the seventy-eighth roll, and that was hours ago. Only a single large box remained, but like the other five, it was packed tightly with rolls of compressed information that dated back to the Kennedy administration. Jensen wondered why in God's name no one had bothered to organize this stuff properly. There was no log, no index, just hundreds of thousands of pages, each condensed down to the size of a postage stamp.

When Jensen finally saw the words *Major Buck Perry* at the top edge of one of the pages, he thought his eyes were playing tricks on him. The contents of the two-page report jolted him like a hard slap across the face; according to the information, a ruthless predator had roamed free for more than thirty years. What Jensen found worse was that unless he intervened, Buck Perry would surely kill again.

The FBI agent reread the report. The gruesome crime scene photos of Chip Peterson flashed into his mind.

Dear God, he had to warn Sarah before it was too late! He had to let her know that Buck Perry had played a pivotal role in her father's death.

He picked up the phone and dialed the State Department. Perhaps Jack Montgomery would know how to find her.

64

"Look, lady," Andy Archer said. "I'm just trying to verify this receipt before I put it in line for payment. I can't believe your hotel charged our client that much for a local call. But it's right here on her receipt."

The clerk in the back office of the Four Seasons rolled her eyes as she held the phone away from her ear.

"I'm sorry, sir, but the hotel charges two dollars for every local call. That's standard policy."

"But this one was made in the middle of the night. Isn't there an off-hours rate?"

"No, sir. They're all the same."

"Well, at least tell me what number it was so that we can talk about this with our client," Archer said disgustedly. "We're not supposed to pay for her personal calls."

Archer heard the ruffle of pages turning. "212-838-8000. That's the Pierre Hotel, sir. It's also within the Four Season's group of hotels."

"That's only a few blocks away for Christ's sake, isn't that right?"

"Yes, sir. Six blocks away."

"Then why'd you charge her two dollars for that call?"

"I already told you, sir, that's our policy. If you want to take it up with the supervisor who's on duty I'll be happy to connect you."

"That won't be necessary." Archer hung up the phone with a smile.

65

Sarah pulled into the underground lot of the Pierre and told the young attendant she would require her Jeep within two hours. She had selected this garage for a number of reasons: it was in midtown, close to both Sam Baldwin's home and office; it was open twenty-four hours a day; and most important, it was an extension of the hotel. When coupled with the information contained in the envelope Walter Jensen was holding, Sarah felt confident that her movements would be sufficiently documented to allow the authorities to accurately reconstruct where she had been, if the need arose.

Sarah walked the six blocks to Fifty-fifth and Fifth, purposely avoiding the zone around the three public phones. She had changed into a tan blazer and put on a pair of dark sunglasses. When she was inside the lavish lobby of the Peninsula Hotel she ran her hand along the lustrous brass banister while she darted up the steps leading to the second-floor reception desk. Once she reached the top landing she searched the expanse of pink marble to make certain no one had followed her inside. Her heart began pounding before her mind fully registered why. There, near the newspaper stand, stood a tall man with a shaved head. Sarah narrowed her focus, preparing to react if necessary. He was in the security business, his body language told Sarah, but she had no way of knowing whether he was a plainclothes employee of the hotel or one of Jack Montgomery's operatives. She hurriedly took the elevator up to the third-floor conference room area, she thought without being seen.

Sarah made her way to the bank of public phones that overlooked the busy street corner three stories below. She chose the phone at the end of the dead-end hallway, closest to the lone window. For a moment she considered checking in with Walter Jensen, then decided to give him a little more time to locate the missing microfiche on General Perry. She dropped a quarter into the coin slot and dialed Sam Baldwin's office.

"Mr. Baldwin, please," she said. She was staring through the white lace curtain, watching the throng of pedestrian and street traffic move at a virtual creep.

"Oh, I see," Sarah said in response to his secretary's answer. "Just tell him his cousin Amy called."

She heard her quarter drop into the belly of the phone with a clang when she set the receiver back onto its hook. She looked behind her, down the short hallway that fed into both rest rooms. There was no sign of the man who had been loitering near the newsstand. Fifty paces away, and around the twisting labyrinth of hallways, were a half dozen conference rooms packed with seminar attendees. Sarah had noticed the small sign directing visitors in the proper direction when she had exited the elevator. When one of these seminars paused for an afternoon coffee break, the rush for the phones would be on. To keep her place, Sarah lifted the receiver and again placed it against her ear. All she heard was a dial tone, although to someone searching for an unoccupied public telephone it appeared as though she was deeply engrossed in conversation. Then she waited for Sam Baldwin to emerge from the lobby of the Baldwin Building.

66

SAM BALDWIN'S heart jumped when his secretary waved the message slip in front of him. She had been instructed to interrupt whatever he was doing only in the event his cousin Amy called. She was not to put it through, but to inform him immediately when the call came in.

"Peterson just called again!" he excitedly told Doug Templeton.

Templeton's drained expression became animated. "Did she call from that same phone at Fifty-third and Fifth?"

Baldwin picked up his private line and clicked the contact button. "That was her, Victor. Did you get it?"

"Yes and no. Our nine-one-one software narrows down the location of any given call in increments. First it recognized she was calling from within New York State, then Manhattan, then midtown. If your secretary had stayed on for another eight seconds, it would've given me the exact location."

"You'll have another chance real soon," Baldwin replied confidently. "Did Hank give you the number of the phone booth outside of the Peninsula Hotel that she's going to call?"

"Yes, sir."

"Good. I want you to monitor that line for the next fifteen minutes and call my cell phone as soon as you've got a fix on where she's calling from. Doug will answer that call and take the location from you. And great work, Victor. You'll be paid a bonus in cash tomorrow."

Baldwin went into his walk-in safe and removed a steel container that was slightly larger than a shoe box. He wished Hank Savage were here instead of Doug Templeton.

"Have you ever fired a gun?" Baldwin asked his future son-in-law.

"Never." Templeton paled, as though he was about to faint.

Baldwin removed a handgun from the strongbox. "This is a Beretta 92 FS. At close range it can blow a hole straight through the underbelly of a cow." He threaded a five-inch-long silver cylinder onto the gun's spit hole. "And this is the best silencer money can buy. It'll muffle any shot so that it sounds like you're punching a pillow."

Baldwin snapped the magazine into place, satisfied it was now primed to deliver thirteen shots in a matter of seconds. "Here," he said as he handed the weapon to Templeton. "The safety's on. If you flick this button toward you it's ready to fire."

Templeton clumsily grabbed hold of the gun, his palms soaked with sweat.

"Put on my overcoat and stuff it into the right pocket."

Templeton grabbed Baldwin's beige raincoat from the tall brass stand beside the office door and put it on. He was practically in a trance, complying with Baldwin's commands by rote.

"Here's my cell phone," Baldwin said. "Leave the building first, and walk down the east side of Fifth Avenue. If anyone's watching the exit they'll be looking for me, not you."

"What should I do when he calls?" Templeton asked, looking like a deer caught in the headlights of an oncoming truck.

Baldwin grabbed him firmly by the shoulders, their faces almost touching. "We may be this close to finding Jessie," he said, his thumb and index finger barely spread apart. "I want you to call Francesca right now and tell her that. And let her know that I'll call her as soon as I can to explain exactly what's going on. In the meantime, you've got to do whatever's necessary to get Sarah Peterson back to this office."

"Suppose she won't come."

"Then you've got to decide what to do." Baldwin's hazel eyes were on fire. "But just remember, if she escapes and goes to the FBI, you'll probably never see Jessie again."

67

THROUGH the sheer lace curtains covering the large picture window, Sarah observed Sam Baldwin briskly exit the enormous skyscraper bearing his name. Doug Templeton had followed him thirty seconds later, but to Sarah he was simply one of the dozens of anonymous faces who continuously poured through the revolving doors.

Sarah tracked Baldwin's movements past Tiffany's, then lost sight of him briefly behind a yellow-and-black Ryder truck when he crossed over to the west side of Fifth Avenue. A moment later he reappeared, shirtsleeves rolled to his forearms and hustling his way through the dense sidewalk crowd. Had she been protecting a head of state from this vantage point, this solitary figure weaving between pedestrians would likely have caught her attention. He looked determined, almost bordering on frantic. Through experience and training, Sarah had learned this was the type of person whom she had good reason to fear. These were the men who refused to accept no for an answer.

Because her senses were on high alert she picked up a sound behind her. Sarah quickly looked over her shoulder. Although she didn't turn fast enough to see who it was, someone had just entered the men's room. The door closed with a gentle thud. She turned back toward the window, still mindful of what might be behind her.

When Sam Baldwin approached the bank of phones below Sarah's vantage point she inserted another quarter into the coin slot. She watched him leap for the receiver after the first ring.

"Hello?" he said eagerly. He was breathing hard, not from exertion, but from nervous excitement.

"Calm down, Mr. Baldwin. I'm trying to help you. You have to believe that if we're going to work together to find your daughter."

"I do." Baldwin transferred his weight back and forth between his feet, unable to stand still. It was obvious to Sarah from the weariness etched on his face that the situation was taking its toll on Sam Baldwin. But as much as she wanted to help him, she also needed to protect herself.

"I'm pretty sure I know how to find your daughter, Mr. Baldwin. But from here on out you've got to be absolutely straight with me."

Sarah intently scrutinized Baldwin's reaction as she spoke. Years of surveillance work had taught her that a person's body language said more about their intentions than their spoken words. If, after observing him, she determined Sam Baldwin was not going to cooperate on her terms, then it would be time to try to pull her neck from the guillotine. She had acceded to Sam Baldwin's desperate pleas not to involve the FBI when that course of action had suited her purposes, as well. But this was his last chance. If he played any games, she decided to place her next call from this phone to Evelyn Dunbar at *The Washington Post*. Then she would call the director of the FBI himself.

Sam Baldwin closed his eyes and winced, then buried his forehead in his right hand. He was fighting off a violent migraine.

"I want to tell you everything, but for a number of reasons it's difficult for me to talk about."

"I can see that," Sarah said reassuringly.

"But I'll tell you anything you want to know."

"Good. Here's an easy one for starters. Do you know for sure that Jessie's been kidnapped?"

"Yes."

"Do you know who kidnapped her?"

"No. Do you?"

"I think so. And he's very powerful."

68

THE narrow green lines on Victor's computer screen glowed against the black background. At first there was a single neon rectangle that changed shape as his NYNEX computer processed fourteen million calculations per second. The large rectangle separated into a number of distinct smaller ones after the count of ten, eventually looking like an overhead view of a city block.

"Come on, baby," Victor encouraged Sarah in a whisper. "Stay on just a little while longer."

As he waited for the telephone company software to triangulate precisely Sarah Peterson's position, he dialed the number Hank Savage had given to him. The mixture of diverse street noises made the conversation almost impossible.

"She's on Fifty-fifth Street, between Fifth and Sixth," Victor said loudly. "Wait a second, here we go!"

A diagram of Sarah's location, as well as the pay phone where Sam Baldwin was speaking, appeared on his screen. The two dots were almost on top of one another, although the phone Sarah was using appeared to be just inside of a building. At the bottom of Victor's computer screen was a grid with all of the information a team of paramedics would need to get to the spot where someone might have dialed 9-1-1, then fallen unconscious before revealing their location.

"She's on the third floor of the Peninsula Hotel!" he screamed, barely able to contain his excitement. "The phone's in the front of the building, directly above the intersection where Mr. Baldwin's standing! She's gotta be looking down at him, probably less than thirty feet away!"

Doug Templeton had been pacing back and forth along Fifth Avenue. When Victor relayed the information to him, he began striding toward the Peninsula Hotel, trying his best not to let Sarah see him running, if she happened to be looking out at the street in his direction. Templeton knew that without the element of surprise, she would surely vanish inside the hotel before he could confront her.

"I'm going over there now," he told Victor excitedly.

"Good luck."

Templeton flipped the cell phone shut and shoved it into his lefthand pocket. With his right thumb he moved the safety switch of the Beretta forward a quarter of an inch. Now his gun was ready to fire, even though he wasn't sure that he was.

69

"ARE you sure the phone was working before?" Hank Savage asked Tom Witherspoon as he hovered behind him.

"Of course I'm sure! Who the hell do you think I was talking to a minute ago? Myself?"

"Relax, Mr. Witherspoon. If I can't fix it I'll get someone up here immediately who can."

The rich indigo ink from the arms dealer's Mont Blanc pen contrasted sharply with the starched white parchment of the Hay-Adams stationery, making Witherspoon's notes easy for Savage to read.

Hank scoured the detailed notes on the desk while he feigned diagnosis of Witherspoon's communications problem. The names of various banks were listed along the left side of the page, with several lengthy account numbers beside them in parentheses. Differing amounts were listed on the right side of the page, which Savage correctly presumed were the current balances in each of those accounts. When Savage saw that the amounts being moved totaled $25 million, or precisely half the ransom demand, his rage rose up from his belly. Still, he knew he had to remain composed, at least for the short term. Sam Baldwin would be disappointed if he returned to New York with only Witherspoon's blood on his hands, and no additional information.

"How dare you!" Witherspoon announced indignantly when he finally perceived that Savage was looking past him, and onto the papers spread atop the antique desk. He stood, ready to confront Savage.

Without saying a word, the ex-marine reached inside his suit coat and removed his Luger. In one fluid motion he pressed the cold steel rim of the silencer against Witherspoon's throat.

"If you make a sound I'll blow a hole right through you," Savage said through his clenched teeth.

Witherspoon stiffened.

"Get onto the floor!"

Witherspoon glanced into the adjoining bedroom, at the suitcase where his own German-made Walther was located.

"Lie down, God damn it!"

Witherspoon propped himself on all fours, then complied. When he was totally prostrate, spread-eagle, Savage patted Witherspoon's body from head to toe.

"There's ten thousand dollars in cash in the bedroom. Let me go get it for you." Witherspoon's words lost most of their urgency in the fibers of the thick shag carpet.

"Where in the bedroom?"

"In the safe."

"Where's the key?"

"Right here, in my pants pocket."

Witherspoon lowered his arm to reach for it. Savage halted the unwanted movement by pressing the gun firmly against his victim's sweaty neck. When Witherspoon raised his arm to where it had been before, Savage rolled him over ever so slightly so that he could remove the key.

"If you move from that position, or speak at all, I swear to God I'll kill you right now."

Savage walked backward towards the walk-in closet, sliding the small key inside the lock without taking his eyes off of Witherspoon. He reached inside the safe, and tossed the rubber-banded pack of hundreds onto the floor. With his Luger remaining fixed on his target, Savage moved to each of the three windows and drew the shades with his free hand.

"It's time for some answers, Mr. Witherspoon." Savage finished the sentence just as he slid the chain into place that locked the suite. The button to the front door was also pressed, ensuring that no unsuspecting chambermaid could use her passkey to get inside.

"Please don't kill me. Please," Witherspoon said desperately. "I'll tell you anything you want to know."

Savage straddled the supine figure, his polished wingtips on each side of Witherspoon's legs. He positioned the gun against Witherspoon's back just in case there were any sudden movements.

"What do you know about Jessica Baldwin?"

"I know she was kidnapped a few days ago."

"Kidnapped by who?"

"I don't know their names, but they were two guys from the Delta Force."

Savage pushed the hard steel against Witherspoon's spine. "What are their fucking names?"

"I swear to God I don't know!" The back of Witherspoon's pale blue pinpoint cotton shirt was now saturated with sweat.

"Quietly," Savage reminded.

"Sorry," he gasped, barely above a whisper.

"Where's Jessie being held?"

"I don't know that either. I thought they were somewhere in France, but I swear I've got no idea."

"Is she still alive?"

"I think so."

"Why?"

"Because there's been a ransom demand."

"How much?"

"Fifty million."

"And you're going to pay that?"

"No. I'm paying half."

"Who's paying the other half?"

Witherspoon paused. "I don't know. I've been kept in the dark myself."

"Does the name Ed Gallagher ring a bell?" Savage asked.

Witherspoon swallowed hard, knowing he had been caught in a lie.

"Does it?" Savage spat.

"He's paying the other half."

"Gallagher's here in the hotel?"

Witherspoon nodded weakly.

"What room?"

"I'm not sure."

Savage stabbed the muzzle of his weapon against Witherspoon's rib cage. "406."

Savage swung around Witherspoon's right side and knelt beside him. Now the Luger was pressed on Witherspoon's carotid artery.

"Why are you and Gallagher paying the ransom?"

"Because of a double-cross by the two Delta Force guys. Money never had anything to do with this until after she was in their hands."

Savage nodded as Witherspoon confirmed what he and Sam Baldwin had deduced. "Who else is involved in this kidnapping?"

Witherspoon rocked his head from side to side. "I don't know. If I did, I swear to God I'd tell you."

Savage grabbed Witherspoon by the scruff of the neck and stuffed the rigid end of the silencer inside the fold of Witherspoon's right ear. "I'll ask you one more time before I kill you," he said softly. His voice was composed, yet firm. "Who?"

Witherspoon considered bluffing but changed his mind. "I swear I don't know."

"You're lying to me, you fucking bastard!" Savage angled the barrel of the gun upward towards Witherspoon's brain. "There are ways to make people like you talk. Very unpleasant ways."

Witherspoon shook his head.

"We're going to stay in this room together until you tell me what I want to know. I don't care if it takes a week." Savage removed a roll of duct tape from his pocket and quickly wrapped it four times around the lower half of Witherspoon's face. There was a knock at the door. He pressed the gun harder against Witherspoon's sweaty head.

"You still have a chance to live. But if you make a sound right now it'll be your last."

70

ANDY ARCHER sat rigidly in a large armchair in the well-appointed lobby of the Pierre Hotel, *The New York Times* folded neatly onto his lap. A look at the parking receipt for her Jeep had confirmed his instinct even though she wasn't registered under her own name. A hundred-dollar bill went an awfully long way with clerks who were making six bucks an hour.

Time was no longer on his side, he knew. But he had few options at this point. Sooner or later Sarah would surface, if not here, then in Georgetown. When she did, he would take care of her. She had left him with no choice. Not only was his pride was at stake, but so was his credibility with Jack Montgomery.

71

"THEY said they'd kill Jessie if I told anyone about her kidnapping."

While Sam Baldwin stalled for time with Sarah, he caught a glimpse of Doug Templeton out of the corner of his eye, both hands tucked inside Baldwin's taupe Burberry raincoat. Templeton was several feet off of the curb, trying to gauge when he could safely hurry across Fifth Avenue. The rush of traffic initially prevented him from seeing Sam Baldwin, but when he found him he nodded. Baldwin noticed the subtle gesture, yet opted not to outwardly indicate the signal had been received. He studiously tracked Templeton's movements while he continued his conversation with Sarah Peterson. When Templeton disappeared through the revolving glass door of the Peninsula Hotel, Baldwin realized he was probably being observed by the woman on the other end of the line. Now it was his responsibility to keep her on the phone long enough for Templeton to corner her.

"I'm trusting you with Jessie's life," he said into the receiver, "and I don't even know who you are."

Sarah continued to study Baldwin. To Sarah, his nervous energy was just as obvious from looking at him as it was from listening to his panicky voice. But she also noticed that Baldwin was deliberately scanning the facade of the hotel; it almost appeared to her as though he were searching the building for a suspected sniper. She turned to look behind her, down the short hallway. It was deserted, as was the immediate area surrounding the bank of phones. Sarah turned back to Sam Baldwin; if he had refused Jack Montgomery's demands, as she suspected, then the decision was obviously chewing him up inside.

"Mr. Baldwin, for the time being your secret's safe with me. So let's work together to find Jessica, because we've each got information the other one needs."

"Fine. Then start by telling me who you are and how the hell you're involved."

"Who I am is not important right now."

"But we can't do this over the phone! We'll have to meet face-to-face so we don't waste time."

"No. I'm willing to work with you, but it's got to be from a distance."

"Why?"

"Because the stakes are too high to do it any other way. And Jessie's kidnappers would kill me if they knew I was talking to you. In fact, I know they're looking for me right now."

Baldwin wondered what the hell was taking Doug Templeton so long.

72

"YES?" Savage asked loudly. He was kneeling on the carpet, staring intently at Witherspoon's face. The ex-marine was fully anticipating that his captive would try to scream for help.

"Room Service, Mr. Witherspoon. Your lunch is here."

"I'm not dressed," Savage answered without hesitating. "Please leave it by the door."

Savage heard the roll-away cart bang against the hallway wall as the waiter angled it beside the entranceway. He tiptoed to the door and leaned close to the convex peephole, careful not to permit any part of his face to touch it. The waiter had already turned the corner toward the service elevator. When Savage looked back at Witherspoon, he was surprised to see that the arms dealer had quietly gotten to his feet and was rushing into the bedroom.

Savage sprinted toward Witherspoon, tackling him around the ankles with a headlong lunge. They both went down in a heap. Savage ferociously whipped his prisoner with the butt of his pistol, but took several punches to the side of the head in return. They wrestled on the carpet, blood gushing from the wounds on Witherspoon's head. The arms dealer finally pushed Savage away with both his feet, clearing a yard of space between them. He reached inside his large valise, knowing exactly where he had stuffed his handgun. Savage recovered just in time to see the black snout of a Walther being swung in his direction.

The ex-marine squeezed the trigger of his Luger four times, aiming at the center of his target's head. All four 9 mm bullets spat from the silencer, barely making a sound. They tore through Witherspoon's brain, leaving an exit wound on the other side of his skull the size of a man's fist. The twisted slugs embedded themselves harmlessly in the wall behind a set of floral drapes and Witherspoon collapsed. There had been no time for him to try to scream.

Savage wiped his bloody calfskin gloves on a plush white towel. When they were clean, he hurriedly gathered up Witherspoon's papers so they could be analyzed in detail in the privacy of Sam Baldwin's office.

He swept the spacious room one last time, making certain he'd left nothing behind. He considered pocketing the thick pack of hundred-dollar bills that lay beside the bed. Then he thought better of it: he wanted there to be no doubt in anyone's mind that Witherspoon had been killed at close range for something much more valuable than money. Now it was time to pay a visit to Room 406. Either Ed Gallagher would confess what he knew, or he would meet the same fate as his friend Tom Witherspoon.

73

DOUG TEMPLETON was completely disoriented. One moment he was in South Carolina, the spearhead on a mammoth project that would enable him to pick and choose his architectural assignments for years to come. The next moment he was wandering through the labyrinth of hallways of one of Manhattan's magnificently restored hotels, a semiautomatic weapon crammed in his coat pocket. As for the woman whom he was stalking, Templeton wondered if he would even recognize her with her clothes on. However, the pathetic image of Jessica bound and gagged focused him. *"But just remember, if she escapes and goes to the FBI, you'll probably never see Jessie again."* Sam Baldwin's callous admonition drove the point home like a dagger to his spine. He was primed to find Sarah Peterson.

Templeton stepped from the crowded elevator onto the third floor, the only person heading toward the cluster of conference rooms on that level. He turned right out of the elevator, quickly spotting the sketch that displayed the layout of the third floor. The black lettering on the gold sign indicated there were three conference rooms down the hall to the right, and one to the left. Straight ahead, and around a corner, were the bathrooms and public phones. At each end of the hallway was an emergency exit.

He moved forward slowly, looking in all directions to determine if anyone was in sight. Way down the hall was a woman smoking a cigarette. No one else was in view.

Templeton approached the corner. The entrance to the women's rest room was in front of him. He inched forward, looking left toward the battery of telephones. She was ten yards away, silhouetted against a twenty-foot-high lace curtain. The side of her face was a blur of features because of the bright sunlight behind her, but he recognized her distinctive pageboy haircut. She was peering down onto the corner of Fifty-fifth and Fifth, one foot up on the picture window's ledge. She was looking down at Sam Baldwin.

"But just remember, if she escapes and goes to the FBI, you'll probably never see Jessie again."

Templeton moved forward, passing the men's room on his left. "Keep looking out that window, lady," he silently urged as he tiptoed toward her. His index finger massaged the trigger in his righthand pocket. It was wet. His hand was sweating. So was his forehead. *Stay calm.*

A black woman in a business suit exited the bathroom to his right and she brushed past him. Before he had time to flinch she was gone, back around the corner to one of the conference rooms.

From five yards away there was no doubt that the woman on the phone was the nude woman in the photographs. He was ten feet away. He slowed his pace, trying to appear as casual as possible.

"And this is the best silencer money can buy."

He closed the remaining distance, wishing his heart would slow down. Templeton could actually feel his pulse throbbing in his throat. He took a deep breath just as Sarah noticed a movement in the field of her peripheral vision. She turned, startled that someone was almost on top of her. Her lack of sleep was now taking its toll. Doug Templeton reached for the phone beside hers, lifting it from the cradle. She was less than a foot away, cornered, with only the window behind her. There was nowhere for her to run.

Sarah instinctively reached for her shoulder harness, but wasn't quick enough. Templeton seized her right hand with his left.

"I've got a gun inside my pocket and I'll pull the trigger if you struggle," he warned. "I swear to God I will." The right side of the raincoat was stretched out in front of him, the loaded Beretta just inches from her rib cage.

"Mr. Baldwin," Sarah said calmly into the receiver. "If this asshole fires, your daughter will be dead long before you have a chance to find her."

Sarah handed the phone to Templeton, her eyes fixed on the bulge testing the seams of his deep pocket. *Stay calm,* she reminded herself, *he's more frightened than you.*

Templeton spoke rapidly into the phone, his left hand cupped over the mouthpiece. He was telling Sam Baldwin exactly where they were. Sarah guessed she only had a minute to act. After that, the dynamics of the situation would be entirely different.

Sarah carefully measured the distance between them, waiting for Templeton to make the mistake she knew he would make.

74

JESSICA used her teeth to tear open the shiny vacuum-packed bag and spit out a small piece of foil. All the while she kept one wary eye fixed on McClarty. They were now alone in the stark quarters that decades ago had served as the lighthouse keeper's family room.

The imposing gun McClarty was cleaning looked as though even he would need both hands to lift it. Its perforated black barrel was as round as the fat end of a Louisville Slugger, the circumference of its handle wider than a beer can. But McClarty had not menaced her with any of his powerful weapons. In point of fact, he handled his military hardware as casually as most people carried silverware, going about his business as if no one else was there. He wasn't vicious like Grizzwald. Yet, there was something intangible about McClarty, something that made her wonder what was going on behind those Charlie Manson eyes. She found his faraway look terribly unnerving.

"Can I ask you something?" Jessica asked him timidly.

"Sure." McClarty's eyes were riveted on her face, but it was obvious to her that his thoughts were drifting in another dimension.

Jessica reached into the open silver bag and picked out a few pieces of dehydrated apples, trying to decide whether to pursue her inquiry. She had never eaten survivalist rations, and she hoped she'd never have to again once this ordeal was over. The freeze-dried mashed potatoes they had cooked on their portable kerosene stove the previous night had the smell and consistency of Elmer's glue. But at least her captors were feeding her. For that she told them she was grateful.

"How come there's nothing in there about my disappearance?"

She pointed to *The New York Times* McClarty had brought back with him from his visit to the train station. Because there was no electricity in their hideout, and Grizzwald did not permit anyone outside except to switch shifts in the lighthouse, the only thing to do was read. Jessica had been certain the kidnapping of the daughter of one of the world's few billionaires would receive notable coverage. She had looked forward to poring over the circumstances surrounding her abduction, to reading between the lines to learn what steps were being taken to secure her safe release. Instead, there was nothing in the newspaper concerning her plight. Her emotions had plunged deep into the abyss of despair, and her reaction was the most primitive of responses: *Survival.*

McClarty smiled in a sinister way, his three-day growth making him appear even nastier.

"There's nothing in there about you because we've made sure that almost no one knows you're gone."

"Doesn't my father know?"

McClarty shrugged. He had already offered more than Grizzwald would have permitted.

Tears began to gather in the corners of Jessica's eyes. "Can I ask you something else, please?"

"Uh-huh."

"What will it take for you to release me on your own?"

"What do you think?" he snapped. This time his frightening stare focused directly on her eyes.

Jessica remained still, afraid to agitate him any further. She was sitting with her back against a cold Sheet-rock wall, her knees brought up near her chin. With her hands clasped together around her legs, she was keeping herself as warm as possible. They had taken off her handcuffs while all three were awake, and given her one of her jackets. Still, the room was bone chilling.

"Answer me!" he demanded.

Keep it simple, Jessica thought. *Don't make any waves.* "I would think a lot of money."

McClarty smiled. "Very good, Ms. Baldwin. Go to the head of the class."

Jessica's better judgment howled at her to end the conversation before McClarty snapped. But the actions of her captors in the last few hours, and the increasingly persistent cramps, made her believe that time was suddenly of the essence. Jessica had heard them arguing in the adjoining room about the utility of keeping her alive. Grizzwald talked of taking her picture while she held *The New York Times* in front of her, then doing away with what he had called "the only eyewitness." Neither man had slept much. Jessica knew her only chance of survival was to drive a wedge further between the two men.

"Can I say one more thing?"

"Go ahead."

"I've got no idea how much money you're looking to earn from this, but I'm willing to pay you twice whatever you've demanded, as long as you release me unharmed. Whether or not you split that with your partner is your decision."

McClarty set his imposing weapon on the dark hardwood floor before squatting down beside her. "And just how much are you willing to pay?" he asked as he gently touched her cheek. Their eyes met.

"You name the price."

"Twenty-five million."

"Done," she said without blinking. "I can have it for you in less than a day." She tilted her head away from him as subtly as possible, trying to avoid his caress.

McClarty stood and laughed out loud. Although he knew Jack Montgomery could not be trusted, the career soldier had learned enough about the Secretary of State's dark side to force him to abide by his word. If McClarty could somehow secure the Secretary's offer of blanket immunity with this one, then he'd be walking the streets as if nothing had happened, with a cool $25 million at his disposal in a numbered bank account in Switzerland. It was starting to sound like a no-brainer.

"What's so damn funny?"

Both McClarty and Jessica turned toward the door at the unexpected question.

"I asked what's so fucking funny?" Grizzwald's strapping frame obstructed most of the doorway, the automatic weapon tucked under his arm looking like a kid's toy.

"We were just talking a little shit," McClarty said with a shrug. "Nothing that's worth repeating."

"I thought I told you not to speak to her." Grizzwald's voice rose. "She can't be trusted."

"Grizz, lighten up. It was nothing. Really. It's so fucking boring in here. We were just making small talk, that's all."

Grizzwald walked toward McClarty and handed him his weapon. "You stand watch in the tower for now, while I take care of her, OK? This'll all be over real soon."

Jessica could hear McClarty's combat boots clomp down the ancient wooden steps as he made his way to the adjoining lighthouse.

"You've been a bad girl, haven't you?" Grizzwald asked.

Jessica shook her head, but said nothing.

Grizzwald reached behind him and removed the Colt six-shooter from his waistband. In it was a single bullet. He slowly approached her.

"Round and round she goes, and where she stops no one knows," he said as he spun the chamber.

75

DOUG TEMPLETON stood as stiff as a statue, more frightened than he thought possible. The phone receiver was in his left hand. In his right was a loaded Beretta. The outside flap of his deep pocket prevented Sarah from actually seeing that he was nervously fingering the cold steel trigger. He tried his best to appear in control of the situation, but his deer-in-the-headlights expression, and the sweat beading above his upper lip, revealed his nervousness.

He watched Sarah carefully, praying she wouldn't do something foolish that would require him to fire. He said to Sam Baldwin, "Yes, she's standing here right beside me." He paused, then said, "I don't know, but I guess so."

Templeton tucked the receiver between his face and left shoulder and said softly, "Give me your gun. Now!"

Sarah cursed under her breath; she knew that had it not been for Sam Baldwin, Templeton would have overlooked seizing her Magnum. The episode only emphasized Sarah's conviction that her window for escape would last only until Baldwin arrived. After that, the game would involve someone else who was obviously quite resourceful.

"I said give me your gun!"

Sarah assessed the availability of her limited options. An emergency exit was just past the entrance to the women's rest room, although Sarah had no idea where the staircase around the corner would take her. A scream would attract *someone's* attention, even though she couldn't see or hear anyone from her vantage point. However, there was the chance that the jumble of nerves who was pointing the barrel of a gun at her rib cage might panic and fire. Almost as important, that choice would inevitably lead to a commotion and the possibility of some sort of police presence. That would have to be her last resort.

"Look," she reassured Templeton. "I don't want any trouble." She slowly reached inside her blazer for her shoulder harness, pinching the ribbed handle of her revolver between her thumb and index finger. She deliberately moved it within his reach.

Templeton grabbed the gun and stuffed it into his left pocket. "I've got it," he told Baldwin. "OK. We're on the third floor, right near the bathrooms. Come right up and help me out."

Sarah uncoiled like a rattlesnake the instant Templeton shifted his eyes to hang up the phone. In her right hand was a tiny canister of Mace she had palmed from Templeton's view. With just a touch of pressure from her thumb, a narrow stream of caustic liquid squirted directly onto the bridge of his nose. The searing pain spread across both of his eyes as if he had been hit with a flamethrower. It sent him crumpling onto his knees. Out of instinct he blindly lunged forward to contain his attacker, but all he grabbed was air.

Sarah easily sidestepped Templeton. Before she had taken five steps around the corner she suddenly stopped. Although Sam Baldwin was nowhere to be seen, she suspected that if she continued down the long carpeted hallway toward the flight of marble steps, a face-to-face encounter with him was inevitable. She reversed her course, opting for the emergency stairwell in the opposite direction.

She forced open the heavy fire door with both hands and descended the stairs two at a time with her head down, concerned that her legs were moving so quickly she'd misstep. When she reached the second-floor landing, the barrel of Sam Baldwin's gun halted her dead in her tracks.

76

COMMANDS filled the screen from right to left, Hebrew letters directing an orbiting Israeli satellite to change direction. The advanced lenses on board the craft normally focused on Syria and Lebanon, scouring enemy territory for any unusual troop movements. With this bird's-eye view, Tel Aviv would have some warning if the Arabs ever again attempted to push the Jews into the Mediterranean, like they had tried to do during the Six-Day War. If that happened, nuclear warheads would rise up from their desert silos. The Israelis had no intention of surrendering the Holy Land to any of their hostile neighbors intact.

But right now all was quiet. Ominously quiet. Perhaps it was the calm before the storm. The Mossad had intercepted a fragment from an overseas telephone call that mentioned sixteen powerful missiles that were "somewhere in the region." The rumor was that these weapons could penetrate every bomb shelter ever constructed.

This cryptic information had piqued the Israeli prime minister's attention. He was desperate to find out where the weapons were being hidden, and who was the intended target. So far none of Israel's paid informants anywhere in the world had been helpful. When money didn't produce the desired results, several dozen Palestinians had been vigorously interrogated in an Israeli detention center near the West Bank. To a man, those Arabs claimed ignorance of any upcoming attack.

Believing his own assassination might be in the works, the prime minister convened an emergency session of his national security advisers. Behind closed doors they discussed the three most possible scenarios for the use of the still-unidentified weapons. The first was a terrorist attack designed to kill as many Israeli citizens as possible. This was dismissed as unlikely. Car bombs were just as effective, and more difficult to detect. The second was a strategic hit aimed at taking out one of the high-level Israeli officials who were participating in the security meeting. Everyone believed the odds of that were strong. The last was a long shot, but one that had the support of several key military advisers. They believed the attack might not take place on Israeli soil at all, but would occur against an Arab neighbor. Not only would Israel be blamed for any large-scale assault that took place in an Arab country, but it would also knock Israel out of what was already a very fragile peace. If a terrorist group wanted to destabilize the region, this would be the perfect way for them to do it.

At the conclusion of the meeting, the prime minister decided to take matters into his own hands. Every square inch of Arab territory was a known quantity to Israeli intelligence. There wasn't a grain of sand in the Middle East they hadn't photographed within the last year. The intricate grid the Mossad quilted with these tens of thousands of images formed the baseline for the Israelis' current probe.

Square mile by square mile, the satellite methodically snapped a picture of everything down below. These images were then relayed one by one to a battery of parallel processors in a fortified bunker outside of Jerusalem. These high-speed computers rivaled IBM's Deep Blue technology and could perform thirty-seven million calculations per second. Each image was then digitally superimposed onto its corresponding one on file to determine whether there were any material differences between what existed in the past and what was there today. If so, the variance would be examined by analysts with the Israeli Defense Forces to ascertain whether a group of missiles was in a position where they hadn't been before.

Iraq, the most belligerent country in the region, was the first country the Israelis examined. Measuring 167,924 square miles, it had taken a team of imaging experts four hours to interpret all of the data from the satellite. Nothing of substance was located. Iran was next. At 636,293 square miles, it would take the better part of a day to rule out the Iranians. After that the Israelis would look at Syria.

The Israelis routinely performed this type of painstaking exercise, but only once made a preemptive strike after discovering a problem: on July 21, 1980, an analyst noticed that huge amounts of steel-reinforced concrete were being delivered to an underground site just outside of Baghdad. Upon closer inspection, it was determined that a nuclear reactor was being constructed that had the potential to produce an atom bomb. The Israelis patiently watched and waited for almost a year, allowing the subterranean cooling tower to be nearly completed. Then, on June 7, 1981, a fleet of Israeli F-15s reduced the building to rubble.

The weapons from *The Hercules* would be afforded no such delay in their destruction. If the sketchy intelligence data the Israelis had intercepted was correct, then the missiles were supposed to be fired soon after their final deployment. Unless they were discovered and destroyed before being launched, the unidentified target now had a life expectancy that could be measured in days. If chemical weapons were included in the mix, then the same was true for all those innocent civilians who had the misfortune of living in the middle of what would soon be a very hot zone.

77

"SARAH, I'll fire if I have to."

Sam Baldwin stood just a few feet away from Sarah, his handgun leveled at her chest. Sarah quickly looked over her shoulder at the twenty steps leading back up to the third floor.

"You may be fast, but not that fast," Baldwin said. "You'll never make it. If I have to kill you to save Jessie, I will."

Sarah raised her hands, seemingly in submission. She was still holding the small canister of Mace, although Baldwin didn't see it. She gauged the proper angle for a dead-center hit, wondering whether there was sufficient pressurized fluid remaining to douse her target.

They stared at each other for several moments, like two wild animals measuring one another before the fight commenced. Just as Sarah was about to press her luck, the import of Sam Baldwin's first statement dawned on her. "*Sarah, I'll fire if I have to.*"

"You know my name?" she asked in amazement.

Baldwin nodded and tucked his weapon into his waistband. Slowly he held his hands out in front of him, his palms facing up.

"I don't want to hurt you, Sarah. I drew my gun only because I thought you'd have yours. Doug's not much of a fighter."

"No, he's not."

"Is he OK?"

"He should be fine in a couple of minutes. This stuff doesn't last that long." She opened her hand and displayed the lipstick-sized container. "He got hit with this."

"Does he need help?"

Sarah nodded. "We should probably see how he's doing."

"I agree," Baldwin answered as they made their way up the steps.

"How did you know I'd take these stairs?"

"It's what I would've done if I was in your shoes." Baldwin smiled. "You expected me to come down that hallway, and up the staircase, didn't you?"

She nodded respectfully. It was obviously no accident that he was one of the world's richest men.

"Listen," he said, "all I've wanted to do for the last three days is to hold my daughter in my arms. But we were worried you'd go to the FBI."

"I understand."

Baldwin extended his hand and Sarah accepted it. Losing her father the way she did was about as bad as it got. Losing a child in the same way was the only thing worse.

"Let's get Doug and go back to my office so you and I can talk," he suggested. "Then you'll be free to leave whenever you'd like." Although he sounded sincere, Baldwin knew his last statement was a promise that would likely be broken.

78

SAM and Sarah were both relieved their confrontation had gone unnoticed and that their trip with Doug Templeton down the staircase that led out of the hotel had been equally uneventful. The sting in Doug's eyes had abated. Cold compresses and an hour or two of rest would make his bloodshot eyes appear normal. He decided to recuperate in Sam Baldwin's apartment until then.

Sarah opted not to make any more small talk during their short walk back to the Baldwin Building, and Sam seemed content to remain silent as well. Everything about the billionaire's demeanor signaled to Sarah that until he held his daughter safely in his arms he would continue to view his situation with bitterness. That was a reaction Sarah understood. She would have felt just as resentful had she been thrust into the same position; perhaps more so. Even though it was completely irrational, Sarah also felt a tinge of accountability for what had happened, now that she was a senior member of Jack Montgomery's staff. Sam Baldwin had died a little the instant he was told that his only child had been kidnapped, died a little more when he heard she would be executed unless he acceded to her captors' demands. Sarah now accepted the responsibility of trying to make the Baldwin family almost whole again while making sure that one of Jack Montgomery's henchmen didn't get close enough to shut her down. It was a difficult balance, one she wasn't quite sure was possible.

"We're in here," Baldwin said. They were just a few feet from the revolving doors of the Baldwin Building. Sarah was standing in the very spot where she had delivered her envelope to the bicycle messenger.

Baldwin guided her directly into his spacious corner office when they reached the building's penthouse.

"Can I get you a drink?" he asked after he closed his door behind them.
"No thanks."

Baldwin took a seat behind his large desk and offered Sarah one of the antique wing chairs with a simple hand gesture. When they had both settled in he asked, "You want to talk first?"

Sarah shook her head. "You go ahead. I'll listen."

Baldwin leaned forward on his forearms and began talking as if he were inside the cathartic enclave of the confessional booth. He held his emotions in check, plowing through the details with an eerie, cold detachment. He imparted the facts without editorializing, even when he confessed to Sarah about the haunting nightmares the mechanical voice had caused him to suffer, and the incredible guilt he had felt from keeping this entire situation hidden from Francesca for two full days.

Sarah absorbed every word without interruption, though she was tempted to break in with questions. After nearly half an hour he had encapsulated the most harrowing fifty-six hours of his life, appearing exhausted when he was finished. He leaned back in his leather chair, searching Sarah's big brown eyes for an answer.

"If we share what we know, we might be able to give the authorities enough to rescue her," she finally said. "I'm pretty sure I know how to find her."

"How?" Baldwin asked. Sarah's optimistic statement quickly revived him, like fresh water drenching a wilting house plant.

"Before I tell you, let me suggest that you go to the FBI, without mentioning my name. I have a friend in their forensics lab who's the best in the business. He'll use my information to tell us the physical location where I think Jessie's being held. From there I suspect he'll get Director Cody to assemble an elite team to free her."

Baldwin pursed his lips and slowly shook his head. "An elite team like the one that descended on Waco and blew up the joint?"

"This is different," she said defensively.

"Or maybe Ruby Ridge? Shooting that pregnant woman and her small boy?"

"Mr. Baldwin, those were mistakes in the past that've been corrected."

"Then let me ask you something that I hope won't offend you."

Sarah widened her eyes and raised her chin, inviting him to inquire.

"On a scale of one to ten, how good is our justice system in sending criminals off to jail?"

"Honestly?"

"Honestly."

"Local law enforcement I'd give a three, the FBI probably a five."

Baldwin gave Sarah a gimme-a-break look.

"All right, maybe that's a little too high. I guess each gets a three."

Baldwin nodded. "Giving you the benefit of the doubt I'd say you're getting closer. Now put yourself in my shoes and suppose that this was *your* daughter who'd been kidnapped. She's the little girl who used to crawl into your bed during the middle of the night when she'd have nightmares, and just being beside you would make the monsters go away. You'd cradle her in your arms for hours whenever a fever would give her the shivers. And she's the little girl who'd hold your hand when you walked along the beach while the two of you talked about everything and nothing."

"I get the picture, Mr. Baldwin, but—"

"Now this little girl isn't so little anymore," Baldwin interrupted loudly. He stood and began to pace behind his desk. "But she still desperately needs help because she's been kidnapped. And then let's just suppose you'd been told that if you went to the FBI, the *first* thing the kidnappers would do is kill her. You with me so far?" Baldwin's detached tone had turned to one of simmering rage. He closed the distance between them, sitting in the wing chair beside Sarah's.

"Now out of nowhere comes a Good Samaritan," he said. His index and middle fingers walked along the edge of his desk like the fingers in the yellow pages ad. "And this Good Samaritan tells you that she doesn't *really* want to get involved, but she has information that'll help you to ferret out these two bastards who think nothing of killing your daughter. Now if you had the means at your disposal to use that information to rescue the person who you cherish most in this world, you wouldn't simply pass it along to some stranger, even if he worked for the FBI, would you?"

"I can't really say," Sarah admitted.

"Especially if you thought that by doing so, it would lead to her immediate death."

"Probably not."

"Of course you wouldn't!" Baldwin shouted angrily as he slammed the desk with his open hand. "To those guys it's just another day at the office. To them it's just another interesting hostage situation that doesn't involve their flesh and blood! And at the end of the day if a few people end up getting killed, well, then, just add their names to the list of statistics. Another 'learning experience' for the textbooks."

"I know those guys don't view their jobs that way. Many of them are my friends."

"I'm sure you're not that naive, Sarah Peterson. You know that the FBI can't be trusted on several levels, not the least of which is in regard to your own personal safety. That's one of the reasons you've kept this situation about Jessie secret these past few days, isn't it? Friends or no friends."

Sarah nodded.

Baldwin stood and walked toward the row of picture windows facing Central Park. He had unloaded on Sarah in a more biting tone than he had originally intended, even though everything he had said was absolutely true. He had to settle himself down. Touching an exposed nerve was one thing, completely alienating the woman who held the only key to Jessica's safe return was another.

A minute or two passed while each decided what to say next. Baldwin awkwardly picked up a picture of Jessica while Sarah looked down at her fingernails. The uncomfortable silence was finally broken when their eyes met.

"I'm sorry if the truth hurts," Baldwin said softly, "and that neither one of us can really trust our government for something as important as this. But I've got the resources, and the motivation, to find those two bastards without screwing things up. Please help me to use those tools. If not for me, then do it for Jessie. Because without us she'll die."

"Why not just destroy the weapons?"

"Because we both know they'd kill her anyway. They're in too deep to back out now."

"You may be right, but killing Hussein is too much of a crap shoot to go through with it. Even the experts can't really predict what will happen if he's assassinated."

"I disagree. My sources inside Iraq tell me that there's no way anyone would use those chemical weapons once Hussein was dead. And the Iranians know the United States would never let them overrun Iraq. But those are things to discuss another day. Right now all I'm worried about is getting Jessie back."

Sarah thought for a moment. Before entering Sam Baldwin's office she had been relatively certain that immediately after their conversation she would recruit the services of the FBI and remove herself from the sticky web she had blindly walked into. The last five minutes had convinced her otherwise.

"Here's what I'll agree to do," she finally said. "We'll take things one step at a time. For *now* I won't go to the FBI, as long as you promise to hear me out before you launch those missiles. I've got access to information that'll convince you that what you're doing will probably turn out badly."

"That's fair enough. You've got my word."

Sarah nodded. "Good. Then let's go to Jessica's house in Greenwich this afternoon so we can find out if I'm off on a wild goose chase. Maybe I'm dead wrong by thinking I can help. And if so, we'll really have no choice other than to go to the FBI. But there's something inside Jessica's place that I suspect will help us locate her."

"How do you know that?" he asked skeptically.

"Because I saw it there this morning. But in order to get what I need we'll have to get inside," Sarah said. "Do you have her keys and know her alarm code?"

"Of course. They're in my apartment," Baldwin said excitedly.

"Fine. I'll wait here till you get back."

Baldwin rose from his chair. "I'm trusting you with Jessie's life. I should only be gone for a couple of minutes."

Sarah remained fixed in the velvet armchair until Baldwin had grabbed his suit jacket and exited the room. Then she wandered toward the doorway. It was there, on a small wooden bookshelf, that a picture of Jessica Baldwin caught her eye. It was clear to Sarah that the little girl on the white pony was the same person whose mug shot had been pulled up on Walter Jensen's screening room viewing monitor. Convinced she was doing the right thing, Sarah picked up the phone beside Baldwin's desk and dialed Walter Jensen's number.

79

"Y O U want to tell me what the two of you were yucking it up about?"

Grizzwald was kneeling beside Jessica, absently spinning the chamber of his handgun. His dark eyes stared a hole through her, even though the tone of his voice was composed.

"Please don't do this to me. Like your friend said, we were just passing the time." Jessica tried to make herself as small as she could.

Grizzwald shook his head in disgust. "Don't you lie to me! I was standing out in the hallway for the last few minutes and I heard the whole conversation!"

"Then you know it was harmless. I offered the two of you enough money to make you both very rich men. What's so wrong with that?"

"No, no, Ms. Baldwin. You offered my partner twenty-five million, not me. You suggested cutting me out of the deal."

"But—"

"Shut the fuck up! I've heard enough of what you have to say."

Jessica turned away from Grizzwald's icy stare, trying her best to avoid any appearance of challenging him. He watched her for several seconds, then strode into the adjoining room. Jessica heard him rummage through one of their bags before returning with an instamatic camera. He thrust the first section of *The New York Times* in her direction and forced her hands to grab hold of the corners at chest level. Grizzwald took three steps back, snapped several pictures, then tossed his camera aside.

"I'll let you spin it," Grizzwald finally said. His arm was extended, his Colt .45 just inches away from Jessica. She looked at the weapon blankly, not sure what he wanted her to do with it.

"Take it," he said. He shoved the gun into the palm of her sweaty hand.

"Please no. Please don't make me do this."

"Right now it's just three squeezes of the trigger. If you won't spin the chamber it'll be four. If I have to ask you again it'll be five."

Jessica reluctantly tightened her grip on the smooth, walnut-stained hardwood handle of the gun, then placed her index finger around the single-stage trigger. She felt confident she could level it between his eyes and squeeze off three rounds before he could overpower her. However, if the lone bullet was not one of those few rounds, she knew he would kill her right then and there. She quickly did the math in her head, weighing the odds.

"It's tempting, isn't it?" he asked as he carefully studied her face. "Three in six for you. If you're really fast maybe even four in six. Those are better odds than you could get in Vegas."

Jessica said nothing, fearful that any answer would be interpreted the wrong way.

"Spin it," he ordered softly.

Jessica raised her left hand and gave the chamber a weak spin. When it came to rest the snout of the gun was still pointing toward her feet. Slowly she moved the gun in Grizzwald's direction, the barrel rising higher and higher. Knees, groin, abdomen, chest. She stopped her arm when a bullet leaving the chamber would be aimed directly into his left eye.

"Here," she said, still calculating how rapidly her index finger could tickle the trigger.

"No, you do it. I want to see you press it against your head and fire."

"I can't."

"Then I'll kill you right now."

Jessica froze in place, knowing she had no choice but to obey him. Still, her arm refused to react to what her mind was telling it to do.

"You hate my guts, don't you?"

Jessica said nothing. It took all of her willpower to keep herself from snapping off as many rounds as she could.

"Answer me!"

"I don't know you well enough to hate you."

Grizzwald smiled. "You're a fucking liar," he said softly. Now he stood directly beside her, his powerful shoulders pressing against her side. She could feel his body heat as he crowded her space.

Jessica's heart palpitated wildly until it hurt, her throat constricted as if a noose had been yanked around it. She could hear herself breathing loudly as she sucked for air. Jessica experienced no flashback in the moment before she knew death would occur, no home movie of the life she had led. There were no family images, no thoughts of what she had accomplished or what might have been. Sheer terror was the only thing that filled her mind.

Grizzwald took a half step backward as she squeezed the trigger for the first time. The firing pin and hammer produced nothing more than a gentle click. She took a deep breath and immediately squeezed a second time. Again there was no explosion. This left one bullet and four chambers with which to hold it. She closed her eyes and clenched her teeth, preparing for the worst. When the chamber rotated without firing she knew she had escaped death, at least for the time being.

"That wasn't so bad, was it?" Grizzwald asked. He deliberately shifted his hand toward hers, aware that the blackness of the exit hole was now staring him in the face. He took his time grabbing it from her, almost daring her to take her chances. For ten seconds he held his hand around Jessica's, not yet prepared to take possession of the Colt.

A million thoughts spun around Jessica's mind. Every nerve in her body was screaming at her to squeeze the trigger as quickly as she could. Surely she could do it at least twice before he could react. Do it, damn it! Next time he'll kill you!

Grizzwald grabbed the weapon and released the chamber from its locked position. A single bullet fell to the floor with a thud.

"How do you like that?" he asked with a smile. "The next shot was the one." He shrugged and added, "I hope by now you realize that you're dispensable. We'll get our money whether or not you're alive."

Jessica dropped to her knees in stunned silence, quietly weeping at how close she had come to death. As she quivered in a tight ball on the floor, she knew the time had come for her to try everything she could to escape.

80

McCLARTY absently climbed the spiral staircase, his mind adrift like the spray of rough surf crashing up against the nearby water's edge. The weather-beaten lighthouse rose to a height of nearly seventy feet, with each of the limestone steps cut into six-inch-high rectangular blocks. The stonecutter who had chiseled the white stones more than 150 years earlier had done his best to make the curved staircase symmetrical. Now thousands of footsteps had smoothed out his work, causing distinct indentations on each step. All of this craftsmanship was lost on McClarty as he thought about his separate conversations with Jessica Baldwin and Jack Montgomery.

When he reached the uppermost landing, he sat down on the top step. The filthy stone was as cold as a block of ice and was moistened with a thin mist of frigid saltwater. Four of the five large windows in the pentagon-shaped watchtower had been blown out by nor'easters over the years and had never been replaced. The ocean breeze whipping through the hollow tower howled as if he were inside a wind tunnel. A few feet to his right was the massive parabolic reflector, which, during the lighthouse's heyday, had steered vessels away from the nearby rocky point. The bulb alone inside the patina-tinted glass was larger than a basketball.

McClarty set down the weapon Grizzwald had handed him and rose to his knees. He was able to peer from this position through the empty squares that at one time had held large windows in place. A narrow catwalk encircled the peak of the lighthouse at this level and was surrounded by a rusted iron railing. From this vantage point McClarty could observe the drawn shades of the family room where Grizzwald was guarding their prisoner. He could also determine whether anyone, including Grizzwald, was approaching the entrance to the abandoned lighthouse. No one was.

McClarty removed a cellular phone from his pants pocket and punched in the same number he had dialed from the train station. Jack Montgomery answered after the first ring.

"I've been thinking about your offer," McClarty said without introduction.

"I'm pleased to hear that. I think you're making a wise move." Montgomery's soothing voice was paternal, yet firm.

McClarty glanced quickly to his left. A trawler far off in the distance had migrated into his peripheral vision. He scanned 360 degrees with his laser-guided binoculars, making certain there were no accompanying vessels. The full catch of fish on board the boat came into focus, relieving his anxiety. "What'd you say?" he asked distractedly.

"I said you're making a wise decision."

McClarty scowled. "I haven't made any decision yet. I said I was thinking about it."

"I see. Then why're you calling?"

"Let's just say I'm weighing all of my options, OK? Now suppose I don't take you up on your offer, Mr. Secretary. I need to know whether you've got our fifty million."

There was a long pause before Montgomery spoke. He knew that once the money was wire-transferred abroad, finding the proverbial needle in a haystack would be easier. Trillions of dollars moved electronically over the phone lines every day. McClarty's communications expertise would enable him to make it appear as though the funds had landed in one place, when in fact they had been parked on another continent. And there was nothing Montgomery could do about that. "Believe me, McClarty," he finally said, "I'm doing everything I can to make those funds available. However, there's been a major complication."

"Oh, really?"

"Yes, really. But it should all be resolved in a day or two."

"You're a sneaky bastard, Montgomery, you know that!" McClarty hissed. He cupped his hand over the receiver so there was no possibility Grizzwald would hear him.

"Calm down."

"No, I won't calm down. I thought maybe we were getting somewhere. But it sure doesn't sound that way now, you fucking asshole."

"For God's sakes, McClarty, please relax. Something happened that was totally unforeseeable. One of the people who was bankrolling this damn mission was murdered this afternoon. He had already raised half of the capital, and the other twenty-five million is in place."

McClarty shook his head. "Is this the treatment I should expect to receive from the mighty Secretary of State, from the VIP who assured me that if I hopped into bed with him he'd make all of my troubles go away? Maybe tomorrow you'll tell me your dog ate your homework?"

Montgomery ran his hands through his thinning white hair. He was exasperated both at Witherspoon's inopportune death and at his impotence to put McClarty back in his place. Still, he refused to raise his voice.

"Listen—"

"No, *you* listen," McClarty interrupted, "I thought maybe we could swing a deal that would work out for both of us. But now I know that you and Buck Perry are getting ready to fuck me up the ass as soon as you can."

"Nothing could be further from the truth."

"*This* is the truth, Mr. Secretary. Your little Miss Cover Girl is still alive, and the press hasn't been tipped off yet about your involvement. But that set of facts won't remain for very long. No, sir. We want our money, and we want it now! And just remember, Jack, time is ticking."

McClarty hung up and smiled as he looked out at the white chop of the ocean. He had taken orders from men like Jack Montgomery for seventeen long years. *Seventeen fucking years*, he thought. Jesus, it was fun to grab the balls of a senior government official, then give them a nice little jerk.

81

SAM BALDWIN returned to the seventieth floor of the Baldwin Building with Jessica's spare key and alarm code in hand. There were more quizzical glances from the secretaries, who at this point were curious to know the identity of the woman whom the billionaire had left alone in his office. Even more than that, the staff in the CEO's office simply wished that life at Baldwin Enterprises would return to normal.

"Mr. Baldwin," one of the secretaries called out from behind a filing cabinet. "Can I talk to you for a second?"

"Yes."

"Mr. Savage just came by to see you. I told him you were meeting with a young lady in your office and that you'd stepped out for a couple of minutes. He's waiting in the media room and said he'd like to speak with you as soon as you returned."

Baldwin dispensed a perfunctory wave of thanks before turning into the windowless annex just down the hall. The fifteen-foot square room contained five small tables and a row of armless swivel chairs that rolled on black plastic casters. On top of the tables were the news wire terminals for Reuters, Dow Jones, Bloomberg, UPI, and AP. The up-to-the-second data was nearly as comprehensive as the information circulating in a top-notch newsroom anywhere in the world. Hank Savage had straddled himself across one of the roll-away chairs, his thick forearms resting on the top of the padded seat back. He was holding the hard copy of an article he had printed just moments earlier.

"How'd things go in Washington?" Baldwin asked anxiously as he closed the door behind him.

"Just fine," Savage answered. "As we suspected, Witherspoon was staying at the Hay-Adams. With a little persuasion he admitted knowing all about Jessie's kidnapping. He said two Delta Force members had actually carried it out. But he absolutely refused to tell me who else was involved."

"And?"

"He had a gun in his suitcase and he tried to kill me. But he was just a little bit too slow."

Savage tore the printout along its perforated edge and handed it to his boss. Baldwin's eyes danced along the three single-spaced paragraphs as he reviewed the UPI report concerning the murder of an international arms dealer at one of Washington's most exclusive hotels. A broad smile crossed his face when he was done reading.

"Excellent work, Hank. That pussy deserved what he got. What about the other guy who was staying there?"

"Gallagher wasn't in his room and I wasn't about to stick around and wait for him. This article says that Witherspoon's body was discovered just after I left. Besides, I knew there was work to be done here."

Baldwin nodded. "That's fine for now. You have Gallagher's home address?"

"Yes."

"Good. We'll catch up with him in due time. Meanwhile, I've got Sarah Peterson waiting for me in my office."

Savage's eyebrows rose. "How in God's name did you manage that?"

"I'll explain everything later. Right now I've got to get back in there before she changes her mind. She's agreed to help us find Jessie."

"That's fantastic!" He handed his boss four sheets of paper that had just come in over the fax machine. "But look at this before you do."

Baldwin carefully studied Sarah's impressive curriculum vitae, the same version of which had been provided to the President the day before Sarah's promotion had been approved. TOP SECRET was stenciled across each sheet, and every career highlight was indented with a bullet point. The few who had been permitted to read it came away with the feeling that the senior diplomatic security agent was one of the country's foremost authorities in the area of counterterrorism.

"Excellent work, Hank. This woman's a pistol."

"And obviously very good at what she does."

"Did your contact at the Secret Service get this for you?" Baldwin asked, holding up the résumé.

"Yes."

"What'd it cost?"

"Twenty-five thousand."

"Wire him another twenty-five tomorrow. We may need his help again."

"Will do."

Baldwin took a step towards the door, eager to get back to Sarah.

"Sam, one more thing before you go," Savage said. "There's something screwy about these news reports."

"What's that?"

"They quote unnamed sources as saying that Witherspoon kept a large sum of cash in his room. Now I know that's true, because I saw the pack of hundreds myself. But I left ten thousand on his floor."

"And the money was missing when the cops got there?"

"Yeah, that's what's so strange."

"You think the maid who found his body took it?"

Savage shook his head skeptically.

"I don't either. My guess is that there are gremlins behind the scenes doing all they can to make this look like a robbery."

Savage nodded.

"Listen, I've got to get back to my office. Peterson thinks there's something in Jessie's house that'll help us find her. We're going out there to check it out and I want you to join me just in case there's trouble. I'm still not sure she can be trusted."

Baldwin left Savage alone in the room, closing the door as he rushed toward his office. His secretary stepped in his path, not wanting to announce what she had to tell him.

"I know it's probably none of my business," she said in a whisper, "but the woman in your office was using the phone a few minutes ago. My panel light was on." She shrugged. "I had the feeling you'd want to know."

"Thanks," he said, and started to walk away.

"One other thing," she added, "I swear I didn't mean to listen, but she must have touched your intercom button by accident. I didn't hear much, but the man on the other end of the line kept mentioning the FBI."

82

SARAH had dropped the phone, overcome by what Walter Jensen had just told her. Her gaze was fixed, but her mind was on fire. The recollections of her father were few and far between. Most were based on old photographs and a smattering of 8 mm home movies she had recently converted to VHS cassettes. She had almost no independent memory of the hundreds of hours she and CIA Special Agent Chip Peterson had spent together. The freshly mowed yard in which they played; their nightly trips to the local ice cream shop; and the school playground where he had died. Those images were all a blur, which was something she had remained bitter about until very recently.

Years of therapy had gone a long way toward mending the damage the assassin's bullets had caused. But those sessions had not been able to fully eliminate the trace of frustration Sarah felt after learning how her father's killer had died. His amphetamine-driven heart attack had been so quick and so painless, and had occurred just minutes after he had completed his assignment. Sarah had always fantasized about slowly torturing her father's executioner to death, reveling in watching the expression on his face as he writhed in pain. His assassin had gotten off the hook way too easily, and there was nothing Sarah could do about it, except to go to his grave and spit on it.

Sarah's bitterness eventually subsided, and the wound it left gradually scarred over. But the words Walter Jensen had just spoken into the phone ripped open that scar like a flick with a lancing knife. Jensen had started slowly, explaining that he had called Jack Montgomery's office in a desperate attempt to locate her. However, his call had thus far gone unreturned.

"No matter what you do, Walter, don't talk to him about this!" Sarah urged.

Jensen agreed, then told her he'd finally found the backup reel that contained the two missing pages to Buck Perry's FBI file. Jensen tried to sound unaffected, but there was clearly something wrong. He mentioned the secret projects Buck Perry had been working on in 1963, allegedly to help with the expanding U.S. military presence in Vietnam. The private meetings with chemical companies, pharmaceutical manufacturers, and rocket scientists. Unbeknownst to then Major Perry, someone inside the CIA had taken a serious interest in everything he was doing.

Sarah absently fiddled with Sam Baldwin's phone cord while she looked down on Central Park. The year 1963 kept coming back at her. "Just tell me, Walter, because I don't have much time. I'm in Sam Baldwin's office right now and he'll be back any second."

Jensen had been talking about chemical warfare and the ability of the military to kill a large number of the enemy with a superenhanced synthetic compound known as pemoline.

"Did you say pemoline?" Sarah asked, utterly astounded.

"And had he been allowed to live," Jensen added, "your father would've eventually figured out that millions of dollars in profits were mysteriously being siphoned off for several secret projects that someone inside the State Department was involved in. But for some reason no investigation ever got started."

That's when Sarah dropped the phone. For a moment she was frozen in place, numb with both fear and excitement. As an adolescent she had practically memorized the details surrounding her father's murder, including the twelve-page autopsy report on his executioner. Before the gunman had walked even half a mile from the school yard his throat constricted and his lungs burned. Thirty seconds later his heart stopped beating, the result of an overdose of the obscure amphetamine known as pemoline that had been boosted with a shot of potassium.

In the back of her mind Sarah had always believed that others had been involved, that the assassin had not acted alone. But she had been repeatedly assured by those in the FBI that she was being foolish, that the case was no more complicated than the original investigators had concluded. Since the case was closed, witnesses had died and evidence had been lost. Even her mother had urged her to move on with her life, but she refused. Leaving issues unresolved had never been part of her personality.

Now she knew Buck Perry had played a part in killing the man who had killed her father. But there were still missing fragments to piece together.

• • •

"ARE you OK?" Sam Baldwin asked when he saw Sarah's peculiar expression and pallor. She stood unsteadily beside his desk.

"I'm fine," she replied softly, trying her best to regroup quickly. "I just heard some very disturbing news, that's all."

"Who did you call while I was gone?"

"A friend."

"The one at the FBI?"

"Don't push it, Mr. Baldwin. I've already stuck my neck out for you."

Sarah willed herself to focus on the present. She had disciplined herself for her entire career to avoid getting distracted from the business at hand, even if a personal crisis presented itself. She had done so after she had thrown Jean-Pierre out on his ear. And she had done so when her best friend lost her battle with breast cancer at the age of thirty-one. Now her anger and her hate and her lust for revenge would have to be put on hold. Once it was safe, she would unleash her fury with a zeal few knew existed.

"Why don't we take my limo if that's OK with you?" Baldwin asked.

"Your limo's fine as long as you can drop me off at my hotel once we get back to the city."

"Of course. Where're you staying?"

"The Waldorf," she lied.

"That won't be a problem," he lied also.

83

"GOOD afternoon, ma'am. I'm Hank Savage, one of Mr. Baldwin's assistants." Hank had just slipped into the backseat of the black stretch limo with Sarah.

"Sarah Peterson." She shook his hand firmly. "Pleased to meet you."

The man who had killed Tom Witherspoon less than four hours earlier sat directly across from Sarah with his back to the uniformed driver. Sam Baldwin sat beside Sarah, on her left. For several minutes they rode without speaking, and Sarah used the time to try to process the crescendo of information she had just learned about her father's death.

"Doug was still at my apartment," Baldwin finally said to Sarah. They had already passed over the Triboro Bridge and were continuing north toward Yonkers Raceway. "He was feeling much better."

Savage stared at the woman across from him. He had been hastily brought up to speed in Sam Baldwin's private bathroom just before the limo emerged from the underground garage. He found it extremely impressive that she had incapacitated Doug Templeton while a gun was stuck against her ribs. If nothing else, it reinforced Sam Baldwin's opinion that Sarah needed to be watched carefully.

"You know I didn't mean to hurt him."

Baldwin nodded. "He knows that, too."

The stilted silence returned for the next few miles. All three made trite comments about the colorful trees blanketing both sides of the Hutchinson River Parkway. The further north they drove, the more prominent were the gray branches of winter that would soon supplant the splendor of late fall.

When the limo slowly rounded one of the entrances to Bruce Park and approached Jessica's tree-lined street, Sarah turned to get a second look at a car that caught her attention. Despite her outwardly calm demeanor, she couldn't believe her eyes. Buck Perry's green Bonneville was parked barely fifty yards away.

Sarah's heart practically jumped through her blazer. She desperately wanted to hop out of the limo and stick her revolver in the general's face, but for Jessica's sake she forced herself to remain calm. From what Sarah knew about the package inside Jessica's front foyer, literally every second was critical. She knew that Buck Perry would be there for her after this episode had run its course. Sarah believed that time was on her side when it came to revenge.

"What's wrong?" Savage asked. His eyes darted in the direction where Sarah was looking.

"Nothing." She maintained a constant bead on the general's car out of the corner of her eye until the road curved. Two minutes later the black stretch limo was parked on Jessica's long gravel driveway.

"Follow me," Sarah said. She strode toward the front door, carefully looking back at the roadway they had just driven. Had she seen the green Bonneville, or anything else that caused her concern, she was prepared to duck for cover and remove her Uzi from her carrying case. In a perverse way she wished for it to happen.

Sam Baldwin quickened his pace to overtake Sarah on the front steps.

He jiggled Jessica's spare set of keys, taking a moment to select the correct one. When he had turned two deadbolts, as well as the doorknob, the large pile of mail behind the door moved as if it had been pushed by an enormous windshield wiper.

Savage lingered on the top step of the porch for a moment, looking out toward the front yard. Years of covering other soldiers made the old habits nearly impossible to break. Besides, Sarah's body language had heightened his sensitivity that something might be very wrong.

Sarah took a few steps inside the vaulted foyer, as did Savage. Baldwin closed the door behind them and locked it.

"It's right here," she said.

Sarah bent down toward the white marble floor and waded through the pile with her hand. Envelopes of every size and shape were tossed together in a scattered mound. When the cardboard box that had formerly eluded her was within her grip she snared it.

"What the hell's in there?" Baldwin asked, looking both anxious and confused.

"You'll see." She turned to Savage and said, "Keep an eye on the front yard while we go upstairs. Something down the street wasn't quite right."

"What?"

"I can't put my finger on it," she lied. "Call it woman's intuition."

Sarah took the spiral staircase up one level, quickly finding Jessica's spacious country kitchen. Her visit earlier that morning had given her a good sense of the huge house's layout. Once upstairs, she pushed one of the highback chairs aside so she could stand directly beside the kitchen table. Then she placed the six-inch-long box on top of the stained pine. Baldwin sat in one of the sage green seats across from her.

"What's this box got to do with Jessie's kidnapping?" Baldwin asked impatiently. He tried to read the upside-down name that was printed in ten-point pica in the return address.

"It's from a company called SatSearch. I visited their facility in Silicon Valley about four years ago in connection with a proposal I was working on."

Baldwin scrutinized her every move, not yet convinced the trip had even been worth the cost of the gasoline to get there. Sarah sensed his distrust as she used her Swiss Army knife to slice through the box's brown paper wrapping. Her blade traced a complete rectangle along the underside of the box, allowing her to easily lift the top away from the bottom. A hand-sized device was inside the bubble pack wrap. To someone who had never seen one of these units before, it probably would have been mistaken for a calculator. Sarah slid her index finger under the inch-long swatch of Scotch tape and removed the ten-ounce instrument from its protective wrapping.

"What the hell's that?" Baldwin asked. He was leaning clear across the table, trying to get a better look at the black plastic device.

Sarah handed it to him. "It's a compact receiver and transmitter. When I saw this thing at the SatSearch R&D lab four years ago it was larger than the Manhattan yellow pages. In two years it'll probably be smaller than a doctor's beeper. Two years after that a postage stamp. Their techies told me they'd be able to shrink their microchips by half every eighteen months."

"So how's this going to find Jessie?"

"Watch."

Sarah turned the device on and a two-inch square microthin liquid crystal display glowed an emerald green. She pushed the Locate button when the word READY appeared in tiny black letters in the upper righthand corner of the screen. It was the largest of the eighteen buttons and the only red one on the faceplate.

"From what I understand, these new machines take less than ten seconds to triangulate." Sarah tilted the device toward Baldwin so he could see, then shifted it back to interpret the readout on the display.

"There you go!" she said excitedly.

Baldwin came around the table.

"It's called the Global Positioning System, or GPS. It's technology that's been around for decades, but that's being used more and more every day. The Coast Guard uses it to pinpoint distress signals. Hunters and hikers use it so they don't get lost, and so do eighteen-wheelers. And that's just the tip of the iceberg. I heard recently that golf courses are using them to measure the exact distance from a cart to the flagstick. That top line is our exact longitudinal coordinate as we're standing here in Greenwich, and the bottom line is our exact latitude. The one in the middle is our altitude, in feet above sea level, which is almost zero. This model's supposed to be accurate within fifty feet anywhere on the planet for those first two numbers."

"So how is *this* instrument going to lead us to Jessie?"

"The short answer is that this instrument won't."

Baldwin blanched.

"I thought you said—"

"The problem is," Sarah interrupted, "this instrument can only tell us where *it* is, not where any others with the exact same frequency are. But what the SatSearch company does is to deliver these units to each of their clients on a regular basis because the lithium battery operating these units needs to be recharged pretty frequently. Their clients then mail the used one back in the prepaid envelope SatSearch sends with each recharged unit." Sarah pulled the folded envelope out of the open box and showed it to Baldwin.

"So if Jessie's got her old one with her, it might've run out of juice by now?" Baldwin asked.

"Maybe. Then we'd be back to square one."

Baldwin sat down in the seat Sarah had pushed aside and ran his hands through his thinning brown hair.

"How do we know if she's got her old unit with her?"

"We don't. But I think there's a way to find out." Sarah pressed the gray Frequency button. A twelve-digit number appeared in an instant on the small iridescent green screen.

"Every single user of the GPS is assigned their own individual frequency, just like everyone gets their own phone number. This is Jessica's," she said, pointing to the screen, "as measured in megahertz. My contact at the FBI can tie into the master control station in Colorado Springs without any questions being asked. It's either that, or we call SatSearch and let them do the work."

Baldwin looked up, through the row of windows facing the Long Island Sound. The rays of the setting sun shimmered off of the dark blue water. He smiled ever so slightly as he thought about how stubborn and naive Jessica could sometimes be. "You know, she always pooh-poohed my suggestion that she get herself a few bodyguards. Said she felt claustrophobic with them around. I gave her everything in the world, but she refused to be treated differently than anyone else. She wanted people to think of her as plain old Jessica, not some billionaire's daughter."

Sarah didn't respond. SatSearch had obviously been Jessica's own way of protecting herself against abduction without anyone knowing that she had taken precautions. Now there was important work to be done, and fast. "You want me to call SatSearch or my contact at the FBI?"

"Do you trust this guy at the FBI to keep this a secret?"

"Unequivocally."

"And you're sure Jessie's kidnappers won't find out about it?"

"Given the power of the people who're involved, Mr. Baldwin, I'm not sure of anything. But my life is at risk, too."

"Then do it."

Sarah reached for her briefcase, then walked toward the butcher block cooking island in the center of the kitchen. Above the four burners was an aluminum exhaust fan with a row of metal hooks around it. On each of the hooks hung black skillets, and copper pots and pans of every dimension. Sarah opened her briefcase so that the stiff leather top obstructed Baldwin's view inside. Beside her cell phone was the microcassette that had started her on this bizarre journey, as well as the sheet of paper on which she had scribbled her notes of that conversation. She removed the tape and surreptitiously placed it into Jessica's silverware drawer. Then she quickly grabbed her cell phone and relocked the briefcase.

"I'll be back in a second," she said, before walking into the adjacent dining room so she could call Walter Jensen. When she reappeared in the kitchen she said, "No problem. He said it should only take him ten or fifteen minutes to tie into the SatSearch computer. He'll call me back as soon as he knows."

Baldwin walked to Sarah and put his arm around her. "Whatever happens, I want you to know that I'm forever indebted to you for your help. If I can ever return the favor, and I mean ever, then just ask. I know this hasn't been easy for you."

"Thanks," she said. She reached up to her shoulder to squeeze his hand. "I have a feeling I may take you up on that offer one day."

For a few moments both experienced a certain tranquility before they knew all hell was going to break loose. If Walter Jensen was capable of retrieving the requested information, then Sarah knew exactly what Sam Baldwin was going to do. If Jensen wasn't, then she sensed Baldwin would probably break down and agree to inform the FBI. Either way, Sarah knew the next twenty-four hours were going to be chaotic. The silence was broken by a shout from Hank Savage.

"Sam! Come here quickly!" he yelled. He was two flights up, somewhere in back of the house.

Baldwin and Sarah dashed up the thickly carpeted stairs, trying to locate from where the cry had come.

"In here!" Savage encouraged, once they were all on the same level.

Sarah spotted him first, in a cavernous room with a solid black marble floor. The room was completely encased under a glass geodesic dome that was supported by several crisscrossing steel beams. Savage was hunched behind a five-foot-long telescope whose powerful lens was pointed toward the back windows.

"Check this out!" he urged, his voice echoing around the nearly empty space.

Baldwin peered through the telescope's round eyepiece.

"You recognize those two guys?" Baldwin asked Savage. He was staring at an old fishing trawler that was anchored in the rough waters of the Long Island Sound, about a mile from Jessica's backyard. The image was magnified so many times that it appeared as though the boat and its two passengers were directly outside the window.

"Yeah," Savage answered. He gently nudged Baldwin aside to get another look. "The guy holding the field binoculars is Ray Dawkins, Captain Ray Dawkins. He's with Special Forces, Eastern Europe."

"How about the other guy?"

"His last name's Krystoviac. I never knew his first. But he's also one of Buck Perry's goons. Krystoviac usually operates out of Central America if I'm not mistaken."

"Oh my God!" Sarah gasped.

"What's wrong?" Savage asked.

"When we were on our way in, I saw Buck Perry's car out by that park. He's one of the people who's involved in Jessica's kidnapping."

"What type of car?"

"A green Bonneville."

Both Savage and Sarah drew their weapons and ran to a bedroom that had a view of the manicured front lawn. They saw nothing out of the ordinary. Then they sprinted down the hallway to get a look at the driveway. The limo was still parked on the crushed gravel, but Baldwin's driver was nowhere to be seen.

"Follow me and stay close!" she ordered. "We've got to get out of here! Now!"

With her Uzi in hand, Sarah pulled Sam Baldwin low to the ground. From what she knew about Buck Perry's marksmen, they could pick off their targets from more than half a mile away. And from what she now knew about Buck Perry, he would order them to fire without giving it a second thought.

84

GRIZZWALD grabbed the scuffed handcuffs that hung from one of the belt loops of his fatigues. He had left Jessica alone for an hour after forcing her to level his handgun at her forehead. Now there were details to be taken care of that required her cooperation.

"Get up," he said to her.

"What're you going to do to me?"

"Shut up and do as you're told."

Jessica stood, her muscular yet slender arms raised slightly, prepared to fend off his attack. She had resolved to take a stand from this moment on to protect both herself and her unborn child, despite knowing that any effort she could muster would be practically useless against the chiseled soldier who was twice her weight. There would be no more free shots at her without some sort of retribution. No more degradation of the type she had just experienced. If she and her baby were going to die, then so be it. But at least they would do so with dignity.

"Stand over there."

She shuffled slowly toward where Grizzwald was pointing.

"Now turn around."

Jessica complied warily, keeping a watchful eye over her shoulder. Grizzwald gripped her left forearm and tightened one of the steel loops around her thin wrist. The cold metal pinched against her skin as the notches clicked into place. Grizzwald ignored her grimace and pushed her against the door that opened into the room. He fastened the second loop to the narrow cylindrical section of the rusty doorknob.

"Now sit down and stay there. If you move from that spot, you'll be severely punished."

"Don't talk to me like I'm a child."

"Don't test me," Grizzwald replied.

Jessica sat at the base of the door, her left arm forced by the handcuffs to remain awkwardly straightened above her head. She heard Grizzwald loudly descend the rickety wooden steps, then hesitate at the stone house's rear exit. He was clearly waiting for something, but for what she wasn't sure. She suspected her captors had booby-trapped the two doors, both to keep her in and to keep others out. Jessica had learned by sitting in silence for the last several days that every portion of the old house made one sound or another; and the distinctive creak of the door leading out to the lighthouse was no exception. Though she prayed someone would finally come to free her, she knew any surprise gained by a clandestine rescue mission would be lost the instant one of her potential rescuers stepped anywhere near the house.

Jessica cautiously stood when she heard the sound that signaled she was temporarily alone. Despite being tethered to the doorknob, she was able to position her body so she could see what was on the other side of the door. That was the adjoining room where Grizzwald and McClarty had spent most of their time. Although it was almost dusk, enough light spilled in from the drawn shades to give her a full view of the two rows of impressive weapons Grizzwald had neatly spread out on the hardwood floor. The scene reminded her of the spoils confiscated in the aftermath of an FBI drug bust. The sheer number and size of the weapons was what Jessica found particularly disturbing, but it also gave her hope: if she could just get her hands on one of those guns with enough time to load it properly, then she could instantly eliminate the gross disparity in brute strength between herself and her captors. She would correct the mistake she had made an hour earlier and fire as many times as she could in as little time as possible.

The sight only increased Jessica's sense of urgency to do something to help herself, and to do it now. With a quick jerk of her left arm she tried to pull the doorknob loose from the door. The rusted knob jiggled ever so slightly, but didn't break loose. The failed attempt succeeded only in causing the handcuff around her wrist to click one notch tighter. Her left hand began to turn a deep crimson as the blood filling her fingers had nowhere to go. As her heart beat more rapidly she could feel the pulse in her wrist pumping harder and harder to release the pressure building on both sides of the cuff. She struggled to free herself, realizing that if given enough time she would eventually be able to dismantle the doorknob and grab one of the weapons. When Grizzwald returned she would ambush him before he could possibly know what had happened. Then she would either flee or take on an unsuspecting McClarty up in the lighthouse.

She twisted and turned the rough metal knob with every ounce of strength her right hand could muster, all the while focusing on the huge rifle lying less than ten feet away. As the corroded doorknob bore into her palm she wondered how long she would have to work on it before Grizzwald reappeared.

85

McCLARTY heard the two-inch-thick steel door to the lighthouse open, then shut with a heavy prison-door clang. He pointed his AK-47 toward the base of the limestone spiral staircase. When he saw the top of Grizzwald's buzz cut round the gray handrail fifty feet below, he lowered his weapon to his side.

"What's wrong?" he called down, before Grizzwald had gone any further.

"Nothing. But I've been thinking about something for the last hour. I decided not to use the walkie-talkie because I didn't want her to hear."

"Where is she?"

"Handcuffed inside. But don't worry about her. After the little session we just had she won't be giving us any trouble." Grizzwald took the stone steps three at a time to the top landing. When he reached the breezy observation deck he took a good look around for himself.

"More activity out there than usual this evening?"

McClarty shook his head. "Same as the last two nights." He scanned the water with his binoculars and said, "A couple of freighters and a few oil tankers way out there. Aside from that it's been nothing out of the ordinary."

Grizzwald was wearing only a white crew neck T-shirt up top; he folded his arms, trying to keep himself warm. It was at least thirty degrees cooler in the exposed lighthouse than it was inside the old stone house.

"I think it's time for us to pick up the anchor and get out of here. We've been in one spot too long."

McClarty nodded. "I agree. I don't trust that snake Montgomery to keel over and play dead."

Grizzwald glanced at his waterproof expedition watch. Aside from giving the time, it also served as a compass and an altimeter. "It's coming on eighteen hundred hours now. I say we move out at midnight. That'll give us six hours to prepare and allow us to leave the area without anyone noticing. The few houses around here are completely dark by ten o'clock."

McClarty set his automatic weapon on the cold stone floor and removed a tattered folded map from his pants pocket. "That's fine. Let's head toward Manhattan just in case we need airport access. We'll pick a spot once we're on the road."

Grizzwald nodded, knowing the decision had been made.

"All the plans for the wire transfer are in place," McClarty said. "The money'll move thirty-three different times before it splits into two separate numbered accounts. There'll also be decoy transfers to prevent any track-ing. I've waited my whole life to pull off something like this. We'll have to send Montgomery a postcard from Fiji."

Grizzwald smiled for the first time in days. "We're almost there, buddy, so don't crack now. It's been an uphill climb, but in twenty-four hours we'll be unbelievably rich. A day after that we'll be six thousand miles from here without a care in the world. Montgomery knows even he can't stop us from leaving the country. Those passports he gave us can be traced directly back to his office."

McClarty allowed himself a slight smile, then pulled the conversation back to business. "I'll call that fool tomorrow at nine hundred hours to give him the wiring instructions. The banks in New York will already be doing business, and the ones in Zurich will be open for another few hours after that. There's a narrow window we can't afford to miss."

"Suppose he doesn't have our money by then?"

"Then his time's up. Don't you agree?"

Grizzwald nodded. "No question about it. We may want to kill her be-fore then anyway." He paused then said, "I'll start to pack up our gear. Let me know if you want some relief."

McClarty shook his head. "It's stuffy in that house and I don't feel like talking to that bitch anymore. If it's all right with you, I'd rather stand watch out here by the water until we're ready to go. Just bring me something to eat in an hour or two."

"Sure thing," Grizzwald said as he hurried down the steps. "I'll see you in a little while."

86

ED GALLAGHER saw the four black-and-whites angled hap-hazardly in the circular driveway of the Hay-Adams Hotel and knew imme-diately that his short walk through Lafayette Park to get some fresh air had spared him an attempt on his life. He composed himself before entering the hotel; he exited the elevator on the eighth floor and saw bright yellow crime scene tape enshrouding the doorway to Tom Witherspoon's suite. Three-piece-suited detectives and beat cops were crowding the hallway, questioning everyone on the floor about what they had seen or heard. A shell-shocked Jamaican chamber maid wiped tears from her cheeks as she recounted the bloody scene she had walked in on.

Gallagher quickly retreated to the safety of the lobby. He demanded that a security guard accompany him to his room so he could pack his bags without fear of being attacked. Although the manager assured him the hotel was absolutely secure, he was more than happy to oblige the request. He also offered to assist finding other suitable accommodations, though Gallagher politely refused the offer. He checked into the Ritz-Carlton under an assumed name, then immediately called the Secretary of State at home.

"Jack?"

"Yes."

"It's Ed. Tom's dead, isn't he?"

Montgomery looked up from his desk to make sure his door was closed. "Yes. He was shot four times in the head at close range."

"Oh, God."

"This is terrible." The Secretary swirled his drink, then took another swig of vodka. None of his secret undertakings had ever unraveled like this before.

"Any idea who did it?"

Montgomery laughed nervously. "If you saw the six o'clock news tonight they're saying it was a robbery."

"You think?"

"No, of course not," Montgomery scoffed, "but that's the spin we're trying to put on it." He paused, then said, "Look, Ed, in Tom's business there are lots of shady characters, and it could've been anyone who had a chip on their shoulder about a deal that went south. But if you want my opinion, I'd be very surprised if Sam Baldwin wasn't responsible."

"Jesus!" Gallagher said. "How the fuck could he have found out about Tom? I mean, he barely had anything to do with this."

"I wish I knew."

"You think one of us is next?"

"That would be my guess, Ed. Baldwin somehow learned about our involvement and now he's toying with us. To him it's become a high-stakes chess game. We can't win and we can't force a draw. Worst of all we can't just topple the board and take all of our pieces home."

"You think he'll go to the FBI?"

"No. I think he'll come after us one at a time." Montgomery ran his fingertips along the confidential twenty-page dossier on Sam Baldwin that had just been delivered by courier from CIA headquarters in Langley. Only the director of the CIA had access to the document.

Gallagher closed his eyes and covered them with his right hand. How he wished he had walked out of that conference room the minute Jack Montgomery had spoken about Jessica's abduction. "For what it's worth, my half of the money's in place. Maybe if he gets his daughter back he'll leave us alone."

"Let's hope," the Secretary replied, even though he didn't believe that for a minute. "I'll get back to you soon with instructions on where the funds should be wired. But you and Betty should try to ride this thing out someplace far away where no one can find you. Once the dust clears we should have a better fix on where we go from here. In the meantime, I'll try to pay Grizzwald and McClarty and get Jessica Baldwin returned to her father as quickly as possible. Perhaps we can put all of this behind us without any additional collateral damage."

"Is that what Tom's murder was?" Gallagher said bitterly. "Collateral damage?"

Montgomery stared at his open laptop. Sarah's e-mail trail had evaporated just as quickly as it had materialized. And Mr. Green had experienced no success after reporting that his presence at the Pierre would soon yield dividends.

"I'm afraid so, Ed. And just because this operation turned out so miserably doesn't mean we did the wrong thing. What we did was right for America and right for us as individuals. Tom's a hero who died for his country. But for now you should watch your back and keep your head down. That's what I'll be doing."

"That's easy for you to say. You've got ten people with guns guarding you around the clock."

"I'm not so sure that works to my advantage. If I sneeze too loud there's a clip of it on CNN. There's nowhere on earth for me to hide as long as I'm Secretary of State."

"I'd still rather be in your shoes, Jack."

"Maybe so, Ed, but believe it or not, all in all right now I'd choose Sam Baldwin's."

"How about Buck? What's he doing?"

Jack Montgomery smiled, but said nothing. The less anyone knew about Sarah Peterson's imminent death, the better.

87

S A M , Sarah, and Hank crouched on the cold concrete floor of Jessica's darkened four-car garage, readying themselves. The side door they were about to spring through was beside the spot where the groundskeeper stored some of his gardening tools. Sam Baldwin had been inside the garage so many times over the past ten years that he had no difficulty guiding Savage to the exit despite the near-total darkness. He knew exactly where his daughter's Alfa two-seater was parked, and where the remainder of her garage junk had been scattered around its periphery. Baldwin's palm was pressed firmly against Savage's back. Sarah was lined up just behind Baldwin, her free hand leaning against the handlebars of Jessica's mountain bike. Her loaded Uzi was in her other. If General Perry was outside, she wanted to feel her gun dance to life like a mat of firecrackers. Revenge, she knew, was indeed a dish best served cold.

Sarah turned off the bell of her cell phone and gave Savage a definitive nudge. "Come on, let's get the hell out of here. We're wasting time."

Savage took a step forward, Sarah and Sam in step behind him. "Let's go," he whispered.

With a twist of the doorknob, Savage felt the bolt latch recess into place. He pushed the door open a fraction, allowing the nose of his silencer to inch its way through the tiny crack. Twenty feet away, in the muted dusk, he could make out the polished front grille of their stretch Mercedes.

"You see anything?" Sarah asked in a whisper.

"No. Just stay on my heels."

"I'm ready."

"Good. Here we go."

Savage propelled all three forward onto the gravel driveway with a sudden burst. As he sprinted toward the sanctuary of their armor-plated limo he spun himself around, his weapon outstretched in front of his body. Sarah did the same, desperately hoping she'd see the general's salt-and-pepper crew cut and a gun in his hands. At least that would make his killing a justifiable homicide.

It was eight strides to the side of the car. Savage got there first and jerked open the back door. He forcefully pushed Sam Baldwin in, then Sarah, the door slamming behind him.

"There's no one out there," Sarah said, as soon as they were all safely inside.

"What makes you so sure?"

Sarah was tempted to tell Savage, "Because I've been doing this shit for almost twenty years." Instead, she simply said, "Because I *am* sure."

Savage lifted his head just enough so that his eyes peered through the base of the window.

"I think you're right."

Sarah sat up and motioned with her weapon. "Look over there."

"I see."

Savage exited the car and strode to the back side of Jessica's house. Interspersed between the manicured shrubs were thick pockets of wild rose bushes. Sam Baldwin's limo driver was fifty yards away, down near the white-latticed gazebo, moving laterally from flower to colorful flower. He was oblivious to what had just occurred on the driveway, taking his time admiring each of the aromatic petals. Savage barked at him, and they both hurried back to the car.

"Drive down this road as fast as you can and don't stop for anything!" Savage bellowed into the two-way intercom.

The driver nodded at Savage through the glass partition, his hands white-knuckled on the steering wheel. Although he didn't really understand why he was being reprimanded, when Hank Savage snarled, he listened. The powerful vehicle lunged forward, pushing everyone against their soft leather seats.

"You're sure you saw Buck Perry's car?" Savage asked.

"It had his government license plate."

"And I'm certain that guy out in the boat was Krystoviac. Maybe they're just watching, but I don't trust Buck Perry as far as I can throw him. He's as slippery as they get."

The Mercedes swerved around the interspersed speed barriers and screeched past the turn where Sarah had seen the green Bonneville.

"It's not there anymore," she said, staring out the back window just to be sure.

Sam Baldwin had plucked a golden nugget of information from the episode. Now Buck Perry joined the short list only Tom Witherspoon and Ed Gallagher had previously occupied. Little by little all of the pieces of the puzzle were starting to connect. Still, the billionaire had an uneasy feeling that he hadn't yet learned the identity of the linchpin of the operation. But when he extracted that information from Sarah Peterson, then all hell would really break loose.

88

THEY were driving south on the Merritt Parkway toward Manhattan when Sarah reached into her pocket to reactivate her phone. The instant she did the ringer jumped alive.

"No, Walter, I'm fine. I really am. No, don't do anything with the envelope." Sarah listened for ten seconds, then said, "I know it rang for a long time! I had to turn it off for a few minutes." Jensen interrupted her before she said testily, "Look, Walter, now's not the time for this. Just tell me what you found out about that frequency."

Baldwin and Savage both watched intently.

"Wait, hold on," Sarah said. She looked at Savage and asked, "Is there a map of New York State in this car?"

Savage's middle finger moved rapidly as he flipped through a dozen neatly folded maps. He found the AAA map of New York and northern New Jersey, then hurriedly spread it onto Sarah's lap. Baldwin reached behind him to turn on the mini halogen lamp below the back window.

"Yeah, I see it," Sarah said into the phone once she got her bearings straight. Her index finger was aimed somewhere on the north shore of Long Island.

"Oh my God, Walter! How'd you have time to do all that?" She listened carefully while nodding her approval. "Hold on, I think there's one in the car."

Sarah turned to Sam Baldwin and asked, "There's a fax machine in here, isn't there?"

"Of course," Baldwin answered. "Give her the number," he snapped at Savage.

Savage leaned over and opened a mahogany cabinet beside his seat. When the fax machine's faceplate was exposed he read the phone number.

"Great job, Walter! I'll call you back if we need anything else. You'll be there for a little while? Great." Sarah listened to what Walter Jensen was saying for a few moments, then turned her head to look at Sam Baldwin. "My instructions are the same," she said firmly, loud enough for the man on her right to hear. "If I haven't called you by nine o'clock tomorrow morning, then give her the envelope and tell her about the microfiche. She'll know what to do." Sarah lowered her voice and added, "She should also try to track down a young woman in Gaithersburg named Marica Rodzinski. Marica's mother passed away a few days ago. But before she died, she gave me some very interesting information about the people who I think killed O'Grady." With that Sarah disconnected the line.

"Well?" Baldwin asked anxiously.

"He located Jessica's GPS signal. It was weak, but he's sure it's the one. If it'd been just an hour or two later he thinks the battery would've been dead. But it's coming from right here," she said, pointing to a spot on the map.

"Can he narrow it down?" Savage asked. The width of Sarah's fingernail correlated to more than six miles on the map.

"Yes. That's what he's faxing to us now. He took the precise coordinates and cross-referenced them with satellite photos of the area the U.S. Geological Society had taken eight years ago. Unless there's been some major construction in that specific spot, it shouldn't make any difference that the pictures are a little stale."

"Who's sending you this stuff?" Savage asked. "Just so we know it's reliable."

Sarah ignored the question.

All three knew Savage had crossed the line by asking such a straightforward question about confidential sources. They also knew it paled in comparison to the one that hadn't yet been asked.

Savage broke the clumsy silence by turning the knob that controlled the six rear speakers to the Mercedes's top-of-the-line Blaupunkt sound system. He tuned the digital radio to WCBS, the all-news station that informed New Yorkers of the world's events every half hour. After a few minutes of weather and traffic reports, the baritone voice recounted additional details of the brutal homicide of a wealthy arms dealer at the Hay-Adams, which he described as "the hotel that caters to Washington's powerful political elite." Sarah shifted her weight uncomfortably when she heard the victim's name. She turned quickly, searching Baldwin's hazel eyes in the narrow beam of the halogen. There was no reaction. Savage's response was as neutral, as he returned Sarah's stare.

"There's something coming through on the fax machine, Mr. Baldwin." Savage peeled the paper away from the roller as soon as the completed image was printed. A second sheet of paper inched through the machine, and then a third.

The first two documents were full-sized aerial photographs. The third contained several single-spaced paragraphs. Although the satellite photographs were in black and white, and had been transmitted hundreds of miles via wireless phone lines, the clarity of the pictures was extraordinary.

Savage set the photos side by side on his knees so that all three could examine them simultaneously. Both pictures displayed the three-story fieldstone structure nestled at the tip of a rocky point. On the back side of the house was a stone lighthouse that rose fifty feet above what appeared to be the overlapping cedar shingles of the roof. Long strips were missing, leaving the building's attic largely exposed to the elements.

"The house looks dilapidated compared to when I last saw it." Baldwin commented. "Jessie and I used to sail past there years ago and, now that I think about it, it's the perfect place to hold someone hostage. It's even got a lighthouse next to it that could be used as a lookout post."

Savage nodded. "It's called Old Field Point," he said as he read tidbits of information from the third faxed document. "Built in eighteen twenty-four, the lighthouse was used during World War Two by aircraft spotters. After the war the town's chief of police moved into the main house with his family. He stayed there for twenty years. After that the building was used on and off by the army for Special Forces training until it was abandoned once and for all five years ago. The town's waiting to knock the old thing down, but they don't have the funds."

"Special Forces training?" Baldwin asked.

"That's what it says."

"And Buck Perry's in charge of Special Forces training?"

"For the past eleven years."

Baldwin smiled as he grabbed both pictures so he could scrutinize the topography. Unless the immediate surroundings had recently been developed, which he highly doubted from how remote this area appeared to be, he observed two approaches to the house. The first was a narrow dirt road, which, according to the tiny legend at the bottom of the photo, measured about a mile in length. The road was lined on each side with huge, swooping oak trees and thick underbrush. The massive limbs of the trees were barren in these pictures, because the photos had been taken when the satellite had looked down on the area during the dead of winter. In mid-October there would still be considerable foliage. The second approach was by sea, over the large boulders that formed the craggy point jutting out into the Atlantic Ocean. Here, too, nature would assist in the element of surprise. Best of all, the satellite photos revealed that the next-closest home appeared to be slightly more than a mile away. Barring an unforeseen visitor, a confrontation would take place without witnesses.

Baldwin handed the pictures back to Savage, knowing his righthand man would soon commit every square inch of the terrain to memory. With most of the information he needed to proceed on all fronts now within his grasp, there was only one loose end to tie up.

"Let's discuss what else you know about this situation," Baldwin said without emotion.

"Helping you save your daughter is one thing. That's why I broke every rule in the book and got these pictures without going through official FBI channels. But as much as I want to, I can't tell you everything yet."

Baldwin took her hand and looked directly into her eyes. "These people are evil to the bone, Sarah. They need to be punished."

She returned his intense stare. It would be so easy to comply with his request; spill the beans on Montgomery, step aside, then allow Hank Savage to exact revenge for her father's execution. Quick. Clean. No blood on her own hands. But something was holding her back, at least for now. If nothing else, she felt compelled to hear from the mouths of Jack Montgomery and Buck Perry why they had choreographed her father's assassination.

"Let's not discuss this now," she said. "Maybe another day. But right now they're bringing you down to their level."

"Stop with the lecture and just tell me, God damn it! Those bastards deserve what they're going to get!" He jabbed his index finger in Sarah's direction.

Sarah shook her head. "I can't tell you yet."

"Why the hell are you protecting them?"

Sarah shrugged but said nothing. For the time being all she wanted to do was to slow things down. In the span of a few days Jack Montgomery had transformed into the antithesis of everything she had always believed he was. In the span of a few hours she had learned there was as much to her father's death as she had always imagined. And she needed time to try to understand how this information fit together.

Baldwin discreetly slid his hand to his right without taking his eyes off of Sarah. He spoke into the intercom, "John, get off at this exit." He leaned back in his seat and clicked the power locks shut.

"Where are we going?" Sarah asked.

Baldwin said nothing.

"Take me back to my hotel, God damn it!" As she spoke she began to move her hand toward the clasp of her attaché case. It would take only seconds to reach the weapon inside.

"I'm very sorry, Sarah, I really am. But the situation's changed since we had that conversation."

Baldwin flicked his head upward. Savage reached for Sarah's briefcase, prying it from her grip.

"You're being stupid, Mr. Baldwin. Think about what you're doing. You'll ruin your life!"

"I'm just trying to get back some of what's been stolen from me," Baldwin replied.

He lifted the phone and dialed his home number. Perhaps all they had learned in the last two hours would prevent Francesca from doing something irrational.

89

"PLEASE, God!" Jessica begged. The muscles in her forearms were already cramping. "Please!"

With each desperate turn of the doorknob, Jessica succeeded in loosening the rusted steel another tiny fraction of an inch. First she gave it a hard twist to the left. Then, instead of releasing the knob once the latch bolt had recessed into the door, she squeezed the rounded handle just a bit more, trying to weaken the metal cylinder at the very spot where the two inch-long Phillips head screws were tightened into the door. She did the same with a rotation to the right, repeating the exercise with additional force. After a dozen vigorous attempts she could feel the metal giving way, but she knew that time was not on her side.

"It's no use!" she cried. The palm of her right hand was pocked with angry blisters, the skin rubbed raw and red.

She gave one final squeeze, groaning like a weightlifter, then forcefully snapped her wrist with a jerk. To her surprise both screws popped out of their holes and the old doorknob fell to the wooden floor with a dull thud. The knob rolled in a tight circle for a few seconds before coming to a halt beside her feet.

Jessica's heart pounded wildly as she rushed to the window. She peeked through the edge of the drawn shade and saw Grizzwald and McClarty standing in the observation point at the top of the lighthouse. Seconds later Grizzwald was gone, heading down the lighthouse steps and back into the house.

Jessica guessed that if Grizzwald took his time, he'd be upstairs in sixty seconds. If he hurried, it would take half that.

With one of the handcuff loops still cutting off the circulation to her left hand, and the other loop dangling limply from her wrist, Jessica grabbed the weapon closest to the door. The Swedish-made assault rifle was slightly more than two feet long and weighed about five pounds. The gray steel barrel was smooth and faultless. Jessica lifted the weapon with a surge of anticipation, trying to determine if it was loaded. There were bolts and clasps and ridges all over the damn thing, but there was nothing that even remotely looked like bullets! She looked for the same type of rounded chambers that were part of the two simple handguns she kept in her house, but this rifle was configured differently.

The back door creaked open and slammed shut.

Jessica raced beside the door that moments earlier had secured her. As she moved, she desperately scoured every inch of the sturdy weapon, turning and twisting it in her hands like a majorette's baton. *Where were the fucking bullets*, she screamed to herself. *This isn't fair!*

She decided to squeeze the grooved metal trigger, to test the powerful weapon while she still had time to discard it if it wasn't loaded. If she pointed an unloaded gun at Grizzwald when he entered the room, she knew he would kill her with his bare hands.

Jessica pointed the nine-inch barrel away from her, closing her eyes in anticipation of the deafening hail of bullets that would fly. Although the explosion would take away her ability to surprise Grizzwald, she was sure she'd be able to get into the hallway and fire at him before he could flee back down the steps.

She curled her trembling index finger around the curved trigger. *Stop breathing so fast!* she told herself. Several deep breaths did nothing to slow her racing heart. She could actually feel her body temperature rise, feel the sweat dripping from the pores throughout her body.

She gently squeezed the trigger. Instead of a violent recoil there was nothing. Nothing! It was as if she had picked up a child's toy. She tried once more, this time with all of her might. Again there was no response. She heard Grizzwald bounding up the steps two at a time.

Ten, nine, eight . . .

Jessica frantically placed the automatic rifle on the floor, trying to line it up in the same spot where it had been before. The instant she returned to her position by the door she noticed the box of 9 mm shells and an ammunition clip beside the window. She quickly calculated that she wouldn't have enough time to get to the weapon, load it, then fire. She threw her head back in disgust, then bent down to retrieve the doorknob and the two screws.

Seven, six, five . . .

Jessica heard Grizzwald's heavy footsteps twenty feet down the hall, the sound of his large, black army boots getting closer. Then he stopped for a moment. Something had caught his attention.

She was stricken with panic while her thumb and index finger worked at a fever pitch to twist the two screws back into place. The first went halfway in just as Grizzwald's steps resumed. This time they sounded more cautious than before. Now he was ten feet away.

Four, three, two . . .

The second screw eased into place, though it also protruded from its original spot much further than before. If Grizzwald took even a superficial glance at it he would know something was amiss.

"What was that noise?" he asked suspiciously as soon as he opened the door.

Jessica looked up innocently. She was sitting where Grizzwald had placed her, with her left arm once again awkwardly raised above her head and leashed to the door.

"What noise?"

Grizzwald narrowed his eyes and quickly counted the line of weapons in the adjacent room. They were all accounted for, but the one on the end seemed to be slightly out of place.

"Stand up," he said angrily. "You and I have some business to take care of."

90 MOST visitors to Sam Baldwin's sprawling East Hampton retreat came away from the experience feeling as though they had been pampered at an exclusive spa. Larger than the Kennedy compound in Hyannis Port, it also abutted a vast stretch of private white sandy beach. For those who preferred indoor activities, the bowling alley, thirty-seat screening room, and indoor tennis courts were among the impressive array of creature comforts that kept even the most spoiled guests distracted for days at a time. However, after the nearly successful attempt on his life in 1984, Sam Baldwin ratcheted up the security level at his waterfront sanctuary. The perimeter of Baldwin's Spanish-style villa was encircled with a twenty-foot-high brick wall to keep out the inquisitive and the uninvited. The red clay roof was wired with motion sensors, as was each corner of the eggshell white stucco exterior. Surveillance cameras were placed discreetly throughout the grounds, often peering between the magnificent rows of azaleas, to ensure the safety of those inside the eleven-bedroom house. Cameras were also fixed atop the wooden utility poles outside the main gate on Apaquogue Road in each direction for more than a mile. All of this information was funneled into the security control room located in the basement of the 18,000-square-foot two-story mansion.

On that Thursday night in October, when Sam Baldwin's black Mercedes limousine came to a halt on the cobblestones of his semicircular driveway, there was no one there to greet him. This visit had been unscheduled, and the house had been virtually shut down after Labor Day, with only a skeleton crew maintaining the premises. Of course, that would change as Memorial Day approached, when the number of full-time workers on the grounds would swell in direct proportion to the temperature. By the time Sam Baldwin's annual Fourth of July bash rolled around, there would be more than fifty people on the billionaire's East Hampton payroll, and the summer season would be in full swing.

"Come inside," Baldwin said to Sarah. They were alone in the backseat of the Mercedes, the car door ajar. Savage had confiscated Sarah's weapons and entered the house to disengage the alarm. Now he was moving from room to room in one wing of the ground floor, flipping on the lights.

"I'm disappointed in you, Mr. Baldwin. When I go out on a limb for someone, I don't expect them to stab me in the back."

Baldwin shrugged. "Look, I wish none of us were in this position. But we are. Now I have to do whatever it takes to get Jessie back, and that includes keeping you here for a little while. I'll do everything I can to make sure you won't be here very long."

"And I'm supposed to believe you this time?"

"This is the only way I can be sure that what we're about to do will be kept secret."

"I wouldn't have told anyone."

Baldwin cocked his head skeptically. "Really? How could I risk Jessie's life on the promise of someone who I'd never met before this afternoon and who won't be completely honest with me?"

They looked at one another under the dim light of the moon, each wishing they'd been introduced under different circumstances. Each felt a genuine sense of respect for the other despite the underlying mistrust that now tainted their relationship. Although Baldwin was not yet aware of the link between them, Sarah knew if and when she chose to reveal that final secret about Jack Montgomery, then the balance of their vengeance would be within reach.

They walked toward the front door, with Sam Baldwin longing to put his arm around Sarah. There was so much about this pretty young woman that reminded him of Jessica. But more than that, Baldwin perceived that under the tough exterior that had been so necessary for her to be so successful at the Secret Service, she was essentially a good and decent person. The warmth he felt for this near-total stranger was a painful reminder of how much there was to lose in the next few hours.

"They're on their way," Savage announced as soon as Baldwin guided Sarah inside the cavernous front foyer. Savage stood halfway down the center hallway holding a cordless phone. He was backlit against the burst of light spilling from the kitchen behind him.

"They're coming by chopper?" Baldwin asked.

"They'll be here within the hour."

"Excellent," Baldwin replied with a smile. "Excellent."

Sarah turned to Baldwin and said, "Whether you like it or not, I'm joining you on the rescue mission."

Baldwin stared at Sarah in stunned silence, then looked at Savage for guidance.

"No. It's too risky," the ex-marine said. "Someone will probably get killed tonight."

"I understand the odds as well as you do. But I've got my own reasons for wanting to go, and they're just as important as yours."

"A few hours ago I obtained a copy of your résumé," the billionaire acknowledged. "I apologize for the intrusion, but we had to learn everything we could about you. From what I can tell from that document, you're an expert on terrorism, but your field skills may not be as sharp as we'll need for this mission."

Sarah recoiled ever so slightly. Aside from being amazed that Sam Baldwin had somehow been able to get his hands on the confidential document, she was somewhat insulted at having to defend her abilities.

"Less than two years ago I was recertified at Quantico as a marksman, level one. Ninety-eight hits out of a hundred with a Steyr-Mannlicher SSG-69 sniper rifle from two hundred meters. Four years ago it was ninety-nine hits. There've also been three separate assassination attempts against foreign diplomats that were thwarted by my on-the-scene actions. I know what I'm doing when it comes to this type of work."

Baldwin looked at Savage.

"Sam, if what she says is true, then she'd actually be a valuable asset."

Baldwin closed his eyes for a moment and rubbed his forehead. As much as he did not want to involve Sarah further, anything that increased the chances of successfully liberating Jessica had to be considered. Besides, he knew he never would have gotten this far without Sarah's help.

"You can come if I have your word you'll keep this a secret if you come out of this alive."

"I promise."

"And there'll be no double-cross once we give you back your weapon?"

"You've got my word."

"Very well. Then follow me."

91

THE phone rang and Francesca Baldwin jumped. Every noise in the sprawling triplex was having the same effect. She had thought about swallowing a Valium to calm her nerves, but the last thing she wanted right now was to feel drowsy. Especially because she was alone. If she missed the call she was waiting for because she had fallen asleep, she knew she'd never forgive herself.

For the past twenty-four hours her husband had been providing her with regular reports, explaining his progress on finding their daughter. This slow drip of information had seemed like the Chinese water torture to Francesca and it had made her much too jittery to leave the apartment even though now the walls felt like they were closing in on her. She remained hunkered down in her bedroom, praying that the news would accelerate and be favorable. Until this ordeal was over, her household staff had been told not to report for work until further notice. She didn't want to face anyone, or have them overhear something that might entice one of them to speak with a member of the press.

Within the last few hours there had been a frenzy of new information, and Sam believed that he and Hank were about to zero in on where Jessie was being held. His call an hour earlier had told her that the rescue mission was on. The instant there was more information he would call her. Until he did, she would remain on pins and needles.

After the second ring Francesca took several deep breaths, then reached for the extension Sam had been calling. The other three telephone lines in the apartment had rung several dozen times during the day, just like they usually did, but Francesca had allowed her answering service to field those calls. There was no one in the world who she wanted to speak with except Sam and Jessie.

"Hello?" she asked tentatively. Her hands shook as she brought the receiver to her ear.

"Hi, Mrs. Baldwin. I'm returning your call."

"Mr. President?" she asked cautiously.

"Yes, Mrs. Baldwin. I got a message that you called me last evening."

"Uh, yes, that's right."

"I'm sorry I didn't get back to you sooner, but I'm sure you'll understand that the new trade accord with China has demanded much of my attention."

The equation had changed since Francesca had called the White House a day earlier and Francesca closed her eyes, searching her mind for an appropriate response. Now that their rescue mission was in the works, there was no reason to involve the President unless it cratered.

"That's very kind of you, sir," she stammered, "but I seem to have forgotten why I called you in the first place."

"Very well, then," the President replied, knowing full well he was being lied to. "If you remember why you called, you certainly know how to reach me."

"That's true, Mr. President. I do. And thank you for calling me back."

"Good night, Mrs. Baldwin."

"Good night."

Francesca returned the phone to its cradle. God, she hoped it would soon ring with the information she wanted to hear. If it didn't, she knew the President would be hearing from her once again, and this time she would remember exactly why she had called.

92

"WE'LL move out as soon as the others arrive," Baldwin said authoritatively.

Sarah, Savage, and Baldwin were seated at a small, round conference table, surrounded by the very latest in communications technology. The six-inch-thick walls around them were painted white, the recessed lighting above them fluorescent. Nothing in this room could even be heard in the vast wine cellar that shared a common wall; Sam Baldwin could transact all of his business in total secrecy while his guests, as well as the staff, could freely roam throughout the house.

"Sam, I know you're anxious to get it on as soon as possible," Savage replied, "but I think you're jumping the gun."

"Why?" Baldwin challenged angrily.

"Because we're not ready to go yet. I'll need time to brief our men on the logistics of the operation."

"Fine. You'll have fifteen minutes."

"And I don't feel comfortable with what we know about the site," Savage said. He examined the aerial photographs Walter Jensen had faxed to them. "Right now all we've got is a general location, but that's it."

Baldwin stood, then walked away from the table. He was clearly angered by what he was hearing. "For Christ's sake, Hank, what the hell else do you need?"

"Sam, I'm as frustrated as you. But if we go in there without knowing exactly what we're up against, then we'll all be dead, including Jessie."

Baldwin stole a worried glance at his gold Piaget. "Witherspoon told you there were two of them holding Jessie, didn't he?"

"That's right," Sarah interrupted. "They're both from General Perry's Special Forces units." The thought of crippling two of his butchers was becoming more exciting as it became more of a reality.

"I'll give you forty-five minutes to gather whatever information you need," Baldwin said, pointing to the sophisticated hardware around them. "And there'll be a five-million-dollar bonus to each of you if you pull this thing off successfully within the next three hours."

Savage stood, a thick, blue vein bulging from beneath his starched white collar. He strode within a few inches of his boss and said, "Sam, with all due respect, you can stick your fucking money right up your ass. I'm doing this because I admire you as much as my own father and because I want to right a terrible wrong. Frankly, I also can't wait to squash those two goons. But I won't send men under my command into a situation where they'll be slaughtered. As soon as I know we have the advantage, we'll go. But not a minute sooner."

"What'll it take to convince you we're ready?"

"I'd like an infrared photo that gives me a fix on what's inside that old stone house. Timing will be critical here, and every second will count."

"Who's got that type of information?"

"The Israelis have a satellite imaging system that's almost as good as ours," Sarah said, "but it's positioned entirely over the Middle East. It'd be damn near impossible to get them to divert it, even for a couple of hours."

Baldwin's eyes lit up. "I've known the Israeli defense minister for more than twenty years. Hank and I had dinner with him in London a few years ago. And one of our foreign subsidiaries helped him develop their anti-tank weapons systems right after the war in 1973. I think it's worth giving Avi a call."

Sarah shook her head. "I don't. The Israelis are paranoid about security, and deservedly so. If Syria or Iran attacked while their satellites were diverted, heads would literally roll. I don't think anyone would go that far out on a limb for you."

"I think she's right," Savage said.

"What about the Russians?" Sarah asked.

Savage's intense brown eyes widened. "Yes, ma'am," he said, drawing out his response. "And everything's for sale now in Moscow."

"You're sure their stuff's reliable?" Baldwin asked. He had transacted enough business in Eastern Europe to know their factories almost inevitably yielded third-rate goods.

"Their satellites are just a notch below ours. And even though their military budget's been slashed, I know for a fact that their aerial detection program has been left completely intact."

Baldwin scrambled toward a fireproof metal filing cabinet and unlocked one of the black drawers. He flipped through a series of Pendaflex folders, then found the one he was looking for. "I'll put a call in to their foreign minister right now. He owes me a huge favor for building an ironworks factory practically in his backyard. He's got a few thousand of his neighbors working there and I think his brother-in-law is the plant manager. If he can't help us, no one inside Russia can."

93

ON the red tile roof of Sam Baldwin's mansion, a cluster of communication antennas silently began transmitting signals to a slumbering Politburo member more than seven thousand miles away. A series of urgent phone calls crisscrossed Russia within minutes of that burst of activity, the last of which was to a fortified communications bunker deep below the topsecret Russian military base on Sakhalin Island. There, a corporal in the beleaguered Russian military obeyed Moscow's unequivocal directive to momentarily turn one of their spy satellites away from Washington and onto the precise latitude and longitude coordinates he'd been given. At the same instant, more than 100 million yen, worth exactly $1 million, was wire-transferred out of one of Sam Baldwin's Bank of Tokyo accounts and into a Malaysian numbered account given to him by Russia's foreign minister. As far as Sam Baldwin was concerned, it was the best million dollars he had ever spent.

94

IN all there were twenty-four color video monitors mounted onto a single refrigerator-sized stainless steel control panel in the villa's soundproof communications room. This row of six-inch-by-six-inch monitors was sloped at a sixty-degree angle for easier viewing and was similar in appearance to the battery of television screens at the security desks of most of the world's skyscrapers, where hidden cameras peered down at every elevator and entranceway. Hank Savage had activated the mansion's vast network of cameras so he'd know immediately when the helicopter had touched down on the seaside landing pad. Savage had also triggered the switch to the AP and UPI newswires, curious to learn if additional details had become available concerning Tom Witherspoon's death.

With Baldwin sitting beside him and continuing to dial through to Moscow, and Sarah carefully studying the satellite photos Walter Jensen had faxed to them, Savage stared at the row of monitors before him. As he anxiously watched and waited, an image on one of the video screens jarred him with rage: there was Buck Perry, sitting behind the wheel of his green

Bonneville. The car was parked under a street lamp along the sandy shoulder of Apaquogue Road, less than half a mile away.

Savage activated the zoom function on Camera 17, bringing the image in even closer. Once he did, he had no doubt it was the crew-cut army general who was carefully surveying an unfolded map. Savage turned off all of the roadside cameras, then stood.

"I'll be back in a few minutes," he said to Sarah.

"Is something wrong?" she asked.

"No," he replied. Then he was gone.

95

JACK MONTGOMERY was alone in his private study, meticulously drafting the letter he decided to leave inside the wide center drawer of his antique writing desk. The large room was completely dark, except for the solitary banker's lamp that glowed an emerald green just a few feet from his hands. Because of Witherspoon's sudden execution, Montgomery conceded to himself that it was just a question of time before Sam Baldwin would figure out who else had participated in Jessica's kidnapping; and the Secretary of State knew that if he was to also meet with a premature, violent death, then a team designated by the President would rush into this room to secure every document that had the potential to jeopardize national security or to embarrass the chief executive. It had happened within minutes of Vince Foster's apparent suicide, and it would happen that way if Jack Montgomery was discovered facedown in a pool of blood. Privacy was one thing, but the deepest secrets of a slain cabinet member were another. Whether Montgomery's confessional letter would ever see the light of day was an entirely different issue. But at least the President would have all of the facts before him. After that it would be his call.

When the phone rang he anxiously answered it. Perhaps his operatives had discovered the whereabouts of his chief of security and this failed mission could somehow be righted. Perhaps McClarty had changed his mind.

"Yes?" he said.

"It's check-in time, Jack, just like I promised." It was McClarty, sounding short on patience. "Is all of our money in place?"

Montgomery closed his eyes and slowly shook his head. It wasn't checkmate yet, but it was close. "Yes, the funds are ready to be wired."

Montgomery waited for the cackle on the other end to cease before he spoke again. "It's unprofessional to gloat, McClarty. I thought Special Forces had more class than this."

"Why don't you shove that Harvard class of yours right up my ass?"

Montgomery somberly listened to McClarty's swagger. Any attempt at a clever reply at this point would be a waste of his time and energy.

"Of course, I'll need proof that she's still alive before I transfer the money. If you put her on the phone that'll suffice."

"No can do. Sometimes you just have to trust your business partners."

"I'm afraid that won't qualify as substantiation, McClarty. I'm sure you can understand my position. Fifty million dollars is a lot of money to pay for a corpse."

"That's too fucking bad, Jack. And if you won't budge on this issue, then my next call will be to the managing editor at *The New York Times* so I can let him know how you spend your spare time." He paused, then said, "Of course, you're a big boy and it's your decision. But I'll have your wiring instructions first thing tomorrow morning." McClarty laughed. "Where's star six-nine going to take you today, Jack? Maybe the county jail instead of the White House?"

Montgomery held the phone against his ear long after the line went dead. He was neither bitter nor angry about this defeat. The old warhorse had been in enough dogfights to know it was impossible to walk away unscathed from every one of them. His only regret was that there was nothing he could do in the short run to prevent McClarty from rubbing it in so blatantly. Revenge would be sweet whenever it eventually arrived. For Jack Montgomery it always did.

The Secretary of State set the receiver on his blotter. He wanted no further interruptions while he put the finishing touches to his letter. When he had scribed the final word he folded the paper into thirds and placed it in a manila envelope. He also placed the latest satellite photo inside. It showed the final preparation of the bunker busters that would soon tear Saddam Hussein into a billion pieces, and possibly send the stability of the entire region into a tailspin.

The envelope was sealed with a quick lick, then simply addressed EYES ONLY to the President.

96

HANK SAVAGE knew every inch of this road as well as the street he grew up on. Every curve, every dip, every telephone pole. Even the exact spot where the double yellow line had faded from tires running over it. The long walks he had taken up and down Apaquogue Road would now work to his advantage. The ex-marine knew that being on home turf wasn't everything when it came to an ambush, but it went a very long way. When coupled with surprise, it was as potent a one-two combination as overwhelming force. But Savage also knew that none of that mattered unless the attack was properly executed.

The surveillance cameras had shown him that Buck Perry's green Bonneville was idling beneath light pole 17, four tenths of a mile from the front gate of the Baldwin villa. A hundred yards from the passenger side of the Bonneville was the darkened summer home of Sherman Haley, a Wall Street bond trader who had earned more cash over the last ten years than the gross national product of several banana republics combined. Skylights and multitiered decks blended together to form one of East Hampton's most envied homes. Across the street, on the driver's side, was a two-mile stretch of nothing but scrub brush and tall sand dunes. If nothing else, there would be almost total privacy for his mission.

Savage crossed Apaquogue Road fifty paces before the S curve that even the Ferraris in the neighborhood took at five miles an hour, making sure Buck Perry could not see him through his front windshield. A quick up and over the four-foot sand dunes allowed him to double back thirty feet behind the Bonneville without being seen. The general was still speaking into his mobile phone, an unfolded map spread across the steering wheel.

Savage maintained his crouched position behind the high mounds of sand for several minutes while he calculated the attack strategy that would have the highest likelihood of success. A shot from his Smith & Wesson semiautomatic would probably accomplish his goal even though the angle was not ideal. He'd have to move forward if he wanted a clear shot at his target, which might expose his hiding spot, and if he missed, he probably wouldn't get a second chance.

Yanking General Perry out of the Bonneville was another possibility, although Savage couldn't determine from where he was standing whether the driver's side door was unlocked. He also wasn't sure whether he could get to the car fast enough without being spotted. Ultimately, he decided to wait for the general to finish his telephone call before combining his two options.

Slowly he crept forward, shielded from the general's view by the string of sand dunes. When the ex-marine was parallel with the Bonneville's rear bumper he stopped his progress. It was time to emerge from his hiding spot and cross Apaquogue Road.

Savage made it safely over the sand without being seen. He stayed low to the ground as his feet hit the asphalt. Ten steps and he was at the driver's side door. He quickly pulled the handle, startling the man inside. But the door was locked. He raised his gun, pointing it directly at General Perry's face. On the passenger seat was a closed briefcase, which Savage knew contained a weapon.

"Don't move a fucking muscle!" he shouted at the general.

Buck Perry froze for a moment, his expression making it apparent that he had been caught completely off guard. He looked at the long silencer that was threaded onto the end of Savage's weapon, then all around the car to see if the situation was one-on-one.

"Now put your hands on the steering wheel very slowly!" Savage barked.

The general complied, placing his hands in the five and seven positions.

"Higher!"

Perry reluctantly moved them to nine and three.

"Now open the door very slowly with your left hand!" Savage said. "But keep that right hand exactly where it is!"

General Perry hesitated.

"You've got exactly five seconds before I blow a fucking hole through this window!"

The general paused, glancing down at his briefcase.

"One . . . two . . ."

Savage moved his weapon into a better firing position.

"Three . . . four . . ."

In one quick motion the general pushed the unfolded map up against the window with his left hand while he shifted the car into drive with his right. The Bonneville lurched forward several feet before Savage blasted the glass into oblivion. The car veered off to the side of the road, stopping ten yards from where it had been parked.

Savage ran up to the Bonneville, cautiously looking inside the destroyed window. General Perry was sprawled across the passenger seat, the back of his crew cut visible. Blood from his left shoulder was pouring onto the fine brown leather. He remained prone for several seconds while Savage opened the door, then wheeled towards the ex-marine. In his right hand was his loaded SIG-Sauers. Savage ducked, using the car door as his shield. Only his hands remained a high enough target for the general to see. But not for long. In a split second six of Savage's twelve blind shots riddled the general's body, which slid beneath the dashboard. The Sig-Sauers fell from Buck Perry's bloodied hands, all thirteen shots still in its magazine.

Savage looked in all directions. There was no sign that anyone had heard anything. He dragged the general's body to the side of the road, a blood-stained toothpick falling from Perry's mouth. A tall mound of sand quickly became his temporary crypt. After the rescue mission was complete, Savage would direct one of Sam Baldwin's choppers to dump the general's weighted corpse a few miles into the Atlantic. As for the Bonneville, it would be parked in the villa's six-car garage until it could be driven to a nearby pier and submerged.

Savage returned to the underground communications room and whispered his news into Sam Baldwin's ear. Sarah barely noticed the exchange. Hank calmly took a seat beside her, once again able to focus on the next task at hand.

97

THE gut-pounding thump of the chopper blades became louder just as Hank Savage walked through the villa's sliding patio door. He remained beside one of the diving boards of the Olympic-sized pool, the massive underwater spotlights illuminating the sparkling turquoise water. From a distance of fifty yards he watched one of the Baldwin Enterprises helicopters hover a few feet above the seaside landing pad. He had activated the intermittent lights around the perimeter of the thirty-foot blacktop circle to accommodate the nighttime landing. As the whirlybird slowly descended, bursts of fine sand rushed away from the steel landing struts while the limbs of the smaller trees sprinkled around the property arched as if a hurricane had suddenly rolled through. The brisk cross winds near the breaking surf always made a safe touchdown somewhat uncertain, even though Sam Baldwin's pilot had set the Sikorsky on this spot a few hundred times. Savage rushed out to meet the chopper when it was securely planted, ducking beneath the gradually slowing blades.

"Good job," he mouthed to the pilot as he flashed an exaggerated thumbs-up.

The pilot winked while he flicked a series of switches to shut down the helicopter's power systems. When only the sound of the nearby crashing waves could be heard, Savage pulled open the oval-shaped door.

"Gentlemen, welcome," he said. He peered inside the darkened compartment. It had been five years since this small group of professionals had been together in one locale, five years since they had all attended an international antiterrorism symposium in Amsterdam. Sarah had also been there, although the CIA had arranged for her participation under an assumed identity. The conference had been sponsored by the governments of eighty Western nations under the guise of conventional information sharing, with lectures delivered nearly continuously for two days in a large auditorium. However, selected attendees at the biannual conference had retired to hotel rooms where unwritten "résumés" were discussed. The services offered by men like the ones in this helicopter could never be publicly acknowledged by any U.S. official, or even reported by the authoritative *Jane's Defense Weekly*; but those within the highest reaches of the world's governments understood that evil sometimes had to be dealt with by unconventional and violent means. As much as this revelation would have shocked the average person on the street, it was an open secret among those in the business of counterintelligence.

One by one the three muscular men disembarked, nimbly bounding through the small door. Savage had lured each across the Atlantic with minimal notice by allocating six-figure wire transfers to designated offshore numbered accounts. Matching transfers were guaranteed after Jessica was rescued alive.

The newcomers were clothed head to toe in black, standard dress for their line of work. They each carried only a stuffed duffel bag, except for the six-foot-three blond Swede, who was also toting a hard-shell case that looked as though it might house a prized pool cue. He was known in certain circles simply as the Eagle for his astounding visual acuity. He had spent two years painstakingly handcrafting the high-precision rifle and mounted night scope inside his narrow marksman's case.

Savage shook the meaty hand of Ben Aviv first, greeting him with a smile. The ex-marine held great admiration for the olive-skinned Israeli, fully aware that Aviv's leadership of the crack "269" Commando unit had played a pivotal role in the successful raid at Entebbe. Savage knew that the five-foot, six-inch, stubble-faced man who was standing beside him had honed his considerable covert skills under the direct sponsorship of the Mossad, even though the Jewish state took great pains to stifle dissemination of the particulars of their innovative tactical assaults. That Aviv had managed to slink inside the Parisian apartment of Hezbollah's second-in-command in December of 1996 to take him out with eight shots to the head was proof enough for Savage that the Israeli's skills were still sharp enough to justify his inclusion on this mission.

The last off the chopper was the tall Englishman. Unlike his colleagues, he appeared to be more of a scholar than mercenary. His horn-rimmed glasses, flushed cheeks, and side-parted sandy brown hair had earned him the nickname of the Professor. However, his appearance, like his amiable demeanor, was deceiving. He had served Her Royal Highness for sixteen years in the M-5, spending most of that time stationed in Northern Ireland. The decision was made at the highest levels of the British government to offer the Professor early retirement with a full general's pension when the fourth IRA terrorist under his surveillance mysteriously disappeared. After two years of sipping daiquiris and chasing skirts in the Caribbean, he found himself incredibly bored and discreetly put out the word upon his return to his London flat that his impressive killing skills were again available for hire, on the condition that the targets were those whom he truly believed deserved to die. The telephone call he had received from Savage satisfied him that those requirements had been met.

"Come inside, gentlemen," Savage said. They silently wound their way through the ganglia of art-filled hallways, then down the steps leading to Sam Baldwin's private command center. They entered the soundproof communications room, all three momentarily taken aback when they saw Sarah adjusting the clip on her Uzi. None of them had worked on an assignment like this beside a woman before.

As the men approached Sarah, she smiled deep inside. She recognized all three from her years of studying the dossiers of potential political assassins. Savage had obviously done his homework, Sarah thought. Although she knew it was going to be awkward working *with* these guys instead of against them, in Sarah's opinion, few better teams could have been hand-picked on such short notice.

"Gentlemen, Ms. Sarah Peterson and Mr. Sam Baldwin," Savage said.

Baldwin pushed his chair away from the round mahogany conference table and stood, momentarily shifting his focus away from the documents that had just been faxed to him from Moscow. He greeted the three professionals to whom he was about to entrust the life of his daughter with a firm shake of his right hand, and a more gentle touch with his left. Each squeezed Baldwin's hand and tendered simply a respectful nod. There would be no small talk about airline food or flight delays. Sarah took notice that none of the foreigners offered their names in response.

"Shall we?" Baldwin asked, motioning to the table.

All eyes turned to Savage. It was clear he was now running the show.

"Yes," he said authoritatively. "Let's get to work."

The five men and Sarah hunched over the pair of infrared satellite images that had just cost Sam Baldwin $1 million. The rescue operation of Jessica Baldwin had officially begun.

THREE

THE SCISSORS

If you want to get someone off your back, stand up.

DR. MARTIN LUTHER KING

98 HANK SAVAGE spoke for thirty uninterrupted minutes, meticulously diagramming the scenario he believed would have the highest percentage of success under the circumstances. In the three days since Sam Baldwin had first raised the possibility of a rescue operation, Savage had run hundreds of permutations around his fertile mind, drawing on every military experience he had confronted both in the classroom and out in the field. In the last three days he had slept no more than two hours continuously, and even those fleeting moments had been haunted by violent flashbacks and sketchy images of missions past that might somehow be brought into play. He sifted through every bit of relevant information as if he were panning for gold, carefully culling the valuable specks from the worthless silt. By the time he had answered his operative's final question, there was nothing else to do but proceed.

Baldwin took Savage aside before leaving the room. The two embraced tightly, knowing they might never see one another again.

"We've done our homework," Baldwin said solemnly. "Everything's going to be OK."

The ex-marine smiled, his boss's words so similar to the ones his demanding father had spoken to him during his formative years. Schoolwork, athletics, even hobbies were observed by his intense father in the same fashion that the taskmaster had carried out boot camp exercises during his days as a drill sergeant at Camp Lejeune. Nothing in the Savage household was permitted to be done halfheartedly or without total preparation.

Years later, as a recruit, Hank Savage had been ordered to heed that same message just as religiously as the marine motto "Semper Fi." But Savage was aware that even more than loyalty, what the marines really stressed was preparedness. It was the marine way, and the only way Hank Savage had ever known. But here he was, poised to lead this group into a life-and-death situation less than an hour after they had all assembled. Although each was prepared individually, as a unit they could not have been less cohesive. There had been no dry run, no time for the team to gel, and absolutely no physical preparation whatsoever. Most of all, he would soon be squaring off with two elite soldiers whose training, both physical and psychological, was equal to or better than his own. He had never faced so formidable an adversary. And for the first time in his life he was virtually certain that at least one of his team members would not make it back alive. Whether it would be Sarah, Sam Baldwin, one of his hired guns, or himself, was a question that only time could answer.

99

MOMENTS before leaving the East Hampton villa, Sarah knelt behind both of the cars they would be using for the next few hours. With the aid of a roll of reflective blue tape, the 4s on the license plates were transformed into As, the 3s into 8s. When she had neatly finished altering some of the best work turned out by New York's prison inmates, a DMV computer run on each plate would have come up blank.

Savage split the group as soon as Sarah's handiwork had been completed. Sam Baldwin, the Swede, and the limo driver used the stretch Mercedes. Savage, the Israeli, Sarah, and the Brit took the little-used Jaguar from the carport. They went their separate ways, the two teams agreeing to avoid all contact with one another until precisely midnight. That would minimize the chance that their cellular calls would be intercepted. Then, and only then, would they communicate. If, for some reason, Baldwin and the Swede were not in place at the appointed time, Savage had been deputized to determine whether or not to scrub the mission.

SAVAGE looked at the illuminated dial of his watch. It was eighteen seconds after midnight.

"Bravo, this is Alpha," Savage announced quietly into the tiny microphone clipped near his throat. "Are you there? Over."

He was crouched in the thick woods, less than a quarter mile from where he estimated the lighthouse would be. He and his three colleagues had waited until the Jaguar had been hidden twenty feet off the shoulder of the remote road before they had smeared a black, viscous sludge on their necks and faces. In the near-total darkness not even their eyes or teeth could be seen.

Savage strapped on his pair of night vision goggles, trying to locate his target. While the bulky optical system cut down his peripheral vision, it magnified the available light more than a thousand times. However, the hundreds of trees between himself and the coordinates he had plotted obstructed his view. He removed the goggles and pressed a small button on the side of his watch. The face of the dial glowed an iridescent blue. It was now a minute past midnight.

"Bravo, this is Alpha," he repeated more urgently. "Are you *there*? Over." There was no reply.

Savage fiddled with the clear plastic earpiece of the collar set, then made sure the compact transmitter fastened to his belt was working properly. The costly two-way communications device was the same type Sarah had used at the Secret Service and the Office of Diplomatic Security to guard her VIPs. Like those purchased by the federal government, the one-watt amperage had a range of only about a mile.

"Where in hell's name are they?" the Brit whispered anxiously. He, like Sarah and the Israeli, had also been fitted with the compact walkie-talkies and could hear that Sam Baldwin had not responded. The Englishman was squatting beside Savage, his feet immersed in a pool of ankle-deep stagnant water. Sarah and Aviv were fifty paces away, across the dirt road and set back ten feet into the woods, crouched behind the trunk of a large maple.

"I don't know," Savage replied testily. He shifted uncomfortably. "I'll give 'em a few minutes before we start without them." Warmed breath spewed from his mouth in clouds of smoke as he spoke. It was freezing, or nearly so.

Savage, like the others, tinkered with his gear while he waited impatiently for Sam Baldwin and the Swede to position their speedboat within range of the lighthouse. He was weighed down by eighty pounds of equipment, all of which was essential. His Sterling Mk5 submachine gun was strapped over his shoulder and was connected to the most sophisticated silencer available. He had affixed clips housing more than two thousand rounds of ammunition around his waist, though he knew if he was required to use even 1 percent of it, then the mission would likely be a complete failure. Jessica would be dead if surprise and precision were not the key ingredients of the attack.

"Come on," Savage whispered into his microphone. "Let's all get a little closer."

The three men and Sarah slogged toward the lighthouse in pairs of two, chilled to the bone despite their skintight neoprene suits. All were wearing night vision goggles beneath their combat helmets. Without them, the sliver of moonlight would have been insufficient to enable them to see even a few feet in front of their faces. After two minutes of slow advancement, Sarah stumbled upon a black Cadillac parked hood first in a row of thick underbrush, about a hundred yards from the lighthouse.

"Looky here," she said excitedly to the Israeli, shining a pencil-sized flashlight on the car. The dark sedan had obviously not been abandoned; it looked as though it had just come off the showroom floor, except for the Hertz bumper sticker. A woman's brown leather handbag was on the backseat; Sarah suspected it contained Jessica's now-dormant SatSearch transmitter.

When the three-story fieldstone structure was a hundred feet away, and clearly visible with their enhanced light, all four took up positions behind the trees. Savage held up his open hand to the others, signaling them to wait.

"Bravo, this is Alpha. Are you there? Over."

Savage could see and hear the water beyond the lighthouse, splashing against the huge jagged rocks that served as the structure's beachfront. Through a crackle of static, Savage heard a reply.

"Roger, Alpha, I read you loud and clear. Over." It was Sam Baldwin.

"Where are you, Bravo? Over."

"We're in position and waiting for your signal. Over."

Savage reached into his backpack and removed a pair of long-range binoculars. Rather than looking like most sets of binoculars, these looked like a 35 mm camera with an attached telephoto lens. They were specifically designed to clip onto a pair of night vision goggles. When linked, they formed an instrument that allowed the user to bring an image sixty times closer with minimal available light.

Savage carefully scanned the horizon, missing the small speedboat during his first pass. He rose up from his crouched position and searched again. There, in the distance, was Sam Baldwin at the helm and the Swede kneeling behind him. "Gotcha, Bravo! Wait for my signal. Over."

Savage pointed to Sarah and the Israeli, directing them to move into a position that had a more favorable view of the crown of the lighthouse. The infrared satellite images provided by Moscow had indicated two distinct sources of heat in the area. One of them was a solitary figure standing guard on the top step of the lighthouse. Unfortunately, from Savage's current vantage point, he could not yet confirm that information with his own eyes.

The Israeli moved laterally to his left, circling behind the three-story house. Sarah mimicked his movements, just a few paces behind; they remained ten feet deep inside the woods at all times. Savage tracked his colleagues' slow progress from tree to tree. In his earpiece he could hear them breathing heavily. When Sarah disappeared from view behind the house, Savage knew it was almost time.

"I can see that bastard. Over," the Israeli whispered into his mouthpiece.

"Is he wearing night goggles?"

"Yes, and I think he's looking right at me!" The Israeli hastily raised his Galil SAR sniper's rifle, then froze in place, anticipating he'd have to fire without being fully prepared. "It looks like he's speaking into a walkie-talkie."

"Shoot him only if you have to, Ben! Sarah, do you have him covered?"

"Yeah, he's in my sights, too." The thought of simply unloading a lethal round crossed her mind before she suppressed it. *Patience*, she told herself. *Patience.*

There was a long, silent pause. "Wait a second, he just looked away," the Israeli reported.

Savage smiled. With both a technological edge, as well as the element of surprise, this first kill would be easy pickings. "Tell me when you're each ready to fire. Over."

Savage turned his long-range binoculars back out at the ocean. He could see the Swede standing at the rear of the boat, his feet spread more than shoulder length apart; the man had obviously heard the Israeli's report through his earpiece and was also readying himself. His handmade rifle was out of its case and six hollow-tipped bullets had been swiftly loaded into the chamber. Each .30 caliber shell was designed to penetrate, then fragment, after impact. The horrific wounds caused by these bullets had made them outlawed by the Hague Convention; but as far as the Swede was concerned, that ban applied only to the conditions of conventional warfare.

"I'm ready," said Aviv. He lay belly to earth with his left elbow serving as a tripod. His Israeli-made sniper rifle was loaded, the safety in the off position. He raised his weapon at a forty-five-degree angle to compensate for the height of the lighthouse tower. From less than eighty yards McClarty was squarely inside his crosshairs. This would be a chip shot for him; he had routinely taken out targets from more than five times this distance with this very same weapon.

"Bjorn, how about you?"

"Ja," he replied, focused on his target rather than on responding in English.

"On my count of three," Savage told them both. "Sarah, cover Ben and watch the back windows of that house very carefully. There's another gunman inside."

"Roger."

The Swede steadied himself, trying to counterbalance for the gentle sway of the boat. From nearly five hundred yards away, even the slightest error would send his shot way off the mark. He inhaled several times deeply through his nose, prepared to hold his breath until he had squeezed off as many rounds as necessary. He had learned that technique from his years of biathlon training, where five shots needed to be fired as quickly as possible after skiing the equivalent of a half marathon. Now, without the challenge of physical exertion, he had brought his heart rate down to below twenty-five beats per minute.

"One," Savage announced clearly.

The Swede closed his left eye, allowing his right to take full advantage of the laser-guided scope mounted atop his rifle. He had aimed at the center of McClarty's chest, then decided to raise the barrel just a smidgen. From this distance it was impossible to determine whether or not his target was wearing a bulletproof vest.

"Two," Savage said deliberately.

Both the Israeli and the Swede curled their index fingers around their triggers and began to apply pressure slowly. Sarah's eyes combed the back windows. If Grizzwald appeared inside the glass she was ready to kill him immediately.

"Three!"

Savage turned his focus toward the front facade of the house. He heard two gentle spits in his earpiece, one a split second after the other.

The bullet from the Swede's rifle soared across the foamy water, then tore a hole in McClarty's breastbone the size of a walnut. Before he could crumple to the ground, the .22 caliber slug from the Israeli's weapon exploded against McClarty's back, propelling him forward as if he'd been forcefully shoved from behind. Both marksmen were poised to discharge their weapons again, but there was no target at which to fire. McClarty was sprawled facedown on the stone floor of the lighthouse. A few feet from his half-closed eyes was his walkie-talkie. A few feet beyond that was the AK-47 he'd been clutching before the sudden attack. He saw the gun through the searing pain that clouded his vision and he tried to reach for it. But it was too far away.

"What's the status of the target? Over," Savage asked anxiously.

"Both shots found their mark," the Israeli reported. "He's down."

"Is he dead?"

"I'm sure he is," interrupted the confident Swede without a trace of an accent. "Mine caught him square."

"Ben?"

The Israeli processed what he had just observed through his scope. "They were both perfect shots."

"But is he dead?" Savage insisted angrily.

"It's impossible to tell from here. But if he's not, he will be soon."

Savage cursed under his breath. He was worried that a wounded McClarty would be able to communicate with his partner inside, further risking everyone's life, including Jessica's. It was impossible to proceed with phase two of the operation without answers to those questions.

"Let's go in and mop up," Sarah whispered to the Israeli.

"Good idea," Savage said.

They darted from the safety of the thick woods, and across the shallow clearing encircling the lighthouse, while McClarty struggled to drag his dying body closer to his weapon. He heard the heavy steel door at the base of the tower creak open, and his eyes widened in anticipation.

"Grizz?" he croaked. "Is that you?"

He was feeling lightheaded but he realized that the noise down below was probably one of his attackers coming inside to finish the job. A rush of adrenaline boosted his diminishing strength.

McClarty dragged his mutilated torso along the cold stone floor with all the energy he could muster, inching ever closer to the AK-47. In his left hand was his walkie-talkie. When he heard the faint sound of muted footsteps getting louder and louder he frantically reached for his weapon with a flailing lunge, snaring the snub-nosed barrel with two of his fingertips. One last scissor kick got him close enough to grab the gun's midsection. He rolled over, straining through his blurred vision to see who was crouched at the top of the steps. The rounded tips of two silencers stared at him. His brain quickly ordered his index finger to respond, but the synapses were just a split second too slow to beat his attackers to the punch.

"Fuck you," the Israeli hissed as he and Sarah simultaneously squeezed their triggers.

A hail of bullets crisscrossed the room in all directions. One from McClarty's AK-47 hit the Israeli flush in the forehead, dropping him like a stone. Sarah kept firing at her target. Her weapon fell silent only when her clip was spent.

Sarah slowly approached McClarty's body and kicked his fallen weapon away from his hand. It slid harmlessly across the floor. She removed the walkie-talkie from his other hand, careful not to press any of its buttons, then reached down and felt for his pulse. When she confirmed he was dead, she leaned over and spat on his blood-splattered face.

100

S A R A H tiptoed down the steps of the lighthouse using the utmost caution, stopping before she pulled open the heavy steel door. The noise from McClarty's weapon had sounded deafening from so close.

"Hank, it's Sarah," she murmured into the microphone of her collar set. "Come around back. Over."

"What the hell happened in there? I thought I heard shots through my earpiece."

"You did. The gunman's dead, but so's Ben."

"Fuck." Savage closed his eyes and paused for a moment. "Are you hurt?"

"No, but I'm not sure I should come out of here. The guy inside might have heard something."

"I'll come around and cover you."

"Suppose this one had time to use his walkie-talkie?" Sarah asked.

"Then we're all in big trouble. Especially Jessie."

Savage slowly circled the house, looking carefully for any outward sign that their presence had been exposed. There was none.

"Come on out," Savage whispered into his collar set. "I've got you covered."

Sarah carefully opened the lighthouse door, then dashed toward the protection of the dense woods. She joined up with Savage when she was barely thirty feet from the main house. Together they circled back to the spot facing the front of the structure where the Professor was still hiding.

"You OK to keep going?" Savage asked Sarah.

"I'll be fine."

"Because here comes the hard part."

"No shit."

Slowly, deliberately, they repositioned themselves so they had a better angle at the front of the house. When they were on the fringe of the treeline, about a hundred feet from the front door, all three spread themselves on the ground, bellies to earth.

"There's a door around back," Sarah whispered to Savage. "My guess is that it's open because it connects to the lighthouse."

"And I saw an old fire escape leading up to the attic," Savage added.

Sarah nodded as she stared at the second-floor windows. The infrared satellite photos from Moscow now confirmed what her own computer-enhanced eyes were telling her: whoever was inside that house was likely in the dimly lit front room on the second floor.

"Nicky, you and I'll sneak inside through the back door," Savage said to the Englishman. "Sarah, I want you to fire this grenade at whatever window I tell you when I give you the signal."

Savage shimmied the camouflage knapsack off his back and quickly untied the flap. He removed a pair of foot-long metal cylinders that easily threaded together with a few simple twists. He handed the weapon to Sarah, who inspected the sighting mechanism on the French-made rocket launcher. The hollow tubes were designed to propel a hand grenade–sized Flash-bang concussion bomb into an enclosed space for the purpose of abruptly incapacitating everyone inside. First came the blinding flash from the ignited magnesium powder. It was immediately followed by the debilitating shock waves from the controlled explosion. When used to deal with a tower shooter, or an airline hijacking that had found its way onto an evacuated tarmac, the concussion bomb generally gave a tactical assault team ten to twenty seconds in which to advance without fear of being fired upon. After that short interval, the effectiveness of the weapon diminished dramatically.

Sarah grabbed the launcher from Savage. Ben Aviv had fired this exact model of launcher more than a hundred times; he was the one who was supposed to assume this task. Now they would have to rely on Sarah's limited expertise.

Savage and the Brit sprinted toward the front of the house, then pressed their backs squarely against the stone exterior. There were no bushes or shrubs to hide behind, no doorways to duck into. Even the slightest noise would alert Grizzwald to two of the easiest targets he'd ever knocked down, especially if McClarty had had the presence of mind to warn his colleague. The next few minutes would be critical.

They inched sideways around the rectangular structure, making as little noise as possible. After spotting the back door Sarah had described, they each took up positions on either side of it. Savage pointed to the Englishman, instructing him to lead the way.

"We're going in," Savage whispered into his mouthpiece. "Sarah, be prepared to fire on my command. And maintain your position even if you think you shouldn't. Be disciplined." For a moment Savage's thoughts drifted back to his elite antiterrorist training squad with the marines. They had referred to their mock-up hostage situations as "killing rooms," where each turn of the corner hid a potential pop-up terrorist. Tap-tap. One to the head, one to the chest. But there was always a second chance during training exercises, and here Savage knew there would be no such luxury.

Sarah rushed forward toward the front door, then threw herself prostrate when she was eight feet below the base of one of the second-floor windows. She blended into the unlit earth as well as a lizard on a tree limb. She remained perfectly inert for the count of ten, her face pressed against the ground. Then she double-checked the launcher, making certain it was ready to fire.

The Englishman set the butt of his automatic weapon against the rear of the stone house, then used both hands to cautiously turn the back doorknob. His gloves were made of soft black leather, and the thin padding muffled any sound made by the old bolt latch. Savage nodded, encouraging him to keep going. He pushed the door open just as judiciously once the latch had been released. Despite the Englishman's care, the rusty hinge creaked. Although barely audible, the sound traveled straight up the wooden steps.

"Mac, you coming up?" Grizzwald asked loudly. The voice had come from the front of the house, on the second floor.

The Englishman froze in the entranceway, looking back at Savage. He could hear footsteps moving toward the rear of the house just above him. They weren't heading in the direction of the staircase. Instead, it seemed as though Grizzwald had walked to a back window to determine if he could still see McClarty standing guard in the lighthouse tower. Savage put his index finger to his lips. As he did, he inched toward the open door in a crouched position, getting ready to cover the Englishman, if necessary. He was back in the killing room, and his pop-up target was just up the steps.

"Hey Mac!" Grizzwald shouted as he walked towards the top landing. "We'll be right down! All the gear is packed and ready to go!"

Savage pointed his silencer up the dark staircase while he quietly handed the Englishman his weapon. Savage squinted from behind the eyepieces of his night vision goggles, eagerly waiting for a different shade of gray-green to appear. He would fire two shots directly into the center of it as soon as one did. But instead of getting closer, the footsteps moved back toward the front of the house.

"Come on up!" Grizzwald called down. "I need a hand with these bags!" When there was no response, Savage heard the rustle of loaded bags being shuffled.

"Here, carry this," Grizzwald said angrily to Jessica.

The sound of two distinct sets of footsteps began to get louder before the Brit could back out of the house. He hid in the foyer behind the open door, his gun pointed out in front of him. Savage quickly retreated outside, positioning himself just beside the door frame.

"Where are we going?" Jessica asked. She was descending the steps in front of Grizzwald, a bulging black nylon bag slung over her right shoulder. Grizzwald ignored the remark. Instead, his attention was focused on the cold breeze coming in through the wide open door.

"Mac?" he asked tentatively.

Grizzwald halted in his tracks when he heard no response, three steps down from the top landing. Jessica continued her slow descent, having no idea that the man behind her had stopped walking.

"Get back up here! Now!" he barked at Jessica. He hurriedly dropped the rucksack in his hands, allowing free access to the weapon that had been dangling at his side from a leather strap.

The Englishman bolted out from behind the door and located the precise spot from where the male voice had come. He fired twice at Grizzwald, intentionally aiming slightly to the right of where he wanted because of Jessica's position. Savage rushed inside the doorway the instant he heard the first shot, poised to cover his colleague. From his position, any clear attempt at Grizzwald would have been too risky because Jessica's paralyzed frame was obstructing his sight line.

The Englishman's first shot tore into Grizzwald's shoulder, momentarily causing him to lose a grip of his weapon. When he recovered his semiautomatic, Grizzwald fired blindly at the darkness. A stream of bullets whizzed harmlessly below the arch of the open door, just above Savage's head. Then one struck the Englishman in the chest. The shot would have been fatal had it not been for his bulletproof vest; the force of the .45 caliber slug slamming against the tightly woven Kevlar broke two of his ribs. The Englishman lunged toward the stairway despite the painful blunt wound, but was too far away to grab Jessica. Grizzwald had already yanked her by the hair back up the steps. Savage and the Professor retreated out the back door, Grizzwald to a second-story bedroom. Both sides now had to decide what to do next.

101

"YOU'VE got exactly one minute to throw your weapons down and crawl to the middle of the backyard where I can see you!" Grizzwald yelled from the second floor. His wounded left arm was wrapped tightly around Jessica's neck, spilling blood all over it. In his right hand was an automatic weapon that could fire a hundred rounds per second. It was pressed against her skull.

"I'll fucking kill you if they come inside again!" he spat into her ear. "You tell them that!"

"Please do what he asked!" Jessica shouted in a shaky voice. "He's got a gun to my head!"

Savage and the Professor looked at one another.

"What do you want to do?" the Englishman whispered. "We can't crawl out back. He'll shoot us."

"I agree."

"And if we go inside, he'll shoot Jessica."

"I don't think he'll shoot her unless he has to. She's his only way out of here alive."

"You've got thirty seconds!" Grizzwald shouted.

"Let's go back in," Savage told the Professor. "We need to know where they are."

He cautiously stepped inside the rear vestibule, the Brit by his side. Instead of going up the back steps, Savage walked through a narrow hallway until he arrived at the foot of the front staircase. He peered up the steps from behind a side wall, searching through his night goggles for a differentiation in the shade of gray-green. There was nothing but darkness. He paused, concentrating on any sound coming from upstairs. There was nothing but silence.

Hank carefully opened one of the small pockets of his leather gun belt, the metal snap making a gentle click as it released. He dipped his thumb and index finger into the open pouch and painstakingly removed a single hollow-tipped bullet. He lobbed the three-inch steel cylinder with an underhand motion just past the top step. As soon as it landed on the hardwood floor with a loud thud, a hail of shots showered the spot where the object had touched down. Savage and the Englishman hurriedly ducked for cover in an adjoining hallway, correctly anticipating that more shots would be fired. Grizzwald's spray of bullets splintered the very spot where Savage had been standing. Then the house went completely silent, neither man wanting to give away his new position. Just as Savage was about to double back up the rear stairway, he heard a faint dragging sound somewhere upstairs. He didn't know if Grizzwald had killed his hostage and was now alone, or whether he was still using Jessica as a shield.

Savage and the Englishman again retreated out the back door, still aiming their weapons at the dark staircase. They considered backing away from the house and regrouping in the woods. But if Grizzwald was wearing night vision goggles and could observe them withdrawing through the darkness, then he'd be able to pick off all of them from the high ground.

Savage maneuvered his microphone closer to his throat and asked, "Sarah, are you still out front?"

"Yeah," she answered. "I'm at the door, waiting for your signal. But I'm coming inside!"

"No! Back away from the house and fire that grenade into the attic window on this side of the house when I give you the signal. As soon as you're done firing you've got to reload and put one more round inside. If you miss with either of those shells he'll kill us all."

"Understood. After my second shot I'm going up the fire escape."

Savage and the Englishman entered the house and slowly began climbing the back stairs. At first the old wooden steps made no sound. When they were halfway up the flight there was a loud creak.

"Now, Sarah!" Savage whispered into his microphone.

Savage heard the gentle whoosh of the compact launcher spitting out its projectile immediately after he had issued his command. A split second later there was a crash of broken glass, followed by a flash of blinding light. Then came the powerful thud.

"Come on!" Savage encouraged the Englishman.

The two men raced up the stairs. When they reached the top landing they spun around the corner and sprinted for the next set of stairs. Just as they hit the first step there was a second explosion, as bright and loud as the first. This time they were close enough to the blast to feel the powerful shock waves in the pits of their stomachs. Undeterred, they forged ahead and crashed through the locked attic door, splintering the wooden frame into a thousand pieces.

Savage desperately searched through the dense cloud of suspended dust for the shadowy figure he knew was inside. He was tempted to simply fire blindly into the opaque darkness, but feared that he'd kill Jessie in the process. He stayed low to the ground, ducking for cover beneath a battered steamer trunk until he had a clear shot at his target.

Grizzwald was on all fours beside the window where Sarah was now crouched, a black nylon bag lying a few feet away. A pair of night vision goggles was around his forehead. He shook his head vigorously, trying to clear his mind; the concussion bombs had only disoriented him for a few moments. Jessica lay motionless facedown on the floor beside him. When Grizzwald was no longer dazed he reached for the bag at his feet. Inside were a dozen hand grenades he intended to loft toward the attic door.

Sarah peered through the blown-out window just in time to see Grizzwald's bloody arm cocked and ready to uncoil. She drained her cartridge into the middle of the thick figure without hesitating, then quickly reloaded and emptied another. Grizzwald fell face first onto the attic floor, harmlessly smothering his loaded hand grenade. When he remained motionless for the count of ten she slowly approached the body, an unexpected feeling of power coursing through her veins. With her own two hands she had cut off one of the tentacles of Buck Perry's awful killing machines. She pressed her fingers against Jessica's neck, smiling when she felt a weak but steady pulse. Soon they'd be able to get her to a doctor.

"Everyone hold your fire," she announced into her microphone. "It's all over."

Savage came out from his hiding spot and joined Sarah. When he noticed the pin from the hand grenade tightly curled around Grizzwald's middle finger he realized how close he had come to his appointment with death.

"Thanks," he said to Sarah as he gently rubbed her shoulder. "I owe you one."

Sarah wrapped her arm around Savage's waist. "Just remember that the next time you hear from me."

102 *Friday*

"WALTER," Sarah said wearily into her car phone, "it's me."

The FBI agent looked at his watch and shook his head.

"It's eight fifty-seven. You made it by three minutes. I was just about to call Evelyn Dunbar over at *The Washington Post*. Is everything all right?"

Sarah stared blankly through the rain-streaked windshield of her Jeep, pondering how to answer Jensen's question. The ramp descending into the Pierre's parking garage was visible in her rearview mirror, and she could see a sliver of the Baldwin Building down Fifth Avenue to her left. She was in that foggy state of mind caused by the combination of overstimulation and sleep deprivation. Time and space were somewhat distorted, and even her own voice sounded warped. For a few seconds she absently watched her windshield wipers rhythmically push water back and forth, gliding along the Plexiglas like parallel metronomes. As much as she wanted to stretch out on some hot sand for a few days, there was still work that needed to be done.

"I don't really know, Walter. I mean I'm fine, at least physically. But I've been to hell and back in the last few hours. To be honest, I feel like I've just had the shit kicked out of me."

"You don't sound so great. Is there anything I can do to help?"

"I'm afraid not. I think I just need a little time to sort this all out."

"Are you in Washington right now? I'd be glad to buy you a cup of coffee and talk about it."

Sarah closed her eyes and massaged her throbbing temples with her fingertips. She was so tired that the thought of rehashing all that had occurred made her head ache. "I'm in Manhattan and should be back in Washington in a few hours. But I'll pass for now on your offer."

"Is that your way of politely telling me to mind my own damn business?"

Sarah smiled. "I promise I'll tell you the whole story. One day."

"OK. Then what should I do with this envelope?"

"Lock it someplace where no one will find it. But I still want you to hold it for safekeeping. There are still a couple of loose ends to tie up."

"I suppose Montgomery's one of them?"

Sarah didn't reply.

"Before you go," Jensen said quickly, "I assume you heard they found O'Grady's body?"

Sarah put her hand over her eyes and shook her head. "No, I haven't heard anything. I've been pretty much out of the loop."

"One shot to the temple."

"Good God. This is a fucking mess."

"It sure is."

Sarah drove south on I-95, thinking about what had transpired over the past day. Less than four hours earlier Sam Baldwin had returned all of her belongings, including the compromising photos Savage had removed from her bedroom. Savage had obviously also rifled through her briefcase, vainly searching for the microcassette that had started Sarah on this wild ride in the first place. To her, it now seemed like days had passed since the triumphant group had returned to Sam Baldwin's East Hampton retreat, intoxicated with enthusiasm over the success of the operation. Only the death of Ben Aviv had dampened the mood.

Sarah had intentionally kept her distance from most of the frivolity, catching clipped glimpses of the various conversations from adjoining rooms. She overheard the description of how the lighthouse and the adjoining old stone house had been briskly cleansed of almost every sign of a struggle, and how the two soldiers' bodies, along with Buck Perry's, had been weighted and dumped far out into the ocean, surely never to be seen again. She also heard the hastily arranged travel plans for the Swede and the Englishman, and she watched them leave before sunrise. And everyone in the huge villa listened to the local news, relieved to hear absolutely nothing about the incident.

Later that morning, Sam Baldwin approached Sarah to offer his driver's services for her return trip to Manhattan. It had been less than a full day since Sam and Sarah had met in the emergency stairwell of the Peninsula Hotel. Baldwin was regaining control of his life, but Sarah could read in his wounded eyes that he still had one last item to take care of, that revenge for Sam Baldwin could not be fully savored until that task was complete. And

Sarah, too, had two demons to purge before her life could begin again. One was Andy Archer. The other, Jack Montgomery.

103

Sarah pulled her Jeep up to the secure entrance of the State Department garage. Any possibility of bringing Jack Montgomery to traditional justice had gone right out the very window she had blown to smithereens with a rocket launcher and a fist-sized concussion bomb. She knew, of course, that prosecutorial ripples would engulf everyone who had taken part in the rescue operation if she brought the kidnapping to the attention of the FBI, and she had been involved in enough criminal investigations to know the whole affair would deteriorate into a media circus. She, too, would certainly be swept into the feeding frenzy in the alleged search for justice. Still, she had no regrets at the action she had taken, for she had avenged, at least in part, the death of the man who had brought her into this world. However, before she stepped aside and allowed Hank Savage to finish the job, she needed Jack Montgomery to answer one simple question: why had he directed an assassin to kill her father?

Gus Johnson was manning the security gate at the underground garage at the State Department just like he did most late afternoons. His paunch jiggled around his gun belt as he twirled his nightstick with the practiced precision of a guard at Buckingham Palace. He pushed his head inside the driver's window of Sarah's Jeep. The three cameras behind him kept constant video surveillance of this particular entrance.

"Haven't seen you for a coupla days," he said to her with a welcoming smile. "I heard you was under the weather. You feelin' any better?"

"So-so." She shrugged.

"You don't look so good. Why don't you turn this baby around and get a few hours of shut-eye?"

"Gotta earn a living, Gus."

"I hear you, Sarah," he replied with a wink. He waved his favorite federal agent through without asking for her credentials.

Sarah nervously stepped out of the elevator and took a deep breath. The Secretary of State's corner office was just fifty paces away. She walked them slowly, stopping in front of Montgomery's office door.

"Marilyn, I assume he's in?" she asked Montgomery's secretary.

"You bet, but he's in the middle of something. He said he didn't want to be disturbed under any circumstances." She furrowed her brow, mimicking the stern face Jack Montgomery had made when he issued that edict.

"Buzz me in, will you? I'll take the heat if you catch any shit from him."

Marilyn reluctantly shook her head. "I'm sorry, Sarah, but I really can't. He looked very serious when he went in there."

Sarah strode behind the secretary's desk and pressed a small white button before the woman could stop her. A buzz sounded, and Sarah darted toward the Secretary of State's mahogany doors before the five-second timer elapsed.

Montgomery was sitting at his desk, obviously immersed in the documents spread before him. The sudden noise of the opening door startled him. His eyes narrowed angrily to see who had the audacity to disobey his orders for privacy.

"I'm sorry, Mr. Secretary," Marilyn said from the doorway, "but she forced her way inside."

Montgomery waved his secretary back to her desk with a flip of his hand and the door closed behind her.

"Planning another kidnapping?" Sarah asked sarcastically as she approached his desk.

Montgomery stood so that he was now several inches taller than Sarah. The first rule of negotiating, he knew, was never to allow your adversary to stand over you. Physical presence *did* matter in situations like this. So did going on the offensive.

"Don't jump to any hasty conclusions, Sarah. You don't know all of the details."

"I think I do."

"Sit down and we'll see."

Sarah measured him carefully, then took a seat directly across from him. This was the side of Jack Montgomery, the tactician behind closed doors, that she had never been able to observe firsthand.

"Just hear me out before you pass judgment."

"I'm afraid that'll be impossible."

"Jessica Baldwin planned her own kidnapping," Montgomery said. "She was a willing participant from day one." He sat down behind his desk, allowing the impact of his shocking claim to penetrate.

"Bullshit."

"She came to me about six weeks ago," Montgomery continued, ignoring Sarah's interruption, "appalled that her father was planning to kill Saddam Hussein. From conversations she had overheard, she realized it was a mission he was embracing. It was exciting for him, a new challenge for a man who'd accomplished more than most people achieved in ten lifetimes. And from the telephone calls I then intercepted, it was clear nothing was going to dissuade Sam Baldwin from pressing forward."

"And you couldn't allow that?" Sarah asked cynically.

"No, I couldn't. Baldwin's plan would've thrown us into a war halfway across the globe, with thousands, maybe millions, of senseless deaths on both sides. Jessica and I decided that her staged kidnapping was the only way to change her father's mind. Unfortunately, she badly miscalculated his resolve."

Sarah stared at Montgomery, the rage in her belly rising by the minute. *You're a fucking liar*, she thought. Blame the victim, declare your own innocence, then spin it until you were blue in the face. What galled Sarah as much as anything was the sanctimony and conviction in Jack Montgomery's voice. He sounded almost believable.

"Then why threaten to kill Jessica?" she asked.

"Because those two idiots Grizzwald and McClarty screwed things up!" Montgomery spat disgustedly. "They were supposed to baby-sit Jessica in a hotel room in Paris for a few days and let this whole affair end with a few of us winking at one another. Only her father would've been kept in the dark, and that's what we intended. But they got greedy."

"Then what about Bill O'Grady? Did he agree to take a bullet through his brain?"

Montgomery slowly shook his head, trying to appear as though he was wounded by the question.

"No," he answered softly. "Buck took on these assignments with a fanaticism that wasn't healthy any longer. I feel terrible about O'Grady's death and was furious when I learned what had happened. It was unforgivable. Stupid. And I promised myself that once this operation was over, Buck and I would never work together on one of these projects again. He'd changed over the years, gotten too full of himself and the power we wielded."

"And what about me?" Sarah asked bluntly. "Wasn't I supposed to end up like O'Grady?"

"Absolutely not! I swear on my son's life that my man's orders were to find you and bring you to me alive. He was nothing more than a courier who was supposed to intercept you before you spilled the beans to the FBI."

Sarah held her anger in check, aware that Jack Montgomery had no clue that she had watched Andy Archer get taken into police custody and had seen his sniper rifle.

"Then what about Jessica? You were prepared to let her die, weren't you?" she persisted. "You could've called in the FBI to find her, but you didn't, did you? And that's because you were more concerned about protecting your own skin than you were about saving her life, isn't that right?"

"No. I knew all along that I had the resources to pay Grizzwald and McClarty if it came to that. I never would've let them harm Jessie."

Sarah folded her arms and released a deep sigh. Jack Montgomery had climbed as high as he had because he was a skillful liar who had a ready answer for everything. She stared at him, her blood pressure rising by the second. For all of the deceptive window dressing the Secretary of State had hung on his recent actions, the fact of the matter was that he had been an accessory to murder. In Sarah's mind it was now time for him to come clean once and for all and to face the punishment he had avoided for so long.

"And just how many people did Buck kill so that your own dirty little secrets would be protected?"

Montgomery smiled thinly: How much did Sarah know? His other activities were all so well planned, so well concealed. She was bluffing, on a wild fishing expedition; if she had known about her father she would have been much more direct. Besides, Montgomery knew about the killings in the lighthouse. Krystoviac and Ray Dawkins, the two Special Forces soldiers, had been on their way to meet Buck Perry on Apaquogue Road when the general had been killed by Hank Savage. They had been a minute too late to save their commander, but they had the presence of mind to follow Savage's car to the lighthouse at Old Field Point and had observed Jessica's emancipation from the dense woods near the lighthouse. To Montgomery, this news ensured Sarah's silence. If she pressed the matter, he would bring her down with him in the blink of an eye.

"O'Grady was the only one," Montgomery replied coldly, "and I've already told you Buck had no authorization from me to do what he did."

Sarah continued to stare into Montgomery's icy, blue eyes, her anger welling up like a volcano. Aside from being a liar of unprecedented magnitude, it was obvious to her that he was completely unrepentant. She had given him the opportunity to confess, and perhaps to explain, if that was possible. In return he had calculated the odds and chosen to deny every-thing. She would get nothing more from this man; certainly not the answer she had sought for thirty-five years.

"My resignation will be effective immediately," Sarah said as she stood to leave.

Montgomery nodded deferentially, still confident she would be power-less to go to the authorities.

"I understand your decision, and I respect it. But bear in mind that I had no complicity whatsoever in Buck Perry's activities. He acted alone, without giving me an opportunity to veto what he intended to do. And he received the ultimate punishment for his foolhardy behavior. Raising awareness of this whole episode will do more harm than good." He paused for a moment, then added, "For *all* of us." He paused again. "Am I being clear?"

"Perfectly," she answered as she strode toward the door. "And just so you know, if anything happens to me, there are people who are in possession of certain documents that spell out in great detail your activities over the last thirty years." She paused, then asked, "Am *I* being clear?"

"Perfectly."

She looked at Montgomery one last time, then turned and left the office.

104

Sarah slowly drove past her brownstone, looking more at the cars parked on both sides of the rain-soaked street than at anything else. Her adrenaline was still pumping because of her conversation with Jack Montgomery. So far there was no sign of Andy Archer's black Explorer, but that was not surprising. If he was in the neighborhood, as Sarah suspected, she presumed he wouldn't have been so brazen as to leave his car within a two-block radius of her home. Confidence was one thing, stupidity another. And no one had ever accused Archer of being stupid. She decided to widen her search.

She was almost certain that Archer would continue to pursue her, even though Jessica was now free and the ball game was all but over. One of the garage attendants at the Pierre had warned her that a sandy-haired man in his mid-thirties had been asking all sorts of questions about her comings and goings. The attendant had been given a hundred dollars as a down payment, and promised five hundred more if he cooperated. A simple nod to the guy in the lobby would signal that the lady in the red Jeep had arrived at the hotel so he could catch the adulterous wife.

The first black Explorer she saw was parked on Twenty-seventh and P. A quick CIB check run by Walter Jensen's secretary confirmed that the four-by-four was registered to a doctor from Virginia who was its original and only owner. Two kids' car seats were buckled in the back, and were strewn with ground-in animal crackers.

The Explorer on Thirty-first and Dumbarton took her another forty-five minutes to find; it had been reported stolen two years earlier and had never been recovered. But there were no tinted windows like the car that had been parked across the street from her brownstone just a few days earlier. Still, she sensed that Andy Archer was nearby. She drove around the corner and called Walter Jensen from her car phone.

"Walter?"

"Yeah."

"It's Sarah."

"Are you back in town?"

"Tying up one of those loose ends we talked about this morning."

"OK. How can I help?"

"Do you have a pen handy?"

"Got it."

"Write down this name."

"Go ahead."

"Andy Archer."

"Done. Now what?"

"If I don't call you in the next fifteen minutes, then call the police and have them put out an APB for him. He's a senior foreign policy analyst for the State Department."

"What'd he do?"

"Nothing yet. But I have a feeling he may try to kill me."

"You're not serious!"

"I am."

"Then why not call the police right now?"

"I've got my reasons."

"Sarah . . ."

"Fifteen minutes, Walter. And not a minute sooner."

Sarah rounded the corner and sprinted up her front steps, her bullet-proof vest snug beneath her navy blazer. She had the feeling she was being watched as she quickly made it to the top landing. When she entered her vestibule she noticed the wilting red roses she had placed there on Tuesday night. Then she saw what she was looking for. Beside the glass vase was a trace of moisture left by the crisscross pattern of a man's wet sneaker. It had almost evaporated. *Almost,* Sarah thought. He was inside, but hadn't been for long. The sight made her furious.

Sarah tiptoed up her steps, carefully studying the closed door that led into her living room. Her Magnum was drawn and ready in case he jumped out, the safety in the off position. She had never imagined that she would be forced to kill someone whom she had once considered a friend. Sarah was convinced that he would stop at nothing until he had evened the score.

When Sarah was halfway up the staircase she heard her cat meow, then scamper away from the door. That was unusual. Big Guy always eagerly waited in the hallway, ready to rub up against Sarah's legs before she even took two steps inside.

"Andy?" she said loudly. "I know you're in there."

She listened carefully, straining to locate Archer. A tiny creak of a floorboard told her he was somewhere in the front of the apartment. It sounded more like someone transferring his weight than actually changing position. She shifted her weapon, trying to track his movements.

"We can do this one of two ways, Andy. Either easy or hard. But we're going to settle this once and for all right now."

Sarah paused for a full minute, waiting to hear another creak. There was none.

"Look out my front window. The cops aren't here yet, but they will be soon." She winced, wishing she could take back her last statement. In the heat of the moment she had presented an option she didn't really want him to take. A conviction would put him away for many years, but it would also give him an awfully long time to seethe. Sarah had absolutely no doubt that once he had served his sentence, no matter how long it was, Archer would hunt her down, more determined than ever to retaliate for all that had happened to him. She decided to turn up the heat, to try to goad him into doing what he had come to her home for in the first place.

"You can either surrender to me, or be humiliated again. Either way, you're going to face murder and attempted murder charges."

Several quick footsteps came from Sarah's office that faced Thirtieth

Street; Archer was obviously looking to see if she was telling the truth. Then she heard him walking gingerly toward the living room door.

"Open that door very slowly and slide your weapon onto the floor!" Sarah ordered, knowing he would never comply. "Then I want to see your empty hands way out in front of you as you crawl out very slowly."

"You embarrassed me, Sarah," an angry voice on the other side of the door said. "I don't like being embarrassed."

"No one does, Andy. No one likes getting killed either."

Sarah waited and waited, sweat drenching her underarms. Both of her hands tightly held her Magnum. Her feet were shoulder length apart, just like she had taught her students. A cornered rat always fought, and Sarah knew that Archer now had nowhere to run.

A squeak came, and then another. Sarah watched the living room door open slowly. She heard a soft thud when the bottom of the door struck the doorstop.

"Maybe they'll cut you a sweet deal if you cooperate," Sarah said as she studied the open door. "And then again, maybe they won't."

Sarah heard Archer spring toward the doorway moments before she saw the barrel of his gun. The floorboard that always creaked when she walked inside gave him away. She waited a split second longer than she normally would have, giving him the benefit of the doubt.

Sarah's first shot landed exactly where she had planned, shattering Archer's forearm and crippling his ability to aim the twelve-gauge shotgun. Archer continued to move into a firing position and he quickly raised the double barrel in her direction, only to be thrown back against the wall from a second shot to the stomach. Still he kept on coming, the fire in his eyes telling Sarah that there would be only one way to stop him. She pumped two more shots into his midsection, sending him flying onto his back. His shotgun fell from his hands, cartwheeling right past her. He groaned and then fell silent.

The smell of spent gunpowder filled the distance between Sarah and her would-be assassin. A few moments later she heard the sound of police sirens way off in the distance. She slowly climbed her stairs, and stepped over Archer's body. She decided to let the police know what to expect once they arrived.

"This is Special Agent Sarah Peterson of the Office of Diplomatic Security," she calmly told the 9-1-1 operator. "I was just attacked by an intruder in my home at 1301 Thirtieth Street."

"Do you need backup?"

"No ma'am. The assailant was armed and I defended myself. He's dead."

She picked up Big Guy and scratched his head. The police would be there any minute.

105 *Two Months Later*

A thick blanket of snow shrouded the island of Manhattan, muffling the frenzy of activity accompanying every Christmas Eve. People rushed out of work long before quitting time all across the crowded city, preparing to feast with their families. For those who lived near Gramercy Park, the early departure from the office gave them hours to frolic in the deep snow with their children before supper. As darkness fell, the block-long plaza was dotted with brightly colored ski jackets and sleds that would soon be retired until the morning. Across the park was the National Arts Club, where a caterer busily put the finishing touches on the hors d'oeuvres for the wedding that almost wasn't.

Jessica and her mother were on the second floor of the hundred-year-old brownstone that had been converted into a private club just after the Depression. Housing museum-quality works in every room, the exclusive organization had sponsored thousands of writers and painters and sculptors over the years. Scattered between the beveled stained glass windows and the gilded cornices were treasures that had been lovingly donated by wealthy members. Upstairs, where Jessica and Francesca were getting dressed, were the private sitting rooms.

"Are you nervous?" Francesca asked.

"A little bit. I just want everything to go as planned."

"If Hank said it will, then it will."

Francesca lifted Jessica's white lace veil so she could stare directly into her daughter's beautiful green eyes. She caressed the smooth, tan skin on Jessica's cheek, trying to wipe away the pain of the ordeal that continued to haunt the twenty-seven-year-old.

"What are you thinking about?" Francesca asked when she noticed her daughter's faraway look.

"Nothing," Jessica replied faintly. She closed her eyes, trying to force aside the image of Grizzwald's Colt .45 pressing against her forehead. No matter how many times she thought back on her successful rescue, she couldn't help but remember the game of Russian roulette Grizzwald had forced her to play. As she desperately tried to banish the recollection, a gentle knock from across the room interrupted her thoughts.

"Come in," Jessica said.

The white door opened and the wedding coordinator stuck his head inside.

"Five minutes," he announced with a practiced smile. When he closed the door behind him the din of two hundred mingling guests faded.

Jessica walked over to one of the windows facing Gramercy Park. Antique gas street lamps lined the swatch of cleared-out space, illuminating the small park with a soft glow.

"It's coming down harder than before," Jessica said as she watched the snow fall.

Francesca approached her daughter from behind and clasped her hands around Jessica's expanding belly. The tests Jessica had undergone after her release indicated that her baby was doing just fine. In the reflection of the window Francesca could see that her daughter's eyes were closed.

"You know your father loves you more than anything in the whole world," she whispered into Jessica's ear. She tenderly kissed her daughter's neck and said, "He stares at that picture in the living room all the time. He doesn't think I notice, but tears well up in that tough guy's eyes whenever he looks at it."

Jessica leaned back against her mother and fought off tears of her own. The photograph Francesca was speaking about had been taken when Jessica was eight years old, riding a painted horse on the carousel in Central Park.

For a few minutes Francesca tightly held her daughter.

"Ms. Baldwin?" a male voice asked. Neither Jessica nor Francesca had heard the wedding coordinator's knock.

"Yes?"

"Everyone's ready."

"Thank you."

This time the noise drifting in through the open door was barely audible. All of the guests had been assembled for the ceremony, and the quartet was playing the Pachelbel Canon.

"You both look beautiful," Sam Baldwin commented from the doorway.

"You don't look so bad yourself, Dad." He was impeccably dressed in a starched white dress shirt and a tapered black tuxedo. His wide smile belied his own excitement and nervousness.

Francesca tenderly lowered the veil over Jessica's face. "Are you sure you're ready?"

"Yes."

As Sam reached for his daughter's hand, the mobile phone in his trousers rang. He looked anxiously at Jessica, then answered the call in the hope it was the one he'd been expecting.

"Yes?" he said into the receiver.

"Sam, it's Hank." In the background was the muffled roar of four American Airlines 757 engines.

Sam winked at Jessica. With his hand cupped over the phone he said, "It's him."

"Sorry I couldn't be at the wedding," Savage said, "but I had some important business to take care of in Montana. I'm on my way home right now."

"I understand."

"I sent Jessie a wedding present and just learned that delivery went exactly as planned."

"Thanks, Hank. That's excellent news." He winked at his daughter, then said, "Jessie's standing right here beside me. I'll let her know."

"Great. I'll see you all tomorrow. Save a piece of cake for me."

Sam Baldwin closed the phone.

"Montgomery's dead," he told his wife and daughter. "A freak hunting accident out in the wilds of Montana. His own rifle backfired on him."

"What a shame," Jessica said with a smile.

"The networks should have the story within the hour."

Hand in hand all three emerged from the elegant dressing room. As they slowly began their descent of the curved carpeted staircase they searched the sea of eager eyes cast upward toward the handsome threesome. Sam gripped the smooth mahogany handrail with his right hand as Jessica's long white train trailed a half dozen steps behind. When they reached the bottom landing they turned right toward the makeshift altar. Halfway down the aisle, Sam Baldwin stopped and leaned close to Sarah Peterson.

"It's done," he whispered into Sarah's ear.

"That's great news," she replied with a smile.

Baldwin kissed Sarah on the cheek. Before taking a step backward he added in a whisper, "This day would never have been possible without you."

The Baldwins resumed their progress toward the altar. By the time all three reached the groom everyone had gathered in a tight semicircle around the couple. The violin had stopped, the room was completely silent.

Sam turned to Jessica and lifted her veil. With his thumb he wiped the tears streaming down her cheeks. "Thanks for everything, Dad. I love you."

Doug Templeton clutched his fiancée's hand and stepped forward toward the minister. Jessica looked past the man who was about to marry them, through the huge picture window just behind him. It looked down onto Gramercy Park. Several dozen passersby had braved the severe elements to gather on the snow-filled sidewalk directly in front of the brownstone, entranced by the storybook beauty of the scene inside.

When the ceremony ended, the bride and groom embraced. The flash-bulbs began to pop just as the initial reports of Montgomery's death started trickling in over the news wires. Soon leaders from around the world would stream to Washington to pay their respects. And in Arlington National Cemetery, just five hundred yards from where the Secretary of State would be buried, Chip Peterson could finally rest in peace.

EPILOGUE

SARAH sprinted the last hundred yards, winded from her eight-mile run along the flatlands of Kansas. Her gray sweatshirt was turned inside out, concealing the large blue silk-screened letters of her former employer. Now that she was a private citizen, the handgun fastened inside her shoulder harness was no longer government issued. Instead, she had obtained a carrying permit, just like any other civilian who feared for their safety. She may have been a thousand miles from the violence of Washington, D.C., but old habits were hard to break.

Sarah pressed her palms against the dusty bumper of her mom's Ford pickup, stretching her hamstrings and calves until they burned. Sweat poured off her forehead. The bite of winter was gone. Soon tall fields of wheat and barley would sprout from barren patches of dirt all across the heartland. Maybe, Sarah thought, she'd look for a job after Labor Day. Perhaps she'd take Sam up on his standing offer to join Baldwin Enterprises. There was no doubt the billionaire respected her opinions; his dismantling of the weapons from *The Hercules* at her behest was proof of that fact. Then again, maybe Sarah would continue to coast, taking a well-earned hiatus from the treadmill of life. For now money certainly wasn't an issue. A $5 million wire transfer into her BankOne account from Baldwin Enterprises had taken care of that worry for a very long time.

She peeled off her drenched sweatshirt and ambled over to the battered mailbox at the end of the driveway. It was the same one that had been there for as long as she could remember. Her mother was inside the house, taking an afternoon nap. Her chemotherapy had pounded her cancer into submission, but it had left her weakened for the last several months. A day didn't go by when she failed to thank her lucky stars for her daughter's extended visit.

A Walmart circular and one from the local Shop 'n Bag were stuffed inside the mailbox. Sarah grabbed the day's delivery, quickly thumbing through it for anything of interest. A smile came to her face when she saw the picture postcard that had been forwarded to this address, along with the rest of the mail that first went to her Georgetown brownstone. A cuddly brown koala bear was on the front. Jessica and Doug were sending their greetings from Australia. In another six weeks their around-the-world honeymoon would end and the responsibilities of parenthood would replace their carefree globe-trotting of the last three months. Sarah intended to visit them in Connecticut after their baby was born.

As Sarah entered her mom's living room she suddenly stopped. The letter she held had a return address from the State Department, with Jack Montgomery's name penned in the upper lefthand corner, though the script did not match his own distinctive handwriting. Sarah examined the postmark. It had been mailed from New York City nine days earlier. She knew Montgomery could not possibly have mailed this, because he had been dead since Christmas Eve.

Sarah gently patted the envelope before opening it, making certain it wasn't booby-trapped. From what she could feel there was nothing more than a single sheet of paper inside. She held it up to the light and confirmed that conclusion. Her curiosity aroused, she ripped the seal and removed its contents.

> *Dear Sarah,* [the letter began,] *You don't know me and never will. To make sure that's the case, I've destroyed both the printer and computer that were used to type this letter. I've also taken every precaution to be certain that you will never be able to learn my identity. I know how good your forensic skills are. But there are no fingerprints on this stationery. Likewise, my saliva is on neither the envelope nor the stamp. A popular brand of bottled water was used instead to wet both. And the stationery this letter is written on comes from a ream of paper that's the most popular brand in the United States. It can be purchased in any office supply store. So please accept this communication at face value without trying to find me, because you never will.*

Sarah absently dropped her Secret Service sweatshirt and the stack of mail, her eyes transfixed on the black ink. She blindly reached for the armchair behind her, settling into a cushion while she continued to read.

Your father was a hero who died for his country. Because those words can no longer harm those who conspired in your father's death, I thought the time had come for certain facts to be revealed to you. How I know this information should be of no consequence. Instead, draw comfort from what I know to be true.

As you know, your dad was stationed in Moscow by the CIA during most of 1962 and 1963. While there, he worked on several matters with a young foreign service agent named Jack Montgomery. Jack and Chip were both bold men. Both loved their country. The rapport they established by the spring of 1963 was one of mutual respect and admiration. Both men understood that the other could accomplish anything that he set out to do.

From Jack's perspective, the world had become a very dangerous place. Communism was everywhere and spreading and the arms race was getting out of hand. Even within our own borders there were a thousand wrongs that needed to be corrected. At first Jack tried to make a difference through conventional routes. His early initiatives went through all the proper channels before they died a slow, bureaucratic death. He found himself stymied at every turn, frustrated beyond belief. He discussed this with Buck Perry, a career soldier he had fought beside during the Korean War. Immediately they discovered they shared the same vision for America and they decided to embark on a daring series of initiatives they knew crossed the line. They started small and succeeded, then quickly started to believe they were invincible. But they also realized they would need the assistance of others for some of their larger plans.

Jack approached your father during the summer of 1963. Jack viewed Chip as an up-and-comer in the CIA, a guy who had a real shot at running the agency one day. Even if your father never made it that far, there was little doubt he was going to be privy to so much secret information that he would be invaluable to Jack's future operations. Chip Peterson was the missing piece to what was shaping up as a very formidable machine.

Chip listened to Montgomery. The concepts that were discussed were presented in such vague terms that no one could be implicated for anything.

Jack knew immediately he had blundered and he made the decision to kill your father. Buck went along with it. They had big plans for the future and weren't about to let one misstep get in their way. When your father traveled to the United States in August of 1963, Jack rifled through Chip's office in Moscow to make sure the trail would dead-end. A few days later the assassination was carried out, and Jack was freed from potential exposure.

If nothing else, I hope you now understand the important role your father played in the course of history. He died so that so many important operations could be carried out. Jack would have begged for your forgiveness if he was sorry, but he had absolutely no regrets about what he did. Of course, he wished your father never would have stumbled into this situation. But as you know as well as anyone, timing in life is everything.

Live long, Sarah, and be proud of your father. And now move on with your life.

A friend

Sarah read the letter over and over, fixed in her chair until darkness fell. When she'd committed every one of these words to memory she struck a match and watched the paper dissipate into nothing more than ash. She was certain she could find the author of this letter if she set her mind to it. But her anonymous friend was right. It was time to move on with her life.

ABOUT THE AUTHOR

STEVE SAMUEL worked as defense counsel for three years on the bombing of Pan Am 103 over Lockerbie, Scotland. He works as in-house counsel for a large corporation and lives in Pennsylvania with his family. This is his first novel.